BETRAYAL

Kay Burley is the longest-serving female newsreader on British television. As host of her daily Sky News show, *Afternoon Live with Kay Burley*, she has covered some of the world's biggest news stories. Her coverage of 9/11 helped Sky win its first TV Bafta. She was on air when Diana, Princess of Wales died, Concorde crashed and the Iraq War began, and her exclusive interviews saw her shortlisted for presenter of the year alongside Jon Snow. Kay is a proud ambassador for Macmillan Cancer Support. Kay's debut book, *First Ladies*, published in 2011.

Also by Kay Burley

First Ladies

KAY BURLEY

Betrayal

HARPER

Harper
An imprint of HarperCollins*Publishers*
77–85 Fulham Palace Road,
Hammersmith, London W6 8JB

www.harpercollins.co.uk

A Paperback Original 2012
1

A catalogue record for this book
is available from the British Library

ISBN 978 0 00 736462 6

Set in Sabon LT Std by Palimpsest Book Production Limited,
Falkirk, Stirlingshire

Printed and bound in Great Britain by
Clays Ltd, St Ives plc

MIX
Paper from
responsible sources
FSC™ C007454
www.fsc.org

For Alexander,
I'm so proud of you.

Acknowledgements

So many people have given tirelessly of their time to help me make *Betrayal* the best book it can be. Dr Shaw at Northwick Park hospital whose expertise was essential. However further detail of his contribution here, would just give away the plot! My colleagues Tim Marshall and Anwar Tambe who guided me through the accuracy of life in Aj-al-Shar. Clive Mills, Andrew Wilson, Tim Gallagher, Duncan Sharp, Nick Ludlam and the wonderful Mick Deane who kept me safe, smiling and broadcasting in Libya while I also struggled to finish the manuscript for this book. Andi, Simon and Pat who offered me refuge when I couldn't face another chapter and Eleonora who simply makes my life easier. Sophie, Deborah and Jacquie who selflessly agreed to read through the first draft with a red pen. Nicola Ibison, the bee's knees; Maurice Lindsay, a wise old owl; Janelle Andrew always so generous of her time and Caroline Michel, the best literary agent in the business. Last but by no means least a trio of the most successful female authors in this genre, Tasmina Perry, Penny Vincenzi and the magnificent Jilly Cooper, thank you ladies for all you have done for me.

Christmas Eve

1

Almost 5 p.m.

Mayfair Safety Deposits

'Get your fucking hands up right now or I'll shoot you. Do it, you stupid bastard.' Growling the words with an energy she had been unable to muster for some months, Lily Dunlop was feeling rather embarrassed and a little shaken by her foul language. Nevertheless she resolutely pressed on.

'I mean it, I have a gun. Do as you're told *right now*,' she continued with perfect diction, stopping abruptly before she added an inappropriate *please*.

Pulse racing and palms sweating profusely, Lily tried her best to hold the weapon still. It was a beautifully refinished Smith & Wesson double-action revolver, .44 Russian, with tasteful mother-of-pearl grips and a six-inch barrel. The pistol was in very good working order, according to her father, who had kept it as part of his ornamental gun collection. She wondered for a moment what he might think of her waving it at the bulk of an irritated security guard in a Mayfair vault. Lily tried to force the image of her father's shocked face from her mind.

Bert Jones glared menacingly back at her. He was livid. That was all he needed, some posh bird with issues just as he was about to close up shop for the Christmas break. Why couldn't it have happened on new boy Jim Solomon's watch, thought Bert, while struggling to recall the protocol for such an eventuality. Passive, that's what he'd try to start with. Until, that is, he could grab the gun and smack her round her stuck-up chops with it a couple of times while they waited for the police to arrive.

Raising both his podgy palms to placate his tormentor, Bert became aware his nylon shirt was inching over the top of his prosperous physique and felt a twinge of embarrassment at exposing a little of his soft underbelly. Not much he could do about it at the moment though; any sudden moves and maintaining his dignity would be the least of his worries. What did this daft bint want anyway?

'Hold on a minute there, love, what seems to be the problem? Whatever it is, we can sort it out.'

Bert paused, aware of a slight nervous tremor in his voice. Consciously lowering his pitch, he continued: 'Come on, love, just be calm and we'll try to resolve this without anyone getting hurt, OK?'

Bert Jones was an affable, obese, father of two who had spent most of his career in the police service – Met Flying Squad, to be precise – and was used to talking his way out of tricky situations. He'd left the force eight years ago, when it came to the Commissioner's notice he'd been receiving bribes from journalists. Bert had been with Mayfair Safety Deposits ever since. His employers offered discreet protection for the portable assets and sensitive papers of the rich and famous. Unlike a bank, the owners were satisfied with a nom de plume, a much welcomed option for many of their customers.

Significant tips from wealthy clients – without any misunderstanding whether he should be receiving the payment – had provided a regular and considerable uplift to Bert's modest salary. Middle Eastern clients were the most appreciative of his finely tuned fawning, and working on Christmas Eve was always particularly rewarding. Tight-fisted Europeans were, however, quite another story and his courtesy with them was tempered appropriately. That was the main reason he had shown little interest in the arrival of the well-dressed and obviously privileged young white woman who'd entered the vault just before closing time. Bert hadn't even looked up from his *Telegraph* crossword to acknowledge her until the silly bint had begun waving a gun around. She had his full attention now.

'Tell me what it is you want, young lady, and I'm sure we can sort it. Then you can be on your way,' continued Bert, in as nonchalant a tone as he could muster. At the same time he slowly lowered one of his arms and leaned a chubby elbow on the reception desk.

Lily stared wide-eyed back at him, unaware the seemingly compliant guard was resting an arm on the solid oak desktop in an attempt to hide his other hand, which was sliding towards a panic button concealed just below the rim. Her head swimming, she was momentarily frozen by fear and confusion. Lily was acutely conscious of sweat building in the nape of her neck, snaking its way down her spine to soak the Emilio Pucci asymmetric gold lace and tulle mini dress she was wearing beneath her heavy winter coat. She thought fleetingly about her dashing and impossibly wealthy banker fiancé, Giles, who would be waiting impatiently for her at the bar of the Soho Hotel, sipping irritably on a Flaming Ferrari cocktail. They were both expected at a drinks reception at Sir Philip Green's London residence in less than an hour. Giles was keen to arrive and leave early. The couple were heading off to his family's Barbados home for Christmas and had secured a coveted departure slot for the Lear Jet at RAF Northolt, a private airport only thirty minutes from central London. The clock was ticking.

Despite her heavy coat, Lily shivered. What on earth was she thinking? It had all seemed so straightforward when she'd been planning the audacious raid in her mind. She'd gone through every detail a thousand times. Into the vault just before it was due to close for the festive break. Point the gun at the guard, take what she so desperately needed from the family's safe-deposit box, then out again, pausing only to ditch her half-hearted attempt at a disguise. Lily had visualised everything, just like it happened in the movies. She had reassured herself that nothing could possibly go wrong.

During a recce the previous month, Lily had noticed CCTV at the entrance to the vault hence the amateurish prosthetics. Her mother must never know that it was her daughter who had retrieved the contents of the box.

In a few hours she'd be heading to the sun with her unsuspecting future husband. Her desperation for the truth, the motivation that had driven her on over the last eight months, would be tucked into her coat pocket. Finally she would know whether her father had dealt her a death sentence while her complicit mother covered up the evidence. The reality was far from Hollywood. Standing inside the entrance of the ostentatious vault, the family's security box finally in her sights, Lily found herself panic stricken. Here she was shaking with fear and confusion while facing a security guard who seemed completely unfazed by Lily pointing a pistol at his flabby chest. Instead of doing exactly as she asked, he wanted an Oprah-style chat. What on earth was she supposed to do now? This most certainly wasn't in the script.

Noticing the panic and bewilderment in Lily's eyes, Bert was confident this was a no-brainer, all he needed to do was lean over a little further and his finger would easily reach the small white box encasing two red panic buttons. Roger, his buddy who should have been at the entrance monitoring visitors but was obviously on his mobile to his bookie as usual, would immediately call the Old Bill. This over-primped little madam would be read her rights quicker than she could say, *'I'm not sure these handcuffs really match this dress, officer.'* With luck, he'd still be home in front of the TV in time for the final of *Strictly Come Dancing*. Bert offered Lily a warm, reassuring smile. Just a tiny bit further across the desk and the little minx would be spooning up porridge for Christmas dinner. He, on the other hand, would be tucking into the Delia style turkey his good lady would be preparing at this very moment. Just needed to keep this girl talking for a few seconds more.

'Seriously, sweetheart, you're making a big mistake. I can see it's not going the way you planned it. I'll tell you what, give me the gun and we'll say no more about it. How does that sound?'

Lily faltered. All of the fury, the desperation and angst that had overwhelmed her over the last few months started to ebb away. Ever since Easter and the emotional explosion with her mother that had destroyed her perfect world, she had been determined to discover the truth. Despite her incandescent rage at her parents, she had clung to an unrealistic hope that there had been some mistake. Surely they would never have kept such a deadly secret from her. Would they?

She was so torn. The devil on her shoulder needed to know the answer. He assured her that her actions were justified and it was the only way she could move on with her life. But growing louder were the protests of the angel on her other shoulder, convincing her that the guard was right, this wasn't the best way to discover the truth.

Lily began to lower her arm.

'Good girl, there you go.' Bert smiled reassuringly, his index finger now hovering just over the buttons.

'You're right, sir. I'm terribly sorry for any misunderstanding. I hope I didn't scare you with this?'

Lily waved the pistol dismissively, increasingly embarrassed at the awkwardness of the situation. What had she been thinking? She'd featured in April's edition of *Country Life*, wearing spring Jaeger and pearls, and now here she was holding up a vault with one of her father's ornamental pistols. How preposterous. Shuffling awkwardly, Lily inched backwards towards the door. Reaching the eighteen-inch thick steel-reinforced entrance she dropped her arm completely and was about to push the pistol back into her pocket and run away as fast as her high pin heels would allow when a piercing scream reverberated around the vault. Darting her gaze past the guard, Lily saw a woman in Middle Eastern dress grasping tightly on to the hands of her two children who immediately joined their mother in a unified pitch.

Princess Almira of Aj-al-Shar and her youngsters had popped into Mayfair Safety Deposits on their way back from a last-minute Christmas shopping trip to Hamley's toy store. The princess was at the vault to collect a rather impressive piece of jewellery her husband had presented to her on their wedding day twelve years ago. Almira had planned to wear the necklace that evening at a small dinner party to be held in their suites at the Mandarin Oriental Hotel. The family had as usual taken a whole floor at the luxurious five-star hotel overlooking the magnificent acreage of Hyde Park with an almost view of the Diana Memorial Fountain. It wasn't quite their first choice. Instead, they had rather hoped to be relaxing in one of the well-appointed apartments at One Hyde Park during this latest visit to London. Unfortunately they had been outbid for the property just last month by

Sheikh Hamad, the foreign minister of Qatar, whose £100 million offer exceeded their own.

Her husband, Prince Ansar, was nephew to the King of Aj-al-Shar, part of the United Arab Emirates. It had suffered significant instability over the last five years and was still recovering from the latest coup attempt. As a result, the family travelled widely and made huge sums in the process, selling gas and oil to Europe. The purchase of a £100 million property should have been of little concern to the royal coffers, but the King had advised against it. Though disappointed, Ansar had of course accepted his uncle's guidance. He was now pondering other more permanent living arrangements while comfortably ensconced in the plush Royal Suite of the Mandarin Oriental, impatiently awaiting his family's return.

In addition to collecting her jewellery, Almira had been instructed by her husband to pick up a plain brown padded envelope from one of their many safety deposit boxes. Unbeknown to the Princess, it contained utility bonds that Prince Ansar planned to gift to his other three wives. She had just pushed the bulky envelope into her handbag and was gathering together her mischievous children when Lily arrived. The appearance of an elegant, slender, twentysomething white woman had aroused little more than envy from the plump princess, until she was about to leave and saw the gun. Almira's scream had been followed by shocked cries from ten-year-old Hafsa and her six-year-old brother Umair.

Bert dropped his head in exasperation. Just what he needed, a screamer when he almost had the situation under control. At this rate he'd never get home in time for Tess Daly. In the momentary confusion his fingers finally reached the panic alarm and he pressed both buttons hard. The piercing sound of the siren halted the screams from the Aj-al-Shar royal family, who immediately looked to the guard for guidance.

'Princess Almira, stay exactly where you are please. The police are on their way and should be here very shortly.'

Turning back to Lily, Bert continued with a smirk: 'Oh, are you in trouble now, missy.'

Lily stood rooted, terrified, to the spot. Within a few moments a second breathless guard arrived at the vault door, and Lily was sure she was about to faint.

'No, Roger, you idiot, you're supposed to dial 999. Go, you numpty.'

The second guard nodded nervously but remained where he was, panting breathlessly. Someone had a gun and was threatening his buddy, should he really just run away or should he try to wrestle it from their grasp?

With Lily distracted by the appearance of another guard, Bert leapt to his feet and lurched towards her, hoping to grab the gun from her French-manicured fingers. But the debutante was too quick for him and pulled the weapon away with more force than either of them expected, sending Bert tumbling backwards, slightly winded.

Lily again pointed the gun this time at Roger, who was standing motionless just the other side of the threshold to the vault. She was desperate to run but he was blocking the only way out. Adrenalin took over. With fight or flight the only options she decided to take her chances and bolted towards the steel-reinforced door.

Glaring at the mad woman pointing a gun and heading towards him, Roger, was not about to have his Christmas spoiled by a bullet-shaped hole in his chest, and sprang into action. Using both hands, he grabbed the edge of the massive door and heaving his whole weight behind it began to shove it closed. Lily, who had no intention of either shooting or staying put, tried her very hardest to push in the opposite direction. Though her arm muscles burned with the effort, it was a completely uneven contest. Lily's slight build was no match for Roger's bulk, and the vault door soon settled snugly into its frame.

Stifling a cry of desperation, Lily began battering the metal in pointless frustration until she was suddenly aware of a clattering sound next to her ankles. Looking down, she saw a bulky bunch of keys by her feet. It appeared the chubby guard was attempting to knock her senseless with the only weapon he had to hand. How very dare he!

'Hey, were you trying to hit me with that bunch of keys? Just stop that right now. I have a gun, you know. You must do exactly as I say, I absolutely insist.'

As she indignantly stood her ground, Lily could feel perspiration starting to drip from her nose and with it the prosthetic she had attached with spirit gum earlier. All pretence of a disguise gone. The false nose, had completely lost its adhesive, and slid unrestrained down her face until it rested just above her top lip. The dimple that she had amateurishly added to her chin had dropped on to her left collarbone. Retrieving it with her free hand, while trying not to think how ridiculous she must look, Lily made a last-ditch attempt at menacing:

'See, see, I have a gun! Be very, very careful, mister.'

Looking at the absurd melting face of the UK's answer to Patty Hearst, Bert was sure he would have laughed if the situation hadn't been critical. Desperate to reach the massive door before it was too late, he raised both hands in submission, stood up slowly and was just about to speak when he was interrupted by a whirring noise followed by a dull thud.

'Damn.'

'What on earth was that?' asked Lily, concerned.

'That, madam, was not good. In fact, it was very bad. Very, very bad.'

Bert glanced across to Princess Almira and her children, huddled at the far end of the vault, petrified of the madwoman with a gun. Little did they know their nightmare was about to become an awful lot worse. If only he'd been a moment quicker in unclipping the vault keys from his belt. If only he'd been able to toss the bunch to his colleague a second earlier. But Roger had begun heaving at the door even before Bert had time to manoeuvre his belt around his ample waist. By the time he'd finally managed to lob the keys, it was too late. Bert turned to address the group.

'OK, people, I need you all to be calm and listen carefully. As for you, posh paws, give me that gun, it's no good to you now.'

Lily stood upright, indignant at the very suggestion. She would do no such thing. What on earth was he talking about; she had a plane to catch.

'Excuse me, but I'm in a terrible hurry. I really don't have time for any more of this nonsense.'

Bert shook his head.

'Believe me. You're going nowhere, sister.'

Confused and with tears welling Lily buckled. She slumped against the metal door looking pleadingly at the guard for answers. Princess Almira was about to scream again but Bert was too quick this time.

'Shhh, no more screaming, there's a good princess. You're making my ears bleed.'

Almira stopped abruptly, mid yelp. There would be no tip for this oaf.

'Right, you all need to be calm and listen very carefully indeed. This is really important. That loud whirring noise you heard a second ago was the timer for the vault and the clunk were the bolts of the lock sliding into position. Contrary to what you thought, missy, I wasn't attempting to brain you with my keys – though, frankly, no one would blame me. In fact I was trying to throw them to Roger before he shoved the door shut. They're the second set for the door you're leaning against.'

Lily stared blankly. She had no idea what the guard was talking about.

'Well, if you could use them to open the door now, please, I would be most grateful.'

'No can do, missy, much as I would like to. The override keys open the door from the outside, but you need two sets. Bottom line is, unless Roger can find another set from somewhere else – which frankly is very unlikely it being Christmas Eve – we're in here for quite some time.'

Bert looked around at his captive audience, pausing in an effort to quell his own rising panic. He used the moment to count on his fingers.

'Right, with the rest of Christmas Eve, Christmas Day, Boxing Day and then the bank holiday taken into account, I calculate that we could be in here for about a hundred hours. That's longer than any of us planned, isn't it, eh? So you'd all better start making yourselves settled, people.'

Almira took a deep breath.

'I mean it, Princess, no more screaming – we'll need the oxygen.'

Almira bit her lip.

'As for you, missy, give me that bloody gun and stay right out of my way or you'll be sorry. Do I make myself clear?'

A stunned Lily did as she was told and handed over the weapon without any further resistance. Bert took it and shuffled back to his desk. Slumping into his comfortable lumbar-support chair, he dropped the gun into a drawer, locked it and picked up his crossword.

'Oh, just one other thing. While we're sorting out the housekeeping, no-one get any ideas about making themselves comfortable on this chair. It's mine.'

Eight months earlier

2

Breakfast time

Upton Park, Oxfordshire

Lily leapt from her Anglo-Indian four-poster bed and ran to
the window, flinging back the curtains to embrace the as yet
untold delights of her twenty-first birthday.

Coaxing open the stiff frame, she peered out across the
rolling parkland of the magnificent family estate and breathed
in the warm spring morning. In the distance she could just
make out what appeared to the naked eye to be tiny flecks
on the landscape, the family's flock of Oxford Down sheep
grazing on the lush rolling hillside. Closer to Upton Park,
the house her parents had called home for the last twenty-
five years, Lily gazed over the more formal gardens and
centrepiece lake originally designed by the master landscape
artist, Lancelot 'Capability' Brown. The gardens were looking
particularly well groomed this morning in preparation for
her coming-of-age celebration. Lily was delighted to see even
at this early hour an army of catering, gardening and house-
hold staff already fussing around the lawns. Gin and Tonic,

17

the family's three-year-old Irish Setters, were darting across the garden chased by Brian the butler, who was trying unsuccessfully to entice them back into the house with the aid of a squeaky toy and a Jumbone.

In the centre of the mêlée, being buzzed by a handsome but earnest young man with a clipboard and a frown, was her mother. Ever since Lily had been a little girl, Catherine had always found her daughter's birthday celebrations impossibly stressful. The British weather in April could offer up a heatwave, heavy snow or every other meteorological option in between. Many a bouncy-castle bonanza had been hastily moved to the indoor tennis court to protect inappropriately dressed partygoers from the elements.

This year for Lily's coming of age, nothing was being left to chance at the Cotswold estate. Her father, Joseph, who had made his fortune in electronics in Africa and the Far East, had bought the 320-room manor house plus stabling for 150 horses from the Fitzrovia family. Descendants of West Indies sugar plantation owners (or slave traders, as her mother more accurately acknowledged, the Fitzrovias had initially been extremely reluctant to sell to a man whose money was so new it was still being printed. They felt Joseph Dunlop was simply too vulgar for words and had quickly dismissed his interest. They had, however, reckoned without the tenacity of the electronics tycoon.

Ever since Joseph had first strolled down the overgrown avenue approaching the house, forlorn after decades of neglect, he had completely fallen in love with it and was not to be deterred. The Fitzrovias' sense of bewilderment was quickly followed by disdain then outrage as Joseph's offer was increased and confirmed in writing by lawyers. Their derision for Joseph Dunlop knew no bounds. Instead of the estate being preserved for future Fitzrovias, this nouveau riche fool felt it was completely acceptable to simply open his

18

Coutts' cheque book and purchase a piece of British history. He would no doubt want to arrive by helicopter, before attempting to demolish the hall replacing it with some hideous monstrosity instead. Worse, he may even consider a tasteless renovation complete with added cafe then open it up for coach parties, TV film crews keen on period dramas, or rent it out to the lower orders for tacky weddings. The only plus side they could think of was that at least he wasn't foreign, but frankly that was hardly sufficient reason to sell.

In the end though, with death duties too big to pay, the Fitzrovias were left with no option and the deal was done.

Despite the previous owners' prejudice Joseph's plans were very different to what they had anticipated and he began a sensitive renovation programme that was to take several years. More than simply tired, the 5,000-acre estate, had been exhausted when he took it over. With significant, his wife would say astronomical, investment Upton Park slowly rose from the ashes to become one of the most opulent private homes in the country. In his quest Joseph had enlisted the support of English Heritage who helped him spend more than £10 million on the refurbishment. When occasionally he baulked at the spiralling cost, officials reminded Joseph of his obligation to preserve one of Britain's finest buildings. They were particularly keen to protect the magnificent interiors and that started with fixing the roof. Repairs to the locally quarried honey-coloured limestone facade were particularly expensive, but with phenomenal vision Joseph was determined to fund what previous aristocratic generations had neglected.

His labour of love hadn't stopped at the house and its grand rooms, some as much as three storeys high. Joseph spent another fortune on a programme of replanting the gardens and grounds of Upton Park. A small army of gardeners were enlisted to help restore the classical landscape of Capability Brown. The artist's subtly altered hills and valleys and naturalistic plantings of trees were gradually rediscovered. Walled, lakeside and bird gardens, as well as an orangery came back to life. A handful of follies were rescued from untended lawns and restored to their previous splendour. Above everything, Joseph's pride and joy had been the planning and planting of a parterre. He had based it on a design at the Palace de Versailles, where he had spontaneously proposed to Catherine soon after they'd met.

With the renovation complete, Joseph's final act of defiance had been to rename the estate. Parrwood Hall became Upton Park, after the ground of his beloved football team, West Ham. His father, Lily's grandfather, had been a labourer who worked long hours at Tilbury Docks unloading grain. He saw little of his family in the week, but every other Saturday during the football season he would take his young son to watch Bobby Moore and Martin Peters among others take to the pitch. Snooty Cotswold neighbours would rather have seen the house razed than be named after a football ground, but Joseph was determined. Throughout his life he had held on tightly to his roots – much to Lily's embarrassment. Even now, she tried very hard to keep her father's humble beginnings from her judgemental friends.

As Lily looked down on the perfectly manicured box hedging her father had designed, she reminisced about her wonderful, charming, loving daddy, who had died so tragically from bowel cancer at the age of just forty-eight. How she wished he could be here now, helping celebrate her big day. Lily had always been a daddy's girl, his little princess. Whatever she wanted was hers. She smiled as she remembered the mountain of gifts he'd surprised her with ever since she was tiny. One of her favourites would have to be the fabric doll with woollen hair and a painted plastic face that she'd yearned for after seeing it in a TV costume drama. But it was a 1960s prop and, no matter how hard her parents tried, they just couldn't find one. Her father had even offered to buy the original from the TV studios without success. Nevertheless, that Christmas among the sparkling pile of presents under the Norwegian Spruce tree was a pristine box with her name on it. Lily tore away the silver wrapping paper embossed with her initials. Inside was the much longed for doll. Her father had finally tracked it down to Pasadena in California. Lily squealed with delight as she hugged her new best friend with her Sixties mini dress, red woollen tights and black patent shoes. A string attached to its back made the doll, which she immediately named Jenny, wish Lily a 'Happy Christmas with lots of hugs and kisses from Mummy and Daddy.'

Lily wondered where the doll was now. Misplaced, along with all the other perfect presents she'd received from her doting daddy over the years. No doubt her mother had stored it safe in a drawer somewhere, or perhaps packed it into a carefully labelled box and put it in the attic. Catherine was a world-class hoarder, nothing was ever thrown away. But her organisational skills were somewhat less impressive, as witnessed by the frenzy on the lawns outside Lily's bedroom now.

'Morning, Mummy,' shouted Lily.

Catherine looked up from the controlled madness surrounding her and smiled warmly at her beautiful daughter who was leaning much too far out of her bedroom window.

'Oh, do be careful, darling, you might easily fall. Good morning and a very, very happy birthday. Did you sleep well?'

Catherine was an elegant, middle-aged woman who had been born into privilege. An original girl in pearls back in the 1970s she'd often featured among the pages of *Country Life* and *The Lady* and had encouraged her daughter to do the same. After studying at Cheltenham Ladies' College and attending the Lucy Clayton Charm Academy, where she mastered the gentle art of flower arranging and the skill of getting out of a car without showing her knickers, along with slightly more useful shorthand, Catherine was expected to marry well. For the nineteen-year-old, that meant little to look forward to other than bearing children and an occasional walk around the family estate before tea, always to be served promptly at 4 p.m. Catherine, though, was more of a free spirit than her parents would have liked, and instead embarked on a completely unsuitable and wayward trip to Europe. Reluctantly, her parents had given their permission, on condition that she return in good time to be considered by some appropriate suitor to be chosen by her father, the 11th Earl Fitzwilliam.

Catherine had loved every moment of her two-month sojourn to the Continent. She was particularly captivated by the energy and charm of Amsterdam, Vienna and Rome, but Paris had of course been her favourite city. On the very last day before returning to the UK, she had wandered aimlessly around the French capital, desperately soaking up the romance. After paying her tourist respects at the Tomb of the Unknown Soldier, she triumphantly climbed all the way to the very top of the Arc de Triomphe. Looking down to the Champs-Élysées far below, Catherine could pick out some of the neon-lit stores of the elegant French fashion houses. Strolling nonchalantly across to another corner of the monument, she gazed out over the craziness of the Place de l'Etoile. The traffic roundabout easily shaded the madness of Hyde Park Corner, but she would still be sorry to leave it for home.

As dusk began to fall, Catherine savoured a last lingering look at the Parisian capital and the majestic Eiffel Tower on the left bank of the Seine.

'Excuse me, miss. I'm sorry to interrupt, but could I borrow a franc? I want to call my mum and tell her I've just met the girl of my dreams.'

Catherine lowered her point-and-click camera and turned to see who had delivered such a corny line. Standing next to her was a young man who almost took her breath away.

Looking up at Lily now, Catherine reflected on how their daughter had inherited her father's charm and good looks.

'So, you slept well, Lily darling?'

'I slept perfectly, thank you, Mummy. Goodness, you look absolutely lovely this morning. How are the plans going for tonight? I'm so-o excited I could burst.'

'Oh, frantically, darling. There's still so much to do, I'm not sure we'll be ready in time. I'm just off with Jerome to make sure everything is as it should be in the Big Top. Do have some breakfast and then come and see.'

'OK, Mummy, will do.'

With that, Catherine hurried across the lawns towards a candy-striped circular tent. Her daughter had adored the circus ever since she was a child. Acrobats were Lily's particular favourite and her mother had tirelessly searched for, sourced and subsequently employed the services of several supple-limbed Cirque du Soleil cast members to entertain party guests for her daughter's big day. The theme: all the fun of the fair. The price tag: more expensive than Catherine had first imagined. The result: the perfect party for her little girl's coming of age.

Guests were to be greeted by actors on stilts with clown-painted faces wearing top hat and tails that draped ten feet to the ground. A gilt-framed canvas of Lily's debutante appearance in *Country Life* – just as her mother had done thirty years earlier – took pride of place on one wall of the glass marquee, which was even at this early hour already set for dinner.

The Marcus Wareing menu trumpeted fish fingers or

bangers and mash, two of Lily's favourite party foods when she was a child. In reality, chefs were preparing goujons of lemon sole with goose fat chips or Cumberland's finest accompanied by an onion jus and mustard creamed mash for the guests of the now older, more discerning birthday girl.

Lily's list included Kate Moss, Adele and Katy Perry, who she'd met in the first-class Lounge at LAX. Her mother's understated but nonetheless essential guests numbered those who were accustomed to entertaining each other on their super yachts in the South of France or at Sandy Lane in Barbados.

Despite Catherine's fever-pitch concern, everything was coming together well. With one last anxious glance at the place settings, she allowed herself to be guided out of the marquee by the efficient Jerome.

As Lily watched her mother reappear from the Big Top she noticed among the ever-growing throng some very serious-looking chaps wearing suits and carrying radios. They could only be Prince Harry's security. She'd holidayed with his group at Klösters in February and he'd been one of the first to respond when the gilt-edged invites were sent out last month.

Lily leaned further out of her bedroom window and, cupping her hands around her mouth, she shouted across the gardens: 'Does it look sensational in the tent, Mummy?'

Her bellow was immediately met by a frown.

'Darling, it's a marquee not a tent, and please could you stop bellowing from the window like a market trader?'

Lily lowered her head to feign acknowledgement at the chastisement from her mother but nevertheless continued.

'Where's Giles, Mummy?'

When Lily woke alone she had assumed her partner must be with her mother in the gardens.

'Giles said he had one or two errands, something to do with Asprey's, and promised he'd be back before lunch.'

Lily let out a squeal of excitement. What a magnificent weekend it was turning out to be.

3

Teatime the previous day

Giles had arrived at Upton Park early, keen to enjoy the build-up to his girlfriend's birthday. He'd initially intended to make a statement by driving up to the hall in his father's Jaguar C Class, bought at auction for £2.5 million. Sadly, the weather was still not quite warm enough for the convertible and instead he'd arrived in a new Ferrari California, part of his latest City bonus. Leaping from the vehicle without a hair out of place, Giles sauntered through the entrance with only a cursory nod to Brian the butler and headed into the Long Gallery where Lily paced with her mother.

'Hello, darling. How are you?'

Giles was still wearing his Wayfarer sunglasses and pushed them nonchalantly on to the top of his head as he strode across to kiss his trophy girl. He considered Lily simply divine, ten-car-pile-up gorgeous. As slender and effortlessly elegant as her mother, her seemingly endless legs were frequently photographed in barely there dresses for the pages of well thumbed glossy magazines. Together they were the latest paparazzi sweethearts, followed almost everywhere they went. For now Giles was the more famous of the two, thanks to his flamboyant splash-the-cash lifestyle It had recently included an ill-advised, 'greed is still good' speech at a banker friend's wedding, quickly picked up by the *Daily Mirror*. But Lily's impish charm softened his brashness making them the dream couple. Giles accepted his mother's view that Lily may not be from quite the right stock, what with her father's laughable lineage, but in her defence she fitted in easily with his friends and was always polite to the staff. Giles stood back to admire her fine features exquisitely framed by naturally highlighted blonde hair which cascaded down to her delicate shoulders before arriving at a pert cleavage. Divine.

'You look absolutely beautiful this evening, my love.'

'Thank you. I wish I'd never agreed to the idea of a party. There's still completely masses to do.'

'Now then, don't be ungrateful, darling. Your mother is doing all this just for you.' Giles pressed playfully on the end of her nose. 'I'm sure she'd rather be making arrangements for summer in the South of France than poring over plans for tomorrow.'

'Oh no, I'm not being ungrateful at all. Mummy knows I appreciate everything that she's done, but goodness it's taken up so much time. Look, she's simply exhausted.'

Giles looked across at Catherine, who stood by a table which could easily seat thirty but whose expansive surface was tonight being used to hold mountains of plans and paperwork for tomorrow. Wandering towards her he slid a muscular arm around Catherine's shoulder, and gave her a warm hug. '*Poor Catherine*,' as his mother always referred to Lily's mother, may have married beneath her but she looked as luscious as ever. An expensive yet understated pencil skirt and silk Jaeger blouse complimented her excellent figure, a string of pearls effortlessly completing her sophisticated appearance.

Looking at the magnificence of Mrs D, Giles wondered what she could possibly have seen in a nouveau riche upstart like Joseph Dunlop. Certainly, Giles's father, Oscar, 24th Baron of Worcester, had been no fan of the 'docker's son', as he scathingly referred to him. When Joseph had applied to join the Garrick Club, Oscar was so appalled at the prospect that he launched a discreet but vigorous campaign to ensure the request was politely declined. Quite simply the wrong sort of chap. Although associating with the Dunlops was risky for family harmony Giles had decided at the ripe old age of 25 that now was the time to be his own man.

While the electronics tycoon was alive, Giles could only admire the lovely Lily from afar. However, since Joseph's untimely death he had been able to slowly persuade his father that the advancement of new money was little threat to their class and any involvement with Lily would have no detriment to the family honour. Prince William's marriage to the great granddaughter of a coalminer had offered him the perfect foil. Oscar though was not so easily convinced and was still struggling to tolerate his heir associating with the daughter of a 'docker's son'.

Giles knew he was risking his father's wrath with plans for tonight but so be it. Leaving his hand nonchalantly draped over Catherine's shoulder, he waved his free arm dismissively at the piles of paperwork.

'Mrs D, this is not for you to worry about. Can't you leave it to the planners and let me take both you beautiful ladies out for an early supper? I'm sure if Joseph were alive he wouldn't want you weighed down with all this worry. What do you say?'

Gazing at the table plans and running orders, Catherine knew that, had Joseph been alive, rather than lifting the burden from her shoulders. he probably wouldn't even have been in the country, but off in some far-flung part of the world. He'd have waited until the morning of the party before turning up at Upton Park in the company helicopter, ready to take the credit and pay the bills.

Catherine smiled up at Giles. Such a charming young man, she hoped he would be honourable, or at least more appeasing to her daughter than the man she had married.

'How sweet of you, Giles, but that is completely unnecessary. Neither of you should be worrying about this admin nonsense. You run off and do something fun while I finish up here.'

Lily sighed with relief at the thought of escape, no idea that Giles's offer was all part of an elaborate plan he had cooked up with her mother earlier.

'Are you sure, Mummy? It looks as though there's still masses to do.'

'Absolutely, darling. I'll have Brian call Jerome the party planner and ask him to come a little earlier tomorrow. Off you go, I'll see you both later.'

'OK, bye then.'

Before Catherine could change her mind, Lily grabbed Giles's hand and whisked him out of the Long Gallery and towards the grand entrance.

'What should we do?' asked Lily, racing through the hallway, Giles a step behind her, holding on to his head so as not to lose his designer sunglasses.

'Well, my love, I have a surprise.'

'How exciting, I adore surprises.'

Rushing down the steps of the ancestral hall, Giles breathlessly opened the passenger door of his new car for Lily before dashing around to the driver's side and firing up the engine.

Lily relaxed into the luxurious tan leather seat.

'Wow, this is wonderful, Giles. Where should we go?'

'Settle back, darling, you'll see,' teased Giles as he slipped the car into gear, the wheels spraying up gravel as the couple sped down the driveway.

They arrived a short time later at Autumn Cottage, a perfect English setting in a secluded corner of the grounds of Upton Park. Giles leapt from the Ferrari and walked around the car to open Lily's door, but she remained perfectly still, all excitement gone. Why had he brought her here? She hadn't been down to the cottage for two years. It held far too many painful memories for her. Surely Giles must know that?

Nestled discreetly on the banks of the River Evenlode, Autumn Cottage had been renovated as part of the extensive work on the Upton Park estate. It was an ideal place for privacy and relaxation and had often been used by Lily's father as his 'thinking space'. Sometimes, as a special treat when she was home from school and he wasn't travelling the world, he would allow her to join him at the cottage for the day. Packing a picnic hamper, they would clamber into a coveted Humber open-top touring car that was kept for the sole purpose of pottering around the estate. They would then trundle down the driveway to spend the afternoon in the walled garden of Autumn Cottage, playing croquet or occasionally messing about on the river. All the while Lily was completely safe in the knowledge that nothing could ever upset her perfect life. It had been her favourite place in the world.

Then her father died and her dreams came crashing down. She had been unable to visit the cottage since. Until now.

She'd forgotten how beautiful it was by the river. Looking through the windscreen and up at the cottage's tall chimneys and mock-Tudor façade, Lily wished for the thousandth time that she could turn back the clock. She would give anything for her father to be beside her now, helping celebrate her birthday. Lily sighed.

'Why have you brought me here, Giles? You know it was Daddy's favourite place. I don't want to be here, please, let's leave.'

'But, darling, this is the ideal setting for what I have planned. Trust me, let's go inside. Everything's prepared.'

Lily felt anxious and unhappy. She would rather be anywhere else but here. Even tackling table plans with her mother sounded more enticing than setting foot inside the cottage after all this time. It would be dusty, cold and full of cobwebs. Everything she looked at would remind her of her father. This was a truly terrible birthday surprise.

Giles could see the panic in his girlfriend's eyes, but he was not to be deterred and held out his hand.

'Come on, darling, you won't be disappointed, I promise.'

'No, Giles, I can't. I just can't, let's go back to the house and join Mummy for dinner instead.'

Giles knelt on the soft ground next to the passenger door of the car. He could feel the dampness from the rain-soaked earth seeping through the knee of his designer jeans. If he didn't convince Lily now, the cottage might be out of bounds forever.

'Darling, trust me, it's what your father would have wanted. He loved it here, you loved it here. There are so many fond memories the other side of that front door. All we need to do is walk across the threshold together and the demons will disappear. I promise.'

Lily looked pleadingly at Giles. At the back of her mind she knew he was right. She really missed the cottage, and with the support of the man she adored almost as much as her daddy, surely now was the time to face up to her fears. Yet somehow she just couldn't.

'I can't, Giles. I'm so scared.'

'I know, my darling, but I'm here.'

Giles tugged gently on her arm, a reassuring smile on his handsome face.

'Come on.'

Knowing he wouldn't take no for an answer, Lily cautiously reached out to him. Gripping his outstretched hands, she stepped from the car and took a few deep breaths to steady herself before walking timidly up the pathway with him. Step after uncertain step Lily wanted to turn and run away, but Giles held her tight. Together they inched closer towards the cottage.

When eventually the couple arrived at the familiar front door, Lily stopped abruptly. She resisted Giles' attempts to persuade her over the threshold. Frightened to go any further.

'Almost there, darling, just a few steps more. Come on, I'm here.'

Having coaxed her this far, Giles was determined she would go inside. Lily paused, screwed her eyes tight shut and stepped forward.

Opening them in the sitting room of Autumn Cottage she could see it was just as she'd remembered it: stylish, but less extravagant than the main house. The centrepiece to the room was a wonderful French fireplace brought from a Normandy market by her mother. Her father had initially hated it but Catherine was not to be deterred and searched long and hard for suitable furnishings to compliment the hand-carved period piece. It had worked. Neutral floor coverings and overstuffed sofas helped create the feeling of a warm, comfortable bolthole. Quaint but not kitsch, it was a world away from the magnificence of the main house.

Relaxing, Lily cautiously looked around the room where she'd spent so many days with her father playing Cluedo or Monopoly. She was surprised how clean and warm it was after months of neglect. The fire had been lit, no doubt by Brian.

'Ah, good,' offered Giles as he strolled across to the fireplace and threw on another seasoned log. 'I was hoping we might be able to enjoy the garden, but it's still a little too cold. Brian said he would make the sitting room comfortable. Sit here in front of the fire, darling, while I grab a couple of things from the kitchen.'

Lily's initial anxiety was fading and curiosity was now getting the better of her.

'What's going on?'

'You'll see,' teased Giles as he led Lily to a fireside armchair before disappearing into the kitchen. A few moments later he was back, standing in the doorway, a cooler bag in his hand and a mischievous smile on his handsome face.

During the drive down to the cottage the light gel on Giles's blond hair had given up its attempt to keep his soft curls in place. The tousled look only added to his utter gorgeousness, thought Lily.

'Hi you.'

'Hi you, back.'

'I love you, Lily, and I want to share something with you.'

Lily was intrigued and stared deep into Giles's piercing green eyes for any clue to what the surprise might be. She felt a moment of concern. Was it good or bad?

'What is it?'

'Come on, let's go.'

'Where are we going now?'

'You'll see.'

Grabbing Lily's hand, Giles started to pull her to her feet but, having taken the momentous decision to enter the cottage again, she was reluctant to leave so soon.

'I was just settling here, darling. It's been so long. Can't we reminisce a little first? What's the rush?'

'Wait and see.'

Taking Lily's hand and holding tightly on to her, Giles led

33

her out of the front door and down to the mooring, where one of the family's boats – *Alfie*, named after her father's favourite dog – had been made ready.

Despite her new-found reluctance to leave the cottage, Lily was equally excited to know what else Giles had planned. Clambering on board the boat she wandered up to the bow and waited for him to join her. Giles had disappeared below deck to deposit the contents of the cooler bag in the well-stocked fridge, which was already bulging with indulgent treats, including a bottle of 1993 Cristal champagne. Within moments though he was back and starting up the engine they set sail.

Standing at the bow Lily had a perfect view of the river as it meandered this way and that. Relaxing into the movement of the boat, she was whisked back to her childhood and the ghost of her father was soon by her side. Feeling a sudden chill in the spring air, Lily reached for a nearby picnic blanket and loosely wrapped the tartan wool around her shoulders. She wondered if the shiver was due to the cold or the memory of her father. So many times he had been the one with a steady hand on the rudder as they spent fun-filled afternoons cruising up and down the river.

Losing her father had been completely devastating for Lily. It was a loss that deepened as the years past and with it emotions she felt she would never come to terms with. While alive, he was forever bringing her smiles and laughter; with him gone, they were replaced by tears and despair. Lily pulled the blanket a little tighter around her.

As the river widened she looked out towards the bank. The land bordering either side was mainly agricultural. A couple of inquisitive cows lazily raised their heads as the boat slid past.

'Moo cow, one, two, three,' whispered Lily, remembering the hide-and-seek game she and her father had played with cattle when she was a little girl. She smiled at the memory, wiping away a tear and then another and another. When she stole an embarrassed glance at Giles, he immediately waved and blew a kiss, which Lily caught and put safely in her pocket. She was grateful that he was giving her the space she needed.

Turning to look upstream at the final smudges of sunlight as it dipped below the horizon, Lily stretched out her hand and felt the breeze against her bare arm. For the first time since her father died, Lily began to accept that she could be honest with her emotions while she was with Giles. She could begin to accept her loss.

'Wrap up warm, darling, you'll be cold,' called an ever-attentive Giles.

Lily reached down to retrieve her blanket, which had fallen on to the deck, and settled on to a cushion to enjoy the final moments before dusk.

A little further on, Giles, sensing Lily's mood had moved from reflective to relaxed, expertly moored the vessel before retrieving a bottle of champagne from the cooler. Strolling up to where Lily was waiting, he opened the wine and offered her a celebratory glass.

'There you are, darling. Happy birthday for tomorrow.'

'Thank you. And thank you for such a lovely surprise. I never thought I would come down here again after Daddy died. I miss him so much.'

Giles put a protective arm around her, pulling her a little closer but saying nothing. He'd brought Lily to the cottage in the hope of putting to rest some of those unhappy memories. The time had come for her to move on to the next phase of her life. One in which he planned to play a major part.

'Darling, I have something to ask you . . .'

He sounded anxious, a little unsure. Immediately curious, Lily pulled away.

'Well, if it's about a birthday gift, I've already told you – I really don't mind. Honestly, something small would be fine. Really.'

Giles reached tentatively into his jeans pocket and produced a small red velvet box.

'OK, well how about this small?'

Lily gasped. They had only been properly dating for a few months. Surely it couldn't be what she thought it was.

'Go on, open it.'

Setting her glass down, Lily rather timidly took the box from Giles's outstretched hand. No it couldn't be. She was being silly. It must be earrings. Turning the box towards her she slowly opened it. Inside was a Lilibet emerald-cut diamond ring. It was easily five carats and had blue pear-shaped diamond shoulders. She recognized it immediately as one of Asprey's finest pieces. Lily was unable to move, her mouth open wide in shock.

Giles filled the silence. 'I would have asked your father if I could, but instead I asked Catherine. She assured me he would have been delighted and gave me her permission . . . Marry me, Lily.'

Lily steadied herself against the side of the boat.

'What, what did you say?'

Giles lowered himself slowly to one knee and continued: 'I said, will you marry me, Lily Dunlop?'

Lily laughed and threw her arms around Giles with such force that they almost toppled overboard.

'Yes, yes, yes, yes, yes. A thousand times yes.'

'Is the right answer,' whispered Giles, recovering his balance and lifting Lily into his arms headed below deck.

Eight months later

4

Soon after the vault closed on Christmas Eve

Mayfair Safety Deposits

'We're not in Kansas anymore, Toto,' whispered Lily under her breath as she stroked the magnificent stone in her engagement ring. Memories of the day her fiancé proposed gave way to the stark realisation she was trapped in a safety deposit vault on Christmas Eve with four strangers.

Desperately frightened, she was already starting to find her surroundings incredibly claustrophobic. After the confusion of the last half-hour it was now deathly quiet in the vault, not even the Arab princess was making a sound. Reluctant to risk catching the gaze of her fellow captors, Lily instead kept her eyes cast down. She scrutinised the deep Berber pile carpet and Moroccan hand-woven rugs and began to wonder how many knots there might be. Studying the carpets inch by inch, she was content to stare at the ground forever.

It was six-year-old Umair, the younger of Princess Almira's two children, who eventually broke the silence. Tugging at his mother's coat sleeve to attract her attention, he asked pleadingly: 'Mummy, can we go home now, please?'

It had been a long day for the youngster who'd spent much of it careering around the biggest toy shop in the world. When faced with floor after floor of brightly coloured surprises he had found himself unable to choose. Eventually though Umair had settled on a digital camera, Steiff panda, Scalextric, a puppet theatre and a Mercedes SL ride on car. His sister Hafsa had chosen more conservatively: a Rubik's cube and a thousand-piece jigsaw depicting an impossibly cute chocolate Labrador puppy half closing one eye. All the toys had been duly loaded into the chauffeured car to be taken back to their suites at the Mandarin Oriental.

On their arrival at the vault, Umair had not only refused to stay in the vehicle with the driver while his mother dashed inside to collect boring papers for his father, he had also demanded to bring all his toys with him. After a rather unedifying tantrum, Umair had eventually been persuaded to leave everything in the Rolls apart from the panda, camera and Scalextric. Hafsa, who had no idea what her brother could possibly do with a car track in a security vault, was dragged along to keep him occupied. A Rubik cube stuffed deep into her coat pocket, her jigsaw puzzle under the other arm, simply because Umair liked the picture and had insisted it come too.

Still clutching the panda, Umair tugged again on the sleeve of his mother's woollen coat. He was tired and frightened and wanted to be reunited with his father as soon as possible.

'Mummy, I need to go to the toilet.'

Princess Almira stared at her young son as he rubbed his huge brown eyes and stuck a thumb in his mouth. A timid, indecisive woman she was terrified of her husband's wrath. When Prince Ansar discovered what had happened to his beloved only son, she would be held totally responsible. The princess was quickly descending into shock and had no idea what to say or do. It was left to her 10-year-old daughter Hafsa to comfort her little brother.

'Excuse me, guard, is there a toilet for my little brother, please?'

'Yup. See that sign, the one that says "toilet"? That's where it is, kid. Oh, and don't drink the water out of the tap. It says "not drinking water" for a reason.'

Shaking his head, Bert returned to his crossword.

Hafsa took her brother's small hand and led him towards the bathroom, continuing with her gentle reassurance as they went.

'We'll be able to go home very soon, Umair. Show me your panda again first though. Have you decided what to name him yet?'

'Squidgy. I'm going to call him Squidgy.'

'That's a good name. Why do you want to call him that?'

Umair spoke in the sort of stage whisper that young children adopt when trying to keep a secret from an adult.

'Because that bad lady's nose has gone all squidgy.'

Lily took a moment to realise the youngster was referring to her. He was right, though: her prosthetic nose was now nothing more than mush. Embarrassed, she hastily wiped the remnants from her face and tucked them into her pocket, where the dimple was already coagulating into the lining.

Returning to her scrutiny of the floor, Lily was desperately concerned about what would happen next. Nothing had gone to plan so far.

Soon the children returned from the bathroom and took up positions on the carpeted floor either side of their deathly quiet mother. Time seemed to be standing still. Glancing at her watch, Lily realised Giles would have been waiting at the bar for almost an hour. He must be absolutely livid. Assuming he hadn't decided to fly to Barbados without

41

her. Surely they couldn't be trapped for too much longer? The guard was obviously just trying to scare them with the suggestion they could be inside the vault for one hundred hours.

Hafsa was anxious that her mother's behaviour was frightening Umair and began a story in the hope of distracting him. As she eavesdropped on the adventures of Squidgy the Panda and a boat trip to China, Lily half smiled at the young girl's obvious care and love. This was what it meant to have a sibling: caring and sharing. If only she'd had a brother or sister, she would have been able to discuss what had happened to her, what their parents had done to her. Then she wouldn't be in this position now. None of this would have happened and she would be on her way to spend Christmas in the sun with her fiancé.

Lily shifted uncomfortably. Her feet and her neck were beginning to ache and she rolled her head from side to side to ease the tension as Hafsa continued with Squidgy's travels. As Lily listened she was sure she could feel the eyes of the scary guard boring into her. She ignored the sensation for as long as possible. Eventually, when Squidgy had reached Beijing and the ultimate prize of as much bamboo as he could possibly eat, Lily decided to risk lifting her gaze. Slowly lifting her head she was immediately confronted by the glare of the angry, judgemental guard.

Bert was more than angry, he was absolutely bloody livid. This stupid, arrogant young woman who had obviously been accountable to no one but herself her whole life had only gone and locked them in the goddamned vault. So much for Christmas with his family! His wife Cynthia would be wondering where he was. A former school dinner lady, she was an excellent cook; and although she'd have her hands full, stuffing the turkey, would still have one eye on the clock. He was always home by 6 p.m. Not tonight, though. And not tomorrow or probably even the night after. Bugger.

Continuing to meet his gaze, Lily tried to speak.

'Could I just say that I'm really terribly sorry.'

'Shut it. Just shut up. SHUT UP!'

The children jumped in alarm as Bert shouted at the top of his voice, but Lily was not to be silenced. She wanted to apologise for the distress she had caused.

'I understand your deep frustration with me. I just have to say that I am so terribly sorry. I didn't mean for this to happen, really I didn't.'

'Blah, bloody blah. You're a stupid, spoilt bitch is what you are. Shut it.'

Bert spat the words and the anxious children edged closer towards their mother.

Stupidly, Lily pressed on. She wanted to apologise to the guard but she also couldn't believe they would be trapped for four days and was keen to know when she would be able to return home.

'May I ask, does our present predicament really mean we will be here all night now, sir?'

Lily's question was more of a plea. Bert glared at her. He squeezed his hands into tight fists, his temper teetering right on the very edge of explosive. He'd already said how long they were likely to be trapped, hadn't she been bloody listening?

'Well, no, no it doesn't, actually,' he growled.

'Goodness, that's a blessed relief,' replied Lily. She wasn't sure what trouble she would be in when the vault door opened, but she had no desire to spend Christmas in this awful place.

'No, we won't be here all night. As I've already said, we will be here much, much longer than that. I told you up to a hundred hours, well ninety-nine and bloody counting now. Weren't you listening earlier?'

'I thought you were exaggerating.'

'Nope.'

It was Almira's turn to voice her concern and with another of her piercing screams. Her sense of shocked bewilderment at her husband's actions when he discovered what had happened now replaced by full-blown hysteria.

Bert shook his head in despair. What a way to behave with her children present. He knew from his police training that the best course of action would be to speak gently and reassuringly to the princess. Well, that wasn't about to happen. She needed to get a bloody grip, instead of losing control in front of her children like that. Cynthia would have had none of it, he was sure of that.

Bert Jones might have been a little more sympathetic to the Princess's plight if he'd been aware of the reason for her sickening concern. Almira lived in constant fear of her husband's wrath and the punishment he would unleash on her if she didn't do his bidding. The initial shock at being unable to safely return Umair to his father's side was now replaced by hysteria at the confirmation it really could take days rather than hours before they were reunited. Hafsa who was no stranger to her mother's histrionics reached for the Princess's hand and spoke gently in Arabic to try to soothe her. Bert was less understanding.

'Shut it! Just shut up, will you. That's not helping. Think about the kids.'

Almira was stunned into silence at his insolence. He had been so charming when they had arrived at the vault and now this.

'I would ask you not to speak to me in that tone.'

They were the first words the Princess had spoken since the drama started and Lily chastised herself for being surprised at her perfect diction.

'Your attitude is not appreciated.'

Hafsa gently squeezed Almira's clammy hand. She knew her mother would be struggling to cope with the magnitude of what the guard was saying rather than his rudeness. Her father would be livid when he learned that Umair was trapped. She hoped that he might also be a little concerned about her too but was less sure of that.

Shrugging off the rebuke, Bert returned to his seat before anyone else tried to claim it.

Hafsa wrapped a protective arm around her brother's shoulder and kissed the top of his head. Her mother had again subsided into a state of bewilderment and said nothing more.

'Hey, Umair, I have an idea. Why don't we play with your new camera? Let's unwrap it, shall we?'

Umair nodded excitedly at the prospect of being allowed to rip into one of his toys and immediately set about attacking the cellophane. As Hafsa released her mother's hand to help him, Almira slumped dejectedly against a wall and slid slowly to the carpeted floor.

Watching the Princess from across the vault, Bert half considered offering her his chair but quickly decided against it. Instead he thought about his Cyn. She would have been much stronger, faced with a situation like this. When Bert left the police, his wife had stoically taken on two jobs while at the same time studying for a degree at night school in order to provide for the family. She was now a teacher in the same comprehensive where their youngest, Tracey, went to school. Harry, the elder child, was a strapping sportsman. He would no doubt be taking the opportunity to fight with his little sister for control of the TV remote while their father was indisposed. He hoped one of them had remembered to feed the dog while Cyn was busy in the kitchen, but would bet good money they hadn't. Bert began to grumble to no one in particular.

'If only I'd managed to lob the keys over to Roger before that idiot shut the door, it would have been a very different story. Then we'd have been out quick sharp. Now look at us.'

Lily wasn't sure if she was supposed to be part of the conversation. She joined in anyway.

'I'm sorry, sir, but I don't quite understand. Doesn't the other guard have his own set of keys?'

Bert ignored Lily and revisited his copy of the *Telegraph*, still open at the crossword. A few moments later, stuck on six across – two words: French for Merry Christmas – he looked up again.

'Two sets of key holders. Haven't done your research at all, have you, missy? The lock needs both sets of keys to override the timer. There's one outside with my buddy, and the other set is there by your feet. Without both sets, the door won't open. The end.'

Lily couldn't believe that escape would be stymied by what seemed such an antiquated system. She was apprehensive about suggesting as much to the volatile guard. It was left to one of the children to ask the obvious question.

'But don't other people have keys as well?'

It was Hafsa who spoke. Having finished unwrapping her brother's camera, she was now trying desperately to prop up her mother, who was beginning to hyperventilate.

'Good point, little 'un. You would have thought so, wouldn't you, but Fort Knox we ain't.'

Bert had some genuine sympathy for the young girl, who quite obviously was the adult in this family dynamic. He offered her a watery smile.

'There are another couple of sets of keys at least, but I know for a fact that one set is with Bill Smith, who as we speak is heading off to the Galapagos Islands with his good lady on a cruise. I kid you not. Likelihood of him having taken his phone with him? Not high, I would suspect.

'The only other person with a set of keys that matches mine is Yonni Sanchez. He was due to go back to Chile with his family for Christmas.'

Lily couldn't believe what she was hearing. It was a totally incompetent system.

'But surely rules state that guards should not be allowed to go on holiday with such important keys, what if something were to –'

She stopped abruptly.

'I really don't think you're in any position to be judgemental, young lady. I suggest you sit right there on your posh suitcase and keep it buttoned.'

Almira, who had been half listening to the discussion, snatched her hand away from Hafsa and was about to cry out yet again when she was interrupted. This time it was Lily.

'I'm sorry, madam, but that's not really going to help anyone, is it? Please do try to think of the children.'

That was it. Bert had heard enough. He slammed his hand on the table.

'I do beg your pardon, Miss Twinkle Toes. I suggest you look at your own actions before criticising others. Let's not forget who got us into this mess in the first place, shall we?'

Lily was unhappy with the continuing aggressiveness of Bert's tone. He certainly had a point, but did he need to be quite so rude in making it?

'I really must ask you to keep a civil tongue when speaking to me, if you don't mind, sir.'

'Shut up, just shut up. Seriously, I don't want to hear another word from you, unless it's "Officer, these handcuffs are too tight." Do I make myself clear?'

Lily dropped unsteadily back on to her suitcase, which was packed with everything she would need for a fortnight in the sun, not four days in a vault, however luxurious.

Umair ignored all the shouting. The youngster was quite used to hearing raised voices between his incompatible parents. Instead he continued to snap away happily with his new camera while chattering in his native tongue with his elder sister.

Bert was less happy. He could feel his blood pressure rising and he didn't have his tablets with him. He'd left them on the bedside cabinet earlier in the day after a little morning glory eased by Cynthia. The memory of his pre-breakfast exertion brought a half smile back to his face. His mood was lifted further still with the recollection of a Twix and a Kit-Kat that his good lady had put into his inside jacket pocket as a lunchtime treat if he fancied them. Thankfully, after two pork pies and piccalilli, he hadn't had room for them earlier.

As quiet once again descended on the vault, apart from the clicks and giggles from Umair, Lily tried to make herself a little more comfortable. Manoeuvring her soft-sided case to a more restful angle, she sat down on top of it and eased out of her shoes. Stretching her legs in front of her, she wiggled her toes to try to increase the blood flow. Six-inch heels were never a good idea, but Giles loved her in platforms. Searching for a tissue in her handbag she attempted to wipe the last remnants of itchy make-up glue from her face before shoving the sticky tissue in the same pocket as the discarded prosthetics.

Lily took another tissue from the pack and began to wipe under her eyes. She had been unaware she was crying until telltale mascara blobs smeared on to the Kleenex. What had she done? Would Giles's anger at her tardiness have given way to concern at her whereabouts? Perhaps she could send him a text message to reassure him she was fine. Lily retrieved her mobile from her bag. No signal. Damn. She began to wonder how Giles's family would react if they found out what she had done, behaving like a common criminal. What would her own mother say when she finally discovered where her daughter was? Would she even care?

Cupping her hands in her lap, Lily remained motionless for a very long time. She could hear the children chattering together while their mother sat alone, sobbing quietly. The guard seemed to be breathing quite heavily and Lily wondered if he was starting to panic too. Either that or perhaps he had a chest condition? Given his size, it was probably the latter. Looking up from under her fringe she noticed it was neither. He was snoring. How could he sleep when they were trapped like this?

With the others occupied, Lily took the opportunity to have a proper look around their sumptuous cell. Though Brian the butler had told her that the family had been renting boxes here for years, it was the first time she had been inside Mayfair Safety Deposits. It was certainly plush. The carpeted floor was dotted with North African rugs and two of the walls were covered with oak panelling. A chandelier was hanging about four or five feet above their heads in the centre of the room, offering enough light to see the rest of the vault clearly. Casting her eye past the sleeping guard she could make out the two other walls, which were lined from floor to ceiling with what her father had previously told her were fully restored original Swiss bank boxes. She remembered the story of how the boxes had been salvaged from the vault of the Swiss Federal Bank. Daddy said their box had originally contained artwork and cash owned by the Nazi, Hermann Göring. Not for a second had she questioned her father's unlikely claim. There was, however, little doubt that in their present incarnation these rows of boxes would contain gold, bearer bonds, official documents, cash and perhaps priceless works of art. Lily had no interest what the other boxes held; she was only concerned about the contents of one.

Scouring the uniform rows, she easily located the brass cover with the number 777. It had hinges to the front and top and inside the padded velvet interior would be what she wanted. Her mother would never have given her the key, not if it contained what she feared it might, and so Lily had stolen it. Now she needed another key from the guard in order to open it, but where did he keep it? If what he said was true, she would have more than enough time to locate it.

Casting her eyes back towards the panelled walls, Lily noticed a water cooler. It was half empty. Would it be enough to last five people for four days? She looked again at the others in the vault. The Princess was still slumped on the carpeted floor, fidgeting with an enormous diamond ring on her little finger. Every other finger was also heavily encrusted with precious stones. Yet despite all these trappings of wealth, Almira's eyes betrayed her fear. Lily wondered whether it was because she was claustrophobic, or did she have other concerns too? The children were still playing together on the floor in front of their mother. Umair was now giggling, distracted from the scale of the drama by his sister. Posing for her brother to take pictures, Hafsa snatched a glimpse at Lily, the look one of curiosity rather than judgement.

Lily immediately looked away, ashamed, and instead glanced at the guard, who was still fast asleep. He seemed so calm and relaxed while she, like the Princess, was starting to fall apart. Lily wondered how within only a few months her life could have unravelled quite so spectacularly. What if it was true? How would she ever be able to tell Giles?

She took some deep breaths to calm herself. Lily was beginning to feel rather unwell. Her plan had been to be inside the vault for less than ten minutes but look what had happened. Panic rising, Lily tried to remain composed. What time was it? She looked at her watch. Only 6.15 p.m., just one hour and fifteen minutes since they had been locked inside. Lily was feeling increasingly hot and flustered and loosened her coat to try to cool down. She needed water and stood to walk the few steps to the cooler.

'Ah, not so fast, if you don't mind. Who says you can have some of that?'

The guard hadn't been asleep after all.

'I thought you were –'

'Yes, I know you did, but I need to keep my eye on you twenty-four seven.'

Lily felt a little affronted at his comment and tried to offer an explanation.

'I feel rather unwell and want some water, sir.'

'Well, in case you hadn't noticed there are five of us in here. As you can see for yourself, with only half a cooler of water left that is nowhere near enough for us to take some whenever we feel like it. So, I decide who gets what and when, if we're not to die of thirst before Wednesday.'

Bert's bluntness caused alarm among his audience, but he pressed on.

'We need to ration what provisions we have and you, missy, are last in line.'

Contrite, Lily returned to her suitcase and sat back down. She was forced to watch as Bert strolled across to the cooler, helped himself to a plastic cup and filled it. He wasn't particularly thirsty but was determined to show he was in charge.

'While we're on the subject, do any of you have any food with you?'

Hafsa nodded helpfully and from her mother's bag produced a packet of sweets and a bunch of grapes. A weird mix, thought Bert. Lily dug into her coat pocket and wiped prosthetic glue from a tube of extra-strong mints before placing them on the table. Bert, who had no intention whatsoever of offering up his chocolate bars to the group, looked down at the meagre provisions.

Mints, sweeties, fruit and only a few litres of water to last for up to four days. Surely it couldn't take that long to find someone else with a key? He sure as heck hoped not, otherwise he might have to start gnawing on the knee of the posh bird. Confiscating the rations, he put them into a desk drawer before tossing the drinking cup into a bin and returning to his newspaper, now being used to shield a copy of *Nuts* magazine from the children.

A few minutes later, as he turned the page to scrutinise the Christmas Babes, he caught Lily's forlorn expression. He couldn't resist a dig at her.

'I hope it's worth it. Whatever it is, I hope it's worth it.'

Lily didn't know what to say. She certainly wasn't about to discuss her motive with a stranger. Instead, she simply repeated her request.

'Could I possibly have some water, sir, please? I do feel terribly unwell.'

'Nope,' spat Bert, and returned to his magazine.

Lily lowered her head in a mixture of embarrassment and self-pity. Until a few months ago she had everything to live for. Her whole privileged life ahead of her. Then the note had arrived on her twenty-first birthday and her world had been destroyed. She still couldn't believe it was true.

5

6.15 p.m.

Mandarin Oriental Hotel, London

'Where are they, Dmitri?'

Prince Ansar stopped pacing the Sovereign Suite and paused at one of the French windows to look out over the silhouette of Hyde Park. The last hope of daylight had long since dropped below the horizon and the winter chill was creating a hint of condensation at the corners of the triple-glazed windows. Inside the suite was warm and comfortable. Despite the five-star comfort Ansar was still piqued that he wasn't relaxing in his new apartment at One Hyde Park instead. The launch party for the most exclusive address in London had been opulent even by his high standards, and he'd loved rubbing shoulders with Bernie Ecclestone and Lord Lloyd Webber, both potentially new neighbours. He would have been happy to pay the increased price tag for the triplex penthouse occupying the eleventh, twelfth and thirteenth floors of the prestigious apartment block, but his uncle the King had been insistent that other more practically priced properties should be considered. The family lawyers were presently in negotiations with the owners of another park-view apartment within the complex and Ansar was determined that this time they would be successful in securing one. He was keen to enjoy the block's private cinema, wine cellar and golf simulator on his next visit to London.

'What on earth can be keeping them so long, Dmitri? Try the driver again.'

The Prince's head of security stood bolt upright, a reverent distance away at all times.

'Sir, the driver tells me they are still not back in the car. The vault was due to close on time but we believe Princess Almira couldn't decide which jewellery to choose. I'm assured that they should be returning to the vehicle within the next few minutes, Your Royal Highness.'

Prince Ansar rolled his eyes; his fourth wife was renowned for her indecision. The Prince found her challenging and tiresome, but she was the only female who had provided him with a son who had lived past his first birthday and so her place within the family was secure. He frowned, impatiently checked the time on his twenty-two-carat gold Rolex and began to pace the room again, stalking from one end of the sumptuous suite to the other, the shag pile on the cream-coloured carpet so deep it covered the lower part of his shoes. Almira would pay for her actions when she did eventually return with his beloved son. She had taken the children out shopping hours ago. All she had to do was spend the afternoon entertaining them while he had business to attend to. How hard could that be in the largest toy shop in the world the day before Christmas?

The royal family's dinner guests would be arriving shortly. Tonight they were expecting twenty-four people, among them Simon Roberts, the new British Ambassador to Aj-al-Shar. Ansar was keen to introduce Umair to the Ambassador.

London was such a safe, friendly place for visitors from the Middle East and he wanted his young son to be made as welcome by the British Government as he felt.

As he strode past the kitchen area he could hear service staff busying themselves preparing for the dinner while an immaculately dressed butler cast his expert eye over the table and added a few final touchs. All that was needed was for the Prince's family to return. Where on earth could they be?

Increasingly frustrated by the wait, the Prince tried to distract himself with thoughts of his Christmas gift he had purchased. The new super car had been delivered to the hotel that morning. It was a million pound Bugatti Veyron in midnight blue and was a consolation present after missing out on the triplex penthouse. He easily justified the expense to the King as a bonus for a particularly lucrative oil deal he had negotiated on behalf of the royal family. Ansar planned to transport the car back to the Emirate in the hold of their aircraft when they headed home to Aj-al-Shar after the holidays.

That was if his wife ever returned with his son and daughter. Pausing at an antique mahogany-inlaid coffee table, he reached down for a copy of the daily *Al Quds* newspaper. Flicking through it, he was pleased to see a photograph of himself with the Mayor of London at Harvey Nichols, shaking hands and smiling for the camera. London was so much more fun than life back home, thought the Prince as he dropped the newspaper on to the table. Restrictions on day-to-day life could be a burden in Aj-al-Shar. At least playing with his new car would give him something to look forward to for a while.

Ansar checked his watch once more and was just about to begin pacing the room again when he was interrupted by a gentle tap at the door. Dmitri glided silently over to deal with the disturbance and a moment later was back by his master's side.

'Sir, the jeweller from Graff is here. Should I ask him to wait?'

Ansar shook his head with frustration. He had organised for the Bond Street jewellers to visit the suite to tempt Princess Almira with appropriate baubles. He had set a $1 million price limit for the store and the representative had arrived with suitable pieces.

'Yes. I'm sure she can't be much longer. Tell the jeweller her limit is now half a million dollars. I do not appreciate Almira keeping me waiting.'

Dmitri was about to head back to deliver the news when his mobile vibrated in his pocket. The head of security bowed slightly and took a few paces backwards. He reached into his jacket and retrieved his gold-plated iPhone, answering the call before the second ring.

Dmitri Boutakov had been employed by the Aj-al-Shar royal family for the past five years rising through the ranks to become a linchpin of Prince Ansar's close protection team. A former member of the Iraqi Republican Guard, Dmitri had escaped the country during the Allied invasion of 2003 before finding refuge in the Emirates. A change of identity, coupled with a ruthless loyalty to Prince Ansar, had been rewarded with both ample remuneration and elite world travel wherever his principal went. Over six feet tall and more solid than any England rugby prop, Dmitri Boutakov nevertheless managed an elegant, composed demeanour. His Jermyn Street suits fitted perfectly, specially tailored as they were to conceal an ever-present gun holster.

The phone call lasted just a few moments. Dmitri listened intently but said nothing. Ending the call, he turned to his master.

'Your Royal Highness, I do have some news on the whereabouts of the family. It seems there has been an incident at the vault.'

Prince Ansar was immediately alarmed, his only concern for Umair.

'My boy?'

'It appears he is still inside, along with Hafsa and Princess Almira.'

Ansar punched his fist against the wall in anger and frustration.

'Get him out now, Dmitri.'

'Sir.'

Dmitri was already heading for the door to begin his work when Prince Ansar's private secretary entered the room.

'Your Royal Highness, the British Ambassador is on the telephone.'

Dmitri paused, his head slightly bowed, waiting for any further instruction. Ansar strode purposefully across to his solid mahogany writing desk. It was a favourite piece of furniture that was transported to wherever he travelled. He picked up the telephone receiver.

'Simon?'

'Your Royal Highness, I'm afraid there has been an incident.'

The Ambassador delivered the words in his usual calm manner. Still, Ansar detected just a hint of concern.

'So I have just been informed, Simon. May I ask for further details?'

'Well, sir, I understand that several people have been taken hostage at the Mayfair Safety Deposit Vaults, among them Princess Almira and the children. We are unclear exactly what has happened at this stage, but we believe the guard may have lost control. A young British woman is also being held.'

Ansar dropped into the desk chair behind him. Within a second, Dmitri was by his side, waiting for any instruction.

'What else?'

'We are still in the process of assessing the situation, sir, but I assure you that the police are doing everything they can.'

'I am sure they are Ambassador. I'm sure they are. However, my only concern is how quickly my family will be returned safely to me.'

Ansar had little respect for any law-and-order service apart from his own.

Simon Roberts detected an air of sarcasm, but continued.

'I most certainly understand your concern, sir. Unfortunately, a definitive answer on when they will be released is not possible right now. At this stage, all I can say is that we are hoping it will be within the next few hours. We are in the process of tracing keyholders to the vault. Unfortunately, the owners of the premises do not appear to have been as judicious with protocol as regulation dictates on the listing of such keyholders. Please be assured though that the relevant authorities are doing absolutely all that can be done. We are hopeful the matter will be resolved satisfactorily and very soon indeed.'

Ansar was only half listening to the Ambassador's placatory words and was instead focused completely on his tone.

'Who is the guard?'

'Unfortunately, Your Royal Highness, I am not at liberty to say.'

Ansar stood and leaned against his favourite desk.

'Who is the guard, Ambassador?'

Although the Prince's voice remained measured, Simon Roberts was left in no doubt that Ansar expected a more helpful response.

'He is a former Metropolitan police officer.'

'Ah, the same police service you would like me to trust with my son's safe return?

The Ambassador ignored Prince Ansar's now more obvious sarcasm.

'I'm afraid the guard was asked to leave the police service several years ago under somewhat of a cloud. However he does seem to have been upstanding since. We do not feel that he will pose a threat to your family . . .'

Simon Roberts paused for several moments, unsure whether to add further detail. Ansar detected his unease and remained silent until the Ambassador spoke again.

'Although we do believe that he may have a gun.'

The Prince sat down slowly and closed his eyes for several seconds. Dmitri moved an inch closer to his principal. Eventually Ansar spoke.

'His name, Simon?'

'I'm afraid, sir, that is not information that I can pass on to you.'

'I must insist, Your Excellency.'

Simon had no interest in a stand-off with a high-ranking member of one of Britain's most important trade partners, but neither would he pass on the name of a UK citizen to a man who would quite obviously be bent on revenge. He attempted empathy.

'As a father I understand your concern, Ansar but as I have said, I'm afraid that is not information I can provide you with at this time. I'm sorry. Let me reassure you again, though . . .'

Without listening to the end of the pointless reassurance from a useless, now former friend Ansar slammed down the phone. Suddenly feeling every one of his sixty years, he leaned heavily on the back of his chair. Dmitri instantly offered a solid arm and guided the Prince to a sofa where he was sure his principal would be much more comfortable. Lowering the Prince gently down, Dmitri clicked his fingers and a large measure of single malt whisky was immediately on offer. Ansar drew heavily from the glass before resting his head back on the sofa and closing his eyes. He felt panic rising from the pit of his stomach. Nothing must happen to his son.

Ansar had until now enjoyed a charmed life guaranteed by financial security that the vast majority of his country's population could only dream of. He had been a handsome man in his youth with features that had matured well into middle age. His playboy lifestyle had been curbed only slightly with each of his four marriages. Being part of the family business, or 'firm' as his uncle the King referred to it, meant everything he wished for was his. But with great wealth had also come crippling sadness as each of his three previous sons died before reaching the age of one. Umair's birth six years ago at St Mary's Hospital in London, chosen by Almira because it was the same hospital where Diana gave birth to Prince William, had brought both joy and trepidation in equal measure. Cared for by an army of nannies, the boy had seemed well and had reached his first birthday without concern. Walking at one and talking before the age of two had been easily achievable milestones for the youngster. Umair was acknowledged by everyone as his father's chosen child. The Prince's other children, all daughters, knew and accepted that Umair was the favoured one, their father's total focus. Ansar was devoted to Umair and it was imperative that the boy must be returned safely to him.

'Sir, sir . . .' He was stirred by the slightly accented tones of Dmitri. The guard had worked hard to soften his Iraqi accent and, after years at school in the Middle East studying English as a second language, his diction was now almost perfect, though there was still occasionally just the slightest trace of his mother tongue. Dmitri had been monitoring the Prince closely and was anxious that he might be descending into shock. Ansar opened his eyes to see his physician standing next to him. But there was no need for medical intervention: he was angry not sick. Sitting up and regaining his composure, he waved the doctor away.

'Tell me what is happening at the vault now, Dmitri?'

The Iraqi hardman waited for the doctor to leave the room before answering.

'Sir, the British police are in charge. As you would expect, they are trying to keep matters discreet for now. However, we also have our own team heading to the vault. They will be there within a very few minutes. This is what you would want?'

Dmitri always had a sub-team of security personnel at his disposal wherever Prince Ansar travelled around the world. He'd dispatched half a dozen men to the vault and more could be flown in from Aj-al-Shar as required.

'Of course. When will Umair be returned to me?'

'Sir, the team will begin work as soon as they arrive. We have already researched Mayfair Safety Deposits with the help of the world wide web. We believe it dates back around a hundred years and from our initial investigation it would appear the vault has had two significant refits. However, the locking mechanism is old. The door is some fifty centimetres in depth. The walls, floor and ceiling are approximately three metres thick. We have also learned that the timing device can be overridden by the presence of two keyholders. We have a team working on locating them and will know more soon.'

Ansar looked straight ahead, staring blankly at a piece of artwork he had bought from Christie's during this latest trip to London.

'Locating keyholders should be a simple task. How long before he is back safely with me, Dmitri?'

The close protection officer paused, aware that only he could be the bearer of such bad news.

'Sir, one of the keyholders is in the vault.'

'The guard?'

'Yes, sir. As a result, we are presently attempting to trace others.'

The Prince continued to gaze at the painting, a Lucien Freud self-portrait.

'How long?'

'Hopefully within the next few hours, sir.'

Ansar stood and walked over to the window. It was now inky black outside and Dmitri could see the reflection of the Prince's face on the glass. A mixture of fury and concern were etched there, a tear welling in the corner of his right eye.

'Sooner than that, Dmitri. Umair cannot stay in the vault all night. Not with his condition.'

While Umair had not been stricken by the fatal illness that had claimed the lives of his half-brothers, he did have a medical condition that needed constant monitoring.

'Who is this guard?'

'Sir, from what I'm being told by our security team with connections to Scotland Yard, his name is Bert Jones. He is a former police officer and has been employed at the vault for approximately eight years.'

'What is his motivation?'

'We are unclear. At the moment it seems there has been no motive for his actions. Our people say he may have . . .'

Dmitri stopped abruptly.

'He may have what, Dmitri?'

'Sir, we are being told he may, he may . . . have just gone mad.'

Ansar wiped the corner of his eye and turned to face his head of security.

'What about the British girl. Who is she?'

'Unclear at the moment, sir.'

'You don't seem to know much, do you, Dmitri? Find out.'

Dmitri nodded, but he had one final uncomfortable question for his master.

'In the meantime, the hotel has asked whether the dinner party should be cancelled, sir.'

Prince Ansar picked up a heavy, ornate Baccarat crystal paperweight from his writing desk and threw it with some force at his head of security. The former soldier instinctively ducked and the ornament smashed to the ground.

'We will have them out by morning, sir,' he offered, before hastily leaving the room.

Prince Ansar shuddered. Blaming it on the winter chill, he increased the air conditioning in the room to thirty degrees. Standing alone, perfectly still, he thought he could just hear the faint hum of the London traffic many floors below. Motorists making their way home to their families, their cars laden with gifts, excited about what the next few days might bring. Looking through the window and across the road to the park, he gazed at the giant, brightly lit Ferris wheel, part of the Winter Wonderland he had taken his children to only yesterday. Umair had loved skating on the ice rink and afterwards had made himself sick with too much candyfloss. The children had insisted on staying for hours, captivated by the energy of the circus and squealing with delight on the helter-skelter and Santa's roundabout. That was less than twenty-four hours ago. Now his beloved son was trapped and frightened. He would expect his father to help him, but for the moment Ansar could do nothing. He banged his hand against the glass.

Crossing over to the Bang and Olufsen flat-screen TV, he began flicking through some of the two hundred channels. Pausing at every news station, he was relieved to see there was no word of the drama in the vault. That was how it should stay. His wife and children must be freed as quickly as possible, without publicity or fuss and then . . . then he would deal with this Bert Jones.

6

10 p.m.

Upton Park, Oxfordshire

Catherine Dunlop had spent her Christmas Eve like every other day of the last eight months, lamenting the pain she had caused her daughter Lily. Why had she hidden the truth from her? Was there more she could have done to help her?

Wandering over to the fireplace, she added another log to the dying flames and flopped into a sofa, careful not to spill a large Hennessy cognac she was nursing. Catherine had been drinking far too much of late, but so what; her life was a painful existence and the alcohol helped her through the night. For the thousandth time that day and the day before and the day before that she considered calling her daughter, but what would be the point? If Lily saw her mother's name come up on the screen she would immediately drop the call. And if by some miracle Lily did decide to answer, what would she say? 'Come home, darling. I'm so sorry. I want to make everything better, I truly do.' Both of them knew that those would be empty words; Catherine couldn't make things better any more.

She took another long draw from her crystal brandy glass and traced with her finger the cognac's journey as it burned down the length of her throat. Pausing to press her hand against her chest, Catherine stifled a sob as she remembered the moment her daughter had learned what her father had done. At first Lily had been disbelieving, then enraged, before storming out of her mother's life – forever, she said. Despite numerous desperate pleas, Lily had refused to make contact since.

Catherine wiped away a tear with the back of her hand and drained the remaining contents of her glass before reaching for the bottle resting on the occasional table next to the sofa. Of course she had wanted to tell Lily sooner, but Joseph had forbidden it. He had insisted he didn't want Lily to worry, that it was the doctors fussing over nothing, it was all a terrible mistake and Lily's health would be absolutely fine.

In her darker moments – and this long, lonely Christmas Eve had been one of them – Catherine realised there had probably been a more sinister motive for Joseph's reluctance. He knew the truth but was ashamed of what he had done. Having spent a lifetime dragging himself up from humble beginnings, he could not bear to die in disgrace. He insisted the eventual diagnosis had been as big a shock to him as it had been to Catherine. At first, neither had been prepared to accept the specialist's prognosis, but within a very short time there was no option. In his arrogance – or was it fear? – Joseph had left it too late for any medical intervention and his condition quickly deteriorated. He had died soon afterwards.

Even after Joseph had gone there was still no concern over Lily. Catherine had accepted her husband's constant reassurance before he died that his condition could not have affected their daughter. The doctors had been worried about Catherine at first, but tests showed she was fine, so Lily must be too, surely? Unnecessary tests would only cause distress. Also, she must protect her family from any potential embarrassment at all costs.

But was Lily really fine? The truth was, she didn't know. Guilt over her inaction now haunted Catherine every day. Why hadn't she just checked?

Walking over to one of the French windows, Catherine leaned against the frame. The restoration work at Upton Park had been so important to Joseph. Every minor detail was imperative to him, down to finding precisely the right colour tone for the window frames here in the dining room. She had spent many happy hours researching the estate's history before painstakingly sourcing suitable finishes. All for what? Catherine's previous enthusiasm for the property, her ideal family life, lay in tatters within these walls.

As she looked out over the well-lit grounds it seemed only yesterday that the lawn had been taken over by the Big Top and glass-walled marquee, the centrepieces for Lily's birthday celebrations. Everything had been just perfect. Her beautiful daughter was engaged to the man of her dreams and Catherine's parents, estranged for so long while her husband was alive, had returned into her life. She wondered what Lily was doing right now, right this very minute. She was aware from Giles's parents, Bridge friends of her mother's, that the young couple were still completely in love and marriage plans were well advanced. Catherine allowed herself the briefest of smiles as she pictured her only child walking down the aisle. Who would walk with her? Who would Lily choose to give her away? This should have been the most wonderful of times for mother and daughter as they planned the flowers, the venue, and the dress . . .

Clearly, Giles and his family knew nothing of Lily's fears. Would the wedding still go ahead if they did? Catherine thought it extremely unlikely. Now it was her daughter who was fearful of a deadly secret. Perhaps she knew the answer by now. If she did, would Lily have told Giles or would she have done as her parents did and kept her own counsel, this time in the hope of protecting her future husband's reputation? Joseph had so many lies to answer for. It had all been so different in the beginning.

Catherine tried to remember that magical moment when she first set eyes on him at the top of the Arc de Triomphe. He was a handsome boy with piercing grey-blue eyes and a strong Cockney accent. On the surface, it was hardly a match made in heaven, but Catherine had been smitten from the start, especially when he opened up his rucksack and produced 'a red rose for the English rose'. Catherine had spent an enchanting fifteen minutes chatting with Joseph about nothing in particular, but when it came to swapping contact details, her upbringing stupidly prevented her from taking the next step. She had watched him disappear into the Champs-Élysées crowd, perhaps forever.

Catherine had returned to her hotel room downhearted. She was travelling with her school friend Arabella Wyatt-Jones and the girls had been due to travel back to London the following day to begin life as brides-in-waiting for an appropriate suitor with a good job and an even better title. It didn't really matter whether they had anything in common with their grooms as long as their fathers approved; all that was expected of them was compliance. The following morning, Catherine and Arabella had taken a last lazy stroll along the Champs-Élysées; Arabella enjoying window shopping, Catherine hoping against hope she might bump into her cute Cockney boy again.

'Come on, Catherine, we need to head back to the hotel.' Unlike her friend, Arabella was keen to return to London and begin her search for a suitable suitor. 'I know you're hoping to see Romeo again, but it isn't about to happen. He could be anywhere. Seriously, we need to pack and make our way to the Gare du Nord. Let's go.'

Arabella had not been with Catherine the previous evening when she'd been taking in her final spot of sightseeing. Given what Catherine had told her, she was relieved. Frankly, the boy sounded rather common.

'Come on, we need to go,' Arabella added, with precision vowels.

Reluctantly, Catherine had to agree. Although Paris was only a small capital city it was unlikely she would bump into him twice in just a few hours.

'OK, OK, you're right, Arabella. I was hoping to see him again but I know it's unlikely. It's such a shame though, that's not what happens in the movies.'

'Really, what does normally happen?' It was the unmistakable East End lilt of Joseph Dunlop, who, having seen the girls from across the boulevard had defied death by dodging through the French traffic.

'Well, normally the hero turns up just in the nick of time.'

It was all Catherine could do to stop herself throwing her arms around him.

'Hi, I'm Catherine and this is Arabella.'

She stretched out her arm, determined she wouldn't miss a second chance to introduce herself. Joseph eagerly shook the hand of both girls.

'Hi, girls, I'm Joseph Dunlop. Tell me, what brings two such beautiful girls to a place like Paris?'

Arabella was immediately bored. What a stupid question. It was almost lunchtime and they needed to return to the hotel to pack. If they were late arriving back at Dover then Daddy's chauffeur probably wouldn't be there to collect them in the Roller and they would have to catch the train to Norfolk.

Her friend's eagerness to leave was completely lost on Catherine, who gazed dreamily into Joseph's eyes while trying to think of a witty riposte to his question about why they were in Paris.

'Well, I work as a croupier in an illegal gambling den and on Saturdays I top up my income by entertaining clients at a bar in the Pigalle.'

Joseph laughed. How was the best way to respond? He didn't believe her for a second, but if he acknowledged knowing about the red-light district, that could be him finished even before he reached first base. Perhaps it was a test? He decided to ignore the reference.

'Anyway, I'd really love to know more about what nice girls like you are doing in the most romantic city in the world. Coffee?'

Arabella had already zipped up her Puffa jacket and, flicking back her waist-length blonde hair, was clearly not interested.

'Yes, we'd love to. Thanks. That's OK, isn't it, Arabella?'

Catherine looked pleadingly at her friend, but Arabella had given this chap more than enough of her time.

'You stay; I'll pack the rest of your things for you and see you back at the hotel in half an hour. Do not be late – or else.'

Catherine nodded eagerly and, tucking her arm around Joseph's outstretched elbow, she headed in the opposite direction to her friend. It was a risk, one that she would never normally take, but for some strange reason she felt safe with this boy.

Returning from Paris, she had continued to see Joseph almost every day and it had taken only a few weeks for her to fall head over heels in love. Within a year she had accepted Joseph's proposal. Catherine knew her parents would be disappointed that she wasn't marrying into the life planned for her, but hoped they would accept that love conquers all. Even so, when the time came to break the news, Catherine was concerned.

Setting off from their tiny flat off the North Circular Road and heading up the M1 to Downcliffe Abbey, her parents' home and the fourth largest family estate in England, she had tried to sound relaxed.

'Excited?' she'd asked Joseph, wanting to appear positive.

Joseph had his foot pushed to the floor of his beat-up old Mini, but they were still struggling to reach 60 mph.

'Sure, as long as he doesn't shoot me for not asking his permission first. What's the worst that can happen?'

Catherine knew her father would be furious, but she hoped that, with her mother's help, he could be persuaded to concede to her wishes.

Sadly, from the very first moment her parents Alistair and Agnes had met her new boyfriend, they had taken an instant dislike to 'that rather common oik'. Joseph was no kinder about her father, referring to him as 'smug' and 'pompous', and occasionally as 'probably the rudest man in Britain'.

Catherine had hoped they would accept Joseph in time, but on the contrary after several extremely unpleasant verbal clashes between her bolshy boyfriend and furious father, her parents had made it clear that they would never approve of her choice of partner. They subsequently refused to attend the couple's unconventional wedding at Chelsea Registry office.

'Your cousin Alice tells me that's where that rather ridiculous warbler from that ludicrous popular music group the Tumbling Stones married. You won't catch me dead in there,' had been her father's riposte when she had begged him to embrace social differences and give her away.

Still, refusing to admit defeat and abandon her dreams of

a happy harmonious family life, Catherine had tried again and again, always without success, to build bridges between her new husband and her beloved father. All her efforts proved in vain as stubbornness and honour overcame any hope of a family bond. The young couple, cut loose by the Earl and Countess, were forced to make their way alone. Catherine took a job answering phones at a recruitment company in the city, while Joseph struggled with the only skill he knew, repairing personal computers for perplexed customers. Although efficient at his job, it seemed a thankless task; clients generally replaced the machine within a few weeks of repair anyway, rendering his hard work and the PC worthless. Finally after months of frustration, Joseph hit on a simple but effective idea that was to change the couple's finances forever.

As customers discarded their machines for newer models, he offered to buy the outdated computers for next to nothing. Building up a stockpile, he then sold the refurbished PCs to eager third parties. At first it was to mates who couldn't afford the latest model. The margins were small, but as technology moved on so did the volume of outdated units and he hit on a much more lucrative market.

Joseph saw developing countries as his Golden Goose, many of which he'd visited while travelling between finishing school and finding a job. If he'd gone on to university he could have called it a gap year; as he hadn't, it was more a shoestring holiday. His parents had warned him that it was a luxury he'd regret in later life and his anxious mother had implored him to go straight into the workplace. They'd died in a plane crash to Tenerife on their first ever foreign holiday before Joseph had made a success of his 'gap year' contacts and his business.

Joseph soon adapted the same computer refurbishment business model for mobile phone handsets and his fortune

71

was made. Within five years he was a multi-millionaire and the proud new owner of Upton Park. Catherine, to the manor born, was once again living the lifestyle she was accustomed to, but still her father had refused to accept Joseph or acknowledge his achievements. Alistair's stubbornness now encompassed his daughter too, and even when Joseph was out of the country, which was often, her parents declined to visit Upton Park. The very name offending Lord Alistair beyond comprehension, once the irony of the choice of name had been explained to him by a friend at his club.

Staying one step ahead as a communications entrepreneur meant that Joseph spent much of his time travelling to East and Southern Africa. By the time he'd made his first few million, he was long past caring what his wife's family thought of him. The estrangement had much more impact on Catherine, who was often alone. Day after day she would find herself walking around the grounds, killing time until tea was served promptly at 4 p.m. – leading the very life she had striven to avoid by marrying Joseph in the first place. Then, during one of her husband's brief visits home from Africa, Catherine had become pregnant. Joseph was already back in Rwanda by the time she discovered they were to be parents, and she was forced to break the news of impending fatherhood to him over the phone. Neither her husband nor her family were at the Portland Hospital nine months later for Lily's birth.

Catherine drew the curtains and walked back towards the enormous table where she had been wrapping the last of the gifts. Her perestroika with her family was improving and for the first time in more than two decades the Earl and Countess would be spending Christmas at Upton Park. It was a bitter irony that this was the first Christmas Lily would not be spending at the estate. Nevertheless, Catherine was pleased they were coming, despite her mother's insensitivity on the phone, commenting that Joseph's death had been such a relief to the family. The choice of words may have been crass, but she understood the underlying sentiment: much as Lady Agnes had longed for reconciliation, it had been impossible while Joseph was still alive. Soon after learning of his death in the obituary columns of *The Times*, Lady Agnes had engineered a meeting between father, daughter and the granddaughter they had never seen. Despite his austere upbringing, Earl Fitzwilliam had thawed at the very first sight of his long-lost girls and the memories of a long and hostile estrangement melted away.

Taking a sip from her replenished brandy glass, Catherine absentmindedly tied the last of the tags to the pile of gifts on the table. Brushing away yet another tear she was interrupted from her thoughts by a gentle tap at the door. It was Brian, the family's loyal butler, who had been by Catherine's side for the last twenty-five years. His knock was unmistakable.

'Hello, Brian, do come in.'

He entered carrying an oval scalloped gallery tea tray complete with a pot of Lady Grey. Setting it down, Brian studiously ignored the half-empty brandy glass on the dining table. His mistress had only recently taken to alcohol. He was sure it was merely a phase after the untimely death of the master of the house and the turmoil with Miss Lily, and would soon pass.

'Thought you might care for some refreshment, ma'am.'

'Thank you, Brian, just what the doctor ordered. Biscuits too, how scrummy.'

Catherine made a show of appreciation for the gesture though she had no intention whatsoever of drinking the tea and would return to her brandy as soon as she was alone.

'Almost Christmas, Brian. The house is looking wonderful, but it's just not going to be the same without.'

Brian instantly interrupted, concerned that Mrs Dunlop might cry and unsure what he would do if she did.

'Is there anything else I can get for you, ma'am?'

He was only too aware of the daily pain Catherine had endured since the disappearance of Miss Lily. He had heard his mistress sobbing uncontrollably many, many times behind the firmly closed door of her bedroom. There was no one to comfort her, she was desperately sad and completely alone. It was no wonder she had turned to the demon drink. Why had Miss Lily reacted as she did? Surely she should have visited a doctor rather than treating her mother that way? This business was none of her mother's making. She was not the one who deserved to be punished.

'My parents will be arriving first thing in the morning, Brian. Anything we've forgotten, it's too late now.'

Catherine smiled knowingly at Brian, safe in the knowledge absolutely nothing would have been overlooked. Every detail would be just perfect for her parents' first ever Christmas at Upton Park.

'Everything is prepared, ma'am.'

'I have no doubt, Brian. I have absolutely no doubt at all.'

With Joseph so often away in Africa, it was Brian who had been Catherine's friend and confidant. Always described him to friends as her rock, and he had witnessed the most intimate parts of her life. In fact, there had been times over the last quarter of a century when she had wondered how her life might have been different if she had chosen the handsome, elegant Brian as her beau. Would her parents have approved more of him than they had of her 'oik'? Despite his position, he was quite clearly from better stock than Joseph and, as Catherine often acknowledged privately, was undoubtedly the second most handsome man she had ever seen after her husband. Even now, twenty-five years on, Brian still cut an impressive figure as he stood ramrod straight in the dining room, dressed immaculately as always in his pristine black tails. Catherine shook the thought away.

'What's with the tails, Brian? There really is no need to be so proper with only me here.'

Brian would never be anything but immaculately dressed. He always wanted to look his absolute best, be his absolute best for her.

'It's late, ma'am, please allow me to complete the wrapping of the gifts.'

'Thank you, Brian, but it's all done. I wonder though if you could just write the tags on these last two, for the postman and the butcher.'

Brian hesitated, concerned. Catherine immediately picked up on his anxiety.

'What's the problem, Brian?'

'Erm, if I might be so bold, perhaps a handwritten note from you would be much more appreciated by them?'

'You're right, Brian, of course. You're always right. Mind you, I shouldn't imagine they would know the difference. Come to think of it, I can't recall what your writing looks like. Lots of notes from cook, but only ever typed notes from you.'

'Terrible handwriting, that's why, ma'am. I should've been a doctor.'

Catherine laughed. Taking out her pen, she scribbled on the tags.

'OK, all done. Perhaps you could help me put them under the tree?'

As the butler moved closer to Catherine and waited to be piled up with presents, he breathed in her exquisite perfume, a signature fragrance she had worn for the last quarter of a century. It always made him feel a little intoxicated. As he continued to stand completely still, Brian noticed one of the beautifully packaged gifts had a tag with Lily's name on it. He hoped against hope for Mrs Dunlop's sake that Miss Lily would realise her mother's actions had been intended to protect her child, someone she loved more than anyone else in the world. Perhaps she would choose tomorrow as the day to return and ease her mother's pain.

It took three fully laden journeys to the magnificent thirty-foot Norwegian spruce in the grand hallway before most of the gifts had been moved to their temporary home.

'The tree looks beautiful again this year, Brian, thank you so much. My parents will be mightily impressed.'

'My pleasure, ma'am.'

As Catherine returned to the dining room to organize the last of the gifts into piles, she looked down at the mess she'd created on the table, which still needed to be set for lunch tomorrow.

'I'm so sorry Brian, it's horribly untidy. I was carried away by the wrapping, some of the Christmas paper is just so beautiful this year. I'll help tidy up after we've put this last lot under the tree.'

Though Brian would have wanted nothing more than to spend another few minutes, an hour or a complete lifetime with Mrs Dunlop, he reluctantly rebuffed her offer.

'I won't hear of it, ma'am. I'll have your tea taken up to your room, ready for you to retire. Be assured the table settings will be in place by the morning. Would you prefer the white or the burgundy napkins set for Christmas lunch?'

'Oh, the white ones, please, Brian; Daddy is such a stickler for tradition, especially at Christmas.'

'Very good, ma'am.'

Brian was about to excuse himself to retrieve the appropriate table linen when Catherine stopped him.

'Just one more thing, Brian.'

'Ma'am?'

Anything, absolutely anything at all for Mrs Dunlop.

Catherine picked up an envelope from the table. It contained a voucher for a weekend break at the Ritz Hotel in Paris for Brian and his wife Beryl. It was a generous Christmas bonus to illustrate just how much she valued their services. There were also gifts for other members of staff stacked neatly in a pile at one end of the vast table. They varied from a bottle of vintage champagne in a brightly coloured festive-themed bag for the chauffeur, to a Champney's spa voucher for the chambermaid. Beryl and Brian were her favourites, though, and she wanted to reward them accordingly.

'Just a small token of my appreciation for you and Beryl.'

'Thank you, ma'am. That is very thoughtful of you.'

Little did Catherine know that under no circumstances would Beryl ever be enjoying Paris in the spring or any other time of year. In fact, she wouldn't even be aware of the gesture. Brian had no intention of leaving his mistress's side unless prised away with a crowbar. He would swap the labels and give Beryl the spa day. The Paris trip would be binned and the chambermaid would receive a book token he'd pick up from W.H. Smith when he was next in Chipping Norton.

'What time is it, Brian?'

'It's well past ten, ma'am, and you have a very busy day tomorrow.'

'You're right. I'll head up. See you in the morning, Brian. Merry Christmas.'

'Merry Christmas, ma'am.'

As Catherine made her way up the double staircase to her bedroom, she again felt the pang of loneliness stalking her. She pushed the feeling quickly away. It was completely her own fault, she had tried to ignore her child's concerns and now she was paying the price. Walking into her bedroom and dropping her watch on to the dressing table, Catherine looked across at the marital bed. It had been a long time since Joseph had loved her. Why had she given in to his ludicrous demands? Why hadn't she acted once he was gone? Now she was the one left with the guilt.

7

10.30 p.m.

Europe News

Steve Stone took aim with an elastic band at a Styrofoam cup strategically placed on the news desk in front of him. He flicked. He missed.

'Fuck it.'

Retrieving the band from the floor and taking aim again, he paused, slowing his breathing and lining up his aim with the centre of the cup. He flicked. This time he scored a direct hit and the cup span off the desk and into the metal waste-paper bin, ricocheting against the sides as it fell to the bottom.

'He shoots, he scores,' Steve murmured to himself before reclaiming the cup and replacing it on the desk. He considered continuing on with the time-wasting game but had already lost interest and instead stood to pace the newsroom for the umpteenth time that night.

There were at least fifty functional desks lined up in five uniform rows each with a computer, two TV monitors and a phone. They all faced a bank of screens which covered one wall of the newsroom from floor to ceiling. The screens were tuned to a myriad of news outlets and agencies both in the UK and around the world. Whenever a big story happened, the newsroom would be glued to the screens, waiting for the first pictures to appear either from their own news crews or letting out a huge collective groan if another news outlet had images on screen first. This evening, the biggest screen was tuned to the final of *The X Factor*, albeit with the sound muted.

Gary Barlow was quite obviously bickering about an act with Louis Walsh and Steve couldn't help but be intrigued. He wondered if he dare risk increasing the volume, but there were two other people in the room and, unsure of TV sound protocol for festive *X Factor* viewing, he decided against. Instead, Steve continued to pace. Being the new boy he had drawn the short straw on the Europe News Christmas rota. Even those colleagues who should have been at their desks had slipped across the road for a festive drink in the Red Lion leaving just Steve, the news editor and an East European cleaner on double time in the twenty-four-hour news room.

Steve had been with the channel for little more than a month. In a previous life he had been a top-notch newspaper hack but he'd decided to take the plunge and make the transition to what he saw as the glitz and glamour of TV news. It had seemed like the perfect next step in his extremely successful career but, as he was already discovering, all that glitters isn't necessarily journalism gold dust. Making his mark at the channel was proving almost impossible. He had still not even had a sniff of appearing on screen and, despite it only being four weeks, he was already considering returning to Fleet Street. At his farewell drinks party at the Olde Cheshire Cheese his editor had warned of the pitfalls of powder-puff TV journalism. She'd said he would regret the move but had magnanimously offered a return to the fold anytime within the first three months. Steve hadn't been sure whether she was being serious or snide, but felt safe in the knowledge that he was definitely making the right career choice.

At the paper, he hadn't worked over Christmas in years – unless he'd been covering a major news story. He remembered being sent out to Sri Lanka to report on the Tsunami on Boxing Day, 2004. Hundreds of thousands of people had lost their lives in the Far East, among them hundreds of Britons. His editor had been desperate for individual, human interest stories, and in the middle of the mêlée Steve had managed to find and exclusively interview a British couple who were still going ahead with their wedding on the island. There were many other exclusives too, including a surfer who had ridden in on the giant wave as his desperate partner watched from their hotel balcony. His paper had wall-to-wall exclusive coverage of the natural disaster and no lead story had been complete without a Steve Stone byline. A report on the plot to blow up a US passenger jet on Christmas Day had been another of his award-winning exclusives, for which he had received many plaudits. But being recognised as Newspaper Journalist of the Year wasn't enough anymore. He had wanted to taste the fruit at the top of the tree, and for him that meant TV news.

Oh, how the mighty had fallen, thought Steve. Looking around the empty newsroom, he realised that vanity meant he had probably made the biggest mistake of his professional life.

'Merry Christmas, mate. Want to pull a cracker? It's the only thing we'll be pulling tonight,' laughed Jim, the news editor, as he waved a limp paper cracker that his youngest had made for him. Steve offered a half-smile and pulled up a lumbar-support seat next to him.

'Sure, why not.'

The two men took a half-hearted tug at the cracker. It

tore easily, releasing a Lego brick which clattered on to the desk. Jim smiled at the thoughtfulness of his young son, Jack, who had tried to brighten up Daddy's evening. He put the piece of red plastic into his pocket before swinging his feet back up on to the desk.

'Not what you were expecting?' he asked Steve.

'The Lego or the job?'

Jim smirked and continued.

'Twenty-four-hour news, it looks really glamorous on the face of it, but, mate, let me tell you, it can be boring as hell. One of the toughest challenges is making sure the newsroom is always manned – or do I need to say personned? – at all times, even when there's nothing happening.'

Steve nodded his understanding. He was in his early thirties and had been a journalist for the past twelve years. A stocky, macho, Essex wide boy, Steve had hoped his rugby-player physique and rakish charm would see him progress from news to sports presenter without as much as a 'join us after the break . . .'

'Ain't that the truth? I'm used to being called in for the big stories, not sitting around waiting for them. I'd completely forgotten about the boring taxi-rank monotony the new boy gets stuck with.'

The two men fell into disinterested silence and Steve sneaked a quick glance at the girl band in the *X Factor* final. Married to the girl of his dreams, he had always been faithful, despite countless offers from women who were besotted by his handsome features and laissez-faire approach to life. Steve had lost count of the number of times he'd been propositioned by other journalists while away on assignment. 'What goes on tour stays on tour' was a come-on he'd heard far too often, but he was a one-woman man. Nevertheless, there was no harm in admiring the *X Factor* view. Especially when there was little else to do.

'How long do you reckon before I get a chance to be on air?'

Jim laughed so loudly he began to cough.

'Well, mate, let's say it doesn't happen overnight. You need to shine on a big story and hope the boss notices.'

That was all well and good, but how was he going to find himself on a big story while stuck working overnights at Christmas while the boss was probably off sunning himself in Barbados or skiing in Verbier? Steve changed the subject.

'Anyway, how do you think Arsenal will get on against City on Boxing Day?'

The news editor immediately warmed to the sporting theme and embarked on a couple of minutes of festive football discussion before the two men again fell into a bored silence.

Steve had been so desperate to leave behind the considered Sunday newspaper approach to deadlines and dive in to the avaricious hunger of twenty-four-hour news he hadn't contemplated what happened on nights like tonight. As he stared disinterestedly at the computer screen on the desk in front of him, it seemed the biggest stories on the wires service were either speculation on who was staying at Sandringham for Christmas with the Queen and Santa's gift-delivering progress around the world, which was being monitored by the NASA website.

'I'm gonna grab a coffee, Jim. Do you want anything from the canteen?'

'It's shut, mate. Ain't nobody here but us chickens . . . and the overnight presentation team.'

'OK. Well, I need to stretch my legs anyway. I have my mobile with me. If the Big One happens, call me.'

'Will do, mate, you can count on it.'

After strolling down the open central staircase and meandering towards the canteen, Steve discovered that Jim was right: there really wasn't anyone else there, apart from the overnight presenter and the studio gallery team. The other journalists who had gone to the pub were either still there or had sloped off home. Loosening his tie, Steve walked tentatively towards the gallery. It was all so new to him. Peering through the double-glazed window of the soundproof door, he could see the director and her team going through the motions. Someone had brought in a tray of mince pies and he noticed an open bottle of champagne on the side. Despite the festive fare, they looked even more bored than he felt.

Steve shoved his hands into his suit pockets and turned to walk through the Europe News foyer, where the larger-than-life presenters' photos smiled down at him. Sid Parker and Suzanna Thomas were the two big beasts in the twenty-four-hour news jungle, the stars of the show. Of course there were other presenters, but those two were top of the tree. Sid had recently signed a five-year deal, moving from *Have a Nice Day UK* to Europe News and for a seven figure salary. It was quite a coup for the news channel and the newspapers had been in meltdown covering the story. Sid posing nonchalantly on the edge of his studio desk, Sid out on the town with a pretty blonde, Sid invites readers into his beautiful home across six pages of *Hello!*, Sid covering his face as he left Mahiki's night club at 3 a.m. He was the new big name in news.

Steve had followed the newspaper coverage with fascination and envy. He'd had his sights set on Sid's job, or the sports equivalent, even before he joined Europe News. Seriously, how hard could it be, sitting reading autocue for a couple of hours and then going home to count the money? What did Sid Parker have that he Steve Stone didn't? Apart from being one of the biggest names in TV with almost ten years' experience in front of the camera covering some of the biggest stories of the twenty-first century, a river-view apartment across the Thames from MI5, and more money than Bill Gates. Apart from that, what did he have?

Steve laughed at his own absurd envy. Sid was due in later to present the breakfast show. It wasn't his normal stint at the channel, but the viewing audience was always massive on Christmas morning. The news anchor had readily accepted when his Head of News asked if he could do the honours.

Steve took a seat in the foyer and waited for the clock to tick towards the end of his shift. As he disinterestedly watched the TV tuned to the station's output, with subtitles on the lower third of the screen, he could see that Santa, Rudolph and the rest of the gang were presently somewhere over the Atlantic. The new boy was about to wander back up to the newsroom for more aimless football banter with Jim when he was distracted by headlights at the other side of the glass entrance doors. Peering through, he could see a chauffeured Rolls-Royce Phantom whisper to a stop. Even from this distance, Steve could clearly make out the Spirit of Ecstasy ornament posing majestically on the bonnet. The suited chauffeur opened a rear passenger door and Sid Parker slid effortlessly from the vehicle. He usually had an Audi A8 to ferry him to and from the studios, but the Rolls was a little festive thank you from the chief executive of the channel for agreeing to work Christmas morning.

'Lucky bastard,' mouthed Steve.

Even at this late – or was it very early – hour, Sid had an air of unattainable supremacy. At thirty-seven, he was the perfect age and attitude for TV. Long-limbed and muscular, his mischievous smile won over any woman he locked on to with his mysterious brown eyes. Stricter than Kate Moss when it came to calorie counting, he was rewarded with a perfect washboard stomach, accentuated by exquisitely tailored clothing. His E. Tautz two-piece wool suit was offering him some protection from the early morning winter chill. The Aspinal silk tie, an early Christmas gift from a hopeful squeeze was draped, undone, around his neck. His shirt, open slightly at the neck, was elegant but neutral.

Steve tugged awkwardly at his own Next tie, a gift from his mum.

Thanking his driver and tipping him with what looked to Steve like a fifty-pound note, Sid glided through reception, removing his suit jacket and hooking it over a finger before nonchalantly resting it over one shoulder. His Turnbull and Asser shirt, now more visible, skimmed a perfect six-pack, making Steve even more aware of his own body. While he considered himself a reasonable specimen, Steve's was less a six-pack, more a Party Seven compared to Parker. Standing he offered a quivering hand to the TV god.

'Hi, Sid, Merry Christmas. I'm Steve Stone, the new reporter. What a trouper, coming in on Christmas morning. Hope you have great plans for later in the day?'

'Thanks, Merry Christmas to you, too.'

Sid's handshake was friendly but cursory. He kept walking, but Steve saw this as his big chance so awkwardly tagged along.

'You're in early for the breakfast shift, aren't you? It's only about midnight or just after. Didn't expect to see you until around four thirty.'

'Who are you, my mother?' joked the presenter, clearly a little irritated by whoever this chap was. He'd been out clubbing and had originally planned to head home for a few hours' sleep around 10 p.m. But with temptation never far away he'd stayed much longer. He'd eventually had to drag himself out of the club at just before midnight and head directly to the studio for a shower and a change of clothes.

'Always thought you were great when you were at *Have a Nice Day UK*. Great move, though, coming to Europe News.'

'Thanks.'

'Wondered if we might be able to have a chat sometime. Not now, obviously, not right now, of course not, but maybe when you have a bit more time perhaps . . .'

Steve paused, not sure what else he could say. Sid kept walking.

'Sure.'

'Wanted to chat about what it takes to be a success in TV, which you, of course, er, undoubtedly are, if I might say so. In a blokey way, obviously.'

Good manners were Sid's trademark and despite becoming increasingly irked by this unnecessary chat, he continued in a friendly tone.

'No problem, mate. Whenever.'

Reaching the stairway, Sid began bounding up two at a time, heading towards his dressing room.

Fastening his tie again, Steve remained awkwardly at the foot of the stairs, staring up at the athletic news god, completely deflated by the exchange. Colleagues used to want to stop him as he walked by. When he was kingpin. Now he was a nobody. Sid wouldn't even remember his name. What a shallow business TV was. He slumped on to the bottom step, his head in his hands, his heart no longer in his job. What had he done?

Steve wasn't sure how long he'd been sitting there or even if he'd dropped off, but when he eventually raised his head he was aware of bleary-eyed staff passing him on the way to the increasingly busy newsroom. It was Christmas morning and he had the weight of the world on his sad shoulders. Walking dejectedly up the stairs with the others, he glanced over to Sid's office. It was filling with sycophantic staff, keen to vie for the attention of the star who was probably in his dressing room showering before preparing for the programme. Turning away, he headed back to the news desk where Jim was still in the same position he'd left him in. The news editor looked at his watch.

'Might as well call it a night, mate. Nothing happening and the morning shift is filing in now – apart from Josie, of course. Surprise, surprise, she's rung in sick, as usual. She does it every Christmas morning, selfish bint. Try to get some sleep. See you at six p.m. Have a tepid turkey butty for me.'

'Merry Christmas, Jim. See you later.'

Steve tugged on his coat and headed towards the car park. The first flakes of snow were starting to fall as he walked outside. Pulling up the collar of his high street purchase, no designer labels for him, Steve hunched his muscular frame against the cold and trudged across the road towards his Mini Cooper S. There was already a light dusting of snow on the roof. If it continued to fall like this it might well cause problems on the roads and he'd have to think about waking early to make sure he'd be in for the evening shift. Steve doubted he could be any more miserable. Arriving at his car, he noticed a beer bottle that had been thrown over the nearby fence smashed into pieces on the bonnet, scratching and denting the paintwork.

'Brilliant. Can this Christmas get any worse?'

Steve kicked a tyre of his car as he fished in his pocket for the keys and clambered inside. Not quite a Rolls-Royce Phantom, thought Steve as he started the engine before flicking on the lights and then the windscreen wipers to try to clear away some of the snow, which was falling a little more heavily now. He was tired, cold and miserable, and couldn't wait to get home. Screen cleared, he was about to drive away when his mobile phone alerted him to an incoming text message. It was probably from his mum. Reaching into the pocket of his suit jacket, Steve retrieved his BlackBerry and looked at the screen.

Merry Christmas. Phone Hursty.

Hursty had been one of Steve's best police contacts when he was on the *The World on Sunday*. The guy had given him some top exclusives, but they were the kind of tips that always involved a lot of further research, which was fine for a newspaper journalist but wouldn't be so useful to him now. Besides, he was knackered and couldn't be bothered making small talk with the former copper who, while a nice enough chap, was also a raging alcoholic. Even though it was only 4 a.m. he would undoubtedly want a pint and expect Steve to pay for it. He ignored the text.

Driving past Trafalgar Square, Steve looked up at Nelson's Column but the snow was now falling so heavily he couldn't make out the Admiral's statue at the top of the 51-metre pillar. Nelson would struggle to see Westminster today, let alone across to his old foes in France. Turning down Whitehall and heading towards Big Ben, Steve noticed a couple of police officers in the security hut at the entrance to Downing Street. It was early Christmas morning and the Prime Minister would no doubt be asleep with his family at Chequers, but the street still needed a police presence. Almost at Big Ben and his phone bleeped again. Another text. Leaning across to retrieve the phone from the passenger seat he could see it was Hursty. Doesn't he ever give up, thought Steve as he dropped the phone into the passenger foot well.

Crossing Battersea Bridge and only a few minutes from home, Steve's phone rang. Noticing there was no caller ID displayed, he was relieved that rather than Hursty it must be the office.

'Steve Stone speaking.'

'Ahhhh, gotcha. Merry Christmas, Steve-o, Hursty here. Fancy a drink? Our usual's open at Smithfield Market. Could murder a swift half.'

The reporter had been outfoxed by the former cop. He might be a piss-head, but Hursty was still as sharp as a tack.

'Sure, why not. But it'll have to be a quick one. I'm back at work tonight. See you in a tick.'

A few minutes later and with no traffic on the roads, Steve was parking as close as he could to The Hope. Although it generally opened at 4 a.m. to serve the workers from the nearby meat market, he had half-expected the pub to be closed on Christmas morning. No such luck; the outside lights were on.

Locking his car, he dashed across the slippery road and into the warm, welcoming interior, glad to be out of the snow. Hursty had of course already arrived and was in the dining room on the upper level with a full English breakfast and a pint of Guinness in front of him. An empty glass was on the table, confirming it hadn't been his first of the morning.

'Flippin 'eck, Hursty, you don't hang about, do you?'

'Hungry mate – and thirsty. What do you fancy?'

Steve cast his eye over the bacon, sausage, fried bread, tomato, beans, black pudding, kidneys and liver with a side order of toast, butter and marmalade.

'Just a cup of tea I think for me, mate. I'm driving.'

Steve pulled up a chair and sat next to his old mucker.

'Anyway, how are you? How's tricks?'

'Duckin' and divin', you know me.'

'Missing the police?'

'Nah, done my twenty-five years, pensioned off. I told ya.'

'I know, mate, just making small talk. What you doin' now?'

'Well, they wanted me to join the British Transport Police. Not doin' that. Can you imagine? Every time I saw my old buddies, they be makin' *toot toot* noises at me.'

Hursty momentarily put down his knife and feigned pulling a whistle on a steam train before returning to his full English. Steve laughed at the insult. He could never imagine Hursty as a BTP officer. He'd been one of the best cops in the business, but time and booze had slowed him to a crawl and the crumpled man that sat slouched in front of him. Weirdly though, he seemed to be wearing some sort of uniform. Poor sod, maybe it was his old police gear and he just couldn't let go. Steve tried again.

'Missing the Met though, buddy?'

'Nah, not really. Got myself a new job . . .'

Ah, of course. He must be some sort of security guard; that would explain why he was up all night. Hursty paused as the waitress came over to clear away the plates.

'Another pint of Guinness, Delores, please.'

Steve had hoped to have been gone by now, but Hursty obviously wanted some Christmas company, exactly what the reporter didn't need. He wanted to go home to bed and curl up with his misery.

'How you finding it, the new job?'

'It's OK. Doesn't have the same perks as being in the police, but it keeps the wolves from the door. How's your new job?'

'It's OK too. I miss the paper, if I'm honest. I hate being the new boy. I might as well be invisible,' lamented the journalist. Sipping his builder's tea, Steve searched for more small talk and thought old scoops would fill ten minutes before he could make his excuses and leave.

'Hey, do you remember some of the stories we broke?'

Steve and Hursty both laughed at the memories that had made front-page news. The story about a premiership foot-baller arrested for dealing cocaine in a top city centre hotel had taken weeks for Steve to stand up but was eventually a brilliant exclusive for the paper. Back then Hursty had been custody sergeant at a central London police station and a great contact. With no inside information, he would have no exclusives for Steve now.

'Yeah, not half. What about that actor stalking royalty?

That was a classic. Worked out really well for both of us. You had a massive story and I made a few bob. Those were the days,' laughed Hursty.

'Yeah, they sure were.'

Steve looked outside at the falling snow and then at his watch.

'Anyway, Hursty, I really have to go. I'm knackered. Have a good Christmas – we should catch up in the New Year, yeah?'

'Sure you don't fancy a swift one? I'm going to have another.'

'Really, I have to get to bed, mate, but have whatever you want. I'll pick up the tab on the way out. Merry Christmas, Hursty. Here you go.'

Steve slid a twenty-pound note across the table. It wasn't much of a gift, but he hadn't been planning on Christmas visits so early in the day.

'And Merry Christmas to you too, Steve-o. You were always a good sort.'

Hursty tossed a book of matches over to the reporter.

'Stopped smoking last summer, Hursty. You should do the same. It'll kill you.'

'OK, well keep them anyway. You never know when they might come in handy.'

'Thanks very much, I'll treasure them always.'

'You just might.'

Steve shook his head. What was the daft old bugger talking about? Must be the booze. He offered a playful army salute and politely shoved the matches in his coat pocket before settling the bill and heading out into the wintry London street.

Dejectedly Steve Stone climbed back into his car, unaware how monumentally the meeting with Hursty was about to change his life.

Christmas Day

8

Early Christmas morning

Mayfair Safety Deposits

The temperature inside the vault had been dropping for hours and it was freezing cold. There should have been no requirement for heating during the Christmas break, and the thermostat had automatically switched off when the timing device secured the door. Thankfully, the electricity was still working and the lights remained on.

The children had complained bitterly they couldn't feel their toes, but had eventually fallen into a fitful sleep. Hafsa had entertained her brother tirelessly by posing for countless pictures on his toy camera and gently convincing him there would be plenty of time to play with his Scalextric later. Umair was now nestled beneath his mother's coat, Squidgy, already missing one eye, was tucked under his arm. Hafsa was lying quietly next to her brother, her arm wrapped protectively around his shoulder, her own coat pulled tightly around her tiny frame.

Princess Almira was awake but lost in thought as she sat

hunched against the cold. She knew that her husband's anger would know no bounds and without doubt be heaped solely on her whenever they were eventually freed from this freezing tomb. She began to shake, unsure whether it was cold or fear.

Her upbringing in the dusty backstreets of Aj-al-Shar had been hard. The family home was small and crammed with her parents and six daughters. Almira's father had always longed for a boy and eventually left the family for a new wife when her mother failed to oblige. The girls were left with little money, but her mother always made sure they were sent off to school with a warm breakfast and a desire for learning. Almira was the brightest of the sisters and struggled her way up to further education before securing a financial position with the Aj-al-Shar royal family. It hadn't taken Ansar long to be smitten by her brains and beauty. Almira at first had little interest in the renowned playboy, but with an army of deprived siblings to provide for she did her mother's bidding and married into wealth and privilege. The contrast – leaving a hovel where she'd enjoyed the support of a loving mother for a palatial apartment where she was nothing more than the fourth and lowliest wife, ever-conscious of her place among the senior wives – was stark. Ansar had soon tired of her and only the provision of a son had saved her from being cast aside completely.

Almira had never adjusted to her loveless marriage. Her frustration and inferiority manifested themselves as either disinterest of high-handedness. These days, she used her brain little and spent her time eating, depressed or shouting at her staff. Though her family no longer wanted for anything, what Almira desperately craved was Ansar's love. After what had happened, she knew the chances of that were nonexistent. She closed her eyes and wished she had chosen a different life.

Bert Jones, who had steadfastly refused to give up his seat even if she was a princess, was slumped over his desk. This time he was sound asleep and snoring loudly.

Lily was still wide awake. She was cold, tired, hungry and continued to feel quite unwell. Realising she would receive no sympathy, she had remained seated on her suitcase with her back against the vault door, her coat pulled tight around her shivering shoulders. Surely they would be out soon? It could only be a matter of time now.

Looking up at the security boxes she tried to distract herself by wondering what might be inside each of them. Undoubtedly jewellery, probably artwork and of course papers that their owners would want to keep private. Scanning the neat rows, her eyes stopped again at box 777. Inside lay the answer to the question that had haunted her for the last eight months. Thinking about her father now, her heart that had once swelled with pride at the very mention of his name was breaking. Lily closed her eyes in the hope of sleep but instead her thoughts immediately returned to the morning of her twenty-first birthday.

While leaning out of the window and chatting to her mother she had seen the mail van arrive. Keen to open whatever the postman had brought for her, Lily had run down the grand ceremonial central staircase and into the oak-panelled entrance hall. Dashing across into the magnificent library she had found Brian the butler already waiting for her with two piles of post.

'A very happy birthday, Miss Lily. There seems to be quite a lot of post for you this morning. All sorts of surprises for the birthday girl.'

'Thank you, Brian, how exciting.'

'What a pleasure it must be to be twenty-one, Miss Lily. I can hardly remember that far back.'

'Nonsense, Brian. You look marvellous.'

Lily gratefully took the piles with both hands and almost skipped across to a seat next to the marble fireplace, an elegant George III piece, acquired during the restoration of the house.

With her eyes screwed tightly closed in the claustrophobic vault, Lily could still visualise the elaborately carved fireplace, which her father had never tired of telling her dated back to the eighteenth century and had cost £300,000. It was worth every penny, he had always added proudly.

Lily rubbed the centre of her forehead and tried to ignore the waves of nausea that had started to overwhelm her. Instead, she pictured again the assortment of cards and good wishes from her aristocratic friends vying for position on the mantelpiece. She even indulged in a half-smile. Everything had seemed so perfect that morning.

'Would you like some breakfast, Miss Lily?'

'Not yet, thank you, Brian, I'm too excited to eat.'

'You must eat. It's going to be a long day.'

'OK. Poached eggs, please, Brian. Actually, only one. Need to fit into my dress this evening.'

'Very good, Miss Lily.'

Brian, in bow tie, white gloves, waistcoat and tails even at this hour of the morning, turned and headed to the kitchen. With her mother busy in the garden, Giles off to have her magnificent engagement ring altered to fit and Brian the butler organising a poached-egg breakfast, Lily sat in silence. She had been looking forward to the party for what seemed like forever. Her mother had taken care of every expensive detail. The florist bill alone was in excess of £20,000. The birthday gifts had already started to arrive. Catherine had bought her an eighteen-carat pink gold Cartier watch or 'timepiece' as her mother always insisted on calling what everyone else in the world referred to as a watch. Catherine had presented it to her daughter a couple of weeks earlier, aware there would be far too much activity on her actual birthday for her to appreciate the gift.

Continuing to open her mountain of cards, Lily thought about Giles. He'd be back soon with her ring and he'd hinted at perhaps another gift too. They were both keen to make the announcement of their engagement at dinner. Giles's parents would be there and she hoped they'd be pleased. He had assured her that his father had given them his blessing. Lily was a little sceptical, but pushed away her concern. The marriage proposal was a dream come true. Finally, she would fit in among the 'People Like Us' set. Giles's wealth and privilege would guarantee her the social standing she so desperately craved.

Although Daddy's little princess wanted for nothing, Lily had an almighty chip on her shoulder. Her snooty friends Lady Anne and Eleonora always took the opportunity to look down their perfectly bridged aristocratic noses at her nouveau riche father. As a result, they often dismissed Lily as an Ivy girl: a social climber who could never really fit in with their upper-class set. She still recoiled with embarrassment at their mirth when she confused Glastonbury and Glyndebourne. Giles's lineage and his ring on her finger would put those snooty noses out of joint.

Curling her feet under her on the Louis XVI armchair, Lily returned to opening her mountains of post until Brian interrupted with her breakfast.

'In a second, Brian. I just want to flick through the rest of my cards. Goodness, there are so many. Did the postman bring all of them this morning?'

'Yes, Miss Lily, all of them.'

There were copious birthday wishes from family and university friends, as well as names she could barely remember from school. Lily stood to place some of the cards on the mantelpiece. Continuing to flick through the remainder of the pile she noticed an elegant white envelope. There was no postage stamp on it, perhaps it had been hand-delivered or given to the postman as he reached the entrance to the estate. It was probably an invite to another celebration.

'Oh, how lovely, Brian, it looks as though there's another party to attend soon.'

'Very good, Miss Lily.'

Dropping the other post on to a side table she eagerly ripped opened the envelope lined with tissue paper. Inside was a notelet with a turquoise, brown and gold firefly motif printed on white woven card. It began "Dearest Lily . . .'

Scanning the handwritten words beneath, Lily paused. She was aware she was starting to yawn and her vision had become strangely blurred. Her hands were cold and clammy and there was a ringing in her ears. The room began to spin. Lily collapsed against the fireplace, her face smashed into the marble, knocking her unconscious, just as her mother entered the room.

Lily sat bolt upright in the vault, visualising every syllable on the note that had destroyed her dreams:

Dearest Lily,

Congratulations on becoming twenty-one. I hope you have a truly wonderful day.

What a great age. So much opportunity and excitement should lie ahead for you.

However, today is also the day for you to learn the truth about your father's death. He was an evil man who didn't deserve to live. In fact, he had such disregard for you his daughter that you too could die soon. I want to tell you why . . .

Lily wiped her forehead with the back of her hand as she remembered the rest of the note. Despite the cold, she felt incredibly hot and clammy. She began rummaging for a clean tissue from her bag, unaware that the children were awake until Hafsa, the young Arab girl, walked across to her.

'I'm sorry to interrupt, but my mummy has forgotten to bring my brother's AEDs and she's very worried about it. The guard is asleep and we are not sure what to do. Can you help?'

Lily looked bemused.

'Of course I will help if I can. What do you need? What are AEDs?'

'Anti-epileptic drugs. We don't have his medication with us. He has seizures without them. What should we do?'

9

7.30 a.m.

Battersea

Try as he might, Steve Stone just couldn't sleep. It wasn't right to be in bed alone on Christmas morning while the rest of the country was wide awake ripping open gifts and feigning delight at Marks & Spencer socks and BHS hankies. He pictured the excitement. It would undoubtedly be accompanied by a backdrop of raised voices fighting over who most deserved the purple-wrapped chocolate in the enormous Roses assortment tin, even if it was only breakfast time. Ah, the joys of a family Christmas.

Steve turned awkwardly on to his side, aware of something weighing heavily on his mind. For a moment he couldn't quite place what was causing him such concern. He was sure it wasn't just the frustration at missing out on quality quarrel time. Then like a speeding train it hit him. He'd made the wrong career decision, a monumental mistake that would mean eating a whole truckload of humble pie before his former editor would give him even the slightest chance of securing his old position back. He wanted to call her right now, right this very minute, catch her with one sock on, one sock off and a purple Roses chocolate stuffed in her mouth and beg for her forgiveness. But, even in the depths of jobseeker panic, he knew that a Christmas Day interruption would be unlikely to receive the desired response. In fact, with Christmas falling at the weekend this year, it meant an extra bank holiday for the nation, so she wouldn't be back in her plush corner office until nine o'clock Wednesday morning. That was three more fitful sleeps away. He made a mental note to be on the phone by 9.15 a.m., promising her his first-born and a pint of rhesus-B negative month after empty-arm month for a year if she'd only take him back.

Steve rolled on to his other side and pulled the duvet over his head. He felt dejected and lonely. His new wife, Jackie, had headed up north to spend the festive break with her family in Yorkshire. 'No point both of us having our Christmas ruined,' he'd insisted when she suggested cancelling her travel plans so they could celebrate their first Christmas as a married couple together in London. Jackie had reluctantly boarded the train from King's Cross the previous afternoon. Steve peeked from under the duvet towards the bedside table and their black-cube LED alarm clock, bought as a wedding present by his sister Rachael. It was only 7.45 a.m., he'd been in bed for a grand total of ninety minutes and despite trying every conceivable position, it was no good, he just couldn't sleep. Propping himself up on one elbow, he reached for the bedside phone and dialled Jackie's parents' number.

His wife worked in the press office at New Scotland Yard. They'd met when Steve had been pushing for an interview with the Commissioner, following up on a corruption tip he'd received. Jackie, keen to protect her boss, had been determined the interview wouldn't happen. Jackie won the

103

battle, Steve won the girl. Eighteen months later they were married, with the Commissioner there to witness the nuptials in the front pew of St Bride's, the journalist's church off Fleet Street.

'Morning, darling. Merry Christmas.'

'Why are you awake?' Jackie was talking with her mouth full.

'I bet it's a purple one.'

'Sorry?'

'Never mind. I can't sleep, and anyway I wanted to wish you a Merry Christmas. Do you like your present?'

Life in Sunday newspapers had been lucrative and Steve had splashed out on a Tiffany diamond-and-platinum eternity ring to celebrate their first Christmas as a married couple. It was almost a year since they'd tied the knot and he wanted her to know how much he loved her every single day in every single way.

'It's absolutely beautiful, love, but can we really afford that sort of extravagance now?'

Jackie was a down-to-earth Northern girl who had always cut her cloth according to her finances. Although their bank balance had been healthy, Steve's move to TV had meant a reduction in salary and she'd rather be able to eat than wear a ring so heavy she couldn't lift her arm. Originally in regional newspapers, she'd moved into public relations for West Yorkshire Police and had quickly made a name for herself. When the Chief Constable, Phillip Hughes-Jenkins, had been promoted to Met Police Commissioner he was keen for her to follow him to London and head up his media team. Jackie had immediately accepted, but still jumped at any chance to visit her parents in Dewsbury. She was planning to stay there until the end of the week.

'Don't worry about the cost, darling, you're worth every penny. Anyway, it's fine, I've decided to go back to my old

104

job. I'm calling the editor as soon as the Christmas holiday's over.'

'Whoa, just a cotton pickin' minute there, big guy! Isn't that a bit hasty? Actually, hold that thought a second, love – Mum's shouting at me to come and help. She wants me to peel the bloody sprouts.'

Jackie broke away to speak to her anxious mother who, with apron on already, had her sleeves rolled up in readiness for a military-style Christmas lunch manoeuvre in the kitchen of the modest terraced house. They were expecting fourteen at the table and her father had been dispatched to round up spare chairs from the loft, the shed, the neighbours and, if absolutely necessary, the vicar.

Steve waited patiently and soon found himself being seduced by Jackie's soft Yorkshire accent. He eavesdropped as she calmly reassured her mother they still had plenty of time to cook the turkey before the army of hungry revellers arrived at 4 p.m. Listening to her relaxed chatter 170 miles away made him miss her even more. How he wished he'd been lying next to his wife when she'd opened her gift this morning. Excitement and delight, followed by huge pleasure would have meant whispers, giggles and failed attempts at hushed lovemaking in her parents' box room. Instead, here he was lying in the bedroom of their trendy South London flat alone. He contemplated tempting her with a little phone sex before laughing off the prospect of his wife trying to relax into sexual pleasure in her mum's hallway with the swirly Axminster and Dulux Apple White walls.

'Hello again, love.'

'What are you wearing?'

'Er, my Debenhams nightie and a pair of fluffy dog slippers with hangy-out red tongues that Mum bought me for Christmas from BHS. Why?'

'It doesn't matter.'

Jackie squeezed the phone a little closer to her cheek.

'I really love my ring. I'll show you how much when you come up on Wednesday. You're still coming, aren't you?'

'Only as long as you promise to wear the nightie and the slippers.'

The newlyweds both laughed at the image of domestic bliss.

'Listen, I have to go before Mum has a coronary, but I'm worried you might do something rash while I'm not there to keep an eye on you. Promise you won't drink and dial.'

'I won't.'

'You will.'

'I promise I won't.'

'I know you will.'

'I WON'T.'

'Seriously, love, please try not to ring the editor until at least Wednesday afternoon when you get here. Then I can tie your hands behind your back.'

'Now we're talking.'

'Don't be smutty, Steve Stone. Listen, I really have to go. Please, please, please don't do anything rash, OK? I really don't want a husband who has blown two jobs in as many months. I might have to take in washing.'

'What does that mean?'

'Never mind.'

'Don't worry, darling, everything will be fine, seriously. Have a wonderful day. Say hi to your parents and I'll see you on Wednesday.'

'Will do. Now don't forget there's a TV dinner in the fridge, you know what to do, don't you?'

'Yeah, just call Gordon Ramsay,' joked Steve, then more seriously: 'I really miss you. Love ya loads.'

Reluctantly, Steve replaced the receiver and flopped on to his side of the bed. What was he going to do to fill his day until he was due at the office in ten hours' time? He began by staring at the ceiling and counting the cracks that the builder who'd renovated their flat had promised to come back to fix as part of the snagging list. Four, five, six . . . He wondered if he'd be able to remember how many without writing it down. He counted them again just to be sure, definitely six. He was confident he would be able to remember six and, hey, if he didn't, they'd still be there for him to count again tomorrow. Perhaps there'd be seven by then.

Bored with counting cracks, Steve turned his head and stared blankly out of the bedroom window. The snow was still falling, though it seemed to be easing a little. He should be able to drive to work without too many problems later on. Great, he could barely contain his excitement at the prospect of another twelve hours with Jim the news editor and his inane football chat. Perhaps he could call his old boss this morning, after all. He could phone on the pretext of wishing her a Happy Christmas then, before putting down the phone, just happen to throw in breezily: 'Oh, by the way, can I have my old job back, pretty please?' Steve cringed at the prospect of her choking on her chocolate before dropping the call. He'd just have to be patient and wait until Wednesday.

Without looking, Steve tried to remember how many cracks there were in the ceiling. Was it six or was it seven? He looked at the clock again: 8.15. He was so bored he could have found excitement in emulsioning the kitchen walls with a cotton bud. Perhaps he should try some press-ups; he'd been letting his fitness regime slip after the push to get in top shape for the wedding, and looking at Sid's rippling abs had made him feel inadequate. Nah, he wasn't quite that bored yet. Perhaps he'd attempt fifty a bit later, and maybe a few sit ups too. Not quite yet though, still a bit early for that sort of exertion. Steve absent-mindedly flicked on the bedroom TV in the vain hope it might send him to sleep.

He'd watched the series finale of *Boardwalk Empire* yesterday and there was nothing else saved on their Sky+ so he scrolled through the programme guide for suitable sleep-inducing fodder: *The Wizard of Oz*, *Casper the Friendly Ghost*, *Home Alone* or *It's a Wonderful Life*. Decisions, decisions, thought Steve, before rubbing salt in his open wound and switching to Europe News to see what his soon-to-be-former employer was broadcasting.

Steve sat bolt upright and turned up the volume. There was Sid in full breaking-news mode.

'If you're just tuning our way, let me update you with the details we have so far . . .

'We're receiving reports of an incident at a security vault in the centre of London. We believe it is the Mayfair Safety Deposit vault. Our sources say there are five people trapped inside. There appears to be a timing mechanism in place which is proving difficult for the police to override.

'We have limited information about those trapped, but Europe News believes they include a family from the United Arab Emirates, a British woman and the security guard who is also British.

'For the latest, let's take you to our live position just outside the vault and our correspondent Jillian Simpson, who's standing by . . .

'Jillian.'

As the reporter began to update viewers by basically reiterating what Sid had just said but with a slightly different intonation, Steve reached over for the bedside phone and dialled Jackie again, this time on her mobile.

'Hello again. Merry Christmas again,' she said with her phone tucked under her chin while scoring crosses in the bottom of peeled sprouts.

'Have you seen Europe News?'

'No, why?'

'You better have a look, Miss "I'm a PR chief but I don't know what's happening on my own patch".'

Mildly irritated by her husband's sarcasm, Jackie put down the vegetable knife, turned down Bing Crosby serenading her mum with 'White Christmas' on the CD player and switched on the kitchen TV. Jillian Simpson was just wrapping up and handed back to Sid in the studio. Jackie picked up the phone and the vegetable knife again.

'Missed it. What's happened?'

'Siege in a central London security vault. Who'll know what's happening?'

'Fred's on call, but I can't imagine he'll have much more than what Europe News is saying on the ticker. Probably won't tell you, even if he has.'

'Once a PR always a PR, my darling.'

'Does that mean you want the ring back?'

'Ha ha. I'm going to make some calls. Speak later. Not too many sprouts – don't want you supercharged by the time I get there!'

Steve replaced the bedroom receiver. His brain was still switching up a gear when his mobile rang.

'Steve Stone.'

'Steve-o, Hursty. Thanks for breakfast.'

His old contact's words were starting to slur. Hursty obviously hadn't stopped drinking when Steve left him, and from the background noise he was still in the pub.

'Hursty, glad you enjoyed it, buddy. It was great to see you, but sorry I'm a bit busy right now, mate, big story. Gotta go.'

'Yeah, I know. Watching it on the telly in the pub. Those matches might be just the spark you need to set this story on fire, ho, ho, ho.'

'What you talkin' about?'

Hursty must be going bonkers. It was probably the beer talking.

'The matches I gave you earlier, mate, remember?'

Hursty paused to steady himself against the bar and draw on his pint. Replacing the glass, he accidentally knocked his security pass on to the floor and bent slowly to retrieve it.

'You still there, Hursty?'

'Yes, yes. Are you watching the telly?'

'I am. What about this box of matches, mate? What does that have to do with this siege or whatever it is?'

'It's not a box, it's a book. You haven't lost it, have you, Steve-o?'

Steve wasn't sure what the drunken old fool was talking about and he really didn't have the time to indulge him any further. He was in full journalist mode and needed to find out more about the story. Facts, facts, facts, it was part of his DNA.

'Look, sorry, Hursty, would love to chat, but I really have to go.'

'Shame everyone is so far away from the action.'

'What? What is it that you're talking about now, buddy?'

'Imagine if someone had the ex-directory number for the vault.'

'Yeah, just imagine. Woo-hoo. Anyway, listen, mate, *It's a Wonderful Life* is on the telly later. Why don't you head home and put your feet up? Mind how you go.'

'Ha, ha, you're a funny guy.'

Steve had had enough of this old soak's ramblings and snapped.

'Seriously, Hursty, I'm putting the phone down now.'

'OK, OK, keep your hair on, but just before you go, I remembered that I wanted to tell you about my new job. I forgot to mention it earlier – my new job, I mean, not the matches. I mentioned those already.'

'Stop. You're rambling, mate. Anyway, you did tell me

about the job. Security, isn't it? Hursty, I'm going to be rude now and just put down the phone. OK, buddy we'll catch up in the New Year. Look after yourself and go home while you can still walk.'

'Well, it was a new job until last night. Didn't follow protocol, apparently. How was I supposed to know? Seriously, Steve-o, how was I supposed to know?'

Hursty sounded as though he was starting to cry. A drunk crying into his beer. Steve slapped the palm of his hand against his forehead.

'Going now, Hursty. Go home and be safe, buddy, but definitely going, going . . .'

'It wasn't my fault, Steve-o; honestly it wasn't, but the owners of Mayfair Safety Deposits didn't quite see it that way.'

The guard almost spat the name of his former employer before downing a good half-pint of Guinness in one slug. Steve gripped tightly on to his mobile. He couldn't believe what he'd just heard.

'Whoa, what are you saying? Are you telling me you work at this vault that's on the news right now?'

'No, Steve-o, I'm not. Aren't you listening? I'm saying I used to, until last night. I wanted to tell you about what happened earlier, but you were in such a hurry to go.'

Steve sat down on the edge of the bed and focused.

'I'm sorry about that, Hursty. I'm listening now though. In fact, buddy, you have my undivided attention. Go right ahead, take your time. No rush, all the time in the world.'

'The book of matches . . .'

'Yes?'

'The ones I gave you?'

'Yes?'

'You do still have them, don't you?'

'Of course,' laughed Steve, jumping from the edge of the

bed and searching desperately around the bedroom for the matchbook.

'They have a phone number on the inside cover.'

'All right.'

As Steve listened he began rifling through the pockets of everything he was wearing last night. Where was it, where had he discarded the damned thing? He couldn't find it in any of the obvious places.

'You do have it, don't you?'

'I've left it in the hallway, mate. Just remind me of the number again, though, would you?

'Sorry, Steve-o, I don't know what it is; I couldn't remember it, that's why I'd written it down in the first place. It definitely has a three at the front . . . or was it an eight? Sorry, I can't remember, that's why . . .'

'. . . you wrote it down. Yes, you said. Why is it important, Hursty? Can you remember that?'

Steve was starting to lose interest again. He wasn't sure he believed Hursty's wild claims about a phone number connected to the vault. There was a big story unfolding and he was talking to a pisshead on his mobile while searching for a box – no, a book – of bloody matches with a phone number on it. What a waste of valuable contact-chasing time.

'Oh yeah, sure I can remember what the phone number is for Steve-o, no need for sarcasm. I'm trying to do you a favour here, buddy, for old time's sake, but if you're not interested . . .'

'Sorry Hursty, go on.'

Steve sat back down on the bed, resigned to another five minutes of slurred fantasy. From what Hursty was saying, he wouldn't have much intel about the vault. For starters, he was new, so not much to tell and anyway, he had been sacked, so no further access to what was happening.

'It's the number for inside the vault. I wrote it down so I

wouldn't forget it in case I needed to ring through to Bert, see if he wanted anything, another cuppa, that sort of thing.'

Steve had to remind himself to breathe.

'Bert?'

'Bert Jones, the guard who's stuck inside with the Arabs and the posh bird. He's not very happy with me you know. Not very happy at all. Still, he has another few days to cool down and get over it.'

Steve grabbed a pen from the bedside table and began writing on the back of an envelope containing the gas bill. He made a mental note about remembering to pay it after the Christmas holiday.

'Bert, Arab family, posh bird, another few days . . . tell me more.'

'The timer on the vault, it won't open until nine o'clock on Wednesday morning, unless they can find a second keyholder.

'Second keyholder? Go on.'

'The police need to find another person with a second set of keys that match Bert's, but it's proving difficult. Bill Smith has gone to the Galapagos – never really fancied it, myself, I must say – and Yoni Sanchez is on his way to Chile. Should be there by now. His brother was one of those miners who were trapped, must have been terrible.'

Hursty was starting to ramble again and Steve needed him to focus.

'Shocking. Anyway, how did your mate Bert get stuck in the vault? Didn't he know the door was about to close?'

'It's a long story. Happy to meet you for a pint later, if you like, and run through it. Anyway Steve-o, not sure how much longer the police are going to leave the line connected. I'd try that number while you can, mate.'

Steve leapt from the bed and began another search for the matches.

'You do have it, don't you?'

'Sure, I told you: it's in the hallway. I'll grab it now.'

'Good-o. Anyway, no need to thank me. A pie and a pint later on would be fine. See ya.'

With that, Hursty abruptly hung up.

Steve grabbed his jeans and shoved one leg in his trousers while at the same time grappling with the laces on his trainers. Where had he put that box of matches? He couldn't find it anywhere. He raced down to the hall, but it wasn't with his keys either. It could only be in the car. Please, please, please, let it be in the car. Grabbing his car keys and snatching his coat, he rushed towards the door before dashing outside. The snow had stopped but a good four or five inches had settled on the roof of his Mini.

Brushing away the mounds of powdered snow from around the door handle, he clambered into the driver's seat. There was no sign of the matches anywhere. Scrabbling around on the passenger seat and the footwell in a blind panic, he still couldn't find them. Think, think, think. Steve paused, leaned against the head rest, both hands on the chilly leather steering wheel, and tried to remember events of earlier. Desperately trying to recall what happened he visualised Hursty handing them over and him shoving them deep into his pocket. Then he paid the bill, then he walked across the road in the snow, then he opened the door then . . . Eureka! He remembered. He'd pushed the book of matches in the glove box; he couldn't remember why, he just had. Grabbing at the latch he paused for a second. Please, please, please be there. He released the catch and the door yawned slowly open. Hallelujah, there it was, exactly where he'd left it. He reached across to retrieve the flimsy book and tentatively opened up the matches. Inside was Hursty's unmistakable scrawl and a series of numbers.

Could it really be the ex-directory number for the vault? There was only one way to find out.

10

8.30 a.m.

George V, Paris

Suzanna Thomas had been whisked to the George V hotel as a romantic Christmas treat by her ever-eager boyfriend, Christopher Peters. In the dim, winter half-light of Christmas morning she stared up at the chandelier in their luxury suite just off the Champs-Élysées. Her mother had already texted to wish her a Merry Christmas and to deliver the exciting news it was snowing in London. Suzanna wondered if it was snowing here too. She'd look out of the window and check in a moment, once Christopher had stopped writhing around and groaning on top of her. His breathing was becoming quicker as he edged closer towards climax. Nearly there now, thought Suzanna wearily. Keen to speed up the laborious proceedings, she wrapped her legs around his arching back and scratched cat-like with ten perfectly polished fingernails into his firm behind. That should do it, she thought. But still her boyfriend continued, thrusting even deeper. Perhaps he's waiting for me, she pondered, while noticing with some

115

irritation that there was in fact a slight chip in one of what she had mistakenly thought were perfectly painted fingernails. If he'd only hurry up, she could fix it before breakfast.

It was time to play her ace. Suzanna scratched even deeper while offering an immaculately timed gasp of feigned coital pleasure. That seemed to do the trick. Moments later, Christopher grunted with sexual satisfaction before rolling contentedly next to her.

'That was so amazing.'

'For me too, darling,' lied Suzanna.

Within a very few moments Christopher was asleep. Keen to leave his side, Suzanna padded to the window to look outside. Yes, it was snowing here too. How romantic. Suzanna carefully closed the Thai silk ruched drapes with blackout linings and headed silently towards the bathroom to fix her nail, leaving her boyfriend snoring quietly on top of the enormous bed. Desperate not to make the slightest noise, she opened the en-suite door a tiny inch at a time. She didn't want Christopher waking up and wanting sex again anytime soon. Tiptoeing into the bathroom, Suzanna reached for the nail polish remover.

Christopher Peters had hoped that Paris would be the perfect romantic venue for Suzanna to finally say '*yes*'. Although a well paid IT consultant, the three-day break was costing far more than his bank manager would be happy with and was his last throw of the dice. Sadly for Christopher, while Suzanna viewed him as borderline handsome and a 'better than staying home alone' partner, she also considered him thick and wet. Ordinarily, having the two basic attributes of fog would not necessarily preclude a romantic union for Suzanna Thomas. The non-starter in the marriage stakes for her was rather that Christopher lacked the vital ingredients for a long and happy relationship: money and power. Although she had readily accepted his offer for a winter break in Paris, little did Christopher know he had no chance whatsoever of being successful in his hope for 'happy ever after'.

Naked, she gazed into the bathroom mirror, carefully scrutinizing her boyish figure from every angle. Elfin was a continuous struggle for the thirty-year-old. TV added ten pounds, which meant she couldn't afford to gain so much as an extra ounce if she was to stay at the top of her game. Checking her pert posterior, Suzanna was pleased to see there was nothing to worry about for at least another day. Reaching for a toothbrush and smothering it in Colgate, Suzanna chuckled at the thought of Sid Parker being stuck with the Christmas morning shift. He'd been poached from breakfast TV at vast expense and was now her co-anchor on Europe News, a corporate decision that frankly she wasn't very happy with. He was an OK presenter and was also OK to look at, but that was the crux of the problem right there: he was just OK. She'd have to have another word with the Head of News when she returned to London. In the meantime, reaching for her back molars with her flexi toothbrush, Suzanna turned her attention to an even more pressing problem and that was preventing Christopher from dropping to one knee. It was her festive mission to keep him upright during all waking hours. She'd lost count after at least four previous almost-proposals and there had been another sneaky attempt which she'd just managed to head off shortly after they'd arrived yesterday. Suzanna gurgled and spat as she recalled the close shave.

Sauntering arm in arm along the Champs-Élysées, breathing in the luxury and chic of the most famous boulevard in Paris, Suzanna had been quite pleased she'd accepted Christopher's invitation to join him for a mini-break here. It was so elegant and sophisticated. A little further along the avenue and Christopher ruined the mood when he suggested they stop at a pavement café. With them both wrapped up against the chill wind, he was keen to sit outside and watch the world go by. Suzanna rather sulkily agreed.

'If you insist, darling. But don't you think it's a bit chilly out here?'

'Oh, come on, it'll be fun and romantic.'

Christopher led a reluctant and wary Suzanna across to an empty table as far away from the shivering Gauloise smokers as possible. He pulled out a chair for her next to a circular brass-topped café table. Suzanna sat hunched and sullen as Christopher wandered inside to track down a waiter. He spotted one warming himself behind the bar with no intention whatsoever of venturing outside. Suzanna pulled her coat tighter in an attempt to keep out the cold and waited impatiently for his return. Her beauty regime did not include winter wind taking off the top layer of her skin. Nevertheless, she was determined not to cause friction so early in the trip, especially as Christopher was picking up the bill.

Her boyfriend eventually returned with two strong black coffees in tiny white cups, the Gallic waiter not even offering to open the door for the crazy Englishman struggling with both hands full and wanting to sit outside.

'Thank you, darling.'

'This is so romantic. I absolutely love it here, don't you, darling?'

'It's a little chilly sitting outside, but yes. Thank you so much for bringing me here.'

The couple fell into an awkward silence while Suzanna took a sip of her incredibly expensive black coffee to try to warm her up and Christopher seriously considered whether they should move inside after all. No, it was bracing but not freezing, and such a perfect setting for him to propose.

He'd already tried: Le Pont de la Tour in the shadow of London's Tower Bridge; the top of the Empire State Building in New York; and for a bit of drama Thunder Mountain

Railroad at Disneyland in LA. Every time he'd be just about to drop to one knee when Suzanna seemed to interrupt, obviously unaware of his motives but nevertheless spoiling the mood. Perhaps here in Paris, the city of love, she would be swept up in the moment and accept his offer of marriage. Looking across the bistro table at her pouting lips that were turning slightly blue in the cold, he wasn't quite so sure.

Watching her boyfriend carefully, Suzanna feared another attempt at *happy ever after* might be about to career her way and was determined to head it off at the pass.

'I hope there aren't any big news stories happening back home that I might be missing, Christopher. I'll be furious,' she half joked.

The timely intervention worked, completely ruining the mood. Christopher reluctantly thought better of it and instead sipped unhappily on his over-priced coffee. Suzanna tried to down hers as quickly as possible, burning the roof of her mouth in the process. A few minutes later and the couple was ready to leave.

'Let's have a stroll around the shops,' suggested Suzanna, standing up and relieved to still be able to feel her toes. Shopping would be much safer territory, as long as she steered a path away from any potential jewellery-store pit stops.

They'd spent the rest of the afternoon bashing Christopher's cards in Louis Vuitton and Lancel. Credit-card crunching was one of Suzanna's favourite pastimes, especially when the card in question was Christopher's rather than her own, and all had gone well. While she waited for Mr Right to come along, Suzanna was reasonably happy to spend quality shopping time with Mr Right-Now aka Christopher Peters. Only when it would have been impossible to carry any more designer-labelled carrier bags did the couple eventually return to the elegant hotel room at the George V. With its eighteenth-century-inspired furniture and fittings, overlooking the Pierre I Courtyard,

Suzanna had to grudgingly concede that the bright airy room was charming, sophisticated and tastefully decorated. Christopher had chosen well and it was certainly more enticing than the alternative: sitting alone in her Knightsbridge apartment watching Christmas TV and eating a Marks & Spencer ready meal for one with a half-bottle of South African Chenin Blanc. She did of course realise that there was a downside: she would have to have sex with Christopher as a thank you, probably several times. May as well get it over with.

Putting down her shopping bags and shrugging the winter fur coat from her delicate shoulders, Suzanna switched to Marilyn Monroe charm. Smiling seductively, she stalked towards Christopher, who stood wide-eyed and excited by the window. Thank goodness this quite obviously won't take long, thought Suzanna to herself, but said out loud: 'Darling, thank you so much for bringing me here. It's so romantic. What on earth can we do to pass the time until dinner?'

Christopher could feel his heart racing. He was the luckiest man he knew. He was in one of the most luxurious hotels in the world and about to make love to his famous TV presenter girlfriend who had a body to die for. Was now the right time to propose?

'I love you, Suzanna. I want to ask you to be my . . .'

Blindsided by the outburst, Suzanna knew she needed to act quickly to head off another bloody proposal. Pressing her forefinger against his lips to prevent him reaching the end of the question, she stroked his mousy brown hair with her free hand.

'No, I wasn't thinking of talking, my darling. Guess again.'

Taking his cue, Christopher reached to release the zipper on his girlfriend's Pucci dress, one of several pre-Christmas gifts he'd bought her. Suzanna in turn stretched to close the curtains.

'Let's leave them open,' panted Christopher, who was finding it almost impossible to control himself as Suzanna stood suggestively in front of him in satin La Perla underwear.

Inwardly, she groaned, as if it wasn't challenging enough, she had to watch too.

'Yes, please, let's,' she whispered into his hair before reaching for his hand and leading him towards the Louis XVI-style bed. As Christopher began to undress, she closed her eyes. It would be over soon. Lie back and think of England.

Suzanna bared her teeth for inspection in the bathroom mirror before turning her attention to her canines and recalling the rest of the previous day.

Late afternoon interlude quickly over, they'd headed out for a surprisingly excellent dinner at L'Espadon. Suzanna had surreptitiously managed to ply Christopher with most of the Merlot and on returning to their hotel suite she'd decided haste could easily be interpreted as desire. She wriggled free from her Alice Temperley cocktail dress almost before the bedroom door had closed. A little drunk and unsteady, Christopher was in heaven and fumbled in frustration with his dinner suit. Suzanna took control and, guiding him to the bed, she pushed him down before entertaining him with a little Burlesque floor show she'd seen Christina Aguilera perform in that film with Cher. Soon after, the wine did the trick and he had fallen asleep. Suzanna had padded quietly to the bathroom to brush her teeth, exactly where she was standing again now. Sadly, last night's aborted romp meant sex this morning had been compulsory, but at least it hadn't included a proposal.

Rinsing her mouth, Suzanna checked for blemishes on her usually flawless skin. She was concerned about damage the winter wind might have inflicted on her face yesterday. The last thing she needed was her make-up ladies having to start covering zits when she was sitting next to bloody Sid Parker. Suzanna was an English rose with an alabaster complexion and ash-blonde hair expensively cut into a tousled mane. Her piercing blue eyes were her trademark feature and seemed to bore through the TV screen, seducing every male viewer who tuned in to Europe News. The female equivalent of Sid Parker.

Suzanna had enjoyed an excellent career so far and was on track to become the next big, big name in British TV. That's certainly what her agent had promised. She'd begun at Europe News as an overnight reporter and her break had come with the arrest of an England rugby player on charges of grievous bodily harm. Suzanna had stumbled on the story by accident while queuing to pay for her weekly shop at Tesco. The player's parents were in the queue ahead of her and she'd overheard them discussing his arrest while they packed their frozen chips. Ditching her trolley and escaping from the store, she'd dashed to her car to alert the news desk and was immediately dispatched to the police station. A film crew would meet her there. Her reporting was first and accurate, leaving the opposition standing, and impressing the boss in the process. Since then she'd brought many benefits to the channel. As well as being stunning, she was also an excellent journalist and her interviews had won countless awards. She loved the sweet taste of success and worked every hour she could before finally making it to the Holy Grail of news anchor.

Unfortunately, Suzanna had never been quite as lucky in love. Her excellent judgement at work didn't translate to matters of the heart and her mother was starting to despair of ever having grandchildren. When he'd first joined the channel, Suzanna had even contemplated the thought of covertly dating her co-presenter Sid. Fortunately she'd realised, just in the nick of time, what a huge mistake that would be. She was riding high in her career and any off-screen dalliance with Sid Parker was certainly not getting in her way. As a result, lust had turned to loathing. The emotion was entirely mutual.

'Merry Christmas, darling. Fancy seconds?'

Christopher's question made Suzanna jump. He was standing naked in the doorway, smiling seductively and quite clearly keen on a repeat performance. What was she doing here? Surely sitting at home alone would be preferable to having sex with a man she couldn't bear to touch her even in the opulent luxury of a five-star Parisian hotel?

'Ooh, yes please! I thought you'd never ask.'

Stroking his bare shoulder she wandered back into the bedroom with Christopher, who was already nibbling awkwardly at her ear.

'Just a second, darling, let me check what's happening at home,' stalled Suzanna, reaching for the remote control to switch on the TV. She couldn't get out of the habit of a daily news fix even when she was away from the office. Tuning in to Europe News, she could see that Sid was on air. Ha, serves him right for staying in town. Undeterred, Christopher was now amateurishly fondling her breasts and Suzanna was about to succumb – sooner we start, sooner it's over with – when she noticed the breaking-news strap scrolling along the bottom of the screen.

Siege at Mayfair vault. Hostages reported.

Suzanna screamed out, making Christopher, who'd reached as far as her super-flat stomach in his ham-fisted attempts at foreplay, jolt backwards.

'What's the matter? What is it, darling?'

Suzanna ignored the question. She couldn't believe what she was seeing. A massive story in London and Sid was all over it.

123

Suzanna was incandescent with blind fury. She'd been completely foolish to leave the country, even at Christmas. Big stories always happened at Christmas. The 2004 Tsunami, Romania executing its President, Dean Martin dying . . . She was sure there were plenty more examples but was too furious to consider them. Sid was the pretty boy, the eye candy for the ladies. She was the proper journalist who should be taking the lead on big stories. Yet here she was, the other side of the Channel, while a siege played out in central London.

'Fuck, fuck, fuck.'

'If you insist,' leered Christopher, moving towards her and further kneading Suzanna's bare breasts.

'Get off me; this is all your fault.'

Suzanna jumped away from the bed as if she had been scalded. A moment later she was tearing around the room, throwing her belongings into a suitcase. Christopher sat shocked and alarmed by the whirling dervish in front of him.

'What are you doing?'

'Look, look at the screen. There's a massive story unfolding and I'm not there. It's your fault for bringing me to this cheap, nasty hotel.'

Crestfallen at the insult, Christopher remained silent. Realising she had probably gone a little too far, Suzanna paused from hurling cashmere into her case. She was going to need Christopher's help to return home, so no point antagonising him. Offering her most seductive pout, she strolled towards him.

'I'm so sorry, darling. I obviously didn't mean that, but I am terribly upset. I really can't be here while Sid is stealing the show back home. I need to be in London, not in Paris. Help me.'

Suzanna sat on the edge of the king-size bed and began to stroke Christopher's arm. He immediately softened.

'But, darling, it's Christmas morning. How can we get

home? Public transport will be limited, if not non-existent, and anyway we're due to stay until Monday. If it's such a big story it will still be going on by then and you can take over and show him how it's done as soon as we're back. What do you say?'

Suzanna felt trapped and furious. Of course she couldn't, wouldn't wait for another two days while Sid made her look a fool. He did fluffy. She did hard news stories. Her frustration once again rose to the surface.

'Don't be so bloody stupid, Christopher. Can't you understand, I don't care if I have to swim there: I'm going home.'

He had no response and a sulky stand-off descended on the room. Suzanna returned to her suitcase and Christopher turned up the volume on the TV.

11

10 a.m.

Europe News

Racing up the by now familiar central staircase at Europe News two steps at a time, Steve Stone reached the top slightly more breathless than he'd anticipated. He was immediately swept up by the excitement of a newsroom running on breaking-story full-octane energy. Steadying the ship was Head of News, Miles Winstanley, who was already in his glass-fronted office having arrived at his desk slightly quicker than the national speed limit allowed. Steve momentarily thought about his old editor and assumed she would also be heading back to London from her Loch Ness holiday home to compile a special edition of the paper.

Directly after Miles, or MW as everyone called him, had received the initial, slightly apologetic interruption from the nervous duty news editor as he was separating quarrelling children from their Nintendo Kinetic, he had been on top of the unfolding story. Sitting in his office he was now monitoring his own channel on all platforms including Internet, radio and iPad, as well as what the opposition and news agencies were up to, while all the time formulating a rolling-news strategy for the vault siege.

Miles was a tall, educated man who had been in charge at the channel for the last five years. He'd started his career straight from Cambridge as a wet-behind-the-ears regional TV journalist. A year of traffic reports and skateboarding ducks, and he soon realised that his double first in politics and history meant his skills lay elsewhere. Miles said goodbye to the front-of-camera role and wisely chose the management ladder instead. Working his way up through the ranks to news editor at Anglia Tonight he quickly moved on to managing editor there. It hadn't taken long for his talents to be recognised by executives at National Network News in London, and it was no surprise to peers when he was appointed the Head of Europe News, the biggest news channel in the continent. Miles was generally well liked by most of his team, and previous on-air experience meant he had an easy, reassuring, no-nonsense manner with precious presenters. Miles expected them to be down-to-earth, integral members of the team until an hour before they were due to go to air. Then he insisted they be treated like divas, TV royalty. Whatever they wanted was theirs. It was a technique that didn't always play well with other staff members but worked like a dream with the talent and the ratings. As a result, his channel picked up countless recognition awards.

Steve wasn't yet sure how Miles or MW – which one should he call him? – dealt with the 'lower orders', but he was about find out. Tapping gingerly on the Head of News's open door, he stood awkwardly on the threshold and waited.

'Yes?'

Miles didn't even look in his direction, acting on the theory that anyone who needed to knock didn't need to be talked to just at the moment.

'Merry Christmas, boss.'

'Thank you, you too.'

With still no eye contact Steve wasn't sure what to do next. Should he just talk, should he wait until spoken to, or simply carry on changing from leg to leg like an arthritic flamingo? Miles continued to look at the mini-bank of TV and computer screens in front of him, totally ignoring Steve's presence. He had plenty to think about. Suzanna Thomas was away for Christmas and the new boy was flying solo. Miles had at first been a little anxious at the prospect of piling so much expectation on a single anchor, even one as experienced as Sid. Miles had been integral in poaching Sid for Europe News after the anchor had dealt brilliantly with the General Election coverage for a rival channel, but the election had been rich in news lines. On this story the police were saying little and, with a cordon keeping any eager journalist a good fifty metres away from the vault, new pictures to talk over for the anchor were extremely limited. Ad-libbing ad infinitum was quite a challenge, but Miles could see from Sid's relaxed demeanour that his worries were unfounded. Relieved, he sank back into his chair. Sid was doing a great job.

Steve decided to give it one last shot.

'Sorry to interrupt, boss. Not sure what I have, but I think it might be useful.'

'Yes?'

Still no eye contact. Steve started to twiddle with his shiny wedding ring. He wasn't used to this sort of disinterest and wondered what to do. Whenever he'd sauntered into the editor's office on the newspaper, he'd been welcomed with open arms, offered a seat on one of the chocolate leather sofas and made most welcome until he was good and ready to leave. Standing here like a plank, Steve felt slighted, perhaps even angry at Miles Winstanley's overt lack of interest in anything he had to say.

Unaware of Steve's embarrassment, Miles remained totally focused on the output as Sid once again reminded viewers 'if you're just tuning our way' and launched into a monologue of the scant facts he'd been provided with. Miles marvelled at how his latest signing managed to make it sound as though it was the first time he'd uttered every sensational syllable. This guy was good. Very good.

Steve had had enough. For a fleeting moment, he considered walking away and ringing his former editor instead. She would probably be at her desk by now too. He was sure the publisher would have flown her down from Inverness Airport by private jet and she would right now be at the helm, helping put together a special edition of the paper. Her response to his call would undoubtedly be much more effusive than this. Steve resisted the very real temptation to call her, at least for now, and pressed on with one last effort at enticing MW to offer him the courtesy of deigning to look in his general direction.

'Think I might have the ex-directory number for the vault, er, MW.'

Miles immediately looked up to where Steve was still standing.

'Really?'

'Yes, really.'

'Go on.'

Man of few words, isn't he, thought Steve, trying desperately to keep a slight tone of sarcasm out of his voice, but failing.

'Thought I might give it a quick call, see if anyone answers. What do you think, er, Miles?'

'NO!'

Miles was immediately on his feet. The damned new boy had no idea how TV worked yet. Unlike newspapers; he needed much more than a notebook and pen to convey the story to an audience. So many times before, print journalists had failed at the first TV hurdle unaware of the myriad technical hoops to be jumped through to make sure an interviewee could be heard by viewers and not just the reporter. MW was also anxious about the veracity of Steve's claim. Years ago as a novice producer he'd learned the hard way by putting to air a phone interview of a man who claimed to have been involved in a plane crash. In fact he was a hoaxer sitting on his sofa watching the story unfold on TV. MW had been carpeted by his executive producer and the experience had made him extremely cautious ever since, especially with a new boy who had no track record of accuracy. Live television meant that if the interviewee was a fake, all of Europe would know about it instantly.

'Doctors bury their mistakes, live TV broadcasts theirs.'

'Sorry?'

'Are you sure it's kosher?'

A whole sentence, thought Steve, things were looking up. He hesitated for a moment. Hursty couldn't necessarily be described as the most reliable source. Steve began to realise what MW had been trying to convey with his weird doctor-and-dead-body reference. If Sid was connected live on air to the number he had in his pocket and it turned out to be a Chinese takeaway in Chingford, then everyone would know about it and his fledgling TV career would most definitely be buried at sea. He paused before deciding there was no going back now.

'Sure.'

'How sure?'

Miles knew better than to ask one of his reporters to reveal a source, but he needed to push Steve hard enough for the journalist to be one hundred per cent confident of the facts. If it was a bogus number then the station would be a laughing stock. If it was legitimate, then it was gold dust.

'My source has never let me down before.'

Steve wanted to make a play out of crossing his fingers but, realising how unconvincing that would look, he instead leaned as nonchalantly as he could against the door frame.

'Why haven't the police dialled it?'

'I honestly don't know,' said Steve, trying not to panic. 'But that doesn't mean we shouldn't, does it?'

Steve could see that Miles had a point. For all he knew, the police would already have disconnected the number, or the line might very well be engaged, with trained negotiators chatting to those inside. That's why he'd suggested trying it first.

Miles stood silently for a moment, eyes locked on to the newspaper hack standing in his doorway. He considered Steve a cocky young gun, too maverick for his award-winning news organization. He had resisted employing him, but had been outvoted by the rest of the interview panel. Everyone wanted to be a TV presenter these days, eager for their fifteen minutes of fame without being prepared to put in the legwork first. There was no question Steve had the looks and the swagger, but did he have the nerve and the talent?

'If I ask Sid to make this call live on air and you make him look like a tit for whatever reason, then you're out. You do know that, don't you?'

Steve was starting to feel a little slighted by the constant disinclination. 'And if it connects him live to inside the vault, what happens to me then?'

Miles relaxed into a wry smile.

'Then you're on the telly, my man, and I'm shining your shoes. Deal?'

'Deal.'

Moments later the two men were walking briskly towards the studio gallery, Miles ignoring any attempt by hassled staff members to divert him from his path.

'MW, I just wondered if . . .'

'Not now, Tim. Speak to Jim on the desk, please.'

A few purposeful strides later and the two men were inside a control room crammed full of bustling activity and intense pressure. It was an environment Steve had glimpsed through the window but had never experienced before. He felt like he was on a movie set and half expected to see William Holden or Robert Duvall walk through the heavy gallery door. In the dim lighting he could see at least three rows of desks, all occupied, facing a wall, every available inch of which was covered by TV screens. Right in the centre was a monitor with a red light over it. It showed Sid, who was talking genially to Europe News viewers via his close-up camera. The gallery itself was a cacophony of controlled noise. Everyone present seemed to have an important job to do and knew exactly how to do it. The Europe News senior director and executive producer, having been called away from their Christmas lunch to cover the story, were sitting in the first row of desks, a sea of buttons and control panels in front of them. To one side of the room another door led off to a specialist sound suite where still more staff were controlling the studio audio. Miles walked across to the executive producer Christine, one of his best. Steve remained wide-eyed at the back of the gallery, frightened to move any further inside.

'Hey, how's it going?'

'Hi, MW. Sid is doing what he can, but to be honest he doesn't have enough to keep it moving for much longer. We're thinking about covering other news for a while after the next break, just until we get more info from the scene or the police. We don't even know who's inside yet. What do you think?'

'Hmm, agreed . . . except that Steve here –' MW turned around, expecting the reporter to be next to him '– or rather there, standing at the back of the gallery, might just have something to spice up our coverage.'

The chatter in the busy gallery subsided for a moment as Christine asked the question everyone present wanted the answer to.

'Really, what is it?'

'The telephone number for inside the vault.'

Every single person in the gallery turned from monitoring the screens at the front of the control room to stare at Steve, who was still standing at the back. He wanted to hide. For the first time the reporter feared that it wouldn't be the right number after all. Hursty was just an old soak and he'd given him the number of his launderette or local Indian or maybe Alcoholics Anonymous. It could be anything, but it certainly wasn't the number that all these busy people were expecting. He contemplated running away, but instead found himself nodding confidently.

Christine was sceptical and voiced the concern of the other seasoned professionals in the room.

'Are you sure, Steve, because if I put it to air and you make Sid –'

'Yeah, all right, Christine, we've already done that conversation in my office. He's sure. Prep Sid, please. And can you also ask Louise to buzz through to online and the radio producers downstairs, make sure they're across the output. We're heading into sound. Steve, come with me.'

As MW walked towards the sound suite, Steve did his very best to follow. Every step felt as if he was walking in diving boots. *What if it's wrong, what if it's wrong?* said a nagging voice in his head. It was a question he would very soon know the answer to. An answer that would make or break his TV career.

Reaching the door to the sound suite, Steve dug into his pocket and with shaking fingers handed the book of matches to MW. Taking it, MW patted him reassuringly on the back, no less apprehensive but much more able to disguise his nerves.

On the other side of the sound-proof glass in the brightly lit studio, Sid had been flogging the siege story for two hours. At first, it had seemed a brilliant news story and definitely worth ruining his Christmas plans for. Now, with no new information for at least an hour and none on the horizon either, he was starting to become frustrated. He had a hot date and hopefully a steamy dessert waiting and was keen to hand over the reins to another, more junior anchor as soon as possible. That was until Christine spoke into his earpiece.

'We have the vault phone number. Being put through to sound now. Not sure what we're expecting. We're planning to take the ring tone live. Let's see. You cool with that?'

Christine was supremely efficient at her job and Sid trusted her implicitly. In a handful of short, succinct sentences, taking less than ten seconds to deliver, he knew exactly what was happening. Christine hadn't troubled Sid with her very real concern that the new boy might be about to make them all look ridiculous. She needed Sid to be confident and assured and '*might*' was a useless part of her vocabulary.

As the reporter at the scene finished her latest update with a 'police are still refusing to tell us any more about those inside or when they may be released. Back to you, Sid,' the anchor sat up a little straighter. Instead of throwing to a commercial break as originally planned, Sid looked directly down the barrel of his close-up camera to deliver the killer line. He was still unaware that in the next thirty seconds he would be made to look like a genius – or a complete numpty.

'OK, Jillian, thanks for the update. Well, let's see if we can throw a little more light on exactly what is happening from this end. Europe News has just received what we believe to be phone access to inside the vault. We're going to try to speak to those being held against their will. Here goes.'

Miles nodded at the sound supervisor, who dialled the number and immediately patched it through to the director. As the ring tone was put live to air, the gallery fell completely silent. The newsroom was completely silent. MW anticipated that every home in Europe watching their coverage would also be completely silent. The phone rang once, twice, three times. Christine, Miles, Steve and everyone else in the room held their breath. Sid continued to look directly into the camera. His warm, friendly, handsome reassuring face offered not a trace of the uncertainty he or the rest of the team was feeling. The phone rang again and again.

In Paris, Christopher had turned up the volume on the plasma a little higher so he could hear above the sound of Suzanna's frantic packing. He was aware of a phone ringing. The strapline on the screen read *Live to the vault*. Suzanna immediately stopped what she was doing and rushed over to the bed. Ignoring Christopher, she sat on the edge and stared at the television, looking directly into Sid's eyes. They'd worked together every day for the last six months. As his on-screen wife she knew all his mannerisms and idiosyncrasies. She detected the faintest hint of panic in his eyes. No one was going to pick up.

'Don't answer, don't answer, please don't answer,' she whispered.

Miles had returned with Steve to the main gallery to listen. While Steve scurried to the very back of the control room, pressing his shoulders against the far wall, MW took up position like a captain on the bridge next to his executive producer. Christine glanced nervously up at Miles, who was anxiously biting his thumbnail. A nasty habit his wife had tried to wean

135

him off ever since they were first married, but he still lapsed in times of extreme stress. He looked back at Christine's worried face, swiftly calculating the options before slowly rotating his hand in a regal wave, indicating they should keep the suspense going for a little while longer.

'Answer the bleedin' phone' was an audible whisper around the gallery, the newsroom and no doubt right throughout the country. Christine spoke softly and reassuringly to her presenter through his earpiece.

'Give it another couple of beats and if there's still nothing we'll pull it. OK?'

Almost imperceptibly, Sid nodded while maintaining his air of friendly confidence for the viewer. Several more rings punctuated the silence as Steve actively planned his escape to Panama.

Miles decided he had heard enough.

'That's it, pull it.'

Christine nodded. She leaned forward to push the button to Sid's earpiece – when the phone was answered.

'Hello, Mayfair Safety Deposits, Bert Jones speaking. How may I help you?'

The whoops of delight in the gallery were immediately silenced by the Head of News raising his right arm. He was keen to listen to every syllable of the exchange.

Sid didn't miss a beat.

'Hello, Bert, this is Sid Parker. How ya doin'? I believe you have a bit of a situation in there?'

Christopher ducked as a water glass Suzanna had been holding smashed against the far wall of the hotel room.

'I need to get back to London NOW.'

12

10.20 a.m.

Europe News

Miles strode across to where Steve was hovering at the back of the gallery. The reporter had thought his career was over but was now smiling broadly while stretching out his hand to be warmly congratulated by the Head of News. In a matter of seconds Steve had gone from zero to hero. He wanted to shout out loud.

MW was delighted.

'We need to talk, superstar, soon as this interview is over.'

Patting Steve on the back, Miles immediately returned to Christine's side, both keen to listen without interruption.

Sid kept his tone measured and controlled, just the right level of urgency without scaring the horses.

'Hi, Bert. To wish you a Merry Christmas would be completely inappropriate, but I just wondered if you could tell us what's happening in there? Take your time, no rush.'

The anchor offered up his well-practised smile to the camera to reassure his audience and waited for Bert's response.

'Sorry?'

Sid tried again.

'I hope you can hear me OK, Bert. It's Sid Parker from Europe News. I believe you have a bit of a situation in there?'

'What, *the* Sid Parker, off the telly?'

Sid feigned humility but confirmed Bert's query.

'Wow, you're my wife's favourite. Can I have your autograph for her?'

Miles winked at Christine. This was going to go well.

'Sure you can, Bert. I'll be happy to fix that for you as soon as you're out of there. Can you tell me though what's happening? I believe you have a bit of a situation you need to deal with?'

'Er, yeah. How did you know?' stuttered Bert, who was hit by a sudden bout of stage fright. His day was getting weirder and weirder. 'Er, sorry, but not sure if I have permission to speak.'

Miles leaned forward and keyed through to Sid's earpiece: 'Keep him talking. We'll put a call in to the vault owners. They're hardly going to say no, are they?'

'We've already spoken to the owners of the vault,' lied Sid, 'and they have assured us that you can tell us what happened.'

There was a long pause while Bert considered what to do. He didn't want to be in any more trouble than he was already.

It was Sid who eventually broke the silence.

'You still there, Bert?'

'Yeah. You know what? I liked you better on breakfast telly. I'm not sure about you on Europe News, though. Are you enjoying it?'

'I am, thanks, Bert,' laughed Sid. 'and you're talking to our viewers right now. I wonder if you want to say anything to your family.'

'Yeah, can I say hello to my wife and everyone else that knows me?'

'Of course, Bert. What's your wife's name?'

'Cynthia.'

Sid jotted down the name.

'All the time in the world,' whispered Christine.

'Any kids?'

'Yeah, two – Tracey and Harry.'

'I bet they're the apple of your eye, aren't they?'

'Yeah.'

'Anyway, Bert, just wondered if you could tell us what's happening where you are?'

Another long pause as Bert tried to compute the surreal situation of being trapped in a vault with four strangers while talking to a famous TV presenter at the other end of the line.

Sid stepped in to help out.

'Tell you what, Bert, should I start by giving you an idea of what we've been told?'

'Sure, why not.'

'Well, we heard there was an incident before the vault closed last night and that you were rather upset with some of those in there. Decided to teach them a lesson and keep them inside for Christmas.'

Bert exploded.

'Rubbish! That's absolute rubbish! Who told you that?'

Incandescent at the allegation, he glared at Lily.

'Oi, Posh Paws – yeah, you. They think it's my fault we're in here, not yours. Come and tell them. Come and tell them it was you.'

Lily was aghast. Who on earth had the security guard been whispering to and what had they said to make him start shouting at her? When the phone rang, she assumed it was to advise them that help was on the way. Who else could possibly have had the number? Shivering with cold, she turned away from Bert's judgemental gaze.

'No, I didn't think so, missy.'

Bert snarled at Lily. He'd just about had enough of her. Not only had she caused all this bloody trouble, he was now getting the blame for it.

'She won't come to the phone, Sid. She's hiding in the corner. But it was her, not me. Who told you it was me?'

Bert's furious tone didn't surprise Sid. He'd been expecting a series of rants from the guard who he was told had finally flipped after one too many well-heeled customers had left him feeling downtrodden.

'OK, OK, don't worry, Bert. It is all right to call you Bert, isn't it?'

'Yeah, sure.'

'Well, Bert, we obviously have the wrong end of the stick. Now's your chance to put the record straight and tell us what happened.'

'Can I talk to the missus?'

'I'm sure . . .' Sid paused and glanced at his scribbled notes '. . . Cynthia will be listening, Bert. You're quite big news, you know. The whole country wants to know what's happening in there.'

'The whole country – what do you mean, the whole country?' Bert's tone immediately changed from anger to anxiety.

'Don't spook him.' It was Christine again. 'Easy does it.'

Sid nodded slightly and continued.

'I'm sure Cynthia will be keen to know you're all right. Are you all right in there?'

'Yeah, suppose so, but could do with getting out of here as soon as.'

'I bet. Who else is in there with you, Bert?'

'Well, there's the little madam who won't come to the phone to face up to the consequences of what she's done. Then there's an Arab lady and her two young children. Must be about six and seven, I would guess.'

140

Bert broke off for a moment, interrupted by a young voice in the background, but was soon on the line again.

'Hafsa tells me she's ten and her brother Umair is six. I have to say they're a credit to their parents, unlike the other little madam in here.

'Can I ask a question, Sid?'

'Sure, Bert, ask away.'

The presenter was settling into his stride. He knew everyone would be gripped by the first interview from inside the vault. He allowed himself a half smile at the thought of Suzanna fuming in her hotel room in Paris. She'd undoubtedly be watching.

'Ask whatever you like, Bert.'

'Who won *Strictly Come Dancing*?'

The gallery collapsed into howls of laughter. Sid just managed to keep his composure.

'The favourite. The favourite won, Bert. You'll be able to watch when you get out, I'm sure.'

'When will that be? Do you know, Sid?'

Sid's tone grew more sombre. He knew that, despite desperate efforts by the police, it had so far proved impossible to trace the keyholders or the owners of the vault. It could be another three days before those trapped inside were released by the timer.

'Well, Bert, it's difficult to say at the moment. All I can tell you is that the police are doing absolutely everything they can to try to get you out, and it shouldn't be much longer now. Can you give us an idea of what happened?'

Bert took a long, deep breath to steady his nerves.

'Er, OK. I was minding my own business, about to lock up for Christmas. There was only one family left in here when some stupid posh bint rushed in with a gun.'

'A gun?'

Sid could hardly contain his delight. This amazing story had just notched up another level.

'Where's the gun now?'

Bert scoffed: 'It's here in the vault, er, doh!'

'Of course, stupid me. Whereabouts in the vault?'

'It's safely tucked away in my drawer.'

'I understand. Can you tell us how you all became locked in?'

Bert began to explain about the timing mechanism and the keys, before stopping abruptly.

'Are we gonna be here for another three friggin' days? Oops, sorry, 'scuse my French.'

'Completely understandable, Bert, but if you could manage not to swear. Don't forget Tracey and Harry will probably be listening, buddy. So, can you tell us what conditions are like in there?'

'They're OK at the moment, but we'll be glad to be out.'

'How's everyone feeling?'

'Well, the kids are keeping themselves entertained with toys they'd just bought. Their mother seems a bit stressed, but coping. As for the little madam who caused all this, she just keeps sobbing. Frankly, she's starting to get on my nerves.'

'What about food and water?'

'Well, to be honest, we're struggling a bit on that score.'

Bert turned away from the group and whispered into the receiver.

'I have a Twix and a Kit-Kat stash, Sid, but they're not having those.'

Once again laughter broke out in the gallery and Sid stifled a snigger.

'What about water, Bert?'

'We do have a water cooler and I'm trying to ration it as best I can, but it's only half-full. I had plenty of thirsty

142

customers on Christmas Eve and it wasn't due to be replenished until after the holidays.'

Sid allowed the moment to linger. Five people sealed in an impenetrable vault with less than ten litres of water and no food. Viewers at home would be making similar calculations. Those rations weren't going to last for another three days.

'As I said, I know the police are doing absolutely everything they can. You just need to hang on in there, Bert, mate.'

In the gallery, Miles looked at his watch. Plans needed to be made for the continuing coverage of the story, and that would involve him ruining the Christmas break for many of his staff.

'Change the ticker to say *developing story*, Christine and update it with every detail we've learned.'

'Good idea, MW.'

Christine didn't look up but instead continued scribbling notes to the text producer, who she'd been briefing for several minutes. How she managed when the Head of News wasn't spoon-feeding her was a mystery.

Embarrassed, MW acknowledged his unnecessary intervention with a wince and, 'Sorry.'

He was about to apologise further when he was momentarily distracted by his mobile vibrating in his pocket. He half-expected it to be the channel's chief executive, congratulating him on what a great scoop they had, but looking at the flashing screen saw it was Suzanna Thomas's mobile. A conversation for later, certainly not now, thought Miles. Ignoring the call, he leaned forward and spoke into Sid's earpiece.

'More info on the others, Sid.'

'Bert, I wonder if you could tell us anything else about the other people in the vault with you. Might they want to come to the phone?'

Bert glanced around grumpily.

'Oi, you. Want to talk on the phone?'

When she realised the call wasn't an announcement of imminent release, Lily had lost interest and slumped back on to her suitcase.

'Oi, I'm talking to you. Sid Parker wants to know if you want to talk to him. Do you or not?'

Lily shook her head decisively.

'Nah, she says no, Sid. And to be honest, I don't think the others will either.'

'Names, Sid, then we can track down the families.'

This time it was Christine speaking in his ear, keen to wrestle back control of the button from her boss.

'OK, Bert. Have you any idea who everyone is? Can I ask their names and where they're from?'

Bert was starting to become a little irritated by the line of questioning.

'It's not *Blind Date* you know. When are we getting out of here?'

Sid, realising he was in danger of losing the guard, hurriedly softened his approach.

'Sorry, you're right. You said you wanted to talk to your wife, Bert. What would you like to say to Cynthia?'

'Is she there with you now?'

'No, Bert, not quite yet. But, as I mentioned, I'm sure she'll be listening. What would you like to say to her?'

Bert paused, considering the best form of words so as not to cause his wife any further concern. She was probably worried sick about what was happening to him. He hit on what he thought was just the right tone and continued with his best telephone voice.

'Cynthia Jones, this is your husband Bert speaking. There is nothing to worry about. I am fine and will be home very soon. In the meantime, please do not forget to feed the dog.'

Again stifled laughter in the gallery. This chap was price-less, thought Miles, as he winked playfully at Christine. There was no need, she'd already forgiven him for his teaching-granny-to-suck-eggs intervention a few moments earlier. MW's phone began to vibrate again and looking at the screen he could see it was Suzanna. He needed to sort it or she would be calling all day.

'I'm leaving you to it, Christine.'

'Sure thing, boss. We'll keep it going for as long as we can and make sure the line remains open until you tell us otherwise.'

'Any calls from the police or the owners shouldn't get as far as you in the gallery, but if they do, direct them to me.'

Miles was pulling open the heavy control-room door en route to his office when he was stopped in his tracks by a piercing scream from inside the vault. He half ran back to his producer's side. Sid hesitated and was about to speak, but Christine beat him to it.

'Wait. Let it breathe.'

Bert dropped the phone and rushed across as fast as his significant bulk could carry him to the opposite corner of the vault.

Prince Ansar who had been glued to the TV screen in the sitting room of his suite recognised the scream immediately as that of his wife. As the tension built, Sid allowed his expression to relax from shock to concern. Exactly what every other viewer would be feeling.

'Wait, Sid, wait a second. Just wait.'

Eventually Bert returned to the phone.

'Hello?'

'Hello, Bert, we're still here. Can you tell us what happened?'

'No, not really. I'm going to put the young girl on, though. Her name's Hafsa.'

'Don't spook her, Sid,' said Christine.

'Hello?' The brittle voice of an anxious young girl came on the line.

'Hello, sweetie. I'm Sid. Who are you?'

'Hafsa.'

'Hi, Hafsa. How old are you?'

'I'm ten.'

'Ten. Well, that's very grown-up, isn't it? Tell me, Hafsa, was that you who I heard being a little upset a moment ago?'

'No, that was my mummy.'

'Your mummy. Why is your mummy upset, Hafsa? Do you know?'

'Yes.'

'Can you tell me? Maybe I can help.'

'It's my little brother, Umair.'

'How old is Umair?'

'He's six and he isn't very well, sir.'

'What's the matter with him?'

'He suffers from epilepsy and he is having a seizure.'

Sid didn't speak. Even he was shocked by the latest revelation. A sick child, trapped with only limited water and food in a vault with a madwoman who had until recently been armed with a gun.

'How he is now?' prompted Christine.

'How is Umair now, Hafsa?'

'He's . . . he's lying down, but we don't have his medication with us. What are we going to do? Can I speak to my father?'

Miles was listening to the young girl from the back of the gallery when his phone vibrated again. This time it was the Metropolitan Police Commissioner, a call he had been expecting for some time. He walked towards Christine and covertly showed her the screen. MW didn't want anyone else to know who was calling. She nodded, understanding he needed to take the call, and MW left to speak to the Commissioner in private.

Christine had been momentarily distracted, by what the Commissioner might be demanding and missed some of what the young girl said. Cursing to herself, she focused again on the output and spoke to Sid.

'Don't freak her, Sid. Ask to speak to the mother.'

A few moments later it was a very English voice that came on the line.

'Hello, my name is Lily Dunlop and this is my fault entirely. I am so very, very sorry. Please make arrangements to rescue this child as quickly as you can. He really is not very well. He needs medical help, now. Please. You have to do something to help him.'

'OK, Lily – you did say Lily, didn't you?'

Sid used his time-honoured skill of repeating a guest's name. It helped him remember it while also making them feel special. Everyone likes the sound of their own name had been a trick he'd learned at *HND*.

'Yes, my name is Lily, but please can we dispense with the pleasantries? This child needs help and he needs it –'

Lily's plea was halted by another scream. This time undoubtedly that of a child.

13

A little time earlier . . .

Upton Park, Oxfordshire

As the clock struck ten on Christmas morning, Catherine was woken by a reverent tap at her bedroom door. Lazily, she raised her arms above her head, stretching out her fingers while simultaneously curling down her toes, encouraging the blood to circulate around her body. Christmas Day, how lovely. Then she remembered. Her first conscious thought, as it had been every morning for the last eight months, was for Lily. Where was she today? Would she call? Please let her call. She missed her so much.

Another, more urgent tap at the door, it could only be one person.

'Come in.'

Brian entered, dressed immaculately as always and carrying a tray of Lady Grey tea, brown toast and thick-cut orange marmalade in a porcelain pot. No butter.

'Morning, ma'am.'

'Morning, Brian, Merry Christmas.'

'Thank you, ma'am, Merry Christmas to you too,' replied the butler as he walked across to a breakfast table positioned next to the sash windows. Ignoring the empty brandy glass and full cup of last night's tea, he put down the tray and drew back the curtains. Catherine squinted against the low winter sunshine as it flooded into the darkened room.

'No papers today, ma'am, but I wondered if you might want to watch the TV news.'

Catherine had first become reliant on news coverage many years before when Joseph was caught up in an attempted coup in Zimbabwe. Mobile communication was impossible, there were no flights in or out of the country, and she had been desperate to know her husband was safe. She had spent countless hours glued to Europe News, the regular live reports from their Africa correspondent her only lifeline until Joseph eventually called to say he was on his way home.

'A little early for that, isn't it, Brian? Not much happens on Christmas morning, does it?'

Brian knew otherwise. He had been glued to the TV since tuning in at 8 a.m. A siege in a central London vault and Europe News had recently made contact with those inside. Mayfair Safety Deposits was well known to Brian as a venue he had driven Mr and Mrs Dunlop to many times previously. A venue he had recently spoken at length to Miss Lily about. Brian had listened intently to the guard's narrative, especially at his reference to 'Posh Paws'. A label that was a little ungracious, but one that had certainly alerted the butler's interest. Brian began to think the unthinkable. No, it couldn't be her. Why would it be her? He was being ridiculous. He'd heard from Alfred, who was in service at Giles's family residence, that Miss Lily was spending Christmas in Barbados. Of course he was mistaken, but still the niggling thought remained at the back of his mind. He felt it best to make Mrs Dunlop aware, just in case.

149

'There appears to be an incident in central London, ma'am. It looks quite disturbing,' offered Brian vaguely, switching on the set despite his mistress's initial reluctance.

Catherine sighed and stretched for a dressing gown before walking over to her tea and toast. Brian had served her breakfast in bed almost every morning for the last twenty years. It was a ritual that had brought some comfort in the months since her daughter's disappearance. Spreading a slice of toast with marmalade she turned to the TV, noticing the breaking news strap at the bottom of the screen: *Siege at Mayfair Safety Deposits. Hostages reported.*

'How funny, Brian, isn't that the vault we use?'

'Yes, ma'am, I believe so.'

Catherine turned up the sound to listen to Sid Parker. Remarkably, Europe News seemed to have established communication with those inside the vault. How strange that the police would allow that to happen. Oh well, it would be something to talk to her parents about over Christmas lunch. As she continued to listen, she wondered who those inside might be.

'How terrible it must be for the poor families of those trapped, Brian. They must be at their wits' end. It's too awful to contemplate, especially at Christmas.'

'Yes, ma'am, terrible,' agreed Brian, as he walked towards the bathroom to draw his mistress a bath. Catherine turned away from the TV to pour herself a cup of tea and was just about to add milk when she heard her daughter's voice coming through the speaker of the set.

'Hello, my name is Lily Dunlop and this is my fault entirely. I am so very, very sorry.'

Lily, it was Lily in the vault. Catherine lost the use of her arms and the milk jug shattered into small pieces, the liquid spreading in all directions and lapping over the edge of the silver breakfast tray. She attempted to stand but couldn't feel her legs; the room was swimming and the image on the TV screen was blurred and unrecognisable. Within a second, Brian was by her side. He picked her up and carried her effortlessly back to the bed, propping her upright with pillows. She was aware of a scream. It was that of a young child. Then silence.

The TV presenter began to speak, but although Catherine was conscious of sound and Sid Parker's lips moving, she couldn't make out any of the words he was saying. How could her daughter have been caught up in this terrible drama? How had she become trapped? Why was she there in the first place? A myriad of questions surged into Catherine's head. Then slowly, through the haze of shock, confusion and disbelief, Catherine realised. Lily must know. She must have gone to try to look in the safety deposit box. But that would be impossible – she didn't have the key.

Catherine leapt from her bed and dashed past a concerned Brian and across to the antique dressing table that had belonged to her mother. Opening up her jewellery box, she rifled through it, discarding diamond rings, cameo pin brooches and gold bracelets that had been in the family for generations. All were tossed on to the carpeted bedroom floor in her desperate efforts to clear a path to the secret compartment at the back of the box. Tugging urgently at the knotted rope handle to the drawer, she pulled it free. It was empty, the key had gone. Catherine rifled through every other drawer and compartment, but it was a pointless search. The key was no longer there. Lily must have taken it. But how had she known where to look? How could she possibly have known what that key was for?

Catherine had been so confident that the key to her guilty secret was hidden away from her daughter for ever. She'd believed that guarding the secret would allow them both to continue on with their lives. After all, there was nothing for either of them to worry about. Lily had seemed well. And the doctors hadn't shown the least concern about her, only Catherine herself. And she was fine. Lily would be too. She had been right not to have told Lily, not to have worried her little girl unnecessarily, not to have brought disgrace on the family.

That was until an evil tormentor had sent Lily that heinous handwritten note on her twenty-first birthday. Catherine had wracked her brain to try to make sense of who could have been responsible for such a wicked act. She shivered at the vivid memory of Lily collapsing into the fireplace that dreadful day, recalling how Brian had carried Lily up to her bedroom and how she had sat by her daughter's bedside while the doctor was called.

Thankfully, Lily's injuries had been superficial and the party could still go ahead. But Lily, faced with a flood of urgent questions she needed answers to, had thrust the note at her mother. Reading it, Catherine was speechless. She began by trying to deny all knowledge of what it could mean, but Lily was not to be deflected. Eventually, in the face of her daughter's wrath, Catherine relented and promised to speak to Lily the day after the party.

The showdown had taken place early the following morning. Unable to sleep, Lily had left Giles snoozing in their bed and rushed down the hall to her mother's room.

Tapping firmly on the bedroom door, Lily didn't wait for a response but strode purposefully into Catherine's bedroom and planted herself expectantly on the edge of the bed.

'I'm listening.'

'Darling, I can explain.'

'Good, because I'm listening.'

'Daddy was very poorly before he died.'

'Aha.'

'Please don't be so aggressive, darling. This is very difficult for me.'

'No, Mummy, this is very difficult for *me*. I have grieved the loss of my father who died from colon cancer. A man I loved more than anyone else in the world. A man I wanted to be with me on my twenty-first birthday to help me celebrate coming of age. Instead, on that very important day I receive a note telling me what happened in Africa could kill me and it's all Daddy's fault.' Lily's anger was beginning to give way to anguish. She tried her best not to cry.

'You must have known Mummy? Surely you must have known? Why didn't you tell me?'

Catherine looked at her daughter's face, contorted with fury and concern. She was desperate to have the note explained, to learn what the cryptic message meant. But if Catherine told her, Lily would be crushed. Besides, she didn't need to know. Catherine reassured herself, as she always had, with the knowledge that the doctors had not been concerned about Lily, only her, and she was fine. Taking her daughter's hands in her own, she began hesitantly.

'Darling, your Daddy was very, very successful and as such had many enemies who wanted to cause him harm. Now he has gone, they can no longer hurt him. So these spiteful, horrible people have turned their attention to you. It is ridiculous nonsense, nothing more. You know what happened in Africa. Daddy saved your life, he certainly didn't want to kill you now did he? Whoever it was that wrote such a terrible thing wanted to spoil your big birthday, but they didn't succeed, did they, darling? We had a wonderful time, didn't we?'

'Which people?'

'I don't know, but I am determined to find out. Please believe me, my darling, there is nothing more to it than that.'

'Yes, but Mummy you saw what the note says . . .'

153

'I know what the note *claims* darling, but it is malicious gossip and hearsay. I do not have and would never keep any secrets from you.'

'Are you really sure Mummy? I want to believe you but the note had so much detail, it's difficult to believe it's not true.'

Catherine subconsciously glanced across to her jewellery box before continuing.

'Please trust me, darling. I have nothing to hide. Now, come up here and give me a hug. I'm quite exhausted by last night and fear I may have drunk a little too much red wine. It was such a wonderful night wasn't it? Come here and show me your magnificent engagement ring again. Oh, it's absolutely exquisite.'

Lily had spent the rest of the day contemplating her mother's words. After Giles had returned to London and her mother had gone into the garden to search for Gin and Tonic, who could be heard barking and were no doubt causing havoc in the half-dismantled catering tent, Lily had spied her opportunity.

Dashing up the staircase to Catherine's room and flinging open the door, she ran across to the dressing table. It had been only a fleeting glance, but Lily had seen her mother's eyes dart towards it when she had challenged her earlier. What was it that Catherine didn't want her to see? Rifling through the drawers but finding nothing, Lily eventually turned her attention to her mother's jewellery box.

Now, staring at the empty drawer, Catherine realised that Lily would know what her parents had been keeping from her. She dropped the drawer on to the floor.

'Ma'am, ma'am, are you all right?'

Catherine ignored an anxious Brian and turned her attention to the TV screen. Her daughter, her baby, was locked in a vault with access to a devastating secret she had tried to protect her from. At that moment she hated her dead husband.

Catherine wasn't sure how long she had remained staring at the TV screen, hoping for any snippet of news on the fate of her daughter but was eventually interrupted from her thoughts by Brian.

'Ma'am, I am sorry to disturb you . . .'

The butler had stood patiently, waiting for his mistress to regain her composure. Whenever she was ready, he would be there for her, but time was ticking on.

'Ma'am, your parents will be arriving shortly. Would you like me to advise them that you are indisposed?'

Looking at the long case clock Catherine realised that Brian was right; her parents would be at Upton Park by noon. She wondered if they too had seen the news and were aware of what was happening with their granddaughter. If they were, would they still come, or would her father feel once again that shame was being brought on the family? Lily making the news in such dramatic circumstances was shocking. Might he turn his face away with embarrassment?

Catherine didn't know what to do. She tried hard to hold her emotions in check, determined not to cry in front of the staff, even if it was Brian, but eventually she succumbed. Tears came in huge dramatic sobs that contorted her slim, elegant frame. Brian at first stood helpless, unsure what action would be appropriate to support his mistress as she disintegrated in front of him. As Catherine crumpled into a second wave of raw emotion and fell to the floor in a sobbing heap, Brian threw away caution and lowered himself awkwardly next to her. After a further moment's hesitation he began to stroke Catherine's hair, which was already wet with heavy tears. Not for the first time, Brian cursed the man of the house, a man who could still cause so much hurt even in death.

'There, there, ma'am, everything will be fine.'

'It won't though, will it, Brian?' sobbed Catherine. 'Nothing will ever be fine again.'

Brian didn't reply.

In time, when there were no tears left, Catherine was quiet. Blowing her nose, she moved to sit on the edge of her bed, conscious she needed to compose herself before preparing for her parents' arrival. If by some miracle they weren't aware of Lily's actions, then they would already be on their way to Upton Park. To cancel Christmas lunch would jeopardise the fragile peace with her father, perhaps destroying it forever this time, and her mother would be forced to take sides with him. If she didn't cancel Christmas then Lily would remain trapped and frightened in that vault while she, her mother, did nothing to help free her. Catherine wasn't sure what could be done to help her daughter, but there must be something. Should she ring the police? What would they be able to do? Besides, it was the TV station who seemed to be in contact with her daughter, not the police. Should she call the TV station instead? But what would be the point? She wasn't prepared to appear on TV, so their help would no doubt be limited. After much mental turmoil, Catherine convinced herself that monitoring the output of Europe News was the best course of action, at least for now.

Slowly standing, she walked across to her favourite place and sat in a winged armchair that overlooked the lawns and on to the rolling hills beyond. This morning the glorious countryside was in the grip of a cold winter's day. A heavy mist hung over the lake. As Catherine listened to Sid Parker, she tried to remember the first time she met Joseph at the top of the Arc de Triomphe. The image was no longer as clear in her mind. Instead, she recalled the hours, days and months alone on the vast estate while he travelled abroad. She had everything she could ever want except happiness.

Catherine thought about how different her life would have been if only Joseph had been loyal to his marriage vows.

'Ma'am I'm so terribly sorry to interrupt. Lord and Lady Fitzwilliam are due to arrive very soon. Would you like me to prepare for their arrival, or would you prefer I call their driver to make alternative arrangements?'

'No. We must continue as normal, Brian. It's a long drive from Northumberland and my parents will want to freshen up when they arrive. We'll take drinks and open gifts in the drawing room. Could you ask Beryl that lunch is ready to be served by 4 p.m.?'

Brian nodded and, turning to go, reached for the remote control to switch off the set.

'Leave it please, Brian. That will be all for now, thank you.'

Catherine needed time alone to think. As Brian closed the door behind him, she remained seated, staring out towards the parterre. Here she was, making plans for a family Christmas opening presents and eating plum pudding, unable or unwilling to help her child. Aloft in her ivory tower, deeply embarrassed by her failure as a mother, Catherine hung her head in shame.

14

At the same time

Mandarin Oriental Hotel, Mayfair

Prince Ansar took a few long, deep breaths. He had failed as a father. His son needed him and yet he could do nothing. How could he not rescue his favourite child from this terrible situation? Would his heir die inside an impenetrable tomb while he stood by, helpless? The Prince closed his eyes.

An hour earlier he had woken from a fitful sleep, still sitting on a silk-covered armchair, a TV remote clenched in his left hand. It took a little while for him to comprehend where he was. The blind fury had arrived a moment or two later as he once again realised his beloved son was trapped. Picking up the phone on the solid walnut table by the chair, it was answered immediately. Within a few seconds his head of security was by his side.

'Sir?'

'I demand to know when my son will be returned to me.'

'Sir, the vault remains locked. We are still attempting to trace the keyholders. We have managed to track down the vault owners before the British police reached them and they are presently being interrogated. There appears to have been a lax approach to the rules, but we are helping them address that now. We remain vigilant to all options.'

Dmitri had been made aware that Europe News had communication with those inside the vault but had been reluctant to wake his principal until more was known. Now was the time to tell him.

'Sir, a television channel appears to be broadcasting from the scene. Would you like to hear what is being said?'

Ansar was furious, as Dmitri had known he would be. This was exactly what he did not want to happen. If this stupid, woolly, liberal country had a state-run television service, all news coverage would be controllable. Irritated, the Prince tuned in to Europe News. The reporter was in full flow, describing what was happening. There was a camera trained on the main entrance and exit, and a helicopter could clearly be heard hovering overhead. So much activity outside and yet these ridiculous people were doing nothing to rescue his son.

As the Prince watched, he'd become aware of a different tone from the TV anchor. It had soon been clear that the channel had exclusive contact with someone inside the vault. At first he had been keen to hear every syllable, desperate to learn what was happening to his family, but he soon tired of listening to the imbecile guard. He was about to change channels in search of other coverage when he'd heard his wife scream. The Prince had collapsed into a chair, his concern not for Almira but dread at what might have caused her to scream. Dmitri dashed across to where his principal was slumped.

'Sir, sir.'

Regaining his composure, Ansar pushed the guard away. The scream could only mean one thing, a problem with Umair's condition. His son had suffered from epilepsy since he was a baby. Despite the best medical care money could buy, he was still consumed by the occasional seizure. Generally these could be well managed with daily anti-epileptic drugs. Almira did have them with her, didn't she? Ansar walked briskly towards his son's room and opened a bedside drawer only to be faced with Umair's medication. How could his mother have forgotten to carry the boy's pills with her?

Grabbing the bottle, he waved it at Dmitri: 'How can we get this to him?'

The head of security knew the answer: they couldn't.

'I will make sure he receives it at the earliest opportunity, sir,' offered the guard, careful not to raise the Prince's expectations while still appearing supportive.

Ansar sat down on his son's bed, lost in thought. For the first time in his adult life he felt powerless. His son needed him, his only son. Surely there was something he could do?

'Put on the TV in here.'

The anchor still appeared to be speaking ridiculous nonsense to the guard, but then he heard another voice. One he recognized instantly.

'Hello.' The unmistakable sound of an anxious young girl.

'Hello, sweetie. I'm Sid. Who are you?'

'Hafsa.'

'Hi, Hafsa, how old are you?'

'I'm ten.'

Ansar had continued to listen as Hafsa spoke about her brother and her mother, and then the appeal from his trapped child:

'Can I speak to my father?'

'Well, I am sure he will be listening, Hafsa. What would you like to say to him?'

The young girl had paused for a moment, careful to choose the right words. Ansar leaned forward to listen.

'Daddy, please help us. We are all very frightened and . . .'

Hafsa was interrupted by another scream, that of a child. Ansar had heard enough.

'Dmitri, it is time for us to take charge. I need this resolved. I want the families of whoever has done this. I want them here with me so we can endure this together. This Miss Lily Dunlop, I would very much like to speak to the mother and the father. Do I make myself clear?'

'Sir . . .'

'Do I make myself clear, Dmitri?'

The sharpness of his master's tone left the guard in no doubt of the consequences if his orders weren't fulfilled.

Without another word, leaving his principal to watch events unfold on TV, Dmitri set about tracing the parents of Miss Lily Dunlop.

15

6 p.m.

George V, Paris

Suzanna was apoplectic with rage. How could the Head of News not answer her call? She had now been trying all day without any bloody success whatsoever. Who cared if he was in a meeting? She was Suzanna Thomas, Europe News's top anchor. From what she could see on her TV screen, this story was massive, the station needed her. Surely her priceless live news experience was required on air as soon as possible? No one does it better, wasn't that what MW always said countless times before? Seriously, how many awards had she won with her scintillating coverage of major breaking stories? What on earth was the matter with MW? He needed to get her on a plane to London and pronto.

Christopher, who had been earlier placated with a quickie sex apology, had continued to listen patiently hour after hour as Suzanna ranted on. With the holiday seemingly back on track, he had originally planned a celebratory meal at the hotel's LeCinq restaurant overlooking the courtyard and garden. He'd read online about the two Michelin stars and the menus drawn up from classic French culinary techniques. Everything was perfect down to the last detail; even the tablecloths, china and silver were all created specifically for the hotel. What better place to propose? Suzanna, however, had other ideas and they'd had to make do with a club sandwich lunch in their suite while the presenter raged on and on and on. Sitting on the gigantic bed watching Europe News hour after interminable hour, Christopher was finally forced to accept that this much planned trip could never end the way he had intended. Any hope that a proposal in the city of love would lead to a happy ever after with Suzanna was simply not going to happen.

Liberating a cocktail stick that was still holding together uneaten quarters of his sandwich and using it to excavate between his teeth, the IT consultant realised his dream was over. Christopher dug out a piece of chicken from his back molar, much to Suzanna's disgust, but he no longer cared what she thought. He felt bereft; plans shredded into tinier pieces than the crystal water glass flung in fury by Suzanna against the wall of the hotel room earlier. She was either unaware of or simply ignoring his despair.

For the umpteenth time she tried MW's mobile: still no answer. That was it. Furious, Suzanna dialled the news desk for the fourth time. An apologetic assistant confirmed that MW was busy in meetings, as he had been all day, but assured Suzanna that he had promised to get back to her at the very first opportunity.

'Who on earth is this?'

'It's Jenny, Suzanna, you spoke to me earlier, remember? I've been called in to help cover because of the vault siege. It's a really big story over here.'

'Yes, I know that, *Julie*, or whatever your name is, otherwise I wouldn't be ringing from Paris, would I?'

'Oh, Paris – how lovely! Are you having a wonderful time, Suzanna?'

'No, *Jessie*, I'm bloody not. I need to be back in London, and I need MW to organise it for me. I absolutely insist that you put me through to him straight away.'

'I'm so sorry, Suzanna, but he's briefing the team and says he can't be disturbed.'

Jenny held the phone a little closer to her ear.

'Sid has been doing such a great job and MW was busy earlier making sure he had a big public pat on the back. Now he needs to brief the producers about what he wants for tomorrow. It's going to be hard to follow today's coverage though, Suzanna. Unbelievably, Sid managed to talk to the people inside the –'

Suzanna had already dropped the call. She was not prepared to sit quietly and allow Sid to steal a march on her for a moment longer. Scrolling through her contacts, she dialled her agent.

'Darling, it's Suzi. Merry Christmas! Hope you're having a really lovely one?'

Without waiting for a response Suzanna pressed on.

'I am absolutely furious. So angry I can hardly control myself, and of course as you know, darling, that so isn't like me.'

'Suzi, sweetie, tell me, what on earth is the matter?'

Nick English had been Suzanna's agent for five years. She was without question his most challenging but equally his most lucrative client. Her hosting of corporate events for pharmaceutical and oil companies, together with copious after-dinner speaking engagements and photo shoots for glossy magazines had brought in top dollar for his agency. However her diva behaviour was becoming increasingly absurd, like calling him on Christmas Day. Nick rolled his eyes at his ever-patient wife, Cecelia. Signalling he would be 'two minutes', he apologetically handed over their toddler

164

son before heading for the privacy of the conservatory. Nick's business strategy with Suzanna was to hold on to her as a client long enough for her to tie the knot. The exclusive pictures would be worth a high six-figure deal with *OK!* and once he had his twenty per cent commission in the bank, that would be a good time to drop her. For now though it made sound business sense to listen to her ridiculous rant.

'I'm stuck in bloody Paris with no way of returning home. I'm watching this vault-siege story unfold with Sid at the helm while I'm holed up in some sort of French doss house forced to watch it on TV. It's simply not good enough Nick, darling. I need to get back to London pronto, but MW won't answer the phone. I'm furious. Doesn't he know I make his channel what it is? I need you to call him right now, darling, and tell him what a big mistake he's making by not rushing me back to London. Otherwise I will seriously contemplate a move to the BBC. I will, I really, really will.'

As she spoke, Suzanna subconsciously stuck out her bottom lip in a childish pout. Witnessing her continuing bad behaviour, Christopher began to question why he had ever contemplated spending the rest of his life with this woman.

Completely oblivious to her boyfriend's judgemental attention instead Suzanna listened petulantly as Nick attempted to placate her.

'Well, my darling, of course they can't cover this story properly without you. Europe News is you and you are Europe News. I'm sure MW will call you just as soon as he possibly can. He's probably snowed under right at the moment, though. This story is massive . . .'

Nick immediately wanted to retract the last sentence. It had been out of his mouth before he'd had time to think.

Suzanna instantly erupted, forcing Christopher to lunge across to grab the crystal glass she was reaching for.

Financially as well as emotionally, he couldn't afford any more breakages.

'I bloody know that, Nick! That's why I need to be back there, rather than trapped here bored out of my mind.'

Christopher took the latest crushing blow without emotion. He had spent three months' salary and four weeks of his life planning the Christmas trip and festive gifts for Suzanna. The Tiffany platinum engagement ring in his pocket bought in Old Bond Street was the icing on the cake. And for what? To be ridiculed by this screaming banshee who, until a few hours ago, he had been desperate to make his wife. He dropped his head in despair.

'Suzi, darling, don't fret. Getting so upset won't help when you do get on air now, will it? Leave it with me for a few minutes and I'll call MW, see what I can do about getting you back to the UK. How does that sound?'

Suzanna softened. At last, a breakthrough.

'Would you, darling? I really hate to interrupt your Christmas celebrations with Cecelia and the little one. Hope he liked the gift I bought for him, but, oh, OK, if you insist, thank you so much. Call me back as soon as you possibly can and certainly within the next ten minutes.'

Putting down the phone, Suzanna returned to packing her pashminas and only then became aware of the heavy atmosphere in the luxury room.

'Anything wrong, darling?'

Christopher couldn't bear to look at her.

'Yes, as a matter of fact there is, Suzanna. Thank you for asking. I think you are behaving abominably towards me. I have tried very hard to make this a trip to remember, but you have been horrible. In fact, you've been an absolute bloody cow, and I think you should be ashamed of your behaviour.'

Suzanna was flabbergasted. Just how selfish could this man be? She was about to respond when her mobile rang.

'Nick?'

'Darling, good and bad news, sweetie. The bad news is that MW is still tied up. The good news, however . . .'

'It better had be good.'

Nick ignored her.

'The good news is that I have a plan for you to get home.'

'Listening.'

'Princess Almira of Aj-al-Shar and her two children are among those in the vault.'

'I bloody know that, Columbo.'

Nick bit his tongue and thought about his twenty per cent commission from *OK!* He knew Christopher was planning to propose so it could only be a matter of months before a big pay day and release from this bitch.

'Think about it, Suzi, sweetie: Prince Ansar's wife . . .?'

It took a moment, but then a huge smile appeared on Suzanna's face as she realised what Nick was driving at.

'Ah yes, you clever thing! Of course. Thanks, bye.'

Nick had been on the verge of asking about wedding plans, before the line went dead.

'You're welcome, Suzanna. Pleasure to be of service to such an appreciative client,' he added, returning to his family Christmas. Suzanna had called at bathtime for the baby. She wouldn't have been aware and certainly wouldn't have cared about parental duties. They'd been taken over by Cecelia while he'd tried to find a solution for his client. It had been Cecelia who'd jogged Nick's memory, reminding him that he'd introduced the TV presenter to Prince Ansar of Aj-al-Shar. Nick had put the prince and the showgirl together as part of a lucrative oil industry conference Suzanna had been hosting. The Prince's family owned the oil company and no expense had been spared to make him feel comfortable in London. Presenting and interviewing during the day, Suzanna was later seated next to the Prince at a sumptuous dinner.

The event had been held in his honour at a Mandarin Oriental function room overlooking the park that evening. Ansar had enjoyed both the dinner and the location, but he was particularly taken by Suzanna's warmth and beauty. As a result, the hotel and the TV presenter had been the Prince's favourites ever since.

Suzanna had completely forgotten Ansar's wife's name. Of course: Almira. Perfect. Scrolling through her phone contacts, she nonchalantly wandered into the bathroom and away from Christopher's earshot to make the call. Utmost privacy was needed for the planned grovel to the Prince in the hope he might show pity and send his plane for her. If Christopher was going to be so beastly to her without any reason whatsoever, then he could damned well make his own way home.

Boxing Day

16

9 a.m.

Montagu Square, London

Sid lay back on to his crisp, white Egyptian cotton sheets, arching his spine to better enjoy the full pleasure of the pretty little thing writhing around in ecstasy on top of him. Chantelle was proving to be very a welcome addition to his stable of willing fillies and was certainly leading the race, at least for today.

Easing ever so gently to one side not only further increased his enjoyment but also provided the added benefit of allowing him to better keep an eye on his HD plasma TV over the crest of her peachy derriere. The volume was muted, of course, though in reality it would have made no difference. He wouldn't have much chance of hearing anything over the noise of this gorgeous little screamer.

His handling of the interviews with Bert Jones, Lily Dunlop and even young Princess Hafsa, who'd put in a surprise guest appearance, had received rapturous approval from MW. The Head of News had made such a fuss of the anchor when he entered the newsroom, which included instigating a round of applause as he walked up the spiral stairs from the studio.

Europe News had replayed the interviews throughout Christmas Day and attention had now turned to tracking down family and friends. MW wanted as many as could be traced to be interviewed live in the studio and as soon as possible. From what Steve Stone was gleaning from the police there was little likelihood the vault would open before Wednesday morning.

Over a relaxed chat in his office, MW had insisted Sid take some time out to recharge his batteries. Reluctantly accepting and with a brief detour via a loft apartment off the King's Road, that's exactly what he was doing now. Chantelle had been only too happy to be collected by Sid in a Rolls-Royce. Use of the luxury car had been extended another day by his appreciative employer. The chauffeur had also rather helpfully conjured up a bottle of vintage Louis Roeder Cristal Champagne and two glasses while Sid had continued on air throughout the afternoon. The glasses and the champagne were chilling in an ice bucket for Sid and any potential companion when he'd slid back into the vehicle. Seeing the car arrive outside her apartment block, Chantelle had taken as long as possible to saunter down the stairs, giving every neighbour left in the road the chance not to miss her climbing into the Rolls-Royce before it sped off. Chantelle had been in heaven as she wriggled excitedly on the drum-dried bull leather seat while sipping chilled vintage champagne. Just wait until she told her flatmate.

When Sid had called earlier in the day to cancel, the swimwear model had been bitterly disappointed not to be keeping their Christmas lunch date at The Ritz. She'd been left with no choice but to spend Christmas Day alone. Her family were in Cornwall and too far away to make last-minute plans to see them. Her flatmate had left last night to join her family in the New Forest. A miserable Chantelle had remained in her pyjamas and passed the time painting her nails while watching Sid on TV.

When he'd called out of the blue later that evening with profuse apologies and the offer of champagne and a sticky dessert at his place, she'd leapt at the suggestion. They were hardly through the door when the TV anchor, high on adrenalin and expensive champagne, had lifted up Chantelle and carried her to his bedroom, undressing her as they went. The morning after they were still there, with Sid's discarded suit lying crumpled on the American oak boarded floor. Chantelle's Hermès silk blouse and Galliano micro mini skirt, which frankly had been little wider than a belt even when she was wearing it, lay on top of his clothes. Dessert had been so good they had decided on seconds and this morning a pre-breakfast pick-me-up.

Sid had taken an immediate shine to the twenty-something model when he'd first spotted her little more than a week ago while in the VIP area at Mahiki. On top of her drop-dead gorgeous figure and unchallenging grey matter, it was a further delightful surprise to discover just what a sexual dynamo Chantelle was. It had taken only the tiniest amount of persuasion to convince her to change her festive plans. The opportunity to spend Christmas Day with Sid Parker had even placated her mother's initial ire at her decision to stay in London. Lying here now, Sid thanked the news gods for shining down on him and happily reflected on the events of yesterday.

After Christine had advised him from the gallery via his earpiece that he should take a break, Sid had immediately headed for the Head of News's office where the executive production team were waiting for him. The heartfelt round of applause from the newsroom was a surprise and he'd offered a humble bow of genuine appreciation as he walked through.

'Brilliant job, Sid. Really top drawer,' began Miles as he strolled into his office. 'We're absolutely killing this story. Carole Smith has telephoned from *Have a Nice Day UK*, asking for some of our audio interview from the vault. Obviously we said yes, as long as they use no more than two minutes, at least one of your questions in vision, and of course give us an on-air credit.'

Sid smiled. There had been much wailing and gnashing of teeth when he'd walked away from the breakfast TV channel right in the middle of his three-year contract. It had been a difficult decision and the promise of a hike in salary to stay had been sorely tempting. Carole Smith had taken him out for an expensive lunch at Scott's to try to convince him what a big mistake it would be to leave. Sid loved Carole and had even tried to persuade her to come with him to Europe News. Although *HND* was a fantastic place to work, he wanted to play on the world stage, and with breaking stories like this one lifting his profile it wouldn't be long before America was calling. In fact, Europe News's US partner had been dipping in and out of their coverage for most of the day, especially when they established the phone link inside the vault. World domination next, thought Sid as he walked over to MW's fridge and helped himself to a Coke Zero. Flipping open the can, he ambled over to a sofa and found an empty seat in the busy room.

'So, what's the plan then, boss?'

'Good question. We're just running through things now, Sid. From what Bert Jones the guard was saying, it looks like this story could run for the next few days at least and that only takes us up to when the vault opens. What happens after that is anyone's guess, and we need to be ready. The country, the continent, the whole world is at home for Christmas. Once the batteries have run out on the Wii and everyone is bored of making small talk with the in-laws, there's nothing better than a rolling news story to drive traffic to us on all platforms. My guess, this story will be an absolute ratings winner for us, but we need to be ahead of the opposition. They'll be doing their best to play catch-up, but we can't allow that to happen.

'We need to *own* this story, so, this is how it's shaping up. For starters, we're planning round-the-clock cover on the camera position outside Mayfair Safety Deposits. Greg, can you make sure we have reporter and crew coverage twenty-four seven on that please? Julia, I'd like your team to commission a series of 3D graphics and an animated news wall showing the dimensions and an artist's impression of inside the vault. We'll need them as soon as possible, please.

'Christine, what's your view on the phone connection? I think we should be more sparing with it and use it to boost interest at key viewing times.'

'Reasons?'

Christine couldn't lose the habit of using as few syllables as possible and Miles laughed at her directness.

'Well, for one, the Met Police Commissioner has already been on the phone. He's absolutely livid, as you can imagine. The sound department still have the line connected, even though we aren't putting it to air at the moment. I'm in the process of brokering a deal so police negotiators can talk to those inside the vault on that established line. That of course is fully dependent on the continuing understanding that we have access at times to be agreed.'

As he took another sip of his Coke, Sid did his level best to listen intently to the logistics without interruption, but it was no good, he needed to know the answer to his most pressing question.

'Where's Suzanna?'

'She's still in Paris, trying to get back, but transport links are proving a challenge. We're doing our best to get her home as soon as possible, Sid.'

Miles watched Sid shift uneasily in his seat. The anchor was keen to keep control for as long as possible, but he knew it could only be a matter of time before Suzanna used her broomstick to fly back over the Channel.

'Don't try too hard, MW. She needs the break.'

'Don't worry, Sid, you'll be on air when anything big happens.'

Relieved, Sid adopted a pose which he hoped suggested that he was cool about whatever decision was made.

'So, back to the Met: obviously the police don't want to cut the line, and if they force us to end the connection we've established there's no guarantee that Bert or any of the others will answer again. Can you believe the Met wasn't even aware there was a phone line inside the vault? Apparently it's only just been installed and the owners had forgotten to mention it. In fact, the owners appear to have forgotten to be in touch with the police full stop. Can't be traced anywhere.'

'How did we get the number then, MW?'

After the briefest moment of insecurity Sid had regained his composure and was keen to be involved in discussions.

'Steve Stone, the new boy. Not sure if you've met him yet?'

Sid shrugged. He'd never heard the name before, making no connection whatsoever with the overzealous reporter who'd buzzed him when he'd arrived for the early shift just that morning.

'Where did *he* get it from?'

Suddenly, the excited hum among the production team ceased and the room fell completely quiet. Sid had committed the mortal sin of asking about a journalist's sources. He must be knackered, thought Christine, who jumped in to save him.

'So, everybody, Steve also says the police are having a devil of a job tracking down the secondary keyholders. He's bashing the phones now to see what he can come up with. Seriously, what sort of Mickey Mouse operation was this Mayfair Safety Deposits anyway, MW? One of the questions we'll need an answer to.'

Miles picked up the ball and Sid winked his thanks to Christine for being there to save him while also using more words than he could ever remember hearing her utter. That was, except in the height of passion.

When he'd first arrived at Europe News, the presenter and his producer had enjoyed a get-to-know-you dinner, which of course involved drunken flirtation. A fling ensued but was over almost before it had begun. It had meant nothing to Sid and he was sure Christine felt the same way. They returned to mutual professional respect without any ill feeling.

'So what about those inside, do we know anything about them?'

It was Jim the night news editor, who, with standing room only, had found leaning space against Miles's door frame.

'Good question, Jim. Thanks again, by the way, for giving me the heads-up earlier. Rescued me from the kids and the in-laws. Steve tells me there are five inside in total. Actually, where is Steve? Get him in here and he can tell us himself.'

Jim disappeared and re-emerged a few moments later with Steve Stone in tow. His greeting from the Head of News as he arrived in the office was very different to the one he had experienced when attempting to attract Miles's attention earlier.

'Ah, you're Steve Stone, welcome on board, mate.'

Sid stood and offered a hand of greeting.

'Thanks, yeah thanks.'

Steve was dumbstruck. He'd been in lots of planning meetings at the newspaper, but none attended by TV celebrities before. *Don't blow it this time* was all he could think of and he reverted to silence in the presence of the TV anchor. Miles stepped in.

'We're planning next steps, Steve, and wanted to know what your contact had said about those inside. The guard gave us names, and we know the young boy is ill, but what more do we know?'

Steve was relieved at the thinking time MW's question gave him.

'Well, I've just been chatting to my contact again. Obviously, he doesn't want to be interviewed on air, but he did fill me in on a few more facts.

'Let's start with the Arab family: they're from Aj-al-Shar. They arrived at the vault about fifteen minutes before it was due to close. The mother is Princess Almira. The kids didn't sign in, but we know she has two children, Hafsa and Umair. The ledger also says there's an older woman who had signed in as the Countess Fitzwilliam. Given the Countess is in her mid seventies, it was clearly a false name. Anyway, we now know it's Lily Dunlop. I can tell you Lily was a "girl in pearls" in *Country Life* earlier this year.'

'Library needs to get that picture.' It was Christine again.

'On it,' offered another member of the team in competition for the shortest sentence of the day.

Steve continued:

'Lily Dunlop celebrated her twenty-first birthday in April. A friend of the royals, she's holidayed with Harry and Chelsy and is engaged to Giles Musgrave-Rose.'

'Isn't he the wanker who . . .' the question came from an anonymous group of journalists gathered next to Jim by the door.

'Yup, "Greed is still good" – that's the one.'

Christine raised an eyebrow to be met by a 'yup' from the picture editor.

'I think I remember this Lily Dunlop. Check the pages of

Hello! – I'm sure I've seen at-home pictures of her there.' MW was thinking out loud. Lily Dunlop, Lily Dunlop . . . he was sure he knew her mother.

'The only other person is Bert Jones, a former copper, colourful history. Wife and two kids, lives in North London. I have the address.'

'I want a crew and reporter outside the house soonest,' said Miles. 'Great work, Steve. I'll let you get back to the phones.'

Miles hadn't forgotten his promise of a congratulatory chat with Steve, but it would have to wait until he was confident this breaking-news juggernaut could stay on the road. As Steve turned to leave, he acknowledged Sid's congratulatory army salute with a ham-fisted gesture of his own. The anchor either didn't notice or politely ignored Steve's awkwardness.

'Brilliant work, well done. Again, welcome on board.'

Now, holding Chantelle firmly around her tiny waist, the news anchor was equally impressed by this morning's onboard entertainment. Sid caught his breath before arching to kiss her between her beautifully enhanced breasts. A moment later he reached the height of pleasure and dropped contentedly back on to his goose-feather pillow. This girl was good.

As Sid reclined in post-coital satisfaction he couldn't help but entertain himself with the thought that Suzanna was stuck the other side of the Channel while he'd been coast to coast Stateside and still managed to squeeze in the first festive fun of the season. It was impossible for life to get any better, thought Sid as he fell into a contented sleep.

17

10 a.m.

Upton Park, Oxfordshire

Lady Agnes was aghast to see her granddaughter's photograph on the front page of *The Times*.

'Your daughter obviously takes after her father. How could she possibly bring such shame on the family? I will never be able to hold my head up at the bridge club again. Pass the marmalade please, darling.'

'Mother, I thought we had spoken about this yesterday. Please can we not continue to be quite so critical of Lily when she is not here to defend herself.'

Catherine's tone was calm with just a hint of pique. Nevertheless, her mild irritation showed a little too much attitude for her father's liking.

'Excuse me, young lady, but I would ask you not to speak to your mother in that manner. See, Agnes, that's what happens when we allow her to marry an oik. What's for breakfast, Brian? I'm famished.'

Lord Alistair had arrived at breakfast later than his wife

after sleeping off an excellent bottle of port from the previous evening. Catherine despaired. Any hope of a sensible conversation with her mother had disappeared with the unwanted arrival of her father at the breakfast table. It was Lord Alistair who had been the first to bring up Lily's incarceration yesterday after listening open-mouthed to the Radio 4 news in the Bentley as they headed to Upton Park. Concern that their granddaughter was being held against her will had been immediately replaced with fury when they had heard a sound clip from the guard commenting on Lily's actions. The Countess had concurred with her husband. They were absolutely furious at the antics of their granddaughter.

Lady Agnes had spent every one of the last twenty years trying to convince her husband to accept an invitation to spend Christmas with Catherine and Lily. He'd only reluctantly agreed after *that oik* had died. The Earl and Countess were close friends of the royal family and it was a matter of continued embarrassment that their daughter had married beneath her. The fact the Princess Catherine was a descendant of coal miners was of no consequence. Now Lily behaving like a common criminal only served to underline the point that no good could ever come from a lack of breeding.

Lady Agnes was an elegant woman of indeterminate age. Nearer seventy-five than sixty, her regular discreet trips to Harley Street had managed to keep the ageing process at bay. Her own parents were not aristocrats. Her father had been a banker and her mother an actress. She had met Alistair at a debutante ball when she was just eighteen and had readily accepted his proposal: 'No point fannying around – let's just get on with it then girl.'

Though not yet twenty at the time, Lady Agnes had found herself running a vast estate in the North East. Alistair was often in London and returned when it suited him. Agnes had accepted early in married life that her role was to support her husband in whatever he said and produce an heir and a spare. Although trying her level best to fulfil almost his every need, heartache and desperation had still failed to provide an appropriate heir. Catherine had been their only child, a fact that Alistair often referred to when the couple quarrelled.

Lady Agnes had long since discovered that food was always the best way to placate her husband.

'Have you decided what you would like for breakfast, Alistair? The eggs are lovely.'

Catherine wondered how her mother could possibly know how the eggs, or for that matter anything else, tasted. As usual, she had eaten like a bird this morning and certainly not even contemplated tasting an egg.

'Excellent, I'll have three, fried. Bacon, two pork sausages . . . no, make that three, please, Brian, and perhaps a spot of porridge while I'm waiting for Cook.'

'Certainly, sir.'

As Brian glided from the room, Alistair stretched across to retrieve the newspaper from his wife's hands. Agnes didn't flinch as *The Times* was taken from her grasp. With her reading material removed, she began nibbling on a slice of dry granary toast instead.

Catherine watched her parents from the other end of the table. She had been delighted to finally have them here for Christmas, but it had turned out so badly. Yesterday she had been on the receiving end of her father's hot temper and this morning she was finding it difficult to maintain eye contact with the Earl. Instead, she looked out through the dining-room window. The downfall of heavy snow had carpeted much of the lawns and a thick rug covered the orangery. Catherine remembered how Joseph had been absolutely delighted when the building had received a mention in Pevsner's guide to historic buildings in England. Looking at it now she was concerned the ageing roof might struggle to hold the weight of so much snow. She must ask Brian to arrange for it to be cleared. He probably already had it in hand.

Gazing out towards the lake, Catherine remembered how caustic the atmosphere had been in this same room just yesterday. It had begun with Lord Alistair's ire.

'Bloody disgrace. No grandchild of mine should act in this way.'

'Please, Daddy, let's eat Christmas lunch first. Cook has gone to so much trouble. We can speak about Lily later.'

'Wouldn't have happened if you hadn't married that bloody oik.'

Alistair banged the table with the base of his dinner fork, part of a Roberts & Belk set secretly bought by his wife as a wedding gift for their daughter. Agnes had made a discreet call to Harrods to purchase the canteen. The only demonstration of love she dared show in defiance of her husband's wishes.

The Earl, who'd attended Eton, Oriel and Sandhurst before a spell in the army, was totally dismayed at his daughter's choice of husband. He had refused point-blank to in any way acknowledge the couple's union.

Brian the butler moved quickly towards the table and placed a linen cloth over the sauce that had splashed from the gravy boat when Sir Alistair had lost his cool. His timely intervention managed to prevent it from spreading any further along the crisp, cotton table cloth.

'Daddy, please don't be so judgemental about Lily. She must be so frightened right now. I can't imagine what must have happened for her to become involved in such nonsense.'

Even if Catherine's suspicions about Lily's actions were right, she was certainly not prepared to share her family secret with her parents. If they had any inkling of what was in the security box, then the fragile family bond she had been nurturing would be permanently destroyed. In fact, if her mother knew the truth it wouldn't just be her father who would be estranged this time. Catherine put down her cutlery and dropped her hands into her lap, twisting her napkin into tight knots beneath the table. Any expectation that her parents would not be aware of Lily's incarceration had been dashed the moment they'd walked disapprovingly through the door to Upton Park.

'Judgemental? She's a bloody disgrace is what she is, Catherine.'

Alistair chewed contentedly on a large piece of succulent turkey, washed down with a significant draw on his Château de Meursault Premier Cru before turning to his wife and continuing.

'I knew we shouldn't have come here, Agnes. Did I mention that John at the club had invited us for Christmas at his table? It would have been a much better option, I'd say. We'll never get another bloody invite now, not after all this nonsense. I mean to say, what will happen when the bloody girl is finally released? Hey? What will happen then?'

Alistair took another long slurp from his Reidel crystal wine glass, spilling a little down his shirt as he pondered.

'I say the only option is to send the bloody girl away. Either that or better still, leave her in the bloody place. Damned disgrace.'

The Earl returned to his lunch.

'Bloody good food, though, my girl. Have to say that for you.'

Catherine smiled thinly and looked in vain for support from her downtrodden mother. Agnes was primly sawing through a chipolata while studiously ignoring her daughter's pleading glances. With only three of them at the vast table, the room fell into an awkward silence. Brian the butler stood to the side, making himself almost invisible until required.

As early as last spring Catherine had agreed that Lily could travel to Barbados with Giles for Christmas. Wary of the Earl's disparaging view, she knew that in the event her mother did manage to persuade him to visit for any part of the festive season, Lily would not sit quietly and hear her grandfather pour scorn on her father's achievements. Nevertheless, Catherine now longed for the alternative of a family argument round the dining table rather than Lily's present fate. She could sense the first tears starting to build.

'May I get you anything else, ma'am?'

Brian, sensing his mistress's distress, was immediately by her side.

'Erm, thank you, Brian. I think I am fine for now. What about you, Father? Can we tempt you with anything else to eat?'

Catherine, like her mother, knew that whatever her father's level of fury he wouldn't say no to food. It had taken years of constant attention to the dinner platter to create his twenty-six-stone bulk, a stark contrast to his wife's delicate frame. Agnes had long adhered to the 'never too rich or too thin' mantra of Wallis Simpson, the wife of Edward VIII. Alistair was impressed by her discipline and still regularly appreciated her body, though Agnes often felt sex with her husband was like being flattened by a tumbling wardrobe, with the key still in the door.

'Don't mind if I do. Might be our last bloody supper if that damned girl causes us any more embarrassment. I knew you shouldn't have married that penniless oik.'

Catherine wanted to stand and scream up the table at her father. Joseph wasn't an oik and certainly wasn't penniless. When they met he had swept her off her feet and made her realise what love could mean. She hadn't been prepared to settle for the life her mother had accepted. Joseph had provided her with what, initially, had been a very attractive alternative. She would never admit to her parents that, by the end, the marriage had been little more than a shell.

As her father once again piled his plate high, her mother took a second minute bite at a roast potato. Catherine stared blankly down at her own lunch. The thought of food made her feel physically sick. She fidgeted with her cutlery instead. Watching her father once again clear his plate, Catherine tried to lift the mood.

'How was lunch, Daddy? I hope you enjoyed it as much as you seemed to?'

'First class. At least you have a decent cook, my dear. I can only assume that Joseph Dunlop had nothing to do with hiring her. If it's going to be our last bloody meal before we're ostracised forever, then I might as well enjoy it.'

Catherine ignored the slight.

'It's traditional pud for dessert. Would you care for brandy cream with that?'

Lady Agnes smiled at her daughter, relieved she was prepared to play her part and indulge the Earl's nineteenth-century idiosyncrasies for just a few more hours. Catherine was less happy. She couldn't begin to understand why she was sitting eating Christmas lunch with her judgemental parents while her daughter remained trapped just a few miles away. What was happening at the vault? She'd had Brian call the police earlier, but they had been able to offer little further information. Would they know any more now? At the very least she should be monitoring the news on television instead of sitting here with her parents and doing nothing to help Lily. But rather than making her excuses and leaving the room, she continued to sit passively listening to her father abuse her dead husband and her trapped child. Catherine had spent so many years being rejected by her parents she was prepared to do almost anything to be welcomed back into the fold. A prodigal daughter given a second chance. For that opportunity she was prepared to pay the ultimate price of leaving her own child to her fate, at least for now. Catherine knew her behaviour was simply unacceptable. She wanted to leap from her chair and run all the way to London, but instead beckoned Brian.

'That was excellent, Brian, thank you. In fact, Daddy has already made room for dessert.'

'Bloody good food, Brian. Compliments to Chef, old boy.'

'Thank you. I will be delighted to pass them on, Sir Alistair.'

Several hours and many, many hundreds of calories later, the family had retired to the drawing room of Upton Park and were relaxing in front of a roaring log fire, laid, lit and tended by Brian. Alistair was snoring loudly, a hefty glass of port set within easy reaching distance for when he woke. Catherine sat opposite her mother, a half-played game of chess spread out in front of them.

Outside the snow had continued to fall throughout the day and Lady Agnes was concerned that if the inclement weather persisted they would find it challenging to make the journey back to Northumberland the following morning. Catherine hoped the god Apollo would be listening to her little prayer and bring some winter sunshine.

'I know it's difficult, darling.'

Catherine was jolted by her mother's softly spoken words. It was rare to hear her voice unless her father was out of the room.

'But all will be well.'

Catherine wanted to scream at the top of her voice that all wouldn't be well. How could it be, when Lily was trapped in a vault while she was playing bloody chess? But her mother would never understand her frustrations. Lady Agnes's role had been to serve her husband for almost sixty years. During that time she had never thought for herself. Not once. Even when Alistair had cut Catherine out of the family, Agnes had done little to protest. Over the years, Catherine had tried hard not to be critical of her mother, but couldn't help wondering how differently she would have reacted to Lily's drama if her own mother had been more effusive with love for her. Perhaps it was time she put her mother's love to the test.

'Mother, Lily needs me now more than ever. What should I do?'

Lady Agnes appeared not to hear her daughter's plea and continued to scrutinise the board. Catherine moved her queen to take off one of her mother's bishops before trying again.

'I need to try to help her, Mother. I have let her down so badly . . .' The end of the sentence trailed away.

Agnes put down the rook she had been contemplating castling with and stretched her hands across the chess table, knocking over her king in the process. Catherine was unsure if it was a mistake or she was conceding defeat. Lady Agnes held her daughter's hand.

'Darling, I understand. I truly do. I cannot begin to imagine how I would feel if it were you that was trapped. I would be desperate, absolutely desperate. What have the police said?'

'They are sending a liaison officer to the house but can do little more than that at the moment. I feel I ought to be doing something more though, Mother. What should I do?'

Agnes paused, staring deep into her daughter's eyes before continuing.

'Well, darling, I would think there is little more that can be done for now. However, Catherine, I would strongly advise that, after so long apart, it would be foolish to make an enemy of your father again. It has taken so much for him to be here today. His pride was mightily challenged by Joseph's behaviour towards him all those years ago. Many times I have tried to bridge the canyon between you. It has taken twenty-five years and the death of Joseph to finally achieve that ambition. Every day of those twenty-five years I missed you, my darling, so I know how challenging the last eight months without Lily must have been for you, truly I do.'

Lady Agnes appeared to be on the verge of tears, but checked herself. Clearing her throat, she continued.

'Nevertheless, our role as women is to support our husbands. That is why despite, your father's view, I did always admire you for standing by Joseph for so many years. You were his wife and that was your duty.'

As Sir Alistair woke from his slumber and reached for his port, Lady Agnes fell silent, repositioned her king and castled. Catherine spent the rest of the evening tortured by her mother's words. She retired to bed exhausted and frustrated by her own inaction.

Sitting at the breakfast table now, her overriding emotion was still one of guilt that she was doing nothing to help Lily. Brian interrupted her thoughts.

'Ma'am, there is a telephone call for you. A gentleman who says he has information which may help Miss Lily. Would you like to take the call?'

18

10.15 a.m.

Mayfair Safety Deposits

It had been more than twenty-four hours since Umair's seizure and after a flurry of concern followed by a night of restless anxiety, the atmosphere in the vault was again calm. Bert had been particularly freaked by the young boy's condition. Watching the child blinking and twitching as his muscles went into spasm, had left Bert helpless and unsure of what to do. But the seizure had quickly passed and Umair had returned to playing with his Panda bear, exactly as he had been doing in the moments before he was taken ill.

Nevertheless, Bert had spent an edgy night keeping a watchful eye on the youngster. Umair was still sleeping now, or was he unconscious? Which was it? Should he go over to check? No, let the child sleep. But what if he wasn't asleep? What if his condition had worsened and he'd done nothing to try to save him? He needed to check, but how could he do that without causing any further alarm?

It had taken Bert a good two hours to calm everyone

down after Umair had been taken ill. Princess Almira had been the worst. Her child's illness seemed to be the final straw for her. She had screamed hysterically as she rifled through her bag, searching for something that quite clearly wasn't there and shouting at her daughter between sobs. Hafsa had explained to Bert that her mother was looking for Umair's medication. Just as Almira's desperation had reached hysteria pitch, Umair had appeared to simply wake up, rub his nose and continue to pull at the remaining one of Squidgy's eyes.

'He'll be fine now,' Hafsa reassured everyone.

And indeed he had been, but looking at him this morning, Bert just needed to make doubly sure.

Ambling across to the cooler, he measured out water into five clear plastic stacking cups, four a little fuller than the fifth cup. Lily, who hadn't slept all night, was watching the guard as he went about his task. She knew which cup would be for her but didn't protest. She too had been completely shaken by the young boy's seizure and was equally anxious to make sure he was fully recovered.

'Morning, Hafsa, how's little Umair today? Here's some water for him and for you and your mother too.'

'Thank you,' whispered Hafsa, taking the cups. 'He's fine, thank you, guard. He usually sleeps a little longer after a seizure, but my mother will wake him as soon as she returns from the bathroom, I'm sure.'

'Gave me quite a turn, I have to say,' conceded Bert. 'Glad he's on the mend, though. Shouldn't be much longer now before we're out of here and then the doctor can give him the once-over.'

'Thank you, guard.'

'Please, call me Bert.'

'Thank you, Bert.'

'You're welcome. I'll leave your mother's water just here

191

on the floor. Make sure you don't knock it over. It's precious stuff at the moment.'

Bert returned to the cooler and, collecting the other two cups, walked back to his desk and put them down.

'Oi, yours is here. Come and get it if you want it.'

Lily realised she should have expected nothing more, but was still stung by the guard's continuing contempt for her. Walking across to collect her cup she attempted to speak.

'I really didn't mean for this to happen, Bert.'

'Well, it did. And YOU can call me Mr Jones if you don't mind.'

As the Princess emerged from the bathroom to be greeted by Hafsa and a sleepy Umair, Bert tucked his paper under his arm and took his turn. Lily returned to her corner of the vault. A lonely walk with no one there to greet her, to reassure her that everything would be all right. She sipped slowly on her water. It had been two nights and they were still here. Surely it couldn't be too much longer before they were freed? She thought about Giles and wondered what he would be doing right now. Would he have gone to Barbados without her, or perhaps stayed at home with the family? Boxing Day, it would be the hunt, of course. His mother was master of the Hothrop Hunt and he had been born to the saddle, almost literally, after Rose had gone into early labour. Her loyal hunter had stood patiently while she was lifted from its back and into the ambulance. Giles had learned to ride practically before he could walk and often tried to convince Lily to join him in the thrill of the chase.

'It's not cruel, we're just exercising the hounds these days and following a scent trail. The hounds can't kill – not since that blasted Tony Blair changed the law, anyway. He's the sort of chap would probably shoot a fox rather than offer it a fair chase. Bloody politicians, know nothing about life in the country.'

192

Despite his cajoling, Lily had always declined Giles's invitation to join him. She was content to hand out the sausage rolls and mulled wine in the car park before the hunt set off, while using the tips Giles had taught her to check for saboteurs among the crowd. Finishing her water, Lily wondered if she would ever visit the countryside again. First, though, she needed to know the answer from inside the security box. With the guard occupied perhaps now was her chance to search for his key?

A shrill whistle made Lily, Princess Almira and her children all jump in alarm. Looking around wildly, Lily realised it was coming from the telephone receiver resting on the guard's desk. Someone was trying to attract their attention.

With the guard still in the bathroom, Lily had no alternative but to answer it.

19

11 a.m.

Mandarin Oriental Hotel

Prince Ansar put down his teacup, unable to concentrate on anything other than when he would see his beloved son again. Umair had now spent two nights within the confines of the vault and still nothing seemed to have been achieved in the attempt to free the child. Last night the police had assured him that negotiators were in constant communication with the vault. They had spoken to Princess Almira and she had confirmed Umair had recovered from his seizure. She had wanted to speak to Ansar. He had refused, asking instead to speak to Umair, but the child was already sleeping. The police had assured Ansar they would contact the vault this morning and report back as soon as they had more to tell him. He had heard nothing. Ansar checked his watch: 11 a.m. His patience was stretched to breaking point. This ridiculous farce could not be allowed to continue. He required immediate action.

He raised his hand and clicked his fingers loudly. Seconds later, Dmitri tapped gently at the door and entered the room.

'Sir?'

The head of security's mid-Atlantic accent, which provided him with an air of respectability when they were in public, was not required in private. It had given way to a thick Iraqi tone betraying less savoury aspects of his CV.

Dmitri Boutakov – or Aban al-Yussuf, as he was named by his parents – was a former lieutenant general in the Iraqi Republican Guard, and had been in charge of close protection at the Presidential Palace. The Golden Division, as it was known, was responsible for directly protecting Saddam Hussein. Occasional foolhardy attempts to unseat the dictator had been quelled ruthlessly and efficiently by Aban and his men. Although his tactics were never discussed, the ruling family's lions were always well fed; Aban had been paid handsomely for his loyalty and Saddam relied heavily on him until the second invasion of Iraq in 2003. The head of security read the runes better than his master, and fled to Aj-al-Shar as the American tanks thundered across the desert towards Baghdad. By the time Saddam's statue was toppled in Firdos Square, Aban had already changed his identity. A little R&R, financed by the gold ingots he'd liberated on his way out of the Presidential Palace, was followed by an intensive English language course. Soon after Dmitri was ready to offer his ruthless services to others who might benefit from a man who knew, no matter how fast a traitor could run, it was never as fast as a hungry lioness.

Now, standing in one of the most expensive hotels in London dressed impeccably in a Jermyn Street suit, specially cut to conceal his Glock 9mm pistol, Dmitri was the image of propriety.

Ansar banged his fist on the table.

'Why have I not yet heard from the police this morning? What is happening with our own plans to free my son? How many more times must I say this, Dmitri? I need action.'

'Sir, I have spoken to the police. They were planning to talk to your family about an hour ago and assure me they will be in contact shortly.'

'I want to speak to my son.'

'I made that very clear, sir.'

'I expected Umair would be home with me by now. You have failed.'

Dmitri lowered his gaze and remained silent.

'Well?'

'Sir, everything possible is being done.'

Dmitri paused, hoping the Prince would not want him to go into detail. In reality, despite his men's best efforts, little had been achieved. Any hope his team might have had of getting close to the vault had been rendered impossible with the arrival of the SAS. Even his most ruthless men knew better than to challenge the red berets. He did, though, have some news.

'We have located the family of Miss Lily Dunlop.'

Ansar had been pacing the room in his Ralph Lauren pyjamas, newly purchased by Umair for his daddy on his mother's credit card and with the advice of his sister Hafsa. Wearing them helped Ansar feel closer to his son until he could hug him again.

'Tell me more.'

'Sir, the family's principal residence is located in North Oxfordshire. It is five thousand acres with impressive security measures. Miss Dunlop's father died relatively recently of colon cancer. Her mother is still alive and is spending Christmas at the house with her own mother and father. There is staff of about a dozen at the house. While it would, in theory, be possible to call on Mrs Dunlop and persuade her to visit you here, I think it may be better to wait a little longer.'

Prince Ansar was tired to the point of exhaustion and

wanted Umair back with him. He massaged his clipped beard and contemplated what should be done. The news that Lily Dunlop's family was enjoying quality time together filled him with a fury he could barely contain. Family meant nothing to Westerners. How could they pull crackers and eat turkey while one of their own was incarcerated? His growing contempt for the British increased a notch further.

'Wait for how long?'

'Well, sir, I have a man at the gates to the estate. He advises there is press interest there already and, despite the security measures in place, at least one photographer almost managed to reach the house before being stopped. I would have thought Mrs Dunlop and her parents will be keen to leave the house quite soon. Her parents live in Northumberland and are expected to return later today, according to my sources. I would expect Mrs Dunlop will depart for London soon after that. She has property in Cheyne Walk, but again there are photographers already outside, so she may not return there.'

'I want her here. Don't lose her.'

'We won't, sir. The photographer being apprehended at the estate offered a useful diversion while we attached a tracking device to the car.'

'Excellent work, Dmitri.'

'Thank you, sir.'

The tracker would make it possible to tail Catherine Dunlop wherever she went. All Dmitri needed was for her to get in the car. With that in mind, he had telephoned the house. It had been easy to convince the butler he had useful information about the condition of Lily that could only be shared with her mother. Dmitri smiled as he remembered Catherine Dunlop's desperate tone when she came to the phone.

'Hello, hello, who is this? What can you tell me about my daughter? When will she be free?'

Dmitri had persuaded the gullible woman he was a senior executive at Mayfair Safety Deposits and it would be in her daughter's best interests if Catherine were to head to London straight away. He hoped to organise an alternative exit from the vault for Lily, avoiding any unsavoury press interest. Catherine had accepted, though hinted family commitments meant she wouldn't be able to leave her home until later in the day. The security guard scoffed. Clearly, not so concerned about her daughter that she was prepared to leave her lovely home immediately. Typical example of Western women, no concern for their children.

They had agreed to meet at the Dorchester Hotel for afternoon tea. There, Dmitri would offer to take her to the vault to explain to her in greater detail his proposition. Within a few minutes she would instead be in the suite of Prince Ansar, feeling his pain. If for whatever reason she decided not to show, then the tracker on her vehicle would allow Dmitri to easily trace her whereabouts.

His plans, however, were to be quickly thwarted.

As Catherine had returned to the breakfast table to check if her father needed more to eat, Brian the butler apologetically interrupted with another telephone call. This time it was a producer from Europe News. How on earth could a television station know who she was or indeed gain access to her private number? Nevertheless, curiosity and good manners prevailed and she accepted the call. During the short conversation that followed, Catherine was offered the opportunity to speak to her daughter live on air. It was something she had briefly contemplated on Christmas morning, only to dismiss the idea as vulgar. Now, with no sleep and precious little news about Lily, Catherine was more amenable. Perhaps Lily hadn't yet opened the security box. There might still be time to convince her daughter how much she truly loved her.

While Catherine accepted the offer from the TV channel, Brian remained hovering just out of earshot on the other side of the study door. He entered immediately Catherine rang the bell.

'Brian, I will be travelling to London after my parents depart.'

'Ma'am.'

'I had originally intended to meet with a Mr Gordon Bennett at the Dorchester for tea, but something else has come up. Please could you telephone and leave a message with the concierge for Mr Bennett, offering my apologies.'

'Of course, ma'am.'

'We will be travelling to the studios of Europe News instead.'

Brian said nothing, simply nodded. He was unsure whether it was appropriate for Mrs Dunlop to be appearing on television. This matter was escalating out of control. If only Miss Lily hadn't behaved so rashly.

As she made her way back to the breakfast table, Catherine hoped that her parents would understand her dilemma. If not, so be it. It was time to be a proper mother to her daughter.

Dmitri was first alerted to Catherine Dunlop's change of heart when Europe News began trailing their forthcoming interview with Lily Dunlop's mother. Seeing the breaking-news strap line, Dmitri had let out a curse in his native tongue, irritated by her change of plan. Even though he knew where she would be, once Mrs Dunlop was within the warren of TV studios it would take him some time to extricate her.

That was the challenge he had been working on when the Prince had summoned him a few minutes earlier. Standing in front of his principal now, the guard had yet to come up with a solution.

'No further delay, Dmitri, I want Mrs Dunlop here with me immediately. Do I make myself clear or do I need to find someone else who can make that happen? When can I expect her here in the suite enjoying my hospitality?'

Ansar's sharp tone focused Dmitri's mind. He told the Prince what he knew.

'Sir, I believe Mrs Dunlop is planning to head to London soon to appear on television at the Europe News studios. I expect to have the plans of the building within a few hours. We should be able to locate her shortly after that.'

'Europe News? The woman is seeking publicity while her daughter torments my family! I do not understand the British.'

Ansar stalked towards his desk and mobile phone.

'However, plans for the studios will not be necessary.'

'Sir?'

'No need to locate plans. Suzanna Thomas will know.'

Ansar had first met the female presenter when she interviewed him two years ago and then joined him at dinner. It was a conference in connection with the Gazprom dispute with the Ukraine and the supply of gas to Europe. Aj-al-Shar guaranteed a supply of natural gas if the dispute intensified. He had been very taken by Suzanna Thomas who had hosted the event and had been a delightful dinner companion. Since then she had been an irregular visitor to his suites whenever he was in London. She would easily be able to explain the best place to locate guests within the Europe News building.

'I will ask Suzanna for the location of the Green Room,' offered Ansar, keen to flaunt his insider TV knowledge.

'Would you like me to take care of it, sir?'

'No. I will do it.'

It had been only three weeks since the Prince had last enjoyed Suzanna's company. He found her refreshingly deferential for a Western woman. He had shown his appreciation with several gifts from Garrard's, including a copy of a ring that Suzanna had admired when it was worn by the Duchess of Cambridge.

Dialling her number, Ansar was surprised to note a foreign ringtone. Suzanna picked up almost immediately.

'Prince Ansar, I have been trying to telephone you for days. Er, I mean, hello, Happy Christmas. How are you, sir?'

Suzanna couldn't believe her luck, finally, some good fortune. She had tried to call the Prince several times on Christmas Day, but for some reason he hadn't been answering his phone. Nick her agent had suggested she keep on trying before turning off his own phone.

With no public transport and no knight in shining armour, there had been no option but to spend yet another night in Paris. For some reason, Christopher was chillier than when he'd taken her to the ice hotel at Jukkasjärvi. Not even the offer of slutty sex had thawed his mood. Suzanna had spent every second since monitoring Europe News and plotting an escape route.

Christopher was still frosty this morning and Suzanna had given up on him. Honestly, he was so difficult and demanding. As soon as good manners would allow, she'd begun trying the Prince's number again but still without success. Thinking there was some sort of Vodafone conspiracy against her, she'd just been checking the Internet for their press office number when by a stroke of luck the Prince had telephoned. Dashing towards the bathroom and closing the door, it was all she could do to prevent herself from launching into a little Snoopy dance on the marble floor as she listened excitedly to the dulcet tones of her on/off sugar daddy. Suzanna just managed to stop herself from singing out loud and instead made appropriate noises of sympathy to the Prince about the fate of Umair.

'Oh my goodness no, that is absolutely terrible. I had no idea it was your family who was in the vault, sir,' she lied.

'I am presently stuck in Paris with no way of returning to London, so I'm afraid I know very little of what is happening. If I was at the office, then of course I would be able to discover more and keep you fully informed. Sadly, stuck here in Paris that is not possible.'

Suzanna wasn't sure how many times to mention 'stuck' and 'Paris' in order to make yet not labour the point.

'Ah well my dear, allow me be the first to offer my assistance. It is simply unacceptable that you are not on my TV screen for such a major story as this. My jet can leave RAF Northolt within say the next hour. It can be with you shortly after that and return you back to London in no time. I will send Dmitri, my security guard, to collect you. He will accompany you directly to the TV station. I assume his access to the studios will be a formality?'

Suzanna was ecstatic. Exactly what she wanted and she hadn't even had to ask.

'Of course, of course, I will be happy to show him around as well, if he would like?'

'How kind, my dear. Please, prepare your things. Dmitri will be with you very shortly.'

Without another word, Ansar ended the call and replaced the phone on to his writing desk.

'I find Suzanna Thomas really most obliging and I would expect her to be treated well. Mrs Dunlop I would like in my company very soon.'

Dmitri nodded and walked swiftly to the hotel exit where a car was always waiting. This morning it would take him the ten miles to west London and just a short jet ride away from resolution.

Suzanna whooped with joy. She should be back in London and in control of Europe News's coverage within three or four hours. Throwing the last few things into her suitcase, she quickly zipped up the Louis Vuitton monogrammed keep-all, yet another gift from her wrecked lover. Glancing across at him, she noticed the look of complete bewilderment on his ashen face.

'You were like this all last night and now again this morning. What on earth is the matter with you? I've managed to organize a lift back to London, so there's nothing for you to worry about. The least you could say is thank you.'

Crushed by the single-minded self-absorption of the woman he had thought he loved, Christopher continued to stare into the middle distance. Yesterday he had been in shock. Today, after a sleepless night, he was broken.

'Aren't you going to say anything?'

Still Christopher was quiet.

'Fine, please yourself. If you're not offering to at least carry my bags then I'm leaving without you. Bye.'

Ha, he had given her the perfect excuse to leave him behind without her looking bad, thought Suzanna as she hoisted the overnight bag on to her shoulder. Without another glance she hurried to the door allowing it to slam rather too forcefully behind her.

Christopher continued to stare blankly ahead, unable to comprehend what had happened. How could his plans for the Christmas break have ended so disastrously?

Suzanna didn't appear to care that he had shelled out an obscene amount of money in an effort to make her happy. Neither did she have any concern for the five people who were trapped in a vault away from their families at Christmas. All she cared about was crushing Sid Parker or anyone else who stood in her way. She was without question a brilliant presenter. It was what had attracted him to her in the first place. But did she really have to be the lead on every single story? Why couldn't she just be confident enough in her own abilities to occasionally allow someone else to take the reins?

Christopher stood and walked to the window. The snow had stopped and Paris looked stunning in her winter coat. At that moment, Christopher Peters was completely crushed. His hopes and dreams in tatters around him in a swish hotel room in the most romantic city in the world. Paris was no place to be alone, no place to be dumped. It would take time for his pride to recover. But he knew that he would pull through this humiliation and some day find real love. Looking out over the rooftops towards the Eiffel Tower, Christopher was equally sure Suzanna would never be happy, that she would always be in search of something more. Today that something wasn't a luxury romantic break in Paris with a man who doted on her but a studio chair in London presently occupied by Sid Parker.

Turning away from the view, Christopher wandered across to the mini bar, took out a beer and sank into an armchair to watch the latest developments on Europe News. Why, he wondered, had Lily Dunlop trapped everyone in that vault?

20

2 p.m.

Europe News

'How's it going in there, Bert? How's everyone holding up?'

Sid Parker had loved his lazy start to the day but, entertaining as Chantelle was, she couldn't keep him from the story.

'Been better. When are we getting out of here? Am I live on the telly, Sid?'

Europe News had agreed to a twenty-four-hour noncommunication rule as part of an agreement brokered with the police. Miles had consented to police negotiators spending time in Europe News's sound suite so they could speak to Bert and the others on the line that had been established by the TV station. There were of course conditions. The police reluctantly agreed the channel could use the line to talk live on air to those inside each day the siege continued. Other stations, including Carole Smith at *Have a Nice Day UK*, had cried foul, but it was Steve's exclusive and, no matter how much the others complained, Europe News was the channel in the driving seat. They had the line and they weren't giving it up.

The police had spent the last few hours talking to those inside, checking on the young boy's medical condition and assessing the mental health of the four others. Now it was the turn of Europe News to be offered their half-hour window, and Sid had been determined he would be the one in the hot seat.

He'd returned to the station a couple of hours earlier to prepare and discovered that, as part of a congratulatory chat with Miles, Steve Stone had been instantly promoted to on-screen reporter. He was presently at the live camera position outside the vault in an ever-increasing cordoned press area. Young police officers with double time and little patience were doing their best to control the throng. Channels from around the world were descending on Mayfair Safety Deposits.

Good for Steve, thought Sid. But unfortunately, watching him on screen, he could see it wasn't going well. Despite wide-eyed keenness and supportive texts from his wife Jackie, it had quickly become apparent that Steve's on-air skills were not yet as impressive as his contacts. He looked like a rabbit in the headlights as he did his best to control nerves, remember his lines and speak as fluently as possible while looking down the barrel of a camera. The more he focused, the more Steve found it impossible to relate to the viewer while peering into a black hole.

Miles could also see the new guy was struggling, but he was insistent that Steve should not be pulled off air completely. He just needed to increase his flying hours. Another reporter had been quickly dispatched to the vault who would interview him side by side. A human being to talk to rather than a camera, just until he learned the ropes.

Sid had no such issues relating to a TV camera and was

very much front and centre in the studio. His few hours off had reinvigorated him and he'd left Chantelle in bed while he returned to the studio for this latest opportunity to speak to those trapped. In the vault, the atmosphere was tense and Bert was doing his best to support the children as their mother slowly fell to pieces.

'Yes, Bert, we are live on air. I believe you've been speaking to the police and that Umair is fine. That's such a relief. How is everyone else?'

'We're OK, but we're all starting to feel the pressure a bit to be honest, especially the children. I'm keeping an eye on the little 'un. I'm worried he could have another epileptic fit. Let me tell you, Sid, it looks pretty scary when it's happening. Poor little bugger.'

'I bet. What about the others?'

'Well, his sister has been an absolute little star. If her dad's listening, he should be very proud of her. Her mother is struggling, but doing her best to hold it together. As for the other one, she was keen enough to talk to the police when they whistled through a bit earlier, but she won't talk to you though, will she? No, she won't, because she's embarrassed. And so she bloody should be after what she's done to us. When are we getting out, Sid?'

Bert's voice cracked and he swallowed hard.

'I know, buddy, it must be tough, but shouldn't be long now. If I could just remind you though: try not to swear as you are on live television.'

'Shit, I forgot.'

'If you could just try to remember, Bert. I know it's difficult.'

'Please get us out, Sid, please.'

Sid offered conciliatory words of comfort and support. In his peripheral vision, he noticed the latest guest being brought into the studio to talk to viewers. He'd been expecting her.

207

She was nervous and visibly shaking and he reached across to put his hand on top of hers, offering a reassuring smile before continuing his conversation with Bert.

'We have someone in the studio who would like to chat to you, Bert. I'm sure you'll be pleased to hear from her – here you go.'

Sid nodded reassurance to his guest, signalling for her to speak.

'Hello, love, it's me.'

A timid Cynthia Jones tried to adopt her most reassuring voice, but it was very difficult. She was desperate to speak to her husband and find out how he was coping, but the last thing she wanted was to be doing it on live television. She'd heard him on Europe News yesterday, and when the studio had called and offered to send a car for her she'd jumped at the chance. Now, though, she was regretting her impulsive decision.

Cynthia had hoped to arrive earlier, while the police nego-tiators were talking to the vault. That way she could have chatted in private to her husband first but Boxing Day traffic around Trafalgar Square meant she'd arrived at the studios a few minutes too late for that. Her police family liaison officer had reassured her if she waited an hour then there would be another opportunity to speak privately. Cynthia was only too aware that Bert's temper was a problem and could sometimes get the better of him, especially when he was under stress, so it was imperative that she speak to him as soon as possible. His anger had ultimately cost him his job at the Met after he'd taken out his frustration on a journalist who wanted to challenge his hourly rate for supplying information. She didn't want him losing his temper with that well-spoken young girl in the vault and landing himself in trouble again. Cynthia decided there was no option but to be on live television.

'Is that you, Cynthia?

'Yes it is, love. How are you?'

'Who's with the kids?'

'Don't worry, love, they're fine. They're with your mother.'

'How's the dog?'

'He's OK. He's been looking all round the house for you, but he's fine.'

'Have you walked him?'

Sid smiled reassuringly at Cynthia, who was growing in confidence.

'Love, I just wanted to make sure you're feeling as calm as you can be.'

'Yeah. When will we be out?'

'Well, love, the police have a charming lady looking after us and when I asked her that question she said they were still trying to contact all the keyholders.'

'They'll be lucky! Yoni Sanchez never charges the battery on his phone. It'll be well flat by now. Bill Smith is in the Galapagos. I told you he was going for his wedding anniversary. We're going to be in here forever, aren't we?'

Talking to Cynthia had made Bert emotional and he stopped to clear his throat and compose himself. His wife, hearing him upset, immediately stepped in to comfort him.

'Now then, love, deep breaths. Of course you won't be in there forever. You'll be out before you know it. But I do want you to promise me that you'll stay calm until they find those keyholders. Think about your blood pressure, love. It's really important that you try to stay as calm as you possibly can. Everyone is doing everything they can. One of the producers here told me that the Prime Minister has even called in the army to look at blowing off the door.'

Sid immediately stepped in. Cynthia was offering up

information that shouldn't have been shared, especially on live television.

'That's not really something we can confirm at the moment though, Bert, so best not to rely on it just yet.'

In Miles's office, his phone rang immediately. It was the Police Commissioner, furious that confidential information had been broadcast live on air. Miles held the phone disinterestedly to his ear as he continued to listen to studio output.

'Sorry, Sid, I shouldn't have said that, should I?'

Cynthia began to shake and stood to leave but was restrained by the microphone cable attached to her crimson M&S woollen sweater. Sid reached for her hand and beckoned her to sit down again.

'Don't worry at all, Cynthia. You were trying to reassure Bert, I completely understand. Anything else you would like to say to him?'

Cynthia reluctantly sat down again and grasped the glass of water Sid was offering to her. Her hands were still shaking as she sipped and Sid took it from her before she dropped it. He repeated his question.

'Please don't worry, Cynthia, take your time. Anything else you would like to say or ask Bert?'

She nodded and continued.

'As I said, love, please be calm until they get you out. How is everyone else in there? Don't be too hard on the young girl, was her name Lily? Such a pretty name. We nearly called our Tracey that, didn't we?'

At the mention of Lily's name, Bert's blood pressure began to rise. He immediately forgot he was on TV.

'Can you believe that stupid little bitch?'

Sid was about to jump in to correct his language but Christine, who was back in the hot seat, spoke into his ear.

'Let it go. He's in full flow. MW will deal with any complaints.'

210

'She comes in here with her expensive clothes and her hoity-toity accent, waving a bloody gun around and gets us all locked in. Then she sits on her posh suitcase – no idea why she has that with her – and starts fiddling with her bloody mobile phone. What's she doing that for? There's no bloody signal inside a metal box, is there? No brains on her either obviously. There's no food in here, hardly any bloody water left, and we have no idea when we'll be out. I'll tell you what, Cyn, I'm bloody fed up to my back teeth.'

'I know, love, I know, but don't be too hard on her. I'm sure she didn't mean for everyone to be stuck in there like this now, did she?'

Bert didn't reply. He paused to wonder why Lily had done what she'd done. What did he care?

'Anyway, make sure you walk the dog tomorrow if I'm not out by then, will you, love?'

'Course I will. How are the little ones doing in there?'

'Well, I have to say I'm a bit worried about the youngster, Cyn, but I don't think there's much I can do for him. Luckily, his sister seems to have her head screwed on and she's been doing what she can to help her mother stay calm. They brought some of their toys when they came in and that's helped keep their minds off things for a bit. We've been putting his Scalextric together this afternoon.'

'Well done, love. I knew you'd be everyone's rock.'

Listening to a dial tone, Miles eventually realized the Police Commissioner had hung up. He put the receiver down and returned to eating a turkey sandwich as big as a doorstop. The interview with the guard and his wife was going well, and he continued to monitor the output of rival channels while contemplating the station's next move.

Miles had been in journalism for twenty years. He'd seen most stories from different angles – at least a half a dozen

211

times. Natural disasters, stock market collapses, serial murders, politicians caught with their pants down, even two royal weddings in one year, but he'd never known five people locked in a vault over Christmas before. As he swung his feet up on to his desk and took another bite at his tasteless sandwich, Miles contemplated comparable stories of humans trapped. Of course there had been the Chilean miners, stuck underground in 2010. Certainly those miners were in much less predictable surroundings, but they were with colleagues and friends who had supported them when they needed it. Those inside the vault came from three different cultures, trapped with little prospect of early escape, unable to see their families for Christmas. What were the psychological challenges they were facing? How would they be coping, not knowing when they might be free?

Miles stared at the TV screen. Similarities to the miners, yes, but still a world apart. Could there be comparisons for a news angle to keep them ahead of the field? Absolutely! He wanted one of the miners on the phone to describe what it was like to be trapped. They'd need an interpreter. Throwing the rest of his sandwich into the bin, he strode to his office door and bellowed across the newsroom to his increasing army of staff who had been pulled away from the bosom of their families to cover the news.

'Meeting, conference room, now, ladies and gentlemen. And can someone find me a Spanish speaker, please.'

As staff flooded into the meeting room it was standing room only for dawdlers. Jenny had popped up to the super-market petrol station to buy as many mince pies as she could reach on the shelves, and a dozen boxes were in the centre of the table. Miles began to liberate a mince pie from its aluminium cup before offering the box to the producer sitting next to him.

'So, people, great job so far. We're so far ahead of the

curve we can't even see Nigel Mansell in our rear-view mirror.'

Some of the younger staff didn't understand the reference to the Formula 1 motor racing legend, but a gentle chuckle from more experienced colleagues was their signal to smile knowingly.

'We really need to stay on top of this fast moving story, everybody. I want to know what the police are up to hour by hour. Actually, leave that to me, I'll call the Commissioner personally. Also what's happening with this cowboy outfit, Mayfair Safety Deposits. I can't believe there's still no sign of any of those bad boys. I need more info on the Arab family. Do their relatives want to talk? The child has epilepsy – what are the risks if he's not out soon? What will happen when the vault is finally open? And, perhaps most importantly, who is this Lily Dunlop and what's her motive?'

Christine was standing at the doorway, prepared to spare two minutes for the meeting before returning to the gallery. She had only one question for Miles.

'Any news from Suzanna?'

Miles shrugged. He'd completely forgotten about her. He really must call her later on.

'OK, well, if you can let me know the plan on presentation, boss. I need to get back and see what Sid is up to with the love birds.'

Leaving Miles and the team brainstorming, Christine returned to the gallery and was pleased to discover that Sid had managed to keep the conversation going between Bert and Cynthia.

'Has the girl said why she did it?'

'Haven't asked her, Cyn.'

'Well, she's obviously distressed, love, otherwise she

wouldn't have done what she's done. She must be really struggling.'

'Don't care.'

'Come on, love. What would you do if it was our Tracey? You know she can be a bit impetuous. Imagine if it was her. You would want someone to support her if she was in trouble, wouldn't you?'

'Suppose.'

'There you are then.'

Bert glared over at Lily. She was slumped on her suitcase as usual. He noticed that she hardly ever moved from the same spot. Glancing across at the children, Umair seemed to be in better spirits today and his sister was racing him on the Scalextric. Bert had helped construct it so it covered almost half of the floor area in the vault, twisting around the water cooler before heading straight for the leg of his desk and turning at the last moment to shoot towards the vault door. Princess Almira watched her children play while contemplating what her future would hold when she was out of the vault and facing the wrath of her husband.

Lily felt she had no future to contemplate. Giles would certainly disown her. Even if he hadn't been watching the news, someone at the hunt would definitely have told him by now. She wondered whether he would try to talk to her via the vault phone, but decided that was highly unlikely. He would feel humiliated and wouldn't be interested in knowing why she'd done what she'd done. Who would look after her now? Her grandparents would be so embarrassed they would want to send her to Timbuktu and leave her there. And what of her mother? Her mother, who had caused all of this. If only she'd been honest, none of this would have happened.

Shifting uncomfortably on top of her case, Lily tried to swallow but it hurt her throat, parched from so little water.

She was feeling increasingly unwell. She wondered again if she was ill. She needed to see what was in the box before deciding what to do. Why hadn't her mother been honest with her? Without warning, the tears came and Lily dropped her head to hide her distress from the children.

Looking across at her, Bert decided he couldn't care less. A bit of humility would do her good.

In the studio Cynthia looked across at Sid Parker's handsome face. Ordinarily, she would have been beside herself to be in the company of her heartthrob, but not right now. She wanted to flee the studio as quickly as possible. So long as Bert wanted to talk to her though, she would stay. She had no choice. Her husband was trapped, and given his high blood pressure and hot temper, he needed her.

'There are loads of presents waiting for you under the tree.'

'I bet. I can't wait to see you, Cyn. I really, really miss you, love.'

'I miss you too, and I love you loads.'

'To the moon and back a million times?'

'Yes.'

'Me too.' Bert choked back tears. The conversation was too much for him to bear. 'Anyway, love, I better go.'

Cynthia also began to cry.

'Try to stay as calm as you possibly can and I'll see you soon. Love you, bye.'

Sid allowed the moment to linger. All viewers could hear were sobs and sniffles. Eventually, Sid reached over and offered a supportive hug to Cynthia Jones, who leaned into his muscular shoulder to hide her face. Sid felt strangely emotional by the exchange. The conversation between Bert and Cynthia had also touched the hearts of all those listening in the gallery and in the newsroom.

One person who didn't appreciate the lovebird interlude was Roxy Costello. She had believed Bert Jones when he'd said his marriage was a sham and he would leave his wife immediately after Christmas. Now here he was, whispering sweet nothings to her on live TV. Well, she wasn't about to put up with that sort of nonsense.

21

4 p.m.

New Scotland Yard.

Sitting opposite the Gold Commander in the incident room at New Scotland Yard, and clearly out of his depth sat the dejected Managing Director of Mayfair Safety Deposits. He couldn't remember how many times he'd told his paymasters that security at the vault needed to be updated. The locking system on the main vault was antiquated, the CCTV was obsolete, and the fail-safes for the heavy metal door were anything but. But they wouldn't listen, more interested in profit than the safety of their clients. There had never been an incident so there was no need to worry. Now all the chickens were coming home to roost leaving Peter Goodyear with questions he couldn't possibly answer.

'I'm listening.'

The Commander had spent the last thirty minutes reassuring the Commissioner, who in turn had reassured the Prime Minister everything possible was being done to release those trapped in the vault. Not only was the siege big news in the UK, it was also front and centre for the King of Aj-al-Shar, whose relatives were trapped inside. The Prime Minister and everyone back down the line to the Gold Commander had been left in no doubt that the King was less than content with the way the situation was being handled. He had hinted that the current multi-billion pound gas deal being discussed between the two governments could stall, perhaps irrevocably, dependent on the outcome of this one incident.

'I said, I'm listening, Mr Goodyear. Guidelines state any system should be capable of being overridden by a professional within fifteen minutes. It has now been almost forty-eight hours and we are still on the outside while several people, including two terrified children, are very much on the inside of your vault. I am waiting for an explanation as to how this can possibly be the case.'

Peter Goodyear sat a little straighter in his chair. When he'd received the inevitable phone call interrupting the family Christmas he had anticipated that this would be a challenging meeting. He'd hoped that everything would be handled by the duty security team and the owners of the vault. However, both owners of Mayfair Safety Deposits had been uncontactable. Peter Goodyear had told anyone who asked that his bosses, Russian brothers, were due to be holidaying with their wives at a seven star hotel in Dubai. However, as well as a helipad and spa, the hotel was also equipped with twenty-four-hour news, which had alerted the brothers to the drama at their vault. Despite countless calls there had been no answer from either of their suites.

With the owners uncontactable, it was their hapless MD left facing the music. Hastily dispatched in a Next suit by his anxious wife, he was currently regretting the addition of a festive tie bought as a Christmas gift by his young children. It played 'Jingle Bells' every time Santa's nose was pressed, and unfortunately Santa's nose was just at the point where he crossed his arms. Acutely embarrassed, he waited for the latest tinny rendition to end before answering the police officer.

'Well, sir, we do have dual-access control. The vault has two locks, which can be overridden with the use of two keys. We do not allow just one person to have single access. This protects the contents of the vault from would-be intruders. This has already been explained by my staff to your officers at the scene.'

'Indeed, but it's a system that doesn't appear to have worked, does it, Mr Goodyear? As we both know for it to be effective, we need the whereabouts of the two personnel who are key-holders, do we not?'

'Yes, sir.'

'Well?'

'Well, sir, unfortunately, at the moment . . .'

Peter Goodyear uncrossed and re-crossed his arms, inadvertently pressing Santa's nose. 'Jingle Bells' interrupted his interrogation and he stared embarrassed at the floor, waiting for it to finish while trying desperately not to mouth the last few bars. Where were those wide-boy owners to face the music? He'd told them a thousand times this might happen. So far there was no sign of a second key-holder. The only keys that could free those trapped in the vault were presently in Bert Jones's pocket on the wrong side of the solid steel door.

As the music stopped, Peter Goodyear unwrapped his arms and sat on his hands.

'As I was saying, sir, unfortunately at the moment there is a problem locating keyholders.'

'Exactly, Mr Goodyear. In the meantime, we are in the process of re-interviewing Roger Hurst, the other guard who was on duty on Christmas Eve. Are we correct in assuming that he was the person with the most contact with Miss Lily Dunlop?'

Peter Goodyear nodded, though he had no idea if that was the case.

'Can you confirm that, following the appropriate protocol, Mr Hurst has spoken to no one about the events before offering a full detailed account of the incident?'

Peter Goodyear knew the protocol. Its purpose was to preserve the crime scene and keep the facts accurate. He also knew that Roger Hurst was a drunk who couldn't be trusted and would sell his own grandmother for a pint of Guinness and a packet of pork scratchings. Hurst had been employed by the owners against Goodyear's better judgement, primarily because he was cheap.

'Yes, sir, it's my understanding that the protocol has been strictly adhered to.'

The commander didn't believe a word of what this dishevelled little man was saying, but he still needed to ask the questions to try to glean as much information as he could. The owners of Mayfair Safety Deposits had not updated the security details on the vault since they bought the place, and the building plans were woefully inadequate.

'Tell me about the vault.'

'Well, sir, the walls are approximately two metres thick, as is the ceiling and the floor. We have twenty-four-hour CCTV coverage of the entrance area. The door itself is eighteen-inch reinforced steel. The locking system is . . .'

'I'm aware of the locking system, Mr Goodyear. What else?'

'There is a recently installed telephone, only to be used for emergencies.'

'. . . and on occasion for speaking to the world via a television station.'

The Met Police Commissioner Phillip Hughes-Jenkins had

been torn to pieces by a furious Prime Minister who wanted to know how Europe News could have acquired the phone number.

'Any idea how the media may have discovered the ex-directory number of the vault at all, Mr Goodyear?'

Though he had no doubt whatsoever that it was Hursty who would have passed on the details for cash, but there would be no point in dobbing him in to the law. The guy was without a job now, anyway. Peter Goodyear hoped the tip-off money had been spent wisely, but knowing Hurst, it had probably gone straight to his pub landlord.

'That is something we are investigating at the moment.'

'Really.'

The Gold Commander was aware of Roger Hurst's background. He had checked up on his police credentials and knew that if he had access to the information he would undoubtedly have sold it.

'Mr Goodyear, we have the army on standby. There is a plan to blast through into the vault because we cannot gain access any other way or at least that is how it would seem. Naturally, our major concern is for the wellbeing of all of those inside, particularly the children. As a result it is ultimately, a decision which rests with the Prime Minister. He has asked me to advise you that if anything untoward were to happen to those trapped inside, then MSD will have some very serious questions to answer. Even more serious questions than are already on the table. Do I make myself clear?'

Peter Goodyear nodded.

'Do you have anything else to say, Mr Goodyear?'

'No, sir.'

'Take a walk, but don't go far. I'm not finished with you yet. Oh, and lose the stupid tie.'

Peter Goodyear felt as if he was being temporarily

dismissed from the headmaster's study but with a blistering punishment to follow. He almost ran to the door and fumbled with the handle before dashing in search of a coffee machine while he contemplated his sentence.

Further down the same corridor, Roger Hurst was slouched in a chair, being interviewed by a chief inspector.

'You're in the shit, Hursty.'

Apparently unconcerned, the former guard shrugged his shoulders.

'How much did you sell the number for?'

'Don't know what you're talking about.'

'The number for the vault. How much did you sell it for?'

'Not me, guv.'

Roger Hurst had spent years interviewing suspects. and wasn't intimidated in the slightest by being called to the Yard.

'Tell me again about what happened on Christmas Eve.'

'I've already told one of the woodentops.'

Hursty used the derogatory term for police officers in an effort to rile his inquisitor. The inspector smiled, enjoying the confrontation.

'Tell me.'

'The posh bird came in and said she wanted to collect something from the vault. I told her she'd have to leave her suitcase with me as it was too big to go through the scanner. She must have sneaked it in when I wasn't looking.'

Hursty failed to mention that he'd walked away from his post to take a call from his bookmaker, allowing Lily Dunlop to take her case and the gun into the vault without being stopped.

'Really.'

'Yeah, really, mate.'

'What did you do when the alarm sounded?'

'I followed protocol.'

'If you'd followed protocol, Hurst, then this situation would never have happened.'

Hursty remained silent. The police couldn't prove jack shit. He knew there'd be nothing on the CCTV. He'd already made sure of that. Christ he needed a drink, though.

'Will that be all then, officer?'

'How did Lily Dunlop manage to get a gun inside the vault when you were supposedly on duty to prevent just such an eventuality?'

Hursty shrugged his shoulders but said nothing.

'How did Europe News acquire the ex-directory number of the vault?'

'Dunno.'

'You're going nowhere until you start to give me some answers.'

Shifting in his seat, Hursty began to pick his teeth with the corner of a book of matches.

A couple of floors up, the Met Police Commissioner sat at his desk fuming. He had been ripped to shreds by the sharp tongue of the Prime Minister, who had demanded he ring back urgently with solutions. He was contemplating what he could tell him when the desk phone rang again.

'Hughes-Jenkins.'

'Miles Winstanley.'

'Winstanley, unless you are telephoning to inform me that you will no longer be broadcasting telephone conversations from the MSD vault, I am not sure we have much to say to each other, have we?'

Hughes-Jenkins had wanted to cut the line, but the Prime Minister had insisted that the freedom of the press meant that, unless the telephone number had been obtained by illegal means, it would be unacceptable to do so. Thus far, despite the interview being conducted downstairs, he had been unable to prove that and the broadcast conversations continued.

Miles, who was sitting behind his own desk across town, was not in the slightest bit intimidated by the Commissioner's tone. They both knew that the officer's request was ridiculous and Miles ignored it.

'No, guess again.'

His irreverence rankled with the Commissioner. His privileged education had seen him quickly rise through the ranks of the Metropolitan Police. The royal family had taken easily to him while he was in control of their close protection. He wasn't about to accept this sort of disrespect from a mere journalist. A journalist who hadn't even had the courtesy to take his call when he had rung to remonstrate about privileged information being broadcast on live television. The PM had been furious.

'I beg your pardon?'

'I said, guess again.'

Miles Winstanley couldn't care less about the Commissioner's frosty attitude. That superior tone of his cut little ice with the man who had been his fag at Eton.

'Should I give you a clue, Phillip, old boy?'

Miles well remembered the school's views that 'we want each boy *to have that true sense of self-worth which will enable him to stand up for himself and for a purpose greater than himself, and, in doing so, to be of value to society.'* He had learned quickly that being a Streetonian would fare much better in the news media. The Commissioner preferred the respect and conformity of the police service.

'I really don't have time for this.'

'Shame, I'm calling for a reason. Won't take a tick. We at Europe News are very keen to know what, if anything, you are doing to get into the vault. Also, how's the hunt for the second keyholder going?'

Hughes-Jenkins sat back in his chair. The audacity of the man! He had been just the same at school.

'Oh really Winstanley? And what might you be trading in return?'

'Positive publicity about how Our Boys in Blue are doing everything they possibly can to bring this siege to a calm and peaceful conclusion.'

'We are.'

'I'm sure you are, but you want my presenters to underline that on TV, and in return I want you to tell me how the plans are progressing to release those trapped.'

'No deal.'

'Shame.'

With the conversation over, both men replaced the receiver with a shake of the head, considered the other's actions a grave mistake, and then rose from behind their desk to address their relative troops.

22

6 p.m.

Mayfair Safety Deposits

The children, having played with the racing-car track for most of the day, had finally tired of it. Umair was hungry and fractious and was trying to pull out Squidgy's other eye. Hafsa tried gently coaxing him to stop, until his stubborn refusals had given way to tears. Princess Almira watched her children but did little to intervene. With every hour that passed, her anxiety increased. Ansar would know by now that she had forgotten Umair's medication. She had tried to speak to him on the telephone to reassure him that the child was well and had fully recovered from his seizure, but he had refused to talk to her. Would he now discard her? Would she have to return to her humble beginnings? Who would feed her mother and sisters? Panic was never far from the surface. She reached into the depths of her cavernous bag to retrieve a nail file. A mundane task she hoped would help to keep her calm.

From the other side of the vault, Bert sat watching the

Princess. How could she sit filing her nails? Her children needed her reassurance and yet she did nothing to comfort them. He thought about his own family. Speaking to Cynthia had made him pine for the children. He hoped they'd be holding up and looking after their mother. Cynthia had sounded calm when he'd spoken to her on the phone; too calm, in fact. Knowing his lady wife, he was sure she'd be putting on a brave face for the sake of him and the children. He had been concerned to learn that his mother was at the house looking after them. Bert hoped she would break with tradition for once and try to be pleasant instead of picking a row with Cynthia. He shrugged. There was nothing he could do about it in here.

When he turned his gaze to Lily, he caught her staring sheepishly back at him.

'What you looking at?'

Lily immediately averted her eyes and began to search in the depths of her own bag before pulling out a Kindle. It was a Christmas gift to herself and she'd downloaded heaps of novels in preparation for her holiday in Barbados. She'd already started John Steinbeck's *Of Mice and Men* and, switching on the machine, attempted to pick up where she'd left Lennie choosing his own puppy in the barn.

Bert shook his head. What a complete bloody mess. His Christmas had been all planned out and now look what had happened. The father of two had been very much looking forward to spending quality time with his family on Christmas Day. He'd bought Cynthia some perfume from a discount shop on the high street and a lovely polyester scarf from Marks & Spencer. He'd kept the receipt, just in case she didn't like it, but Bert was sure that wouldn't be the case. Cynthia was easily pleased and would be happy with whatever made Bert happy. He'd left it to her to organise the children a joint present: a Nintendo Wii. He wondered if they'd be playing with it right now, rather than worrying about their old dad trapped like a caged animal. Cynthia and the kids had been due to head up to Yorkshire today, Boxing Day, to visit grandparents who, as an incentive for reluctant kids to make the journey, had been instructed to buy specific games for their new Wii console.

Sadly, Cynthia's parents were allergic to Rob the family dog, so Bert had agreed to stay in London to look after the German Shepherd cross. It was such a shame, he'd told Cynthia, because he really enjoyed spending some quality time with her parents. She had marvelled at his big-heartedness.

In reality, the break from the family would give Bert the opportunity to attend to his lover's Christmas wishes. Roxy was the voluptuous and extremely popular barmaid at the Dog and Duck, who had taken a shine to Bert the very first time she'd set eyes on him. When her marriage had fallen apart, it had been Bert who offered her a shoulder and then much more to cry on. Their affair had flourished and eventually he had even told her that he loved her, but had failed to add that he would never leave Cynthia. In fact, he'd more or less promised the exact opposite. Tricky, but he'd figure out a solution somehow. Bert wondered what Roxy was doing right now. He hoped she hadn't heard his lovey-dovey talk with Cynthia on Europe News.

'Excuse me, sir.'

Bert looked up to see Lily standing in front of him. This posh bird was really starting to get on his nerves. How dare she interrupt the start of a five-minute fantasy involving Roxy, a pint of Newcastle Brown, and some intimately placed Wotsits. Bert had already forgotten the promise he had made to Cynthia about attempting to be more understanding with the girl.

'Look, minxy chops, I don't know how you haven't got the message yet. Let me tell you straight, in a couple of days at the most you'll be swapping posh nosh for prison porridge. Armed robbery and kidnap, it's never going to look good on your CV, sister. You're heading to jail for a very long time, so I suggest you go over there, sit back down on your designer luggage and just keep your big mouth shut, *capiche*?'

Armed robbery and kidnap? That wasn't meant to be what happened. All she wanted was what was in the security box. Lily rocked unsteadily on her six-inch Jimmy Choo heels and leaned heavily against Bert's oak desk. The guard was unimpressed by what he considered to be amateur dramatics.

'I'm terribly sorry, but I really don't feel very well at all. I wonder if I might be able to have just a little sip of water?'

Bert's immediate reaction was to say no, but seeing the colour drain from Lily's face he decided to relent, this once. He stood just in time to catch Lily as she fainted, but not before she'd banged her chin on the top of the desk. Shit, not another sick kid! The vault was starting to look like a scene from *Casualty*, thought Bert as he lowered Lily's limp frame to the floor. Hooking his foot around his chair he managed to manoeuvre it from behind the desk and shove it under Lily's legs in an effort to lift them higher than her heart. He loosened her coat and checked her airway. She was hot and clammy, but her breathing seemed OK.

The thump of Lily's chin on the desk had alerted the children. Umair started grizzling and then came over with his sister to see what was happening. When they saw that Lily was bleeding they both began to panic.

Bert's parental skills immediately kicked in.

'Hafsa, bring a beaker of water, if you would precious. and you Umair, you little monkey, I need you to make sure that car track is still working. I want a quick race in a second.'

They scurried off to their errands. With both children occupied and the Princess staying well away from the sight of blood, Bert quickly had the situation under control. Within a few moments Lily began to come round. She seemed spacey and unsure, and for the first time Bert could see absolute fear in her eyes.

'You OK, missy?' His tone was softer than before.

Lily's lip was bleeding profusely, but taking a closer look Bert was confident it would soon settle.

'Don't worry, love, it's not that bad. Just a bit of a thick lip, you'll be fine.'

However when Lily caught sight of a small pool of blood on the carpet next to where she lay she immediately began to panic.

'NO, the children. Keep them away.'

In her alarm, Lily almost screamed her instruction as she attempted to crawl over and cover the bloody patch with her own body.

'Whoa, stay calm It's only a bit of blood. It's not going to kill anybody.'

'Keep the children away, make them go away, I will clean it up.'

Bert wasn't much for the sight of blood either but this girl's reaction was a bit over the top. Nevertheless, he took a handkerchief from his trouser pocket and threw it over the stain to hide it from the youngsters. Didn't need them flipping over a tiny bit of claret as well.

'Sorted. Now, here you go, missy, sit up and have a sip of water you'll feel better in no time. It's a bit stuffy in here, no wonder you feel a bit queasy. Not really enough room for all of us over the whole Christmas break,' added Bert, before he could help himself. 'Anyway, not to worry, eh.'

'Thank you, thank you.'

Lily sat up and took the plastic cup with both hands. She felt panicky and claustrophobic. Was it the start of her symptoms? What if her worst fears were true? She didn't yet know the truth. In the meantime, she needed to protect the children.

Lily rummaged in her suitcase and, finding a holiday sarong, she threw it on top of Bert's handkerchief before taking another sip of her water.

Bert watched her, concerned. What was all that about? Despite his best efforts, her vulnerability made his fatherly instincts rise to the surface. When the Arab youngsters, seeing that Lily was sitting up and apparently OK again, came over to offer their support – which largely consisted of sitting cross-legged next to her while staring mesmerised at her swelling lip – Bert wondered how to occupy the inquisitive children so he could speak to Lily in private. Attempts at a distraction with the Scalextric had been short-lived and looking over at their mother he realised he wouldn't be able to count on her help. The Princess was shaking her nail polish in preparation for the second coat of her manicure, seemingly unaware of the drama unfolding under her nose. Bert didn't notice she was trembling with fear and on the very edge of losing all self-control.

After a brief mental struggle, he decided on the ultimate sacrifice. Pulling the Kit-Kat out of his inside pocket, he beckoned the youngsters closer. Hafsa and Umair's eyes lit up at the sight of a Western chocolate bar. They were seldom allowed them and were completely overexcited at the prospect of tasting the forbidden goodies. He glanced over at their mother again before whispering to the children.

'Shhh, I've been saving this as a special treat for you. Don't tell your mother. Take it over to the other corner, then she can't see. Make sure you share it, mind, or there'll be no more.'

Given that he'd already eaten the Twix when everyone else was asleep, there wouldn't be any more whether they shared or not, but his words were out of habit, from speaking to his own children.

'After you've eaten it, let me know and we'll play the car

231

game again. I want to be the red one this time, OK? I think it's faster. You can be the black one, Umair, and Hafsa can be the race official. I'll be two minutes.'

The children were absolutely delighted and scurried away, keen to organise their race and keep the contraband hidden from their mother.

At last, Bert was able to turn his attention to Lily. On the whole, he considered himself a sensitive man, though of course he could be an animal in the bedroom, especially when Roxy wore those Ann Summers panties. Nevertheless, he knew when a woman was hurting and he could tell just by looking at Lily crumpled in front of him that she was in a great deal of emotional turmoil.

'Come on, up you get, love. Let's sort you out.'

Bert gently eased Lily into a more comfortable sitting position, leaning her fragile frame against one of the legs of his desk. He took the cushion from his chair and as gently as a sixteen-stone man with fingers like Cumberland sausages was capable of, he placed it behind Lily's head. Lowering himself awkwardly on to the floor next to her, he took a few moments to catch his breath from the exertion. Bert wasn't sure if Lily would want to tell him what was on her mind, but he knew enough about women to realise it didn't take much scratching the surface for the flood gates to open. The question was, where to start?

For the first time looking at Lily as a young woman rather than his evil captor, he could see the pain etched in every inch of her face. She was quite obviously a privileged girl who had certainly not experienced the challenges that life had thrown at him. But she was haunted by something. What could have happened for her to behave as she had and risk spending a very long time in jail?

Bert looked across to the children, who were doing their best to hide what was left of the chocolate bar, most of which was spread over Umair's face, while organising racing cars with sticky, chocolate-covered fingers. They needn't have worried. Their mother appeared to Bert to be totally disinterested in anything apart from how quickly her nails would dry. Now was his chance for a chat.

'How you feeling, love?'

'Much better, thank you.'

'Have another sip of water.'

Lily raised the clear plastic beaker and sipped delicately.

'There you go, colour back in your cheeks in no time, missy.'

Lily tried to smile, but she felt she was teetering on the very edge. It was so much more difficult to remain composed when the guard was actually being kind rather than beastly to her. Without warning, the tears began to fall. The harder she tried to stop herself, the harder she sobbed.

Oh Christ, not bloody waterworks, thought Bert, who was hopeless at dealing with women's tears. He immediately melted and leaned over to rest his chubby hand on Lily's delicate shoulder. He was shocked by how thin she was.

'Now then, love, it can't be that bad. You've made a mistake. I'm sure with a good lawyer you'll probably get off with a suspended sentence. Your dad will be able to afford the best brief in the country, I've no doubt.'

The mention of her father stung Lily back into self-control. Bert noticed the immediate change in her. His years of police interrogation flagged up the most likely cause of her torment. He waited for a few moments. Should he press her? What difference did it make anyway? After all, it wasn't really any of his concern. Lily, meanwhile, continued to look at the floor where the handkerchief and the sarong were covering the bloodstain. Bert tried again.

'I have a daughter, not that much younger than you, actually. Tracey's her name and she hasn't 'alf caused me some

233

trouble at times. Sometimes I've been so angry with her I've had to leave it to her mother to deal with. But you know what, whatever's been done, whatever harsh words might have been said, time passes and before you know it everything is all right. I'm sure it will be the same for you and your dad. A good cry and you'll feel much better about things. It's like they say: "The soul would have no rainbow, if the eyes had no tears."'

Bert paused for effect, chuffed at remembering the Native American proverb he'd read on a poster on the Central Line tube on his way into work.

'Really? I suspect, sir, that perhaps Tracey would feel differently towards you if, rather than wise words, you had handed her a death sentence.'

23

6.45 p.m.

Europe News

'Lady Catherine, thank you so much for joining us here on Europe News. If I may just introduce you to our viewers. Ladies and gentlemen, this is Catherine Dunlop, the mother of Lily Dunlop, who is presently trapped inside the vault at Mayfair Safety Deposits. Whatever the circumstances of her incarceration, I'm sure every parent can identify with the depths of despair you must be feeling, knowing your child is trapped with no means of escape. You, Lady Catherine, can do nothing to ease her suffering. How are you coping?'

Watching from his office, Miles thought Sid was pitching his delivery the right side of sugary – just. He was an absolute godsend for this story and easily justified his astronomical transfer fee from *HNDUK*. No wonder Suzanna Thomas was so furious that Sid was having it all his own way. Her continual phone calls had been starting to grate, though he hadn't heard from her for a couple of hours. The one time he had tried to return her call, about an hour ago, her phone was switched off. He would try her again soon and sort out her transport back to London. She was as big a star as Sid at the station and needed to be handled with kid gloves. Miles's plate spinning of temperamental talent was challenging for him at the best of times, and especially when the channel was leading the pack on a story like this one.

A little while earlier he'd faced another difficult challenge when he'd slammed down the phone on Phillip Hughes-Jenkins following their testy two-minute conversation. It had rung again almost instantly and Miles thought it was either Suzanna pestering or the Commissioner squaring up for Round Two.

'What?'

'Sorry to interrupt you, MW, it's Daphne here in reception.'

'Hello, Daphne. Merry Christmas,' he said softening his tone. 'Hadn't realised we'd dragged you in, too. Thanks for giving up your holiday.'

'No problem, MW, my pleasure. I wouldn't normally bother you directly, but all the phones on the newsdesk are engaged and I think this might be important.'

'Go on.'

'Well, MW, there's a lady in reception who says her name is Catherine Dunlop. She says she would like to be able to speak to her daughter and she's been told we might be able to "facilitate" that, were her exact words. Apparently we sent a car for her, but there's no one in reception to meet her. What would you like me to do?'

MW missed the last part of Daphne's question as he dropped the receiver on the desk and sprinted for his office door. Taking the steps down to the foyer two at a time, the Head of News was finding it difficult not to be too judgemental about his newsroom team. They should have been circling the car park like Disney vultures waiting for her arrival. What were they thinking of? Thundering into reception, he arrived just as Catherine was heading for the door.

'Mrs Dunlop, Lady Catherine, just a moment.'

But Catherine had already lost her nerve. All the way to the studio she'd been replaying her father's reaction when she told him what she planned to do. First he'd tried to dissuade her by warning that she would regret her actions. Catherine's response had been that she had already regretted her actions for long enough since Lily left and she was determined to speak to her daughter now, even if it meant doing it on live TV.

'I'll disown you, my girl, I'm warning you. A TV station is no place for you to be.'

His words were still ringing in Catherine's ears. He was right, she thought now. A TV station was no place for her to be. What a ludicrous notion to even contemplate speaking to her daughter for the entertainment of the nation. They had plenty to say to each other, but not like this.

MW caught up with Catherine as she reached the glass doors to the forecourt and began to search for her chauffeured vehicle. She hoped it might take her to the Dorchester to meet up with the official from Mayfair Safety Deposits after all. Perhaps he hadn't received the note from the concierge and would still be waiting for her.

'Mrs Dunlop, Mrs Dunlop, if I may introduce myself. My name's Miles Winstanley and I'm the Head of News here.'

Miles offered his hand and Catherine unenthusiastically shook it.

'Let me say I can't begin to imagine how you are feeling.'

'Of that I have no doubt, Mr Winstanley,' replied Catherine.

Miles pressed on: 'I do, however, completely understand your reticence at the thought of appearing in front of a television camera.'

He paused for a moment, trying to gauge the reaction

from Catherine to what he'd just said. He couldn't let her slip away, not now. Everyone wanted to know why Lily Dunlop had behaved in the way she had, and her mother would surely be the one person who would know the answer. As he looked deep into Catherine's eyes, Miles knew he was losing the battle. He could well imagine the conversation she would have had with family and friends before setting off for the studios. Nevertheless, he needed to convince her to stay. Can't let her go, can't let her slip away, think, think, think.

'If you understand my concern, Mr Winstanley, then I am sure you will not want to keep me standing in this winter chill any longer and allow me to leave.'

'Of course, Lady Catherine. May I call you Catherine?'

Catherine ignored the familiarity and Miles was duly chastised.

'It is very cold out here. Please wait inside and allow me to find your vehicle for you,' continued Miles, speaking a little more sotto voce as he politely guided her away from the steady stream of Europe News staff heading into the building.

'I would prefer to wait here, if you don't mind.'

'Of course – as you wish. I'll be just a moment.'

Scanning the parking bays at the front of the building, Miles contemplated his options, rapidly dismissing every idea he had to keep her here. He decided he had no choice but to divulge information he had shared with no one else in his professional career. Walking back to where Catherine stood shivering in the cold, he attempted his last roll of the dice.

'I know you are worried about the reaction of Lord Fitzwilliam.'

Catherine was shocked. How could this man know who her father was, or indeed how he might react?

'Forgive the familiarity, but the Earl is a friend of my own father, Robert Winstanley-Garwood. They were associates at the Bullingdon Club and, more recently, in the Prince's Trust. In fact, I believe they dined together at the Garrick just last week.'

'Ah, you're the son who . . .'

'Sullied the family name by earning a living in media.'

'Pleased to meet you, Mr Winstanley. I'm sorry I hadn't made the connection.'

'Please, call me Miles.'

'My parents mentioned you only this very morning when I told them I was considering an interview. I didn't know you were involved with Europe News though. It's reasonable to say you have made quite an impression on my father.'

Both laughed at the obvious slight.

'Indeed, so I believe from my own father.'

'So, Miles, as you will know from personal experience it would be a rather big mistake for me to be involved in any way with the media.' Catherine began to search once again for her car. 'It has been a pleasure meeting you, Miles. If I might ask you to escort me to my vehicle, it's a little slippy under foot still.'

'Of course, Catherine.' Miles took her arm and guided her towards a vehicle at the far end of the car park. 'Given my miscreant profession, I can completely understand your anxieties about being interviewed.'

Catherine smiled and nodded but said nothing, concentrating instead on staying upright on the treacherous road surface.

'Working in journalism has been a constant bane for my family and the subject of many heated dinner-table discussions between my father and me. If I'd gone into banking or property or the law, that would have been much more acceptable to Father. Yet for me, media is by far the most gratifying.'

Again Catherine nodded while leaning unsteadily against

Miles's outstretched arm for both physical and mental support.

'I'm sorry we brought you all this way on such a fruitless journey,' he continued.

'Never mind, no harm done,' was the most Catherine could muster.

'As I always say to my parents, I suppose the one thing about working in journalism is that I feel I can make a real difference to peoples' lives sometimes.'

'Really, how so?' shivered Catherine, relieved to see they were now just a few steps away from the salvation of the chauffeured car. Opening the door and gingerly guiding her off the slippery road surface and into the comfort of her vehicle, Miles played his ace.

'Well, I may be of constant disappointment to my somewhat judgemental parents. I certainly don't make millions in the City or have the ability to change the law of the land – all of that is true. But what I do have the power to do, and where I can make a difference, a real difference to people's lives, Catherine, is to be able to reunite a desperately distraught young girl with her equally devastated mother. That I do have the power to do, and that's why I sleep well at night.'

Catherine stared up at the Head of News. She noticed for the first time what a handsome, strapping chap he was, but more than that he had an honest, open face. He really wanted to help her be reunited with Lily. He could make it happen and she was sure he would look after her. She would be safe with him. This kind, intelligent young man had the power to deliver what she most wanted. Wasn't that exactly the reason she had defied her father and reluctantly come to the TV studios? Why would she reject the offer now it was being presented to her? Catherine rested her head on the seat and thought for a moment.

On her way down from Oxfordshire, she had first gone to the vault in Mayfair in the vain hope she could speak to Lily from there. However a cordon and heavy police presence, along with a baying group of journalists desperate to pounce on anyone who could contribute anything whatsoever about the story had meant she remained in the car. The driver had been instructed to take her on to Europe News, where she hoped to be reunited by telephone with Lily. Now Miles was offering her that opportunity.

'You're right.'

'I know.'

'Will I be in safe hands?'

'The very best.'

As he watched Catherine being comforted on set by his suave anchorman, Miles allowed himself the indulgence of swinging his feet up on to the desk and settled comfortably in readiness for the next chapter to unfold in this never-ending saga.

'Hello Lily, it's Mummy.'

Catherine's voice cracked before she could say more and Sid immediately stepped in with his stock anchor phrase.

'Take it slowly, Lady Catherine. We've all the time in the world, no rush.'

When Bert had heard the pitch whistle coming from the telephone receiver he'd hoped it was Cynthia back to talk to him again. He had been shocked to hear there was someone who wanted to speak to Lily. Perhaps it was her father, keen to say sorry for whatever it was he had supposedly done. Bert thought Lily's reference to a 'death sentence' was a little dramatic, but that's what young girls were like. Anyway, it looked as if it was all about to get sorted; hopefully her father also had the number for a damned good lawyer, because she was certainly going to need one.

When Lily took the phone and he saw her face crumple,

Bert realised not everything was going to be happy ever after. Not yet anyway. He ambled across and put his hand on her shoulder. In the studio, Sid was adopting a similar pose. Catherine composed herself and sat up a little straighter. She tried again.

'Lily darling, please don't be angry. I'm sorry to talk to you in this manner, but I just had to let you know I'm here, I miss you and I want to help.'

At Upton Park the Lord Fitzwilliam almost fell off his Queen Anne chair. He had forbidden Catherine from appearing on television, absolutely forbidden it and yet she had defied him. When she left the house he had assumed she would drive around for a while and then return with her tail between her legs. Brian had served lunch and then tea, but still there was no sign of the girl. The short winter day had long since given way to a frosty inhospitable night and Agnes had convinced him they should not risk the roads in the dark. While he was waiting for Cook to make dinner, Alistair had flicked on the TV.

'She bloody went and did it, Agnes. I warned her not to, but she did it anyway. She's no better than Winstanley-Garwood's son. I can't bloody believe it.'

Alistair was about to change channels, but his wife stopped him.

'Let's listen, darling,' whispered Agnes, wanting to hear what Catherine and Lily would say to each other.

'Want to help, Mummy, want to help? Why now? Why didn't you want to help when you could have made a difference, why didn't you help me then? No, all you were interested in was yourself and Daddy's reputation. And now it's too late.'

Lily was furious and shouting so loudly down the phone line the sound technicians had to reduce the audio levels to cope with her outburst.

Alistair looked aghast at his wife. 'Do you have any bloody idea what they're talking about, Agnes?'

His wife shook her head but said nothing, riveted to the screen.

'No, darling, no, it isn't too late,' pleaded Catherine. 'As soon as you are out of the vault we can start afresh. You have your whole life ahead of you. We will have the checks, the tests done, and I am sure all will be fine. You misunderstand the situation.'

'Do I really, Mummy? I don't think so, do you? I have the key to the security box, the key you tried to hide from me, and I know the number. I'm going to look inside and then we'll see, won't we?'

Lily didn't want to admit to her mother that she had been frightened to look inside the box up to now. Once unlocked, there was no going back, and she was terrified.

'That won't prove anything, darling.'

'We'll see, won't we, Mummy?'

Lily leaned heavily against the wall. She was still feeling woozy after her fall and the conversation with her mother was just too much.

'Lily, Lily, are you still there? Can you still hear me, darling? I love you.'

'Well, I hate you, Mummy. I hate you.'

'No, darling, you don't, you are angry – and I understand why – but you don't hate me. I'm your mother.'

'No, what you are is my tormentor and I have nothing more to say.'

'No, Lily, no, don't go. Lily, can you still hear me, darling?'

Lily could no longer control her anger. Fury that had built up over the last eight months had finally found a vent. With an energy she didn't realise she had, Lily slammed the receiver against the wall, again and again, smashing it into useless pieces. Holding what was left of the handset she ripped the rest of the phone from its mounting on the wall of the vault, immediately disconnecting the line.

The finality of Lily's actions was met with varying responses either side of the thick walls. In the vault, Bert clenched his fists and felt his blood pressure rise so high he thought he might explode.

'You stupid, stupid bitch.'

The children, alarmed by Lily's action and Bert's response, both ran quickly across to their mother. For the first time since they had been trapped, Princess Almira reached an arm around each of them. She was aware that such anger in a man could have terrible consequences. Pulling her children closer, Almira lowered her head and waited.

Sid picked up as smoothly as he could after the explosive confrontation, trying to reassure Catherine and the viewers that all would end well.

Miles was desperately embarrassed. That had not gone at all the way he'd planned. Swinging his legs from the desk, he walked to his office door and shouted 'meeting room now', summoning all those within earshot. Like everyone else who'd been listening to Lily and Catherine, he wanted to know what was in that security box. And with the line dead they needed another way to find out.

Killing the sound on the TV in his suite, Prince Ansar retrieved his cell phone and dialled Dmitri. With the phone cut off he would no longer be able to have regular police bulletins on his son's health. Someone must pay. The close protection officer answered before the second ring.

'Sir.'

'Where are you?'

'Over the Dover Cliff Whites. We should be landing shortly, sir.'

'You should have returned already.'

'There was a problem at Border Control, sir. Miss Suzanna had left her passport in the hotel safe.'

'Resolved?'

'Yes, sir, Miss Suzanna is on board.'

'Good. Bring her directly to the hotel, and then I need you to travel to the TV studios and pick up a package for me. You may need a little help.'

'Very good, sir.'

Dmitri put down his phone and smiled. His employer's reference to 'a little help' was code for the tongue-loosening skills Dmitri had honed under Saddam's regime.

Two hundred miles north and Alistair's curiosity now had the better of him.

'Brian . . .'

'Yes, Your Lordship?'

'Do you have any blasted idea what's in the damned box?'

'No, sir.'

'Bloody mystery. Dinner ready yet?'

'I will speak to Cook now, sir,' offered Brian, leaving the room hastily.

As he closed the door behind him, Brian paused to compose himself. He did indeed know what was in the security box. He was the one who had put it there on Lady Catherine's instruction. She had sworn him to secrecy and he had only ever told one other person.

245

24

7 p.m.

Bethnal Green, London

Easing her voluptuous chest into a Primark black lacy bra, Roxy Costello was not a happy camper. He'd said he was leaving that trout for her. Hadn't he promised he was only staying with her because of the kids? Didn't he assure her that she was the only woman he had ever truly loved and soon they would be together forever? Now here he was, talking all lovey-dovey to that bitch, and in front of millions of people too. Well, she wasn't going to stand for it.

Massaging Body Shop banana butter into her ample thighs, Roxy reached for her matching black lace panties and wriggled her generous derriere into them.

How could he, how could he? This was to be the Christmas they would spend so much time together. Then, just as soon as his wife was back from Wetherby in the New Year, he was going to tell her it was all over. Roxy had already cleared three drawers and a whole wardrobe rail in her IKEA bedroom furniture.

She looked at herself in the circular bathroom mirror. She liked what she saw. She was no longer a spring chicken but her skin was still plump and relatively line free. Her enhanced hair colour flattered her green-grey eyes and she was confident her signature Boots Number 7 Red Carpet lipstick made the very most of her full pout. Roxy was not about to take this nonsense lying down. It was just a silly wobble from Bert while he was trapped inside the vault. What else was he going to say when he was forced to speak to Cynthia on the phone? He could hardly say he was leaving her, could he? There's always a simple explanation for everything, thought Roxy, as she gurgled mouthwash and spat into the basin.

Baring her teeth to check they were clean, Roxy calmed herself with the memory of the last time she'd seen Bert. He was all man in her eyes, and the way he made her feel with only the tiniest amount of Viagra was definitely worth fighting for.

Adding the finishing touches to her Pacific green eye contour, Roxy returned to her bedroom – or love den, as Bert liked to call it. Opening the wardrobe, she scanned the rail before choosing an appropriate outfit for another night behind the bar at the Dog and Duck. She settled on a tight corseted bustier and a satin thigh-skimming skirt with a pair of fishnets that had only the tiniest of holes in them. Finding a clear nail polish in her bedside cabinet, she added a dab to either end of the ladder to prevent it running. Finally she checked her look in the free-standing full-length mirror that Bert had bought her for Christmas. Roxy liked what she saw. Sticking her finger in her mouth and slowly withdrawing it to remove any excess lipstick which might otherwise mark her teeth, she switched off the TV that had been permanently tuned to Europe News. 'Bye for now, my love.'

Grabbing her coat and moon boots before tucking her slingbacks into her handbag, Roxy headed for the bar.

* * *

Sitting in the rear of the Bentley Mulsanne, Suzanna felt cocooned from the frustration of the last forty-eight hours. Of course Prince Ansar would make everything all right. They had become occasional lovers almost as soon as they met, a relationship that was gratifying for her on so many levels. She'd been showered with jewellery and now had returned from Paris in a private jet. In return, Prince Ansar had been rewarded with the sort of sexual experimentation that she was sure none of his four wives would ever consider even in their wildest dreams. She wriggled her feet into the deep-piled carpet of the luxury vehicle and allowed her fingers to run across the soft leather stitching. Glancing at Dmitri sitting next to her, Suzanna was a little perturbed at his familiarity. Shouldn't he be seated with the chauffeur?

'Thank you so much for coming to collect me. I really appreciate it. I hope I haven't dragged you away from your family over Christmas?'

Dmitri sat bolt upright, careful to stay an appropriate distance away from his principal's sex toy. He would have felt much more comfortable sitting in the front but he needed information urgently and time was running out. Suzanna had spent most of the short hop from Paris in the bathroom of the aircraft, giving him no time to talk to her. This was his final chance.

'Not at all, miss. I am only glad to have been of assistance. Prince Ansar would like me to take you straight to the hotel, if that is convenient?'

Dmitri was adopting his mid-Atlantic accent for the conversation.

'Of course, Dmitri, of course.'

'I will then be heading to the TV studios, madam.'

'Really? Why do you need to go if I'm not there? Wouldn't it be better to wait for me?'

Dmitri was already one step ahead.

'Prince Ansar has been invited to appear on Europe News tomorrow in order to speak to the children in the vault. He has asked me to take look at the layout of the building, purely for security reasons.'

The guard, noticing Suzanna's pout, continued.

'He wants me to make it clear that he will only be interviewed by you and as such is keen to avoid any contact with Mr Sid Parker. Perhaps you can advise of any less frequented routes around the studio area where Prince Ansar might arrive and leave without being too obtrusive?'

Suzanna was delighted at the prospect of interviewing Ansar and at the same time stiffing Sid. Turning to face Dmitri, she suggested a back entrance to the studios often used when she didn't want the staff to see her arriving without make-up and with freshly washed, wet hair.

'Thank you, miss, that is most helpful.'

By the time the car arrived outside the Mandarin Oriental, Dmitri had everything he needed to know. Still wrapped in her warm winter coat, Suzanna skipped past the deferential doorman and made straight for the hotel lift to take her to the Prince's suites. Arriving at the door she was delighted to see Ansar already waiting for her.

Having escorted her to his principal, Dmitri bowed slightly and was about to leave when Suzanna stopped him and dug into her bag.

'Oh here, Dmitri, my security passes. Should make your access to the building a little easier. Don't forget to bring them back though, I'll need them.'

Dmitri nodded and melted away. With now just two of them in the room, Ansar wandered over to where a bottle of champagne was chilling. Suzanna felt a tingle of anticipation and looked coquettishly at the Prince from under her false eyelashes while gently chewing on her bottom lip.

'Prince Ansar, thank you so much for coming to my aid. You truly are a knight in shining armour.'

The Prince stood several feet away from Suzanna, admiring the view.

'You're welcome, my dear.'

'To show my appreciation, I have brought you a gift back from Paris.'

'Really, my dear. May I ask what it is?'

Suzanna eased her slender shoulders from her coat and allowed it to fall to the floor. The space in the aircraft bathroom had been limited and the lighting was also a challenge but having balanced on the basin to look at herself in the circular mirror, she'd liked what she saw. Her skin presented without a flaw and her hair had been enhanced by Russell just before she'd left for Paris. Her Estée Lauder make-up, charged to Europe News expenses, was perfectly applied. Her lip gloss was a little heavier than she normally wore but that was how Ansar liked it, and anyway it matched her outfit. Suzanna had banged her elbow on the wash basin as she squirmed and tugged at her costume. There had been just about enough room for her to change. Now, standing before the Prince in the hotel suite, the tight squeeze had definitely been worth it.

Taking a step forward, Ansar was immediately and obviously delighted by her attire. The barmaid bustier and thigh-skimming satin skirt was exactly what he'd hoped for. While he expected grace and elegance in public, slutty Suzanna was his preference in private. He knew she wouldn't disappoint. She had originally bought the outfit for Christopher in the hope his overexcitement at her in corset and suspenders would shorten the sexual experience. For Prince Ansar her hope was exactly the opposite.

Reaching into his desk drawer, Ansar popped a 'blue diamond' and opened his arms to his TV temptress. She stalked towards him, teasing her forefinger with her over-glossed lips. Leaning seductively over his desk, Suzanna cupped her breasts, pushing them closer together, further enhancing her cleavage. The Prince swept his arm across the antique desktop, clearing a space for her to perform. Suzanna clambered on top of the desk gouging the wood with her heels as she did so. Unconcerned, the Prince sat back to watch the show.

Suzanna smiled, enjoying herself. She could already feel the diamond on her finger.

Strutting towards the bar tables to collect empty glasses, Roxy's mood had lifted considerably and she decided a little light flirtation was in order. Leaning seductively forward she was met by a cheer of appreciation from regulars as her cleavage tried its best to wrestle free from her corset.

'Come on, Roxy, give us a show, love,' coaxed one of the men clearing away the beer mats from the bar table.

'I'm yours for a Double Diamond, dahlin',' she teased in response.

25

10 p.m.

Mayfair Safety Deposits

The conversation with her mother weighed heavily on Lily. Before they had spoken, she had been sure she no longer loved her, perhaps even hated her, and was quite prepared to spend the rest of her life estranged from her family. She had planned on building a new life with Giles and his family. She felt safe with him and was positive he loved her as much as she loved him. Lily wondered what Giles would be doing right now. It certainly didn't appear he had made any attempt to speak to her on the phone line, but was that really so surprising? He would be mortified by her behaviour, especially since he had no clue as to the reason. Of course she had been planning to tell him what she had most feared. She had the whole thing clear in her mind and would tell him everything before the wedding. She just hadn't managed to find quite the right time yet. And now it was too late.

For the first time Lily had to accept that she was keeping a secret from Giles for the same reason her mother had from her:

to protect the one she loved. Was it really fair to judge her mother so harshly when, faced with the same dilemma, she had behaved in exactly the same way?

Just two days ago everything had seemed so different. Lily had been preparing to spend a couple of weeks with her husband-to-be at his family's Caribbean home. His parents planned to join them after the hunt and in time for the New Year celebrations on the island. It was to have been the ideal opportunity for them all to be together ahead of the wedding and for any last-minute plans to be finalised. One thorny issue was bound to raise its head, as it had done several times already. Giles's parents had been a little sniffy that Lily's family was making no contribution towards the wedding costs.

'There is nothing wrong with that except that convention is such that one might presume they would have been keen to make some input,' had been Giles's mother's view.

Lily knew that her own mother would have been delighted if not desperate to pay for every single item of the wedding ten times over, but Lily did not want Catherine involved in any way. Not after what she had hidden from her. So it was left to Giles's mother, Rose, to help make plans, and for his father to stump up the cash.

The arrangement was not without tension. Rose had been the one with her when Lily had gone to choose the dress. A big mistake from the outset. The bride spotted *the Dress* the moment she walked into the bridal store. It was a vintage gown of peachy pink brocade, shot through with a pale silver thread. Her mother-in-law had been less sure and thought it a little unsophisticated, but conceded, 'It's up to you, dear. It's your day.' Lily, picking up on the slight, was so desperate to please that she had ultimately chosen the gown Rose preferred instead.

It had been the same with the church. Lily wanted intimate,

Rose had gone in search of a chapel big enough to accommodate three hundred guests. 'Plenty of trees in pots too, don't you think, Lily darling, just like Kate Middleton did with the Abbey. Didn't it look simply magical?'

The reception was to be held in the grounds of the Musgrave-Rose family estate and involved several interconnecting marquees. Giles's sole task had been to take charge of the cocktail menu; he had been keen to have his City friends' favourite Flaming Ferraris included. His mother had happily agreed. The top table had been a particularly vexed issue and was on the agenda for further discussion in Barbados. Lily felt the plans for her big day didn't really involve her, but as long as Giles was happy then so was she. All she wanted was to spend the rest of her life with him. But that was before she had done what she did. Would Giles still want to marry her when the vault finally opened?

Being trapped had given her so much time to think. Minutes felt like hours and hours like days. The wait for Wednesday morning seemed interminable. Looking aimlessly around the vault, she stared mesmerised as the crystal lozenges on the antique chandelier created a light prism on one wall of the vault. Her melancholy was suddenly interrupted by a loud clunk, followed by a continuous whirring noise which lasted for several seconds. Lily leapt to her feet and turned to see the bolts on the huge vault door start to slowly move and slide. Adrenalin flowed to every part of her body. Her fingers and toes began to tingle. What was happening? Finally the keyholders had been traced. Thank goodness, thank goodness. They would soon be free. She would be able to explain everything to Giles and hopefully he would forgive her. It seemed to take forever but eventually the huge reinforced door swung open on its enormous hinges.

'It's open, it's open, we're free!' Lily shouted to the others. Ignoring her belongings, she kicked off her shoes and ran towards the open door. Giles was standing at the other side of the threshold. He hadn't rejected her after all. He couldn't speak to her on the telephone because he was here, waiting for her when she came out, desperate to make sure she was safe. Everything was going to be all right. Lily raced towards her fiancé, keen to be wrapped safely in his outstretched arms.

But something was preventing her from moving. Bert had grabbed her arm. He didn't want her to be free; he wanted to keep her captive in the vault. He was determined the police would arrest her and she would be held accountable for her actions.

'Let go, please, let go.'

Lily tried to struggle free, desperate to leave her Mayfair prison and be reunited with Giles, who was standing with his arms wide open, beckoning her. But Bert refused to let go.

'No, stop now. Lily, stop.'

Lily tried again to break free from his grasp.

'Please, let go of me. Come on, everyone, quickly, the door's open.'

But Bert wouldn't release his grip.

'Stop it – you're upsetting the children. Stop it right now or I'll have to slap you.'

Lily woke to find Bert shaking her.

'Wake up. It's a dream, love, it's just a dream.'

Staring around wildly, Lily was aware of the alarmed, tearful faces of the children. She was still inside the vault and the door was firmly locked.

'I'm sorry, I'm so sorry, I thought the door had opened.'

Lily hid her face, embarrassed at what had happened. Bert offered her a reassuring hug. He, too, was feeling the strain, though he hadn't yet succumbed to nightmares.

With Lily now wide awake, the sleepy children returned to their mother.

'Don't worry, it will soon be over.'

Bert wished he believed that. What could be taking the police so long, thought Bert This girl was buckling and there was little he could do about it. Time for another chat. Loosening his grip on Lily's shoulder, he slid his bulk awkwardly down the wall until he came to rest next to her on the carpeted floor.

'So, should we take the money or open the box?'

'Sorry, I don't understand your question.'

Bert's reference to an old UK game show was lost on Lily and she looked at him, mystified. He pressed on.

'Which box should we open? Should I take a guess? I'm good at this; give me a second while I think about it . . .'

Casting his eye along row after row of hundred-year-old bank boxes, each with its unique numbered brass cover, Bert tried to picture which Lily's family box might be. Having eavesdropped on her conversation with Catherine, he was desperate to know what the Dunlop box contained.

All the boxes opened in a uniform way: a metal flap to the front with hinges on the top. Inside, they were lined with padded velvet, a garish touch introduced by the present vault owners who felt it added a certain elegance. The colour choices were either black, green or burgundy, and Bert often entertained himself by guessing which colour his clients would have chosen when customising their box. He was sure that the interior of Lily's family box would undoubtedly be black. Each lock required two keys to open it and often the second was left in the vault at MSD for safekeeping. Lily must have one key in her possession, but she would also need his key.

'If you tell me which box it is, I will probably have the second key. Then we can have a peek inside.'

'You do have the key, I know you do,' interrupted Lily.

She'd done her research and was aware the box needed two keys. When she had searched her mother's jewellery box she had only found one. Lily had later been told that the guard had the second one. She knew she wouldn't be able to open the box without the guard's help, willing or otherwise. That's why she'd brought the gun.

'Yeah, I figured that was why you came in here, all guns blazing.'

'I'm sorry about that.'

'Water under the bridge now, love.'

Lily said nothing. She was still dazed and confused after her dream.

'OK, I give up; at least tell me which number it is. Is it on the top row?'

Lily pulled her coat a little tighter around her and continued to ignore the questioning.

'Go on, love, which one is it? I can have a quick rifle through the keys we hold here and we'll have it open in a jiffy. That's why you're here, isn't it? That's what you said to your mother.'

Lily nodded.

'Seven seven seven.'

Bert's eyes immediately darted along the numbered boxes, scanning up and down the rows; he noticed 777 towards the back of the vault, about fifteen boxes up from the floor.

'It's over there.'

'I know.'

'I know you know. What's inside?'

'A family secret.'

'Why don't you want it to stay a secret?'

'It will prove whether my parents lied to me. Whether they were content for me to die rather than sully the family name.'

Lily had lobbed the emotional grenade without even bothering to look up. Instead she pulled up her knees closer to her chest and wrapped her arms more tightly around them.

'That's why I want to see what's inside.'

She rested her tiny chin on top of her raised knees. No tears, no tantrums, no emotion left.

Bert looked pityingly at her. He had always done his best to protect his own children from harm. Even when he was sacked from the Met, he had still dressed in his uniform every day under the pretence of going to work. It had taken six months for him to find this job, and only then had he announced over a Sunday lunch that he'd decided to retire from the police. His children had never known there was anything wrong, never needed to worry. This young girl, who to the outside world had a life of ultimate privilege, had been weighed down by a burden he would never have allowed his own children to have experienced. He wasn't sure what she was talking about, what this secret in the box might be, but he knew she was hurting and that she considered it her parents' fault. He reached out a podgy hand and placed it on the top of Lily's. They sat silently side by side for a long time watching the children and their mother sleep. Finally Lily turned to look at Bert.

'I need to know, Bert, but I'm not sure if I want to know.'

The guard wrapped an arm around her fragile frame and Lily crumpled into his chest. He wondered if he'd ever find out what was in the bloody box.

'So, what's in the box? Ideas, please, people.'

Like Bert, MW had been consumed with curiosity about the contents of the box when he'd called a conference meeting a few hours earlier.

'Diamonds,' offered one of the overnight editors, who had just started his shift.

'Nah, why would diamonds be "life-threatening"?'

The room buzzed with energy and ideas.

'How about if they were blood diamonds,' suggested another. 'The family stole blood diamonds and the African owners have put a price on Lily Dunlop's head.'

'You've been watching too much Miss Marple, Colin. Any other ideas?'

'State secrets from a former or developing super power, India or maybe China,' was a suggestion from one of the reporters. MW laughed.

'And you, Vince, have been reading too much Ian Fleming. OK, everybody, obviously more coffee and Quality Street required. Get your thinking caps on. This is still the only story in town.'

MW was about to share with the team the overnight Christmas Day blockbuster audience figures when he was interrupted by the sports editor.

'I wonder if I might make a quick point here, please, MW?' Robert cleared his throat and continued without waiting for approval. 'I accept that the vault may be a huge story, but there is other stuff around as well you know. The sports team have an interview with the British Taekwondo champion. He's expected to do really well at the Olympics and, given that it's on home turf, I'm sure viewers will find it very interesting. It took mega discussions for us to secure it. I promised the Lord Coe it would definitely get a run over Christmas.'

Stifled sniggers from the news team confirmed the sports editor's concerns that the Taekwondo champ could be Jackie Chan, and he still wouldn't be appearing on a TV screen anytime soon.

'Now then, Robert, you know the drill: never make promises. It'll run in the New Year,' was the only consolation for the crestfallen sports man as MW handed round a family tin of chocolates.

'So while we wait for these flavanols to kick in, let me tell you what I know from the Met. Bottom line is they are still no closer to finding the other keyholders.'

This drew a chorus of groans and jeers.

'I know, I know, I'm starting to sound like a broken record.

259

Last I heard, they've dispatched a couple of coppers to the Galapagos Islands, lucky chaps, to track down one of the vault guards.'

'That's just a jolly,' barked Jim, incensed. 'By the time they get there, the vault will be open anyway. What a waste of my tax dollar.'

His colleagues banged the table in agreement.

'OK, OK, maybe it's something we could put a piece together on once this is all over, but in the meantime, the army are preparing to "blow the bloody doors off",' joked MW in his best Michael Caine accent. No one laughed. Embarrassed, he continued.

'Seriously, though, that would need the OK from the PM, and he's worried about the kids, especially the sick one. We'll keep an eye on that. Any other thoughts, people?'

As Europe News staff brainstormed in the conference room, downstairs in the studio Sid had just thrown to a commercial break and was now thanking Catherine profusely for her second interview of the day. She had been devastated when Lily cut the line and had been desperate to flee from the studio, but Sid had convinced her to stay on and talk about her daughter. Ten minutes of coaxing from Sid had provided viewers with a greater insight into the Lily her mother knew. A fun-loving, kind, gentle girl who had made the biggest mistake of her life. Eventually, after he could milk no more from her, Sid had thrown to another commercial break and Catherine immediately stood. This time she was determined to leave the set, and Sid had to accept that there was nothing he could say that would persuade her to stay any longer.

Instead, he asked, 'How are you feeling, Lady Catherine? I can't begin to imagine how stressful this is for you. Lily sounded strong, though, that must be of some relief.'

'Yes, thank you.'

Catherine fidgeted with her lapel, keen to remove the microphone as quickly as possible. Sid persisted.

'Thanks for staying on, Lady Catherine. I know it must have been a terrible shock to you when Lily, erm disconnected the line, but I think expressing your love in such an honest open way will be very beneficial for her when she is released from the vault.'

'She won't have seen it though.'

'No . . . still, we'll give you a DVD,' was the best response Sid could muster on the hoof. Lily would probably never be aware of her mother's outpouring of love on Europe News, but it was great for the viewers.

Catherine smiled thinly at the attempt to console her. When Lily had ended the call, that should have been her cue to flee, but she had stupidly agreed to stay and talk about her own feelings. She was now completely regretting the decision to appear on television at all.

'Thank you, Sid, thank you. I hope chatting to you about the good qualities my daughter possesses may reassure the public that she is not an evil girl. However, I am not at all sure that speaking to my daughter earlier helped her.'

'Oh, on the contrary, I'm sure that it did. Very much so.'

Sid paused for a moment before covering his mic and continuing in a quieter voice.

'I wonder if, after a short break, you might want to talk in more detail about what's in the box.'

Catherine ignored the question. She had already said too much and had no intention of discussing family secrets with a stranger.

'Would it be at all possible to have a cup of coffee?'

Sid realised he had lost her for now and there was no point in pushing this broad any further. There was no hurry; he had plenty of time to reel her in. Women always yielded to him eventually. She was quite a looker for her age. He'd try a bit of harmless flirting after she'd stretched her shapely legs.

'Of course, Lady Catherine, of course. Cheryl the floor manager will show you to the Green Room. Take your time.'

Catherine had reached the heavy studio door with the obliging Cheryl scurrying along like the Mad Hatter next to her when the floor manager was interrupted by urgent instructions into her headset from the director.

'I'm so sorry, Lady Catherine, I just need to hand over some new scripts to Sid. If I could ask you to wait here for a moment, I'll be right back.'

Catherine smiled at the stressed young girl who she guessed was probably about the same age as Lily.

'No problem, my dear, I will wait just outside the studio door, if I may. It's a little too hot in here under all these bright lights.'

As Cheryl dashed back to where Sid was sifting through a pile of scripts, Catherine wandered out into the coolness of the corridor and began to inspect the larger-than-life photographs of presenters lining the walls.

'You seem a little lost, madam. Can I help you?'

'No, not at all, thank you. I am just waiting to be guided back to the *Green Room,* I think it is called, where I believe I will find coffee. The floor manager will be back in a moment to show me the way.'

'Ah yes, the Green Room. It's this way, madam, I can show you. There's some fresh coffee just made. Perhaps you would also like something to eat? We have an assortment of sandwiches available.'

'That's very kind, but I am fine thank you. Just a coffee, that's all.'

'Coffee it is then. Please follow me.'

Catherine fell into step with the helpful young man.

'Tell me, where are you from? I think I can detect a slight accent? Are you Russian?'

'No, madam, I am from Iraq. My name is Dmitri. Pleased to meet you. The Green Room is just this way.'

Tuesday

26

8.20 a.m.

Europe News

Looking at the studio clock, Sid stifled a yawn behind his hand. Good job they were in a break. It was early and he'd only just returned to the studios, but after another night with little sleep he was starting to feel the strain.

Last night he'd been too wired to head home straight away and had jumped a cab to Mahiki. Stepping inside, he was immediately mobbed by clubbers who'd been glued to Europe News coverage of the vault siege. What did he think was in the box? What was Lily's motive? Would the army blow the bloody doors off? The gag hadn't been funny the first half-dozen times he'd heard it and didn't improve with the slurred delivery of a Hooray Henry sloshing vodka shots over his sharp suit, but he laughed heartily anyway. Accepting a congratulatory glass of champagne, Sid headed for the roped-off VIP area where some of the usual crowd were chatting with a little more elbow room.

'Darling! You don't call, you don't write, the flowers have stopped.'

Sid turned around to see one of his regular squeezes shimmying towards him. All thoughts of last night with Chantelle vanished as he slipped a tentacle around the girl's micro waist.

'Aggie, love of my life, invader of all my dreams. Where on earth have you been hiding? You haven't returned any of my calls. The letters I'm sure are piled up behind your door and, as for the flowers, I'm single-handedly keeping Jane Packer in business, darling.'

Both laughed at the charming but obvious mistruths. Aggie St John Smith was looking particularly stunning in a Thai silk Prada dress so short that she couldn't possibly sit down and still maintain her modesty.

Within the hour, Sid had been easing her out of it in his bedroom. He'd left her sleeping there this morning while he headed to work.

The floor manager wandered over to him.

'Morning, Cheryl. Did we ever find out what happened to Lady Catherine last night? Did she just bottle it and do a runner back up the M40 to Oxfordshire?'

'Dunno, Sid. She'd said she was only taking a break for a coffee but I couldn't find her anywhere.'

Cheryl had been with Europe News for five years and had worked her way up from runner to senior floor manager. She was pretty and articulate and had her sights set on high table. Newly single after ditching her two-timing sound recordist boyfriend, she'd had a secret crush on Sid ever since he'd arrived at the station. Sometimes presenters did fall for their floor managers and, even if he didn't fancy her, perhaps he could help make her a star. After all, hadn't Christine Bleakley started out as a floor manager?

'By the way, did I tell you how gorgeous you look today? It's all I can do to keep my hands to myself.'

Cheryl blushed and dropped her chin, turning her head mischievously to one side.

'Get a room, buddy.'

It was Christine's voice in his ear. She had been eavesdropping the studio chatter.

'Coming out of the break in thirty seconds, Sid. Can you throw to Steve Stone outside the vault this morning for us?'

Sid groaned.

'Don't worry, he has Julia standing next to him to talk to so there'll be no more rabbit-in-the-headlights stuff. And don't moan. MW says we're to look after him, so behave. We all had to start somewhere. Coming to you in ten seconds.'

'Did you say he was outside the vault?'

'Yup.' The moment they were back on air, Christine immediately returned to her monosyllabic delivery.

'Hello everyone, a very good morning. You're watching Europe News with live continuous coverage of the Mayfair Safety Deposits siege. Let's get the very latest from outside the vault, and our crime correspondent Steve Stone is there with reporter Julia Morris. Julia . . .'

As Julia picked up from Sid's throw, the anchor was distracted by his Head of News wandering into the studio. Checking with the floor manager that Sid's microphone had been faded out, MW walked on to the set. He'd hoped to catch Sid before he went on air but had been in conference when the anchor had arrived at the studios and by the time he was free, Sid was in make-up. What he had to say needed to be said in private.

'Good night's rest? You're doing a sensational job, Sid. Quick chat in my office? Ten minutes or so?'

Sid could tell by MW's tone that, while it wasn't exactly an order, a chat in his office at the bottom of the hour was non-negotiable.

'That would be great.'

'Excellent. Sophie can take over for a while. After the key points at eight thirty we're going to run a back half-hour catch-up on everything's that's happened so far. so she'll literally be linking in and out of the breaks.'

'What's going to happen at the top of the next hour? It's prime time, the viewers will be tuning in in their droves.'

'Come and have a chat.'

Sid didn't like the sound of that and immediately suspected Suzanna's dark forces at work.

'Pick up, Sid,' instructed Christine in his ear.

'Thanks, Julia, thanks, Steve . . .'

Ten minutes later, dropping into a luxurious sofa in MW's office, Sid accepted a black coffee from the boss.

'Great job with the mother last night, Sid. Shame about the phone line but, hey, we had a good run. The police say they are no nearer to finding the keyholders, and the army are anxious that semtex might spoil everyone's Christmas. We don't know what's wrong with the girl and if it's a dickie ticker they can't risk her pegging it. Don't suppose Lady Catherine confided in you, did she?'

'No. Weirdly she did a runner. Went to stretch her legs and never came back.'

'Yeah, I heard. I came down to find her and have a chat, looked everywhere, no sign. Was it something you said, buddy?' MW laughed.

'Well, not sure, boss. But I have to say, I don't usually have that effect on women.'

'She's old enough to be your mother, Sid. I can see your point, though. Certainly still a looker.'

MW prided himself on his effortless ability to strike just the right tone with each of his presenters. He paused, allowing the laddish chat to reach a natural end.

'So, the police negotiators tell us that, given the last time they spoke to the vault before the line was cut, they're confident those inside will have enough water left – just. They might not be enjoying a slap up festive bird with all the trimmings, but they won't starve either. Anyway, if stories about the guard are to be believed, he's as big as a small semi in Salford. They can chew on him if they get peckish.'

'Any news from the Arab father? He's a prince, isn't he?'

'Yes, he is and no, nothing so far. We know he has suites at the Mandarin Oriental, but trying to get to him is harder than tracking down the Home Secretary for a quote.'

'What about the PM?'

'Great idea. Why didn't I think of that, silly me.'

Both men laughed. As the banter reached another natural pause an uneasy silence descended. Sid knew that MW hadn't called him out of the studio to chew the fat and trade jokes about whether Europe News had tried for an interview with the PM. He took another sip of his coffee and waited for the other boot to fall. They continued to sit in silence, MW not sure how to approach his star anchor with the news that would infuriate him, Sid half guessing what was coming but not prepared to help out his boss. Eventually, it was MW who cracked. Still adopting the Streetonian mockney that came just as easily to him as rubbing shoulders with Catherine and her aristocratic friends, he pressed on.

'Seriously, mate, you've been absolutely brilliant. Why not have a break with the family for a while and come back for the vault opening tomorrow?'

Sid allowed himself a wry smile and another mouthful of hot coffee. Why hadn't they had this conversation last night? He could have stayed in bed with Aggie rather than flirting in the studio with Cheryl.

'Mate, thanks, but I'm fine. The odd half-hour break like this and a good sleep overnight is fine.'

Sid paused and waited for the next move in this game of three-dimensional chess. MW couldn't stall any longer.

'Suzanna's back.'

'Better late than never, I suppose. Did she have a good time in gay Paris?'

'Sid, cut me some slack here. She is also one of our main presenters and she wants to be involved in the biggest story we've ever covered. We've never pulled in a larger collective audience on a rolling news event.'

'What do you suggest, MW?'

'She'll be taking over at the top of the hour and you can have a bit of downtime with the family.'

'Sounds like it's all already sorted.'

'It is.'

Without another word, Sid finished his drink, put down his cup on the glass table in front of him and stood to leave.

'I'm on my mobile, MW.'

He walked towards the exit without turning to see the undoubted relief on his boss's face. He'd decided to make it easy for him.

MW sighed. He'd been unhappy about hoofing Sid, but the call in the early hours of the morning from Suzanna's agent had taken him by surprise. He'd sleepily agreed that a different perspective, a woman's angle, might be just what the viewers needed. In make-up, Suzanna was almost ready. Last night's barmaid's outfit had been replaced by an Armani Collezioni two-piece.

Sid was too angry to head home to Aggie straight away. He'd known better than a confrontation with MW – there was no way he'd have come out the winner – so for now, acquiescing was his only option. Still seething, he slid into the rear seat of his chauffeured Audi.

'Where to, Sid?' asked his driver.

* * *

Suzanna was on cloud nine as she made her way to the studio. The previous evening, Prince Ansar had been demanding, insatiable but nevertheless reasonably enjoyable. Afterwards she'd been a little disappointed that there was no invitation to stay the night in his suite, and with Dmitri tied up elsewhere there was no-one available to take her home. Still, mission accomplished. She was back in London and back in charge.

Arriving home scantily dressed to an empty flat with no heat and no food in the fridge had been deflating. Running a bath, her thoughts had turned briefly to Christopher at the George V in Paris. If only he'd known how to behave properly, he could have been back in London by now. Silly man. Not for a moment did Suzanna consider that Christopher didn't want to be in London or within a thousand miles of her, ever again.

Towelling herself dry, she checked the bedside clock and saw that it was just before midnight, still an acceptable time to ring her agent.

'Hi Nick, darling – weren't asleep, were you? Good. Just arrived back in London, sweetie, raring to go. What news from MW, all sorted for tomorrow?'

Nick English propped himself up on one elbow and tried to rub the sleep from his eyes. Disturbing his Christmas Day had been bad enough. Calling in the middle of the night was a new low, even for Suzanna Thomas. Aware that his wife was trying to rest between regular painful overnight bouts of baby teething, Nick dragged himself from the marital bed and padded towards the landing.

'Suzanna, it's midnight. I can't believe you're calling this late.'

'Don't be precious, darling, I don't have time for precious. It's taken me days to get back to London.'

Nick sat on the top stair looking out through the landing

window and across into next-door's garden. The snow was still thick on the ground and a deep carpet covered the wishing well. He saw it every morning when he walked down the stairs. He wished he could soon be free of Suzanna Thomas. The baby began to grizzle and Nick put his head in his hand.

'Listen, Suzi, it is not acceptable to call at this hour. I haven't heard from MW, I will call him again tomorrow.'

'Nonsense! I need you to phone MW now and make sure I'm on air for prime time tomorrow.'

Trying to make his point forcefully while also keeping his voice to a whisper, Nick hissed into the phone: 'That is not going to happen, Suzi; you are being completely unreasonable.'

'Oh, Nick, don't be so difficult. You should be congratulating me, not chastising me. Christopher proposed,' lied Suzanna. 'We're going to make lots of lovely money. Anyway, can't stay chatting, sweetie; have to get my beauty sleep ahead of tomorrow. Text me to let me know you've spoken to MW. Night, night.'

As Nick banged the wall with his fist, the baby announced he was ready for attention.

'Why aren't you asleep?'

'Dunno, I'm just not tired.'

'Well, you should be. TV stars need to get their beauty sleep, you know.'

Steve Stone sat on the edge of his bed and pressed his mobile closer to his ear.

'I'm crap, Jackie.'

'No you're not.'

Jackie had spent every moment that Steve wasn't on air on the phone to her husband trying to reassure him that he wasn't crap at live TV. She might as well return to

London for all the quality time she was spending with her parents.

'I am.'

'Look, Stephen Jonathon Stone, you most certainly are not. You are learning a new trade. You can't be brilliant at it straight away. You will get better and better, but for now you are really very good. OK?'

'Do you really think so?'

'Yes, I really think so.'

'I love you.'

'I love you too, and I'll love you even more if you let me get some sleep.'

'Sorry, love, but I just knew you'd be honest with me and tell me if I was crap. Are you sure I'm not crap?'

'Sure.'

'Positive?'

'Steve, I'm going to sleep now. Then I can reassure you all over again first thing in the morning. OK?'

'OK, but you would tell me?'

'Yes. Good night, love.'

Jackie ended the call before she was drawn into another decreasing circle of self-doubt from her husband. They both knew he was totally rubbish on air, but now wasn't the time to tell him.

Steve lay back on top of his bed, safe in the knowledge he wouldn't have a wink of sleep ahead of being crap on TV again tomorrow. And this time it would be Suzanna Thomas in the studio. He'd been warned to watch out for her.

'Who is Steve Stone?'

Suzanna had only been in the studio for five minutes and was already feeling testy.

'He's the new crime correspondent, Suzanna. It was

275

his contact who gave us the exclusive phone line into the vault.'

'OK, let me talk to him.'

'Well, you can't speak directly to him – he's finding it a little difficult to communicate down the barrel. You need to throw to Julia, who is with him at the vault and she'll chat to him from down there.'

Suzanna snapped. She hadn't dashed back from Paris so someone else could conduct interviews on her show.

'Nonsense, Christine. This is my show and I would like to carry out the interview with Steve Stone. Our viewers would also like it to be me who carries out the interview with Steve Stone. Do I make myself clear, Christine? I think I do. Now sort it.'

A few moments later Suzanna swapped her scowl for a smile as the credits rolled, signalling to viewers the top of the hour at Europe News. A wide shot of the studio, the voice of god announcing 'This is Europe News with Suzanna Thomas', followed by a close-up of the presenter, and she was off and running.

'Hello, everyone. Welcome to Europe News. It's nine o'clock and the top story this hour continues to be the siege inside Mayfair Safety Deposits. All five people remain trapped inside. Let's find out the latest from the scene. Waiting to speak to us this morning is our crime correspondent, Steve Stone . . .'

Switching on the portable TV in the kitchen over breakfast Jackie could see from Steve's rabbit eyes that someone had moved the goalposts. She reached for her mobile, set it on the work surface next to her tea and toast, and waited for it to ring.

27

9 a.m.

Mayfair Safety Deposits

'How you feeling about stuff this morning, love?'

Bert had ambled across to Lily, who was sitting in exactly the same position where he had left her last night.

Sleeping had been easier since the temperature in the vault improved. During a conversation with a police negotiator before the phone was cut off, Bert had asked if the heating could be switched back on. It was now considerably warmer and much more comfortable, though the children were still wearing their coats.

Hafsa and Umair had woken a couple of hours ago and were busy playing with their toys. Hafsa was concentrating so hard on a Labrador puppy jigsaw that she didn't notice her brother hiding key pieces in his mother's bag. Late last night Bert had seen the Princess pop a couple of blue pills that were without doubt illegal in the UK. She was now dribbling slightly between her collagen-enhanced lips.

Lily, on the other hand, looked tired and wan.

'I'm OK, thank you, guard.'

'Bert, you can call me Bert, OK? That's my name, says it right here on my name badge.'

'OK, thank you, Bert. I'm feeling a little better this morning, thank you.'

'How are you feeling about opening the box? We going to do this thing or not?'

Bert offered her a hand up in the hope they would wander over to the boxes and open 777. Lily looked to the floor and remained seated on her case.

'I don't know. I don't know if I want to know.'

Here we go again, thought Bert.

'But last night you said you did. Come on, love, it's why you came, isn't it?'

'Yes, I know, but, now I'm here . . .'

The end of Lily's sentence trailed away and Bert knew, rather like the vault door, it would be some time yet before the box was opened. Damn, he was fascinated now, desperate to know what was inside. Last night they had been on the verge of opening it. He'd found the second key to Box 777 clearly marked and hanging from a board containing several hundred others. They'd walked together across to the rows of security boxes and had even gone as far as to push the library ladder into position, only for Lily to lose her nerve at the very last moment. Without another word she'd returned to her suitcase, where she was still sitting now.

Bert strolled across to the water cooler, returning with two plastic cups half-full.

'Want to talk, love?'

'Yes, I think I do, Bert.'

'OK, should I stand, or will it be a while?'

'It'll probably take a while. Have a bit of my suitcase to sit on, if you like.'

Looking at the space offered, Bert laughed. He certainly

wasn't about to risk his weight on such a flimsy bit of nonsense. Sliding on to the floor again was a destination too far. Instead, he opted to drag over his office chair, positioning it next to rather than in front of Lily. More supportive, less confrontational, he thought.

'Right, well, I'm sitting comfortably, so you can begin.'

A bit of levity always helped when his daughter had something awkward to say to him.

Lily began hesitantly.

'I love my mother and my daddy. Well, I did love them, but I don't know if I still will after I look in the box.'

As she blurted out the words, Lily was unsure of where she was headed. Bert patted the top of her hand.

'Start at the very beginning, love. We have all the time you need.'

Lily took a deep breath, sipped from her plastic cup and allowed her mind to wander back to her late teens. She remembered how her father was travelling all the time and she often didn't see him for months at a time. With her eighteenth birthday fast approaching, Lily had grown increasingly anxious her father might miss it as he had so many other birthdays. For her, like every other teenager, eighteen was an important milestone and she desperately wanted him there. Her mother, keen to manage Lily's expectations, had prepared her for spending her big day without her daddy. He had been in the middle of a major electronics deal in Rwanda and probably wouldn't be able to return to Oxfordshire in time. Joseph, however, determined not to disappoint his baby girl, organised a surprise last-minute trip to Africa so that she could join him. Lily had been beside herself with excitement. She had never been to Africa before and to see animals in their natural habitat while also spending quality time with her father was a birthday surprise beyond belief. Three days later she was sitting with her mother in the BA lounge at Heathrow surrounded by piles of hand luggage.

'Seriously, Mummy, do we really need all of these bags?'

'We most certainly do, darling. Life in Africa is not quite what we're used to in the UK, you know. I want to make sure I have everything I need to keep you safe.'

Lily shrugged. She knew that there was always a risk of contracting malaria or dengue fever during a visit to Africa, but she still wasn't sure carry-on luggage that was better stocked than A&E at John Radcliffe Hospital was completely necessary. As their flight was called to Nairobi and on to Kigali, her mother was not to be deterred and Lily was forced to lug countless pieces of hand luggage. Leaving the lounge Lily descended into a teenage sulk which her mother either didn't notice or chose to ignore.

Arriving fifteen hours later at Kigali's basic airport terminal with only very limited facilities available, Lily began to appreciate for the first time her mother's concern. As they waited for their baggage to be offloaded, Lily could see her father, standing the other side of Immigration. She desperately wanted to run to greet him but was thwarted by a glass divide and a Rwanda law that relieved her and her mother of every plastic bag in their luggage. They were banned in Rwanda, a detail her father had failed to mention. Thirty minutes later and Lily could wait no longer. Leaving her mother to gather up shampoo, body lotions and other belongings strewn across the arrivals hall floor, she ran the few yards to where her father was waiting to greet them.

'Daddy, Daddy I've missed you so much. You haven't been home for ever. I've loads to tell you.'

Lily was swept up into her father's bearlike hug and she knew everything was all right with the world. A few moments later they were joined by her mother, who was content with a cursory peck on the cheek before the family headed to a waiting vehicle. As their driver negotiated the busy traffic and kamikaze motorists on their way to the Serena Hotel, her father began to run through a rough itinerary for his girls.

'I thought we might head up to see the silverback gorillas in a couple of days' time. We can move really close to them and I believe two of the families have new babies. It does involve quite a bit of trekking on foot, but nothing my girls can't cope with. Before that though, I've organized for George to drive us to Kibuye. It's on the edge of a beautiful lake; there's a speedboat there and it can take us over to one of the uninhabited islands for lunch. What do you say?'

'Brill, Daddy. Sounds great.'

Catherine squeezed her husband's hand, pleased that he had made some effort to make Lily's trip one to remember.

'Why are we staying in a hotel, Daddy, rather than at your house?'

'I thought it would be more fun, and you'll love the pool at the Serena,' smiled Joseph, failing to mention that his African lover had taken up residence at his palatial property. He had finally found someone whose insatiable sexual desire matched his own, so Kozi stayed put and his family were provided with suites at the best hotel in the city instead.

'Oh, lovely. I can't wait to jump in the pool. How exciting. I love you, Daddy.'

'I love you too, baby girl. We're going to have such fun.'

The following morning, Lily woke very early and, flinging open the curtains to her hotel suite, was met with a stream of bright sunshine. It was already a beautiful day. Keen to set off to the lake as soon as possible, she cantered down the hotel corridor and tapped lightly at the door to her parents' room. There was no response. Lily knocked another three times before her rather flustered mother eventually came

281

to the door. From the expression on her face it was quite obvious her parents had been quarrelling.

'Everything OK, Mummy?'

'Yes, darling, everything's tickety-boo. Daddy and I have a wonderful timetable all planned out.'

Joseph and Lily were to travel without Catherine to the lake and then meander via Kigali to see the gorillas, picking up her mother on the way.

'But I want you to come to the lake too, Mummy. It sounds bliss.'

'I have a terrible migraine and quite a temperature. I think a couple of days by the pool here will be the best medicine. Take lots of photographs for me, would you, darling.'

Lily had been reluctant to leave her mother, but Catherine had insisted and after another half-hour of unsuccessful persuasion, still with no sign of her father, she headed down to the foyer. He was already waiting for her at the entrance to the hotel.

'Morning, baby girl. Bags packed? Mummy's not too well but I'm all set – let's go.'

Lily clambered excitedly into the back seat of the Range Rover, her father sliding in next to her, and George set off. The temperature was becoming warmer by the minute; she hoped her mother would remember to wear enough sun cream. Peering through the car window Lily was surprised how lush and green some parts of Kigali were. The rapidly growing city was bustling, noisy and colourful. As they made their way down from the hilltop, covered in skyscrapers and giant cranes busy constructing more, and into the valleys Lily was delighted to see farmland right in the middle of the city. Tea plants were growing in every green space they passed. She couldn't imagine that ever happening in London.

A few miles out of the capital and her father was already on the phone. Lily entertained herself by taking in the scenery and planning what they might do once they reached Lake Kivu. A few minutes later, as they climbed higher and higher up the mountain road away from the capital and closer towards the lake, Lily turned to ask how long their journey might take. Her father was still speaking intently on the phone, so she leaned forward and tapped George on the shoulder.

'I'm really hot, George; could you put on the air conditioning, please?'

Lily was used to being driven to and from her Buckinghamshire boarding school by Howard the chauffeur. He had three girls of his own and was quite accustomed to chatty teenagers who followed one question with another and always needed the answer straight away. Lily felt safe with Howard. She had no clue how different road discipline could be in Rwanda. Instead of chatting while keeping his eyes on the road as Howard did, George turned to the back seat to speak to Lily.

'Sorry, Miss Lily. What did you say?'

The last thing Lily remembered was her father's shout as the Range Rover careered towards a completely inadequate crash barrier and beyond it a sheer drop down the side of the mountain road. Then nothing.

Waking up in a hospital bed, Lily had no idea where she was. Turning her head, she saw her mother's anxious face melt into tears of relief.

'Darling, you're awake.'

'Mummy . . .' Lily found it almost impossible to speak. Her throat hurt and she couldn't lift her head.

'Don't try to talk, darling. Everything is fine.'

'What happened?'

'There was a terrible accident. You've lost a lot of blood, but everything is going to be fine.'

'Daddy?'

'Daddy is fine, darling. He fared much better than you did, my love. I can't believe he didn't check you were wearing a seat belt . . .' Catherine paused; this was no time for recriminations. Lily was alive, that was all that mattered for now.

'How did I get here, Mummy?'

'You were in a small clinic near the lake. You were very poorly, darling, and had lost an awful lot of blood. Daddy managed to donate some of his, enough until we could get you back here to the main hospital in Kigali. He's a bit weak, but he's OK. You can see him soon. Daddy saved your life, darling.'

Bert noticed that Lily was crying.

'Why are you crying love? That's a very touching story. I don't understand why you're so cross with your father. Sounds like he's the reason you're here.'

'Exactly,' sobbed Lily as she took another sip of water from her clear plastic cup.

As the town hall clock struck 10 a.m., Roxy glugged from her water glass and flopped back on top of the duvet. She winced against the penetrating noise, screwing up her eyes and holding her head in pain. She'd spent most of last night swigging straight from a whisky bottle and feeling it burn all the way down to her stomach. Looking across to the bedside table, there was less than half of the ten-year-old Laphroaig single malt left. It had been a Christmas present for Bert. Well, he wasn't bloody having it now. Roxy had opened the bottle as soon as she'd returned from the Dog and Duck last night and had drunk well into the night before eventually crying herself to sleep. This morning, suffering the consequences of too much booze, she lay back on her pillow and closed her eyes. Could it really be true that he had no intention of leaving his wife?

In her own mind she had reconciled the conversation with Bert and Cynthia as his attempt to placate her on national TV but listening to the boys in the pub chatting about it last night had made her think. Roxy opened her eyes and wiped away a mascara-streaked tear. Surely her dreams couldn't end in tatters again; Bert had made her so many promises and she'd believed every single one of them. Why would he lie? He wouldn't. She was sure that this time it really would be her turn to be truly happy. She deserved it. All those others had been lying bastards, but not Bert, not her Bert. Of course he meant every promise he'd made. It was her and not Cynthia that he loved to the moon and back a million times.

Roxy sat up and blew her nose. Those boys in the pub were wrong, she knew it.

There was only one thing for it, a showdown with Cynthia Jones. She was going to walk right up to her front door and put that silly woman straight.

28

At the same time across town

Mayfair

Catherine woke with a start, still wearing her clothes from last night. For a moment she couldn't remember where she was. It was a bedroom she didn't recognise. The bedcovers were fine Egyptian cotton and the pillows where undoubtedly white goose feather and down, but the decoration was not to her taste. Then she began to remember. Last night she had been treated civilly but firmly by a man she first met in the corridor outside the studio at Europe News. He had ushered her past the Green Room and along a snake of corridors before emerging into the cold winter night of Boxing Day and straight into the rear seat of a waiting Bentley. Any thought of resistance was immediately quashed by the sight of a gun half-hidden under the man's coat. The car doors were locked as soon as she was inside and they left the studios at some speed. Catherine had asked many questions in the ten-minute journey from Europe News to the Mandarin Oriental, but this man, who had been charm personified in the corridor, became mute as soon as she was in the vehicle.

Once at the hotel, Catherine had been led past the kitchens and up a back stairway before being shown into a bedroom of the royal suite. The man then spoke for the first time since she had been bundled into the car. He asked her lots of questions that she couldn't answer. While he hadn't harmed her, he had left her in no doubt that he might. After what seemed like hours of pointless threats, she had been locked in this room. Exhausted, she had finally fallen asleep.

Catherine leapt from the bed and dashed towards the window. She was in a hotel suite several storeys up; there was no escape. She ran to the bedside phone, but it was dead and her mobile had been taken from her the night before by that rather sinister young man.

Catherine was startled by a tap at the door announcing the arrival of the same man. Dmitri had been waiting for her to pick up the bedside telephone.

'Why am I here?'

Dmitri didn't reply. Instead he signalled to Catherine she should follow him. Walking into the sitting room of the suite, Catherine was greeted by another man she didn't know. Perhaps he was the owner of the vault. She was no doubt about to find out.

Prince Ansar was sitting behind his desk and rose to greet Catherine. Dmitri had been careful to bring her a convoluted route through the hotel that avoided CCTV. No one except Ansar and Dmitri knew she was here.

'Mrs Dunlop, thank you so much for coming. I hope you had a comfortable night. I'm so sorry I wasn't able to great you personally last night when you arrived. I trust Dmitri was accommodating. May I offer you some tea?'

'You must forgive my ignorance, and I have no desire to

appear rude, but I have no idea why I am here or indeed who you are, I'm afraid.'

'Excellent. Tea, Dmitri, please – and a little privacy for a few moments.'

As the guard left, Ansar beckoned for Catherine to join him on one of the sofas in front of the fire.

'Please sit, relax. Let's talk for a while. Allow me to introduce myself. I am Prince Ansar of Aj-Al-Shar.'

'Very pleased to meet you. Have we met before?'

'Not that I am aware of, Mrs Dunlop. But our families are acquainted.'

'Really?'

'Yes, in fact they are in each other's company right at this very moment. My son and daughter, along with my wife Almira, are presently being held against their will by your daughter Lily in the vault of Mayfair Safety Deposits.'

Catherine gasped and steadied herself against the back of an overstuffed sofa.

'Why am I here?'

'I thought we might visit for a while. It is something that you British do very well. Take tea and chat, make small talk, I think is how you call it. That is what we should do, Mrs Dunlop, chat for a while.'

'I'm terribly sorry, as I have said, I don't wish to appear rude, but I must insist I am allowed to leave immediately.'

'How is it that you take your tea?'

'Seriously, I really do insist. My daughter is unwell and she needs me.'

'Mrs Dunlop, my son is unwell. He needs me. Your daughter is holding him against his will. I'm afraid you must stay here in order to redress the balance.'

Any further protest was quietened by the return of Dmitri carrying a tea tray. As he placed it down in front of Catherine, she immediately noticed the Glock 9mm that had been under his coat last night. It was now added to the tray, leaving her in no doubt her objections were futile.

'As you are here, Mrs Dunlop – and once you have finished your tea, of course – I wonder if you would mind answering a few questions. For that I will leave you in the capable hands of Dmitri. I understand you were tired and unable to help last night. I hope, having rested, you will be a little more willing this morning. If you'll excuse me.'

As Prince Ansar rose to leave, Catherine began to panic and tried to follow him towards the door but immediately felt the steely grip of the guard's hand firmly squeezing her shoulder.

'If I could ask you to remain here please, Mrs Dunlop. I must begin to question you further about the motives behind your daughter's behaviour.'

Catherine turned her face away from her tormentor and walked towards the window. She gazed out across a picture-postcard scene of Hyde Park covered in a blanket of snow. She could see families walking together along the banks of the Serpentine just as she had done with Lily so many years before. There were times when they had been so cold after playing in the snow that only a hot chocolate with whipped cream and marshmallows on top could warm them. Thoughts of her daughter whisked Catherine back to Lily's bedside in a basic Kigali hospital. Lily had lain motionless for hours, drips from her arms, tubes connecting her to machines that monitored and beeped. Her face as pale as the sheets tucked around her. Her injuries included a severe gash to her upper leg and internal injuries that had resulted in an urgent need for a blood transfusion. The car had crashed through the flimsy roadside barrier and down the mountainside before ploughing into a cluster of Eucalyptus trees that prevented it from plunging into the valley another hundred metres below. The accident had claimed the life of George the driver;

Joseph had suffered shock and sustained a broken arm but was otherwise fine.

Catherine had been by the pool at the Serena Hotel, unaware of the accident for several hours. It had been left to Lily's father in his shocked state to supervise his daughter's treatment. He had been anxious about blood contamination in a developing country and had at first refused. Only after the medic's insistence that Lily would die without a transfusion had he reluctantly consented for the procedure to go ahead. Thankfully Joseph knew he was the same blood group as Lily, A positive, and had readily agreed to donate to his daughter. The procedure had taken place promptly and she had been transferred to Kigali soon after.

'How is she?'

It was Joseph. He had been wheeled into the room to be near his daughter.

'She's sleeping. What on earth happened?'

'I really don't know. I was on the phone to the office and the next thing we were careering headlong over the cliff edge. I remember the car smashing into a tree line and it seemed to stop our fall, but George wasn't wearing his seat belt and went through the windscreen. The doctors told me that his body was found at the bottom of the ravine.'

'Lily wasn't wearing her belt either. What on earth were you thinking?'

Joseph ignored the accusation from his wife. He knew he had been foolish and didn't need her to judge.

'I just remember us coming to a juddering halt. The front seat stopped Lily crashing through the windscreen, but she was knocked unconscious. When I looked in the front of the car, the windscreen was broken and George was gone. I couldn't move, I couldn't reach her, I thought we were going to die. Then I heard voices calling to us. The car behind had British tourists in it, they saw what happened and rang for help.' He looked across at his daughter, lying motionless in her hospital bed. 'I feel so guilty, my poor baby girl.'

Joseph hung his head and Catherine softened.

'You mustn't blame yourself, darling. If you hadn't been with her, the doctors say she would be . . . well, she would not be with us. The transfusion saved her life, my love.'

Catherine patted the top of his hand, as much emotion as she was willing to offer. Any love for him had long since died, wilted on the vine. There had been a time when Joseph was her reason for being and she had willingly given up everything, including the love of her family, to spend the rest of her life with him. They had been deliriously happy and the arrival of Lily had completed their joy. But as his business continued to grow, taking him away from the family home more and more often, Catherine's sense of isolation consumed her. When infrequently he did return home the couple would squabble and Joseph would soon find reasons to leave again. That was exactly what had happened as soon as Catherine and Lily had arrived in Rwanda. A disagreement in the hotel room had led to a heated argument and Joseph's desperation to be as far away from his wife as soon as possible.

Lily had almost died and Catherine blamed herself. If she hadn't quarrelled with Joseph then she'd have been with them in the car and perhaps she would have been able to prevent the accident or at least done something to help. She certainly would have made sure her child was wearing a seat belt. At that moment, Lily stirred and Catherine dashed to her side.

'Darling, you're awake, thank goodness.'

Looking out at the families playing in the snow in Hyde Park, it all seemed such a long time ago. If only Catherine had known what might happen to Lily, she could have done something sooner. Now it might be too late. Joseph was dead and she had no one she could talk to.

Catherine looked out across the park and wondered how this terrible situation would end.

'So, Mrs Dunlop, if we may continue . . .'

Dmitri slowly removed his suit jacket and placed it on a chair. He walked across to Catherine and stood much too close to her. Catherine began to breathe a little faster. What was he going to do? Did anyone know she was here? Surely Brian or her parents would wonder where she was.

'I wonder if I might ask you once again, Mrs Dunlop, why has Miss Lily behaved in such a foolish manner?'

Dmitri's accent had hardened from clipped mid-Atlantic to thick Iraqi dialect. It scared Catherine even more than the weapon.

'Your daughter's actions are causing great unhappiness and concern to Prince Ansar and his family. He is a patient man, but his patience is not boundless, Mrs Dunlop. He expects some answers from you – one way or another.'

Catherine continued to maintain her composure. This man had not harmed her, but his tone was descending into one of menace. She felt caged and confused; tightness in her chest was making it more and more difficult for her to breathe.

'I have all day, Mrs Dunlop. I am in no hurry.'

29

7.30 p.m.

Leytonstone

Roxy was breathing much too quickly as she manoeuvred her ageing Vauxhall Astra into Wendover Crescent. She had never been to Bert's home before, they'd always met at her place, and she was unsure of the number. She knew he had recently painted the front door emerald green and Cynthia had bought a brass lion-head knocker from Homebase.

Changing into second gear, she slowed her car to a crawl and peered through the snowy windscreen at the houses set back slightly from the road. Black, black, brown, blue, black, red, no sign of a green door. Roxy reached the end of the crescent and turning her car around began to drive slowly along the opposite side of the road. Black, black, red, green. Green, there it was, Bert's house, but she was too far away to see the door knocker. Perhaps there could be more than one house with a green door. She was about to drive past when she saw a woman at the window. It was Cynthia closing the curtains in the front room. Roxy immediately recognised her love rival from a photograph Bert had kept of the two of them in his wallet. That was until she'd stolen it and hidden it at the bottom of her knicker drawer when he was asleep.

Roxy again drove past and turned the car around before parking at the other side of the road and switching off the engine. Wiping away condensation from the inside of the windscreen, she thought she could see a couple of other people sitting in their cars outside the house. They must be journalists, thought Roxy. The vault siege was a huge news story and no doubt Cynthia was being hounded for a quote. What did she expect after appearing on Europe News, silly bitch. Looking past them, Roxy was aware of a police officer walking down the garden path away from the house and towards the front gate. She spontaneously ducked lower in her seat. Roxy hadn't even contemplated the police being here and she felt her resolve weaken. Reaching for the keys in the ignition, she hesitated, almost driving away, but her determination to find out the truth about Bert's promises was a huge motivation for her to stay.

Roxy sat in the car for at least half an hour, watching the house, the policeman and the journalists. What to do? As the minutes passed the temperature dropped and, with the engine switched off, there was no warmth from the heater. It was almost freezing even inside the car. Roxy knew she had to either confront her love rival or go home, but with the vault due to open tomorrow she needed to know the truth. Confrontation it had to be.

Opening the car door, she marched straight across the road and up to the gate, where the police officer stood barring her way. The barmaid didn't break her stride; she was used to dealing with tricky situations in the pub and an officer who was quite obviously young enough to be her son was no match for her.

'Hi, how is she?'

'I'm sorry, madam, you can't go any further.'

'Don't be daft, officer, Cyn's my cousin. I've just been on the phone to her and she's asked me to come round. She's fed up with all these journalists bothering her and wants a bit of company.'

As the journalists, alerted by the arrival of a stranger, began to clamber out of their cars, Roxy pulled her mobile out of her coat pocket.

'Do you want me to give her a ring, then she'll have to come out to convince you and have her picture taken by all these photographers. That's not going to go down too well back at the station, is it?'

The young officer was confused and intimidated by this larger-than-life woman. He moved aside and Roxy, her heart racing, walked up to the front door, knocked and waited. She was aware of a couple of photographers taking pictures of the back of her head, but it was too late to turn back now. Cynthia was soon at the door, but rather than opening it she called from inside the hall.

'Hello?'

'Hello.'

'Who is it?'

'Hello, Cynthia, you don't me, but I know you.'

'Are you a journalist? How did you get past the policeman? I've said as much as I'm going to, now go away.'

Roxy was not to be deterred. She'd brought the photograph she'd liberated from Bert's wallet and, taking it out of her coat pocket, she delivered it through the letterbox.

'We need to talk, Cynthia.'

A moment later the door opened, prompting a barrage of flash photography, and Roxy was hastened inside before it was quickly closed behind her.

'Who are you?'

Cynthia looked shocked and confused by the arrival of a busty brunette wearing far too much make-up and carrying a photograph of her and Bert in her pocket.

'How did you get this picture? Do you know my husband?'

'We have a lot to talk about. Are you going to just leave me standing here in the hall?'

Cynthia didn't move, one hand on the bottom post of the banisters, the other on the opposite wall of the hallway, effectively barring Roxy from moving any further into the house.

'The children are having their tea. What do you want?'

'I want to know what's going on with you and Bert.'

'What on earth do you mean? Bert's my husband. I don't know who you are, but I think you had better leave. The children are very upset about what's happening to their father and they don't need anything else to distress them. Least of all something that looks like you.'

Roxy felt her blood pressure rising; her hands were clammy and her cheeks began to flush. Looking around the hall she could see signs of Bert everywhere. His walking shoes were by the door next to the dog's lead. Cynthia had her hand on top of his coat on the banister at the bottom of the stairs. There was a framed wedding photograph of him with Cynthia hung in pride of place on the wall opposite the hall mirror. How could this be? He was about to leave Cynthia and the kids for her. This woman must be delusional.

'No, I'm not leaving, I'm not going anywhere, but Bert is.'

'I beg your pardon?'

Roxy's confidence was growing and she rolled up her sleeves just as she did whenever she was dealing with a tricky customer who she wanted out of her pub. Leaning nonchalantly against a wall, she continued.

'So I'll ask you again, what exactly is going on with you and Bert, then? You know he doesn't want to be with you any more, don't you? It's time for you to let go, love. He's mine now. You're history – just face it and let him leave. It'll be easier for everybody.'

Cynthia had heard enough.

'What on earth are you talking about? I don't even know your name, but I want you out of my house right now.'

Cynthia's raised voice had alerted the children, who left their half-eaten fish fingers, chips and beans, much to Rob the dog's delight, and appeared together at the entrance to the kitchen.

'What's up, Mum? Is it another journalist?'

Tracey had been particularly protective of her mother since her dad had been locked in the vault.

'No, love, it's fine go and finish your tea. I'll be through in a minute.'

Tracey and her brother reluctantly returned to the kitchen to finish what Rob had not managed to steal from the table while they were gone. Cynthia returned to her unwelcome visitor.

'If I have to ask you to leave again madam, I will throw you out.'

Roxy moved menacingly forwards.

'Oh really? You really think so.'

Roxy's tone had hardened from 'tell me everything I'm an understanding barmaid' to that of a hard-nosed East End gangster's moll. Cynthia, though increasingly anxious about this deranged woman's presence in her hallway, stood her ground.

'Yes, I really think so. I want you out of my house right now.'

Roxy leaned closer to her nemesis, not in the slightest intimidated. This was the showdown she had been determined to have and she wasn't about to buckle. Bert was hers and this silly woman needed to face facts.

'I'm going nowhere until you realise that it's all over between you and my Bert. You need to let him go, he's mine now.'

Cynthia had heard enough. However frightened she felt, her children were in the house and she needed to protect them from this madwoman. Lurching forwards and pushing past Roxy in the tiny hallway she managed to reach the door and fling it open. Ignoring another barrage of flashbulbs, she shouted down the pathway.

'Officer, if you have a moment, please?'

Roxy knew she was beaten.

'OK, OK I'm going, but you haven't heard the last of me.'

Storming past the photographers and journalists shouting questions at her, Roxy ran to her car.

'Who are you love?' 'Why are you crying?' 'What's happening in the house?'

Roxy ignored them, locked her door and drove away, tears and fury making it almost impossible for her to see the road ahead.

Wednesday

The day the vault opens.

30

7 a.m.

Europe News

Having spent twenty-four hours away from the studio, Sid was chomping at the bit to be back in the hot seat. Suzanna had been in control throughout the day yesterday, but now it was his turn to talk the nation. Perhaps even America would be tuning in to Europe News this morning. At home, Sid had spent every waking hour watching Europe News coverage. Well, every waking hour that hadn't involved Aggie, who had easily overtaken Chantelle as his favourite Christmas present. He was certainly planning to see a lot more of her once today was over, but first things first. Strolling confidently up the central staircase, waving and smiling to those who wanted to catch his attention, Sid sauntered airily into MW's office. Glancing at the giant plasma screen he noticed with some satisfaction that Suzanna was not on air. Today was the big day, the day the vault was due to open, where was she? Who cares? thought Sid, relieved the Head of News had finally come to his senses and realised he was the man to take viewers through the unfolding drama.

'Hey.'

'Hey, relaxing day off?'

'Great, firing on all four now, though. What time do you want me on air?'

Avoiding Sid's gaze, MW didn't immediately respond. The presenter was instantly alerted to a problem.

'You do want me on air, don't you, MW?'

'Sure.'

'So, what time? Vault's due to open at nine, isn't it? I'll head down to make-up about quarter to, hot seat by ten to. The viewing figures will be massive.'

'Sure will.'

MW's conversation remained stilted and Sid looked directly at him as he fiddled awkwardly with a bent paperclip while studiously avoiding eye contact.

'What's going on, boss?'

MW was about to launch into a convoluted attempt at face-saving when Suzanna appeared in the doorway.

'Sid! Happy Christmas, handsome. I hope you had a really lovely one. Hey, by the way, thanks for looking after the shop while I was away. You did a supremely average job.'

Sid wrinkled his nose and blew Suzanna a kiss. What a bitch.

'Why are you here, lover boy? Shouldn't you be at home watching how it's done by the professionals?'

What was she talking about? Watching at home? Today was the day that the vault opened. He'd stepped aside yesterday, but today was a completely different ball game. Sid turned to MW for clarification. Suzanna spoke first.

'Oh, you haven't told him yet, have you, MW? Silly me for spoiling the surprise. I'll leave you to it – have to dash to make-up.'

'Don't rush, sweetie; they need all the time they can have with you.'

Suzanna ignored the insult and disappeared down the corridor with an airy wave. Sid turned again to MW and waited for an explanation. He'd made it easy for him yesterday. No fuss, no drama. Not today.

MW fiddled even more anxiously with the paper clip before tossing it into the metal wastepaper bin and retrieving another from his desk stapler.

'I want you down at the vault for the opening, Sid.'

'Really?'

'Really.'

'Go on.'

Sid was furious and monosyllabic questions were the most he could muster without exploding.

'It's her gig, Sid.' That was it.

'It quite blatantly is not *her* gig, MW. I have nursed this story since it first began. I gave up my Christmas. I coaxed the mother, the wife, the guard into interviews that every other channel was gagging for. She was on air yesterday when precisely nothing happened. All she did was make that poor sod Steve Stone look like a numb nuts, blinking wide-eyed down the fucking camera. This is my story, MW. I did it all. It's *my* fucking gig.'

Sid slammed his hand on the desk, infuriated. His adrenalin was pumping and he wanted to storm from the room, but this time he was determined to stay and fight.

'I know all of that Sid, but Suzanna has secured an interview with the Aj-al-Shar royal family as soon as they are released. It's a fast-moving story and that's the interview that everyone wants now, buddy. Her agent says the exclusive is dependent on Suzanna being in the studio to host the release. We can't afford not to agree. Sid. Come on, mate.'

Sid was incandescent with rage. He couldn't believe he

had been outflanked by Suzanna bloody Thomas. She'd shafted him royally, quite literally, and there wasn't a thing he could do about it. He struggled to feel some sympathy for Miles. Of course the channel wanted the royal interview, everyone would, but still . . .

'OK, I get it, but come on, MW, couldn't we at least co-host?'

'Her agent says the Prince has insisted on single presentation. He thinks Suzanna has the caring human approach that he wants to see as his family are finally freed.'

'You've got to be fucking kidding me, right?'

'That's what's going to happen, Sid.'

Sid slumped dejectedly into a sofa. Why hadn't he contemplated an interview with the Prince and his family? For some reason he'd found himself much more interested in the fate of Lily Dunlop. Although she was the villain in this story, responsible for the incarceration of four innocent bystanders, one of them a sick child, she had nevertheless seemed so vulnerable when he'd listened to her speaking to her mother. He'd scrutinised the 'girl in pearls' *Country Life* shot of her that had been on screen while she spoke. Curious, he'd googled her afterwards. Details about her were quite limited. She was the fiancée of that idiot Giles Musgrave-Rose. There were some images of them together, and he had found another of her at the Debutante Ball at Le Crillon hotel in Paris. The guest list at the annual invitation-only event included celebrities and international aristocracy, among them Lily Dunlop who easily stood out in the group photo. She was absolutely exquisite in her off-the-shoulder Alice Temperley gown, her dazzling smile shining out from his computer screen. Turn a different corner, thought Sid. But then he'd immediately corrected himself. What was he thinking of? She was a wrong 'un and was going to jail for a very long time.

Contemplating his response to MW's decision, Sid

absentmindedly looked up at the plasma to see Steve Stone, the inexperienced crime correspondent, reporting live from the vault. He wasn't getting any better, poor chap. It had been an amazing scoop from the new man and he deserved credit and a bonus, but Sid wondered if the journalist would ever have what it took to be an on-air reporter. Studiously ignoring a sheepish MW, he turned up the sound and listened to the latest update.

'Erm, well, we are expecting that probably the vault will most likely be expected if everything goes to plan to undoubtedly be probably opened this morning. Well, when I say this morning I think probably; well, almost definitely be around nine o'clock, I would think if I'm not very much mistaken.'

Steve paused and stared desperately into the camera. Sid winced as he watched. Beads of sweat were now clearly visible on Steve's forehead and top lip as he once again launched into rambling and unfocused explanations of what was expected later in the day. Sid muted the sound to save further embarrassment.

He had an idea.

'So, boss, you want me to go down and help him out?'

MW almost jumped from his chair. He'd never imagined that Sid would actually agree to being sent out in the snow to be a glorified reporter while Suzanna ruled the roost.

'You sure?'

'Yup, that poor bloke could do with some help.'

'Mate, I owe you.'

'You're not wrong. Anyway, will it just be the Suzanna I'm-ready-for-my-close-up Thomas show, or will I get on the telly too?'

'Guaranteed. The sooner you're there, the sooner you'll be on.'

'In which case, I'm on my way.'

As he left MW's office, Sid almost collided with Suzanna

305

heading back from make-up, keen to make sure the deal she'd brokered was being honoured.

'Leaving?'

'Yup.'

'Enjoy the show.'

'You too. Oh, one thing though, honey, make sure you spend a little tiny bit more time in make-up before you go on set – don't want to scare the viewers, do we? And you are going to change, aren't you?'

Suzanna was about to respond to Sid's barb when her mobile rang. She could see from the caller display it was *Tiffany*, her codename for Prince Ansar. Turning on her heel, she headed for the privacy of her own office and closed the door before answering.

'Hello, good morning, sir.'

'Good morning, my dear. Thank you for your time and attention over the last couple of days, it has been most enjoyable. I trust you enjoyed last night equally as much as the night before?'

Suzanna smiled. She had been wrapped up in pyjamas, a sleeping bag and a duvet in her ice-cold flat when the Prince had called last night. Why did the boiler always have to break down at Christmas when all the plumbers had gone home for the holidays? By the time Dmitri arrived to collect her, she'd managed to shower and change into an elegant McQueen gown, much more appropriate attire for dinner at Claridge's with Prince Ansar. Later, retiring to his suite, Suzanna had been far hotter than she had back in her chilly flat.

'I enjoyed every moment, Your Royal Highness.'

'How are the earrings?'

Suzanna reached up to her earlobe to touch the Caresse d'orchidées par Cartier earrings embedded with twenty-two diamonds and thirty-two coloured stones. She'd counted

306

every single one of them twice when she'd returned home last night.

'They are simply exquisite. Thank you, sir.'

'I will be otherwise engaged for the rest of today, as I'm sure will you, my dear. I wonder, however, if we may meet some time tomorrow?'

'I would be delighted.'

Suzanna hesitated. *Now, ask him now.*

'Perhaps before that, Prince Ansar, I wonder if you might consider a few words on camera with the family after their release?'

Ansar was taken aback.

'Suzanna, my dear. I am surprised you felt it appropriate to ask me such an inappropriate question. As you should know, I am most reluctant to court publicity. I would have considered any interview extremely unlikely and I would be disappointed if you felt the need to ask again.'

31

8.40 a.m.

Mayfair Safety Deposits

Bert was nervous. He'd gathered everyone together to talk through what was likely to happen when the giant bolts slid back at 9 a.m. He didn't want anyone panicking and he certainly didn't want Umair having another funny turn. Looking around at his fellow captives he was confident they had all fared pretty well over the four days, under the circumstances.

'Right then, everybody, today's the day. We have twenty minutes to go before the vault opens. I will talk you through the details in another ten minutes or so, but now is the time to collect up all your belongings and be ready, OK? I just want to say that, much as I've loved being in your company, it's almost time for me to return to the bosom of my family.'

Umair sniggered at the reference to bosom and was immediately quietened by his elder sister. After his initial attack, even though he had been without medication for four days,

308

the youngster was relatively happy and relaxed. Hafsa was relieved that it was almost over.

'We're going home to see Daddy today, Umair. What are you going to tell him about what we did?'

'I'll tell him that a very bad lady trapped us in here and we wanted to go home but we just couldn't.'

'Out of the mouths of babes,' said Bert as he checked his watch. Another twenty minutes then the timer would automatically release the vault bolts just as it had locked them in four days earlier. The police never had managed to track down that second keyholder and Bert knew there would be a whole heap of trouble for Mayfair Safety Deposits heading down the track once this was all over. He hoped his job would be safe, though. After all, he'd done everything possible to try to avoid the siege. The young boy seemed fine now; his sister was calm and quite obviously the family rock. As for their mother . . . well, she had been content in her own little world, grooming and preening and generally ignoring the needs of her children.

'Don't forget to collect your toys together, kids. Make sure you have all the jigsaw pieces back in the box and the Scalextric is neatly put away, Umair.'

The children nodded and scurried around retrieving car parts and cardboard. Turning to Lily, Bert could see the debutante was dreading this particular 'coming out'. Looking at her now, he couldn't help feeling sympathy for her plight. Only once throughout their entire time in the vault had she touched on her problems, before clamming up again. They'd almost opened the security box twice, but each time she'd bottled it at the last minute, returning to her suitcase and turning her face to the wall. They were all the same, these stiff-upper-lip types. Cynthia was always telling Tracey, 'There's nothing a good cry won't fix.' Shame this girl didn't have the same relationship with her own mother.

'You all right, love?'

'Yes, thank you, Bert.'

Just for the hell of it, Bert thought he'd give it one more go.

'It's now or never, missy. Do you want what's in that box or not?'

'No, thank you.'

'Sure?'

'Positive, thank you, Bert.'

Bert shrugged, defeated. He was feeling dehydrated and had a stinking headache. A gallon of Thames Water with a whisky chaser was certainly on the cards as soon as he was out of this blasted vault. At the thought of whisky, his mind immediately turned to Roxy. He wondered how she was and how excited she would be to see him again. Bert indulged in a quick raunchy Roxy moment, picturing the ample barmaid in his favourite dressing-up outfit that he'd bought her from Ann Summers. Wondering how long he could safely leave it before making excuses to Cynthia and heading for the Dog and Duck, Bert again hoped Roxy hadn't heard his lovey-dovey talk with the wife. That would be difficult to explain away to the woman who thought he was about to leave his family for her.

As the minutes ticked down, Lily was feeling increasingly anxious. Trapped in the vault for the last four days she had begun feeling strangely safe, knowing that reality was the other side of an eighteen-inch-thick steel-reinforced door. Real life couldn't hurt her in here. She didn't want to leave. For starters, the repercussions of her foolish actions, would mean she would be in an awful lot of trouble with the police. Then there was the wrath of her grandfather, who would be appalled that she had brought such discredit to the family name. As for Giles, he would probably have already run away to Barbados by now and no doubt he would never want to speak to her ever again. Then there was her mother. The brief conversation on the phone had confused Lily. She had been sure she never wanted to see or speak to her mother again, but now . . . now she had had time to think, Lily wasn't quite so certain. She felt frightened and vulnerable and was desperate for love, comfort and reassurance. Was that a mother's love? Lily checked herself. If her mother had truly loved her, then she wouldn't have hidden secrets away in that security box. Lily began to repack her suitcase in readiness.

Outside the vault, just a hundred or so metres away Sid had just arrived at the TV live presentation point. The media were four deep in a cordoned-off press pen. Further back, barriers had been erected to prevent excited members of the public from pushing forward when the vault opened and the captives were released. Even further back, police incident tape sealed off all approach roads. Sid had been stopped at one by an over-eager PCSO who was insistent he couldn't proceed without a photo-ID press pass that proved his identity. Any confusion had been quickly smoothed over by the arrival of a Met police sergeant who had always had a crush on Sid from his days at breakfast TV. He autographed her notebook and posed for a quick camera-phone pic before heading towards the press pen.

Stopping only to shake hands and slap backs with colleagues from other channels, Sid eventually located the Europe News crew in their taped-off area of pavement. The spot had been baggsed four days earlier and, although reduced in size as other crews had arrived, was still a prime spot to witness the main event.

'Hey, chaps, how's it going? Brilliant location, top job, well done.'

Steve Stone had mixed emotions at the arrival of the main anchor. Disappointed that he wouldn't be allowed to talk over live pictures of the final release, but realistic enough to know it would go more smoothly with Sid around. He sent a quick text to Jackie to tell her he'd been big-footed. She'd immediately responded with: *All part of the learning curve. Watch and learn. ILY.* He was slightly pissed off at her response. She obviously didn't think he'd been any good after all. He was just contemplating leaving to avoid any further embarrassment when Sid Parker walked across to him.

'You, Steve Stone, are a top man. What a great job you've been doing.'

'Thanks, Sid, I really appreciate that.'

'Big favour, mate – I know you must be absolutely knackered, but can I ask you to hang around for another hour or so and we can chat over the live pictures of the release? I know it's a big ask, but if you could, I'd really appreciate it.'

'Sure thing.'

Steve was absolutely delighted at the suggestion, as was Sid, who knew with the two men doing the lion's share of the coverage from the vault, Suzanna would have little hope of being involved. Steve surreptitiously sent another text to Jackie to advise her he would be appearing after all. *Brill. I'll be watching*, had been her instant response.

Back at the studio, Suzanna tottered on to the set in the highest Louboutin heels Cheryl the floor manager had ever seen. Europe News was airing a half-hour background piece, which, apart from updating viewers on what had happened over the last four days, also allowed the studio to prepare for the big release. Cheryl buzzed Suzanna, making a fuss and checking she had everything she needed.

'Good morning, Suzanna, need any help with the microphone lead?'

Suzanna ignored the underling. Didn't the silly girl know she was 'in the zone' and shouldn't be disturbed? Turning up her earpiece to hear more clearly the director and producer in the gallery, Suzanna took her seat on the sofa. It was 8.43 a.m., technically still breakfast-style sofa presentation for the twenty-four-hour news channel. That suited Suzanna just fine, but MW had other ideas. He had wanted her to sit behind the daytime desk to offer a more hard-news impact to the coverage. Suzanna was having none of it. She'd argued that viewers would be used to a definite look at certain times of day and it shouldn't be changed whatever the reason. In reality £500 shoes and a Bruce Oldfield dress weren't being hidden behind moulded plastic furniture.

'You all set, Suzanna?'

MW was in the gallery, leaning forward to speak to his presenter through the director's microphone.

'Yes, thank you, MW.'

'We're going on air two minutes early so we can take the vault opening live at 9 a.m. Not sure what we will be able to see, but we need to mark the top of the hour properly just in case they all run out screaming "We're free, we're free."'

'Unlikely, MW.'

'Indeed so, Suzanna. Anyway, I'll leave it to Christine to explain the plan. Remember, it's a marathon, not a sprint. Pace yourself. Good luck.'

MW was about to head back to his office when he remembered why he'd come down to speak to Suzanna.

'Oh, just one other thing: what time do you need to leave for the Prince Ansar interview?'

Suzanna didn't miss a beat.

'Ah yes, I spoke to the Prince a little earlier this morning. He has suggested I call again once the siege is over and his family are safely home.'

'Excellent, well done on securing that, Suzanna. It's a total coup. Great work.'

Suzanna smiled and readjusted her lapel mic.

'Fifteen minutes until we're back on air, everyone. Are we ready to rehearse the top of the show?'

Christine was more than a little miffed that Sid had been deposed. Although their brief fling had meant nothing to him, Christine was still very protective of Sid and she would make sure he would have equal airtime from outside the vault, whatever MW might say.

'OK, Suzanna, let me brief you on what's planned. We'll start with specially commissioned opening titles and then mix through to you in the studio with a name check.'

'Will it be just my name? We aren't mentioning anyone else, are we?'

Christine rolled her eyes at the director, who did his best to stifle a snigger at his presenter's insecurity.

'As MW agreed with you, it will be just your name at the top of the show, Suzanna.'

'Good. Go on.'

'Opening titles, your name and then a big hello.'

'Then?'

'Then we'll be live at the vault as the captives are finally released. The police have moved the media well back, but we still have a prime spot.'

'Pity it's wasted on that Steve Stone. He was absolutely terrible yesterday, wasn't he?'

From her comment, it was obvious Suzanna was unaware that Sid had been dispatched to Mayfair Safety Deposits. Christine wasn't about to tell her.

'Let's see how it goes, Suzanna.'

'Yes, let's.'

Suzanna looked up at the studio clock: 8.50 a.m. Almost her time.

As the clock ticked down, Lily was cowering at the far end of the vault, her coat wrapped tightly around her. Poor kid, thought Bert. The moment had passed, she was going to be tortured for ever about what was in that security box. Hafsa and Umair were picking up the last pieces of the Scalextric and trying without success to fit them back into the box. Their mother was returning from the bathroom. Now was the time for his briefing.

'So, listen up, everyone. When the vault opens, we need to stay well away from the door, OK? It should be absolutely fine, but I'm not quite sure what's happening just the other side of it. Since we lost the phone line . . .'

Lily bowed her head and Bert moved quickly on. This wasn't the time for recriminations and anyway the kid was screwed up enough.

'. . . the police don't really know what's happening in here. They might come in a bit mob-handed. Kids, you stay behind me. Lily, you'll be the one they want to . . . hmm, talk to the most, so whatever happens offer no resistance. Princess . . .'

Bert looked towards the Princess, who was as usual showing very little interest in anything that was happening around her. He didn't bother to finish the sentence. He was totally unaware that Almira was absolutely petrified. Within an hour, Ansar's wrath would be unleashed on her.

Bert continued.

'Right kids, over here with me. Who wants a quick game of I-spy?'

Lily stayed exactly where she was at the opposite end of

the vault, her attention drawn to box 777. That was why she was here. That was why she had risked and lost everything: in order to know what was inside. The contents had the answer. It was now or never. As Bert spied with his little eye something beginning with 'V', Lily moved unnoticed towards the truth.

32

8.50 a.m.

Gold Command, Lambeth, South London

Every screen in the control room was switched to CCTV cameras monitoring the roads around the vault, or to news channels monitoring the police. Not since the London riots had there been so much interest in a rolling news story in the capital, thought Phillip Hughes-Jenkins. Striding purposefully around the control room, his confident air hid an intense concern about the outcome of the next couple of hours.

The Prime Minister had left him in no doubt that he thought the police handling of the siege was unsatisfactory. He had returned from Chequers, leaving his family at the Buckinghamshire Estate, in order to vent his fury that the drama could not have been brought to an end before now. Eventually, it had been the PM's decision not to use explosives to blow a hole in either the door or the side wall. Ever since communication with the vault had ended abruptly thanks to the rash actions of Lily Dunlop, there had been no way to warn those inside to move away from any explosion.

'So, everyone if I could have your attention, please . . .'

Hughes-Jenkins was speaking generally to the room. Although everyone knew exactly what was about to happen and what was expected of them and their teams, the Commissioner wanted to underline the importance of the next few minutes.

'The door will open very shortly. There are reports of a firearm, but the presence of children means we will not rush in mob-handed. The negotiators will speak to the kidnapper through the open vault door. Hopefully she will hand over her weapon and not resist arrest.

'We plan to take all of the captives out together and there are paramedics on standby. Remember, the boy has epilepsy and will need immediate attention.

'The press are penned about a hundred metres away, though of course they have cameras focused on the vault from elsewhere, including the hotel across the road. We have increased the cordon accordingly.

'Any questions, or is everyone happy?'

Roxy Costello wasn't sure where she was. She'd spent the night driving around central London aimlessly, struggling to come to terms with her confrontation with Cynthia Jones.

All the promises he'd made in the height of sexual passion, all the guarantees as she'd brought him to the very edge of satisfaction with her flexible tongue and deft fingers were all just lies. They had been planning to be together forever. No more lonely days and even lonelier nights wondering if she'd ever find true love. After three failed, childless marriages, this time it was the real thing. And now Roxy had found herself once again alone. Her parents were both long since dead and her judgemental siblings wanted nothing to do with her, contemptuous of her marry-go-round. Four years ago, after the collapse of her most recent marriage, she had moved to

London from her native Sunderland. She'd rented a flat above a launderette in Bethnal Green, and after jobs as a cleaner and supermarket checkout operator finally found work she enjoyed as a barmaid. At least in the pub she was surrounded by people who wanted to chat, especially when her ample cleavage was on show. She had happily conformed to the expected dress code and lapped up the sexual innuendo from delighted customers. Roxy felt wanted and revelled in being the centre of attention.

Bert, though, had been different from the rest. He was a regular at the Dog and Duck, but apart from the occasional game of darts, he kept himself to himself. His usual routine had involved a pint of London Pride at the bar, maybe two on a Friday, then home. Gradually, they had begun chatting and Bert had easily convinced Roxy his marriage was an unhappy one. She'd heard it all before, of course, but she believed it from Bert. Over the next few months he began to come into the bar more regularly and stay for longer, lamenting his unhappy home life. Last Christmas when Cynthia had taken the children up to her parents and Bert had been left home alone, Roxy had offered to make him something to eat.

'No one should be alone at Christmas,' had been her innocent offer, unaware that Bert had purposefully dispatched his family in the hope of a little festive cheer with a raunchy barmaid. He had arrived at the door of her tiny flat laden with gifts, champagne, chocolates, a silver bracelet from TK Maxx and a beautifully packaged box with a large golden bow on top.

They'd eaten lasagne and drunk far too much wine before Bert finally agreed she could open the box.

'What's inside?'

'Have a look and see,' slurred Bert playfully, struggling to control his desire.

Excited, Roxy ripped open the wrapping to reveal a Superwoman costume from Ann Summers.

'That's what I think you are, Superwoman.'

Roxy had been delighted by the reference and had rushed to the bathroom to change. By the time she'd returned, Bert was already in his Santa boxers emblazoned with *I only visit naughty girls* on the crotch. Roxy had laughed all the way to the bedroom.

Over the last year, their relationship had blossomed and Bert had promised he would leave his family to be with her. Roxy couldn't have been happier. Finally, after three failed attempts, she had found the man of her dreams. They were meant to be together. It was fate. Even when she'd heard the lovey-dovey talk with Cynthia on Europe News, Roxy still believed Bert was her destiny. He had to talk like that to her, of course he did, but he didn't mean it, obviously not. Only after she'd been to the house, seen the way the family lived, realized they were still very much a unit, did Roxy know that Bert's promises had all been lies. Once more her world was being ripped apart because of a man.

Well, she wasn't prepared to take it anymore.

'Excuse me, madam, you can't park here.'

Roxy was startled by a tap at the window. A young police officer was attempting to attract her attention.

'Sorry?'

Signalling for Roxy to roll down the window, the officer continued.

'I'm afraid you can't park here, madam. You'll have to move on.'

'Why not?' Roxy was in no mood for surly officialdom.

'This area is cordoned off. The security vault is literally about to open and we must clear the whole area so the ambulances can get through. No one can be here. I'm afraid you'll have to move on.'

Through her tears, Roxy stared past the officer to the police tape beyond. She had driven around until dawn and eventually stopped, not knowing where she was. Her car was less than one hundred metres from the entrance to Mayfair Safety Deposits. Bert was almost within reach. Whatever the officer said, Roxy had no intention of going anywhere.

33

8.55 a.m.

Mayfair

Catherine stared out of the window of her gilded cage at the Mandarin Oriental Hotel. She was once again alone, imprisoned. That frightful guard had gone away, but warned, threatened, that he'd be back.

From her lofty position she could almost see the vault where her only child had spent the last four days frightened and alone. Her guilt knew no bounds. Why hadn't she realised something was wrong when her daughter was taken ill with appalling flu symptoms soon after the accident? She'd dismissed it as a reaction to hotel air-conditioning. If she'd acted then, none of this would have happened. Why, when she knew what her husband had died of, had she tried to hide the evidence? When Joseph first fell ill, she didn't think, didn't realize the implications. Sitting by his bedside as he fought to the death the illness that could also threaten her daughter's life, she still didn't understand. The signs were all there, if only she had wanted to know, but she had chosen to turn her face away. So far as the rest of the world was concerned, he had died of colon cancer, a terrible disease that they could have done nothing to prevent. It was a tragedy.

The doctors felt differently. When they had signed the death certificate, she refused to look at it or accept their diagnosis. For months she had rejected any suggestion that his death could have been due to a different cause.

Catherine still remembered exactly where she was when she had finally plucked up the courage to face the facts in black and white. She vividly recalled sitting in her favourite spot by her bedroom window at Upton Park, staring out across the rolling fields and to the horizon beyond. The grounds had looked so beautiful; Joseph would have been delighted at the fruits of his labour. His death certificate lay on her lap, folded in three and tucked inside an anonymous white envelope. Slowly removing it and placing the envelope on a side table, Catherine had sat for most of the afternoon afraid to look, the certificate taunting her, daring her to read it.

Joseph had died six months earlier and, though their final years had been unhappy, Catherine still missed the love they'd once had. When she'd learned of Joseph's cancer, Catherine had done everything to try to save him. The best medical assistance money could buy, coupled with love and support she hadn't realised she still had for him. When finally there was no hope, they had embarked on a last cruise aboard the *Queen Elizabeth*, a trip they had always promised each other but had never seemed to find the time for before. As they arrived at Southampton, Joseph had been captivated by the majestic vessel with its black-and-red Cunard Livery. Catherine recalled how he had regaled her with memories of visiting Tilbury Docks with his father when he was a child.

The first thing to catch her eye as they boarded the boat was a frieze depicting the bow of the original *Queen*

Elizabeth. It had been designed by Viscount Linley and completely dominated the three-storey Grand Lobby. Joseph, though frail, was mesmerised. During a month-long cruise of the Caribbean they were relaxed and cosseted in one of the grandest state rooms onboard. It had been an elegant last hurrah.

Returning to England, the couple had kept the secret of his illness even from closest friends. Joseph, always a private man, had not wanted any fuss and it was left to Catherine to be his constant companion. They became inseparable, with Joseph increasingly reliant on his wife's presence. As his illness bowed him, Joseph was plagued with nightmares and feelings of terror. Doctors advised Catherine to be open with her husband and not be frightened by the inevitability of his death. As Joseph became more and more frail there had been discussions about him moving to a hospice to make his last days comfortable and pain-free, but the cancer was in an obscene hurry to claim its victim. At the end, and with Catherine by his side, Joseph found courage, dignity and peace. Emotions that had often evaded him while he was alive.

When it was over, Lily had grieved for her daddy, but death to a teenager was a remote event so many years off and she had seemed to recover relatively quickly from her loss. However, within a few weeks, Lily had begun complaining of tiredness. Catherine put it down to delayed grief. Preparations for university life were no doubt also weighing on the youngster's mind. Lily had studied hard at school and, with excellent A-level grades, had gained a place reading politics at the London School of Economics. She should have been on cloud nine, at the coveted place but instead she seemed listless and exhausted. Her mother feared glandular fever and was keen for her to see a doctor, but Lily was reluctant. 'I've been around too many doctors over the last few months of Daddy's illness' had always been her stock response.

Catherine accepted her daughter's resistance and when Lily left for university she retreated into her own bereavement. Her grief was plagued by a recurring nightmare in which she was sitting in an anteroom at a hospital, a handsome young doctor holding her shaking hands, tears streaming down her face. Her daughter was lying motionless in a hospital bed in the next room. Catherine was aware that the doctor was talking to her, comforting, advising her, a piece of paper in his hand, but try as she might she couldn't hear what he was saying. It had woken her many times over the months.

Eventually, Catherine realised what the nightmare meant. She finally had to face the truth. So here she was, sitting in her favourite spot, her husband's death certificate was folded on her knee. It was the same piece of paper that was always in her dream. Garnering all her emotional strength, Catherine unfolded the paper. Still she couldn't look at the typed letters on the formal document. As night fell, she decided to return the document to the envelope and burn it. That's what she would do: destroy the lie. But she couldn't. She knew that, unless she looked, confronted her fear, the nightmare would recur, for years, perhaps for ever.

Catherine closed her eyes and bent her head forwards. Opening them again, she scanned the document. There it was in black and white. Joseph Anthony Roderick Dunlop had indeed died of colon cancer resulting from his body's inability to fight HIV/AIDS.

Catherine felt no emotion. She refolded the paper and placed it back inside the envelope before putting it into a desk drawer. She looked out of the window towards the parterre and began to make sense of her nightmare. When the young doctor had sat her down in a quiet room and tried to tell her that Joseph had died from HIV/AIDS, she'd refused to listen. Warnings that she needed to be tested for the HIV virus fell on deaf ears. Catherine had tried to erase any reference to the illness from her mind. It still carried such a stigma in polite society. Her father, both her parents, would be shocked and appalled that her husband, their son-in-law, had contracted a killer disease from a black woman in Africa. The very idea was too abhorrent to contemplate, and so Catherine had pushed it to the back of her mind. But her subconscious would not let it lie and now she faced the truth.

In the days after reading the death certificate, Catherine had sought medical help. Doctors, concerned she could have been infected by her husband, insisted on tests. She'd been embarrassed by her attendance at the sexual health clinic, but the HIV clinical nurse specialist had reassured her that there was no humiliation in caring for her health. Her finger had been pricked and a blood sample taken. The fifteen-minute wait for the result had seemed interminable, despite the presence of a counsellor who offered comfort and support throughout. She could still remember the specialist's smiling face as he confirmed she was HIV negative. That had been the end of the matter. Nothing more to worry about. But still the nightmares had continued and eventually, agonisingly, Catherine realised why.

The accident.

Was Joseph infected before the car accident in Africa? If so, that would mean he would have been HIV positive before the transfusion. Had he known all along? The doctors had given Catherine a clean bill of health, but they had known nothing of Lily's transfusion.

At the beginning of the year, she'd returned to confide in Dr Henry. He was immediately concerned about Lily. He'd asked and then insisted that Catherine bring Lily to see him and undergo the same tests. Catherine had left the clinic focused and determined to help her child, but her resolve had weakened on the journey home from Harley Street. By the time the car turned into the gates of Upton Park, Catherine had once again refused to accept that her daughter might be at risk. The blood transfusion had been more than two years ago, there was no chance she could be infected. If she had been, there would have been signs before now. No, the cause of Joseph's death could not harm her daughter. It was her secret and it would remain that way. It was simply nothing that Lily needed to be concerned about.

Catherine wanted Lily to remember her father as the strong loving man that had cared for her all her life. Again she resolved to burn the incriminating certificate. It was only after confiding in the one person she could trust in the whole world, Brian the butler, that she had decided against. She told him about Joseph's illness and the potential threat to Lily, along with the presence of the death certificate. He had been concerned for Lily's health, but had offered to deposit the document in the Mayfair vault where Lily would never see it.

Catherine shook her head at the memory. She should have burned it when she had the opportunity. Straining to see past Hyde Park, she tried to look over towards the vault. After eight long months she finally knew where her daughter was. What she didn't know was whether Lily was HIV positive. If Lily did see the certificate, would it matter? Lily would know how her father died of an AIDS-related illness and that her mother had tried to cover it up. But so what? There was still hope for their relationship. Lily would be fine.

Catherine reached for the TV remote control to watch her daughter be released from the vault.

34

08:57:30

Europe News

The gallery clock showed thirty seconds to the start of the show. Everyone was ready. The director checked the outside broadcast sources, the sound recordist checked Suzanna's microphone, and the director's assistant checked the clock and began to count the programme to air.

'Ten, nine, eight, seven, six . . .'

'Here we go, Suzanna,' whispered Christine. 'Good luck.'

'. . . five, four, three, two, one.'

'Roll titles,' instructed the director.

As the specially commissioned opening titles were put live to air, Suzanna sat a little straighter on her sofa. She felt strangely nervous but, as always, in control. As the director cut to her close-up camera, Suzanna offered a warm, reassuring smile to her audience.

'Good morning, everyone. Welcome to Europe News and live coverage of the end of the siege that has dominated our coverage throughout the Christmas period. Finally, it's that time. The vault at Mayfair Safety Deposits is about to open. Let's take a look at the scene.'

Outside the vault, Sid stepped away from the camera to offer a live shot of the scene without him in it. He could hear the programme output and Suzanna in his earpiece. She was calm and considered with just a hint of urgency in her voice. Sid had to accept she was a first-class presenter, if only she wasn't such a bitch.

All around him the tension was tangible as reporters and film crews communicated with their studios and the wider audience beyond. Photographers had also arrived in their droves with metal step ladders which they scurried up, hoping for a view above the TV cameras. Everyone wanted the money shot of vault villain, Lily Dunlop. Until then there would be graphics, interviews and illustrations to seduce the viewer.

Back in the studio, Suzanna was already playing with an electronic illustrator, highlighting relevant places on a map of the area.

'As you can see from this map, the vault is in a built-up area. The police are positioned here, our camera positions are here and here, and the ambulances are here.'

Suzanna used a stylus to draw circles in various colours to differentiate between the media and the emergency services. She was calm and confident and not yet aware that, rather than sitting at home watching how clever she was, Sid was at the vault and about to appear on air. He ran through his choreographed plan with his crew.

'Right, chaps; I'll start off with a sit-rep and then introduce Steve, who can talk us through what the police might be doing. Is that cool?'

The cameraman nodded his camera in acknowledgement and was immediately chastised down his earpiece by the director back at the studio.

'We're live on your pictures, Neil. Hold it steady, buddy.'

Neil dropped his head in embarrassment. He was one of Europe News's best operators, but tension was mounting outside the vault and he'd lost focus for a moment. It wouldn't happen again.

Sid, who had also heard the director down his own earpiece, pulled a face in acknowledgement and mouthed 'Sorry, my fault,' to the mortified camera operator. Sid looked around him. There was literally no room to move. Banks of TV crews from all around the world were squeezed into an area not much bigger than his sitting room. Behind them were photographers balanced precariously on ladders and further back still a curious public keen to have the first glimpse of the kidnap heiress.

'Top spot here, Steve. I know you've been freezing your nuts off for the last few days, but you've done a great job, mate. Ready to go on air?'

Steve Stone accepted the praise but any potential smugness was immediately replaced by sweaty palms and palpitations at the thought of being on camera again. He knew, despite what Jackie had said, that he had been crap on his own. Now he was anxious about how his being interviewed by Sid might appear on TV. Suzanna was coming to the end of her explainer and soon it would be time.

Watching Suzanna Thomas on Europe News in her kitchen across town, Cynthia Jones was still reeling after the visit from that barmaid strumpet. She didn't believe a word of what the little minx had said, but she was nevertheless unnerved by the ferocity of the woman's tone. Bert was a loving family man and any woman would be delighted to have such a doting husband by their side. Roxy whatsername had no doubt set her sights on Bert down at the pub and was obviously jealous and revengeful when he'd said no. Boiling the kettle, Cynthia checked her mobile. She wasn't due back at the school where she worked for another fortnight, but her phone hadn't stopped ringing since news broke of Bert's fate. Calls and texts from family and friends had been punctuated by messages from journalists. She had no idea how they'd tracked down her number, but she certainly had no interest in speaking to any of them.

Making her tea, Cynthia peeked out of her kitchen window. There were still hordes of photographers outside. The police had asked if she wanted to be moved to a more discreet location while the vault was opened, but she was not prepared to be hounded out of her home by either reporters or strumpet barmaids. What she really wanted was to be at the vault, but her police liaison officer had advised against it, telling her that she would be mobbed by the media. There'd be no opportunity for her to speak to Bert anyway until he had been whisked from the scene. So she had decided to stay at home. Walking back into the living room, where the curtains had remained closed in an attempt to provide some privacy over the last few days, Cynthia sat down in her favourite chair and turned up the volume on the TV.

'You OK, Mum?'

It was Tracey. She walked across and sat on the arm of her mother's chair.

'Fine, love – are you?'

'Yes, Mum. It's nearly over. Dad will be home by lunchtime.'

'I know, love. I've thawed out some fillet steak and there's some oven chips in the freezer ready for his lunch. I bet he'll be famished. Where's our Harry?'

'On his PlayStation.'

'Go and get him, will you, love, there's a good girl. We'll all watch together, shall we?'

Tracey squeezed her mother's hand and bounded out of the room to call her brother. Cynthia leaned over the side

331

of the armchair and stroked Rob the dog, who lay obediently by her side.

'Soon now, boy. He'll be home soon.'

Rob looked up at his mistress, thinking whatever dogs think.

Across town Prince Ansar was surrounded by his entourage, including Dmitri.

'Bring Mrs Dunlop to me.'

Catherine was escorted into the room a broken woman. The guard's mind games had forced desperate memories she'd tried to bury flooding back to the surface, but still she had refused to discuss her daughter's medical condition with a stranger. Being in Prince Ansar's presence incensed her.

'I really must object in the strongest possible terms at being held here against my will.'

'Mrs Dunlop, I am surprised at your tone. Surely you would prefer to take a seat next to me and watch your daughter's safe release? But if you wish to return to your room, that is up to you.'

Catherine knew that was an offer she would not be able to refuse and took the seat next to him.

'Not long to wait now until we are both reunited with our children.'

'Then I can leave?'

Catherine was desperate to run barefoot all the way across Hyde Park to the vault to be reunited with her child. Whatever had happened in the past, they would be able to work it out together. It was not too late to make amends.

'Of course, of course. All I ask is that you stay for a short while longer after the vault has been opened and until your daughter comes to my home to enjoy a little of my hospitality.'

'How ridiculous! Why would she do that? What do you want with her?'

Prince Ansar ignored the questions and continued to stare at the television.

'Look, Mrs Dunlop, look at the countdown clock at the top of the screen. The doors are about to open, finally, finally. I wonder how my children are after being kept against their will for four very long days by the actions of your selfish daughter.'

Catherine was about to respond when the Prince raised his arm, keen to listen to Suzanna Thomas.

'Shhh, Mrs Dunlop, Suzanna is speaking. Please do not interrupt her.'

In the studio, Suzanna was just easing up a gear, capitalising on the mounting tension.

'OK, Suzanna, throw to the vault, please,' instructed Christine.

Suzanna ignored her. She wasn't about to allow that useless Steve Stone to screw up the big moment.

'If you're just tuning in, the safe door at Mayfair Safety Deposits is about to open. Trapped inside for the last four days are an Arab princess and her two children, the vault guard, and a young British woman by the name of Lily Dunlop, who will have some serious questions to answer from the police. Though Scotland Yard has said little, it's thought she was responsible for all five people being trapped over the Christmas period. You may have heard Lily Dunlop and the guard, Bert Jones, being interviewed on Europe News over the last few days . . .'

'Throw to the outside broadcast, Suzanna.'

Christine wanted Sid on screen. Suzanna was waffling and the action was at the vault, not recapping on what had happened in the past.

'If not, let me just remind you what was said . . .'

Realising that Suzanna was planning to ad lib over the

pictures from the vault herself and was playing for time until the director cut up the pictures of those freed, Christine was furious.

'OB *now*, Suzanna. Do it, please.'

Still Suzanna ignored the instruction.

'Well, it began when one of my colleagues was able to speak to . . .'

'Throw to the vault, Suzanna, right now.'

This time it was the unmistakable voice of MW, and from his tone Suzanna knew that she had lost the battle, for the time being at least.

'First, however, I just want to bring you the latest from the scene and our crime correspondent, Steve Stone.'

'No, Suzanna – it's Sid.'

Viewers were saved from the fury in Suzanna's eyes by the director cutting to live pictures from the scene, but her anger was plain to everyone in the gallery.

'Fade out her microphone,' ordered MW.

Leaning forward again to speak through the director's microphone, he said, 'Suzanna, quick chat outside the studio, now please.'

As a livid Suzanna stalked from the set, Sid, who was unaware but could have guessed at the tension back at the studio, moved effortlessly into commentary mode, starting with a show and tell.

'Thanks, Suzanna. There is now less than thirty seconds to go until the Mayfair Five, who have been holed up with little food and water throughout the Christmas period, are released. We're not sure how quickly we will see them once the vault door is opened, but let me give you an idea of what we can see at the moment.'

While the camera panned around as previously choreographed with Neil, Sid began to describe the scene in Mayfair, the presence of the ambulance crews, police marksmen, and other officers in public-order uniform at the cordons.

'We're not sure of the condition of those inside the vault. You may remember, the young boy, Umair, was taken ill during his time inside. He suffers from epilepsy and I'm told medics will be keen to check him over just as soon as they can.

'With me is Steve Stone, our crime correspondent, who first broke the story on Christmas Eve. Steve, what do we know about what's been happening inside the vault, and what plans the police have when the door does open?'

Once again, Steve felt like a rabbit in the headlights, but somehow looking at Sid rather than down the barrel of the camera seemed to make talking live on TV a little easier. He began stiltedly but soon fell into his stride.

'Well, initially we had a pretty good idea of what was happening inside because of the open phone line. However, once the line was disconnected, communication was impossible. Up until then we believe from police negotiators that the atmosphere inside the vault was relatively calm. The children had passed their time playing with Christmas toys. Their mother, however, seems to have been deeply traumatised by events and has struggled to cope. Bert Jones, the security guard, has been pretty relaxed throughout, regularly checking on the others and rationing water from the cooler to make sure everyone has a share.

'The girl, Lily Dunlop, had done little more than sit on her suitcase. She did appear to be unwell and Bert Jones had been trying to comfort her. Before the line was disconnected, we learned that Lily Dunlop was trying to retrieve something from a security box belonging to her family.'

Looking at his watch, Sid gestured a wind-up signal to the reporter and picked up the commentary.

'Thanks, Steve. Well, with the time now at exactly 9 a.m.,

you're watching Europe News and continuing live coverage of the Mayfair Safety Deposit siege. The drama has unfolded over the last four days and the police will be about to enter the vault. Within a few moments the Mayfair Five will be released from a vault that has been their jail cell for four long days and nights. The reason, still unclear, but if Lily Dunlop's action centred around a secret in her family's safety deposit box she must know the answer by now.'

Listening intently, Catherine let out a loud gasp.

'What is it that she wants, Mrs Dunlop?'

Ignoring the Prince's question, Catherine continued to focus on the Europe News coverage.

'We're waiting to hear what's happening,' said Sid, 'but as you can see from the pictures we're bringing to you live, there is still no visible activity at Mayfair Safety Deposits. What will the police be most concerned about, Steve?'

Steve was relaxing into his commentary role and picked up smoothly.

'The main concern for the police now is the gun.'

'Of course,' interjected Sid, 'the gun. Tell us more.'

'Well, as you know, Sid, the gun was thought to have been used by Lily Dunlop to threaten the security guard when she first arrived at the vault. However, with the line disconnected, the police have no way of knowing what is happening inside, making their actions even more challenging. Does the guard still have the weapon? Has Lily Dunlop managed to reclaim it? Very real concerns for officers as they try to bring this siege to a successful conclusion.'

'How on earth did she manage to get the gun into the vault without it being detected, Steve. Do we know?'

'Good question, Sid. Police are presently working on the theory that the airport-style metal detectors at the entrance of

336

the vault were not working. Anyway, as I said, officers are unsure of the whereabouts of the gun, so even though the door will be open about now they will be cautious about entering with a potential live firearm in play.'

Prince Ansar turned again to Catherine.

'Please be assured, Mrs Dunlop, that if your daughter's continuing actions further delay the safe release of my children, the consequences will be severe.'

Sid checked his watch and picked up from Steve.

'Thanks, Steve. It's been a long four days for those inside, but their ordeal is about to come to an end. By my watch, the door is now open.

'As Steve was saying, the police are reluctant to rush into the vault. Although Lily Dunlop seemed shocked and confused when she spoke to us live on Europe News from inside the vault, remember this is potentially still a hostage situation.

'If she hands over the gun without any further resistance, then we believe all five people will be brought out simultaneously. As you can see, there are five ambulances on standby to take them to St Thomas's Hospital where they will be treated for dehydration and shock. We are not sure what charges will be brought against Lily Dunlop, but we would expect at least kidnap and false imprisonment . . .'

'Quite fucking obviously, Einstein,' Suzanna mouthed, furious. Any chastisement, quickly followed by attempts at appeasement by MW, had been useless. He'd brought her out of the studio to save her from herself and, judging by her present behaviour, it had been completely the right decision. Returning to the set, MW at her side, she'd been forced to watch Sid on a monitor as he hosted the coverage from the scene.

'Why did you fucking send that fucking wanker?'

337

'Suzanna, we are in a live studio, the director may cut back to you at any moment. Temper your language accordingly, please, or we'll need to step outside again. You wanted to do the studio presentation; you can't do everything. This story will run for days yet. The studio presentation is yours. Relax, sit down, enjoy the show for now.'

'I should be doing everything, all of it. It's a fucking disgrace.'

'Don't push it, Suzanna, OK.'

MW left Suzanna in the studio and returned to the gallery.

Inside the vault, Bert had grouped everyone together. While he knew that Lily should have been made to move away and stand alone so she could be easily overpowered, he couldn't bring himself to insist. Despite everything he had grown fond of her. Now he was anxious what might happen to her when the police moved in.

Gathered tightly together with Bert, slightly ahead of the arrow-shaped group, they waited. The Princess began to sob quietly and then with much more volume. Hafsa comforted her mother and held firmly on to the hand of her brother, who in turn clutched his panda. Lily stared straight ahead towards the door.

'Remember, everybody, stay calm. We're nearly there, it's almost over, we'll be home soon. There may be some shouting and some rushing around, policemen with big helmets on, but don't be frightened. I'm in front of you and I won't let them hurt you.'

On the other side of the door, a dozen officers in protective gear with body shields were also waiting. Ahead of them stood a negotiator with direct communication to the head of Gold Command.

On Wednesday, 28 December at 9.03 a.m., 180 eternal seconds late, the massive bolts slid open.

35

9.04 a.m.

Outside Mayfair Safety Deposits

Roxy had been shocked by the young officer tapping on her window and was finding it difficult to focus. She hadn't slept all night and her mascara-smudged face was testament to the tears she'd shed. Parking up her car in the early hours, she'd somehow found herself in a side street between the press and public cordon. Completely disorientated and unsure which direction to choose, she had decided to leave her vehicle and walk towards where the press was gathered. It was a massive throng of madness, hundreds of journalists who all seemed to be talking at once. Some were raising their voices above the mêlée to try to make themselves heard, which resulted in their neighbours simply doing the same.

As she mingled among them, no one seemed to take much notice of her. Roxy found it difficult to see past the bank of cameras and bobbed up and down a little to try to catch a glimpse of her lover, her man, who had in reality always been someone else's. Roxy had embarrassed herself beyond measure with Cynthia. Photographs of her snarling and crying, rushing away from Bert's house would probably be in this morning's newspapers. She would never be able to hold her head up in the Dog and Duck again. Roxy knew she would have no option but to pack up her things and move on in search of another location, another job, another set of false promises.

Straining on to her tiptoes, she could see very little except the rakishly handsome chap from Europe News. The one who used to be on *Have a Nice Day UK*. Roxy struggled to remember his name. He was interviewing someone while standing in front of a camera, but she couldn't hear what they were saying.

As Sid listened to Steve Stone advising viewers about what police would be doing just outside the door of the vault right now, he scanned the sea of faces packed in around him. Seldom had he been involved in such a big rolling news story. Looking towards the back of the group he noticed an inappropriately dressed woman with a tear-stained face and an ample chest. His journalistic sixth sense immediately kicked in. As Steve continued, Sid silently beckoned the producer and whispered in her ear.

'That woman at the back, find out who she is.'

Steve, instantly distracted by Sid's lack of eye contact, stopped speaking. The accomplished presenter didn't miss a beat.

'How will they move them from the vault to the hospital: together or separately? What's your best guess, Steve?'

With that, the crime reporter was off again and Sid half glanced across to where his producer was speaking to the clearly distressed woman. Even if she was involved in some way with the story, was she in a fit state to be put on TV?

That would be for his producer to decide. Steve continued describing to viewers how he expected police to move as quickly as possible to remove all those in the vault. The mother and her children would probably be kept together, the guard and Lily Dunlop separate.

As Steve reached the end of his point Sid sneaked another glance across to where his producer was. If other news organisations knew this woman might have something to do with the story they would try to snatch an interview with her before Europe News could put her on air. He offered a surreptitious *thumbs up, thumbs down*? The question was met with a nod from his producer and the two women slowly made their way through the throng towards Sid.

'Thanks, Steve. With the time at just after 9.05 a.m. we can assume that the vault door has now opened. As we await the next move by the police, let's speak to a woman who is quite clearly anxious about the outcome.'

As Roxy was moved in front of the camera, Sid was handed a scribbled piece of paper with her name on it.

'This is Roxy Costello. Hello, Roxy, we can see you are clearly distressed. Do you know anyone inside?'

Roxy nodded but struggled to speak.

'Please take your time, Roxy. Just tell us who it is that you know and why you are so upset?'

Roxy could feel the police tape separating the press from the scene fluttering against her hand. She clung on to it and looked up into Sid's eyes.

Watching at home, Cynthia gripped the handle of her tea mug and held on to her daughter's hand. It was the vile woman who had been ranting in her hallway last night. What was she about to do now?

'I love him, but it's the end of my dream. The end of everything. I don't know what more I can say.'

Other TV crews, alerted by Roxy's sobs, began to train

341

their cameras on her. Yet another angle to this never-ending story.

Less than a hundred metres away, Bert's heart was racing faster than his doctor would have thought good for an over-weight middle-aged man. The door had opened, but nothing had happened. No shouting, no rushing in, nothing.

'Hello?' he shouted tentatively, the rest of the group cowering behind him.

Nothing.

'Hello, anyone out there?'

The others huddled even closer together. Bert was about to speak again when a disembodied voice spoke first.

'Hello, my name is Susan Thorpe. Are you all safe?'

'Yes, we are.'

'Are you all standing altogether?'

'Yes, we are.'

'Where is the firearm?'

Bert had completely forgotten about the gun. It had been forever ago since it was waved at him by Lily. She had seemed so intimidating then; now she was just a frightened young woman with a shedload of emotional baggage.

'It's in my desk drawer.'

'Are you standing near the desk?'

'No.'

'OK, Bert, we would like you to come out one at a time. The children first.'

The youngsters immediately clung tighter to their mother and Lily grabbed on to Bert's arm.

'The children would prefer to come out with their mother, and I will come out with Miss Dunlop.'

Bert squeezed Lily's arm. There was plenty of aggro coming down the track for her; the least he could do was walk the few yards to the handcuffs with her.

342

'Is that OK?'

Bert heard nothing for a few moments, during which time the negotiator – Susan, did she say her name was? – was clearly discussing tactics. He waited winking at Lily and blowing raspberries at the children.

'Bert, we would ask that you and Miss Dunlop come out first.'

Bert looked at the group. That seemed sensible: keep the children safely out of the way until Lily had been arrested and was frogmarched to jail, do not pass Go, do not collect Daddy's fortune.

'OK, OK we're coming now, but please be aware that Lily is unwell. I can support her, but can we have medical assistance?'

'There are ambulances and paramedics waiting, when you are ready.'

Bert took Lily's arm and helped steady her wobbling limbs. Lily's head was spinning. She felt sick and confused. She grabbed tightly on to Bert's hand until he thought she would stop the blood flow.

'OK, love, few deep breaths. I'm here, all will be fine. It's all over now. You'll be right as rain soon. Ready?'

Lily felt anything but ready, but nodded and began a few faltering steps. She was sure she was about to faint and leaned heavily on to Bert's shoulder as he wrapped a protective arm around her. Poor cow. As they moved closer towards the door, the children were reluctant to stay behind and rushed to Bert's side.

'Don't leave us here, Bert. Come on, Mummy, let's go. Bert will look after us.'

Bert stopped and the door opened a little further.

'Are you sure about the firearm, Bert?' said Susan Thorpe in as measured a tone as she could muster while shouting through the door towards the group.

'Yes, but the children are terrified, as are the two women. Please be aware that we are all coming out together.'

More silence as Susan Thorpe waited for guidance from Gold Command.

'OK, Bert that's fine,' shouted Susan Thorpe. 'Take it slowly, no sudden moves.'

With women and children hanging from every limb, Bert almost laughed out loud at the instruction. He was finding it hard to walk, let alone move suddenly.

'Slowly does it, everybody. Where's your panda, Umair? Oh, there it is. Hold on to your sister's hand and be a good boy.'

As the group eventually reached the open door and moved tentatively outside until they were just a few steps from the exit on to the street, they were instantly surrounded by police.

Through the glass door, Sid had seen the police move into position and could just make out the Mayfair Five. He interrupted Roxy immediately.

'The siege is over. The siege is over. The group are moving towards the street exit surrounded by police officers. There they are, we can see them clearly for the first time as they move out on to the street. They're moving slowly as a group, a close-knit unit. The guard, Bert Jones, is in the centre; he appears to be supporting Lily Dunlop, his arm around her. The children are holding hands and their mother is sobbing. It appears the police are allowing them to walk to the waiting ambulances together as a group.'

As Sid commentated, Roxy looked past the presenter and towards the vault. There was Bert, she could see him. The man who had been her life, her reason for being over the last year, there he was, standing in the street bold as brass with his arm around another woman. She could bear it no longer. With all eyes on the Mayfair Five, Roxy ripped through

344

the *Police Line Do Not Cross* tape and, with more speed than her frame might suggest was possible, charged in Bert's direction, screaming with fury.

Hearing Roxy's voice, Bert looked up to see the barmaid hurtling towards him. She reached him a moment before she could be stopped by officers, her eyes wild, her determination for revenge overwhelming. Roxy felt the kitchen knife in her hand, the one she always kept in her coat pocket for protection during the journey home from the pub. Screaming, she plunged it deep into Bert's chest.

'You bastard, you lying cheating bastard. I hate you, I hate you.'

Lily cried out, scratching at Roxy's face to try to stop the attack as police moved in to restrain the barmaid.

'Back inside,' shouted the officer in command. The sobbing children were snatched from Bert's weakened grasp, as was their mother. Lily was frogmarched back inside the entrance to the vault as Roxy was shoved against the glass frontage. Bert's limp body slumped to the floor. Blood spurted from an arterial wound. He needed urgent medical attention, but with the situation not yet under control, paramedics stayed back, leaving one of the police officers to administer emergency first aid to try to stop the bleeding.

Sid remained calm and with measured tones described to viewers at home what he could see and hear.

'Roxy Costello, who we were speaking to just a few moments ago, appears to have had some sort of grudge against the guard. It would appear she had a sharp implement, perhaps a knife, in her coat pocket and the guard is now on the floor. From our position, which is approximately eighty to one hundred metres away, it looks as though he's receiving emergency first aid for a serious wound to his chest. Police are now restraining Roxy Costello and, as you can see, paramedics are standing by to attend to Bert Jones. Other members of the group have temporarily sought refuge in the doorway of the vault while police bring the situation under control.'

Sid was about to continue when a loud scream stopped him. There was confusion everywhere. Bert was bleeding on the pavement, a wild woman was being restrained by police, and now it was the Princess who was screaming. Everyone looked frantically around for the reason. It was Umair: the youngster was suffering another epileptic fit. Hafsa was holding tightly on to her little brother's hands, controlled panic in her eyes. With agreement from the police, paramedics dashed towards the child. He was lying on the ground just a couple of metres away from where Bert was already being treated.

'Don't worry, everything will be OK,' Hafsa tried to reassure her little brother as her mother carried on screaming at the top of her voice, any last vestige of self-control now gone.

Roxy, who had been slammed up against the glass frontage of the vault, had handcuffs slapped on to her wrists and was immediately bundled into a police van. Lily, who was completely unable to grasp what was happening, stood trembling at the sight of Bert badly injured and lying motionless on the ground. Blood pumping from an arterial wound in the guard's chest spattered over her shocked face. She tried to wipe clear her eyes as strong arms swept her to one of the waiting ambulances which immediately whisked her away.

As medics took control of Bert and Umair's treatment, a hysterical Princess Almira and concerned Hafsa were quickly escorted into a second ambulance. Blue lights flashing, it sped past the press pen at speed, the Princess's screams from inside the ambulance still clearly audible above the siren.

Sid, who had said nothing during the last two minutes, allowed the drama to play out without interruption. The cameras that had followed the police van and ambulances now panned back to the scene. Bert and Umair both lay motionless on the floor outside the vault. Neil the cameraman was right at the end of his lens's capability. He needed to keep the camera incredibly still, and with mayhem around him that was a challenge. Sid stood to one side of the camera, remaining silent, watching the medics do their work.

'We'll come off it if either dies,' was the most Christine said in his ear.

After several more minutes of treatment it was clear both were still alive but very poorly and the decision was taken to move them. Bert and Umair were quickly gurneyed into two more waiting ambulances and rushed past the press pen under armed escort to St Thomas's Hospital. Neil lingered on the image of the ambulances departing from the scene. A few moments later, Sid calmly stepped back in front of the camera and began to speak.

'So, the vault is finally open. The Mayfair Five have been released. Lily Dunlop has been taken away by ambulance. Bert Jones has been stabbed in the chest and needed emergency first aid on the pavement here at the scene. A woman has been arrested. Prince Umair of Aj-al-Shar has again been taken ill, perhaps another epileptic fit. He, too, required urgent medical assistance and has been whisked away under armed police escort to hospital. His condition unknown.

'We'll be right back after this break.'

Prince Ansar looked towards Catherine, who was sitting aghast.

'Be in no doubt, Mrs Dunlop, I will hold your daughter totally responsible for whatever happens to my child.'

347

Thursday

36

8 a.m.

Europe News

'It's now twenty-four hours since the siege ended and what a dramatic conclusion to a desperately challenging four days. Let's get the latest from outside the hospital where we're joined by Michael Montague.'

Suzanna was composed and in control. She had thrown a gold-plated hissy fit after the release of the Mayfair Five turned into a stabbing and medical emergency, all of which dramatically unfolded without the benefit of her presentation skills. MW had appeased her by promising any aftermath coverage was hers.

'Michael, what's the latest on those at the hospital?'

'Morning, Suzanna, let's start with Bert Jones, the security guard. Bert, who's forty-seven and is married with two children, was stabbed in the chest with a small kitchen knife by a woman we believe to be his mistress. Roxy Costello was arrested at the scene and is now being questioned by police at Paddington Green station.

'As viewers will remember, Bert Jones was initially treated on the pavement outside the vault as police struggled to restrain Ms Costello. He was later rushed to intensive care here at the hospital and underwent several hours of emergency surgery. Doctors say he has lost a lot of blood and suffered a heart attack during the incident. His condition is described as critical.

'Also, Suzanna, you'll recall that the actions and arrest of Ms Costello prompted an incident involving the young Arab boy, Umair. As viewers may already know, Umair, who is only six years old, suffers from epilepsy. He did experience an attack during the siege inside the vault and suffered a second episode when caught up in the drama with Ms Costello. Doctors say he is unwell but will offer no further update. His father, Prince Ansar of Aj-al-Shar, is by his bedside, and his sister, Hafsa, and mother, Princess Almira, are also with the youngster.'

Michael paused and Suzanna took up the slack.

'What of Lily Dunlop, the young woman who some have suggested is responsible for the whole incident?'

'Indeed, Suzanna. Although taken into police custody, she is also being treated here at the hospital for an unspecified condition, though my sources tell me it is HIV/ AIDS-related.'

Michael had been dating a nurse at St Thomas's who'd offered the information after checking the family history on the NHS database when he'd rung to ask what she knew. MW had been listening to the breakfast round-up in his office while eating a bacon buttie. Spluttering, he leapt to his feet and using his desk phone rang the gallery producer.

'For fuck's sake, Christine. Confidential medical informa- tion, broadcast around Europe. Are you trying to get me sued? Shut him up. I'm coming down.'

Suzanna also knew that the line from the news correspondent

was a revelation too far and immediately jumped in to save the station from any further embarrassment.

'OK, Michael, thanks, back to you soon.'

Suzanna threw to a commercial break as MW arrived in the gallery.

'OK, everybody, quick regroup, shall we? I just want to say that we have completely monstered this story. We have wiped the floor with the opposition. We have left no angle untouched in our determination to inform the public. Please, please, please let's not drop the ball now. That includes not speculating on TV on what may be wrong with Lily Dunlop. I think we are all agreed on that?'

Christine the producer knew the Head of News was right. Although she was not directly to blame, the mistake had occurred on her watch and she was furious with herself.

'Great job, though, people. Let's stay as focused now as we have been for the last five days.'

As the director's assistant counted down to the end of the break everyone in the gallery turned to face the bank of TV monitors, focusing on the one marked 'TX': the image that viewers saw at home.

Giles Musgrave-Rose was watching from the family's London home, a double-fronted Notting Hill townhouse that his parents had previously hinted might be passed on as a wedding gift. Not any more. He hadn't seen Lily since the night before they were due to fly away to Barbados for Christmas. They had arranged to meet at the Soho Hotel before travelling on for a quick hello/goodbye at Sir Philip Green's drinks party. He'd waited for over an hour at the bar, but no sign of Lily. She hadn't answered her mobile and, despite constant BBMS messages, nothing. Frustration gave way to anger, fury and then concern as he ordered a second and then third drink at the bar. Where on earth could she be? What had happened to her? Had she been in an accident? His father had called to say he was in danger of missing his allotted take-off spot for Barbados at RAF Northolt unless they hurried. Giles had apologised before suggesting the pilot should be stood down and he and Lily would fly commercial the next day or stay for the Boxing Day hunt and then head out after that. By the fourth drink, Giles was panic stricken. He began calling everyone he could think of who might know where Lily was. Most of their friends were out on the town or celebrating at home with their families. No one had heard from her. Eventually, Giles had no choice but to head home. Switching on Bloomberg to check the closing markets, he noticed the breaking-news strap at the bottom of the screen – *Siege in Mayfair vault . . . hostages reported* – and was immediately alarmed. Lily had mentioned something about collecting something from the family vault before meeting him at the bar. As he turned up the sound, his mobile had rung. It was the police.

He'd spent the next four days hiding from the press at the estate. The Boxing Day hunt was awkward for his entire family, everyone there avoiding the obvious elephant in the room, discussing every subject under the sun except Lily over sausage rolls and mulled wine. They'd been relieved when it was time to head off to trail a scent – and definitely not under any circumstances a fox.

His father had tried to speak to him man to man, but Giles was confused and angry and had spent most of the Christmas break either in his room or riding on the estate. Why had she done this? How could the dream be over before it had begun?

Yesterday the vault had opened and he'd caught a glimpse of Lily as she was frogmarched towards a waiting ambulance. Giles was distraught. His immediate thought had been to leap into his sports car and drive down to London to be with her. But be with her where? In hospital, in a police station, in jail? Instead, he'd saddled up Rum Baba, his favourite grey stallion, and rode until it was dark. Shouting at the top of his voice as he galloped across the frozen fields, Giles wanted to ride far away and hide. Eventually returning to the stable block, he was greeted by his two German Shepherds, Dow and Jones. He was very happy to see them.

'Hello, girls, you'll never let me down, will you?'

This morning as Giles sat by the fire with Dow and Jones watching Europe News coverage, he was aware of his mother's reassuring hand on his shoulder.

'I'm afraid it's all over, darling. There's no coming back from this,' said Rose resolutely. 'Unfortunately, you can take the girl out of the East End, but you can't take the East End out of the girl. She may have had a good education, but this is what happens when the breeding isn't right.'

Rose waved her hand at the TV screen as Europe News once again showed images of Lily being led away from the vault by police. Giles nodded, his expression fixed as he watched the reporter outside the hospital update viewers on the condition of those who'd been trapped. He couldn't believe what he'd just heard about Lily.

'That poor little Prince. If anything happens to him, it will be Lily's fault.'

'Yes, Mother.'

Rose had entered the room too late to hear the report on Lily's condition. HIV/AIDS: Giles was in complete shock. He had no comprehension of what that might mean. Would she die? Would he die? The girl he was due to marry, the woman he had made love to so many times before, was possibly HIV positive. Bolt upright and ashen-faced, he was overwhelmed with anger, fear and uncertainty.

Giles began to shake and then sob. The dogs were immediately at his side. The swagger, the über-confidence of moneyed youth, deserted him. He felt as if he had been handed a death sentence. How could she have done this to him? In that moment, he was his mother's little boy and he needed her support.

'Mummy, Lily has AIDS. I need to go to London. Will you come with me? I need you.'

'Ah, just a moment, darling, I'll call your father.'

Spraying hot coffee all over his bed sheets, Sid turned up the volume a little louder on his bedroom TV. HIV, so that was what was wrong with her. Poor kid. HIV positive at twenty-one. No wonder she was spiralling. Was it confirmed or was it speculation? Either way, Michael should have been more careful about saying it on the telly. MW would be furious. Sid's compassion had been quickly replaced by journalistic curiosity. If she was HIV positive, what did that mean for her, for her family and her sexual partners? How did she catch it? What was the connection with her father?

This was another brilliant twist to the never-ending saga of Vault-gate. After eighteen hours of continuous and successful coverage from outside the vault, he had accepted MW's offer of a couple of days off. It was time Suzanna did some work! Waking late, he'd been watching Europe News coverage from bed when Michael Montague had dropped the speculative bombshell about Lily's condition. Lying back on his plumped-up pillows, Sid scrolled through the news websites and newspaper broadsheets on his iPad to check what rivals had on the story. His brain was already formulating a plan.

Originally he'd intended to head out to the Crown Hotel in Amersham for a three-night New Year celebration with Chantelle, who, after a close-run race, had now pipped Aggie at the post. The Crown was her must-visit place ever since she'd seen the four-poster scene with Hugh Grant and Andie MacDowell in *Four Weddings and a Funeral*. They'd watched it together on DVD during a relaxing Sunday morning wake-up. Sid hoped they could revisit some of her more enticing moves in the famous four-poster later that evening. Unfortunately, all that would now have to be put on hold. St Thomas's Hospital was the only date he planned to keep. Sid reached for his mobile to text Chantelle with the bad news.

Cynthia checked her mobile for messages from the children. Putting it back into her pocket she stroked the top of her husband's hand. He was in a serious condition and unaware she was at his hospital bedside. Cynthia noticed on the portable TV that Europe News was reporting from outside the hospital.

'. . . as far as the security guard is concerned. His condition is serious but stable. His wife is with him. Roxy Costello, who we interviewed before the vault opened, has been arrested and is being held by police over an assault on Bert Jones. We believe she was the lover of the guard.'

Cynthia muted the sound and looked at her husband's crumpled body – her own pain felt just as real.

37

11 a.m.

St Thomas's Hospital

Lily had been drifting in and out of sleep ever since she'd arrived at the hospital and woke up aching and confused. It took a few moments to realise where she was. The average-sized room was spotlessly clean and incredibly bright. There was an overwhelming smell of hospital. On the other side of the opaque glass door she could see the outline of what were obviously police officers. As the memory of the last four days began flooding into her consciousness, there was a tap at the door and a nurse entered.

'Good morning, Lily. My name's Eimear. How are you feeling?'

'Quite woozy really.'

'Not to worry, you're in the best place. We'll have you up on your feet in no time.'

'Am I in terrible trouble?'

Lily nodded towards the door, but the nurse avoided the question. Her job was to care for her patient's physical wellbeing until she was fit enough to leave the hospital. The next steps were for others to decide.

Another tap at the door and a doctor entered.

'Hello, Lily, my name is Dr Shaw. May I sit down?'

Lily nodded and the doctor pulled up a chair next to her bed. He appeared friendly but professional. The nurse hovered nearby. Lily was unsure what he wanted to say.

'Lily, I am aware from reports that you have some concerns about your health?'

He knew. Lily was unsure how he knew, but he did. She was relieved to be able to finally talk about her concerns.

'Yes, yes I do.'

'Is that something you would like to talk to me about?'

'I'm not sure really, but probably. Will you be able to help me?'

'Well, Lily, I am a specialist in the treatment of HIV/AIDS and I will be happy to talk to you about any anxieties or concerns that you may have.'

Lily didn't know what to say. After all these months of not knowing what to do. Whether she might be infected, whether she was infected. This doctor could help her.

'How do you know?'

'I've looked at your parents' medical records . . .'

'I don't know if I am infected.'

'Why do you think you might be?'

'I believe my father may have died from an HIV/AIDS-related illness.'

'Indeed so. Do you know what happened to him?'

Lily was relieved to be able to speak openly to someone who wasn't fazed by the possibility she could be HIV positive.

'Not really. My mother has always said he died from colon cancer, but I don't know. I never saw his death certificate. I think my mother may have tried to hide it from me because she knew and she wanted to keep the truth from me.'

'What raised your suspicions?'

'I'd rather not say.'

'Your mother has told you she is not infected?'

'She has never discussed it with me.'

'Why then do you think you might be?'

'I received a blood transfusion from my father after a car accident.'

'Well, Lily I understand your concerns but we screen blood here in the UK, so it's unlikely you could have been infected in that way.'

'It was in Africa.'

'They also screen their blood products.'

'It was in a remote village hospital several years ago.'

Dr Shaw and the nurse glanced at each other.

'OK, first of all, I need to say that we cannot determine whether you are infected unless we do a blood test. It involves a finger prick and we can have the results very quickly after that. What is important to remember is that HIV/AIDS is a manageable condition that can be treated with anti-retroviral therapy.'

Dr Shaw was keen to continue reassuring his patient.

'In every country that uses ARVs there has been a dramatic drop in HIV-related deaths and illnesses. The treatment works no matter how you were infected. Taking ARVs exactly as prescribed will reduce the virus in the body to tiny amounts, but it does not completely get rid of it. In other words, it is a condition that many, many people can now live with rather than die from.

'Of course you may not be infected. We would need to carry out the blood test to confirm that.'

Finally, it was the conversation Lily had been working up courage to have for eight months, ever since the note card had arrived on her birthday. She was desperate to take in everything the doctor was saying.

'What does the blood test do?'

'It measures your immune system, and it also tests for viral loads. That means how much virus, if any, is in a small sample of your blood.'

'If I am infected, how quickly will I be able to start treatment?'

'That depends. It's best to have the blood test first and then we can discuss next steps after that.'

'What if I go to jail, will I still be able to continue with treatment?'

Dr Shaw was not prepared to be drawn on the young girl's fate.

'As I say, Lily, we need to carry out a blood test to establish whether you have the virus first.'

'How long before I would know the result?'

'By later on today, provided you are agreeable to having the test.'

Lily was unsure what to do or what to say. A pin prick and she would know if she had contracted HIV from her father. As simple as that. Yet it was the most difficult decision she would ever have to make in her life. Dr Shaw remained silent, waiting for her decision. Eimear the nurse moved a little closer and held out her hand, which Lily immediately took.

'Eimear is an HIV clinical nurse specialist. Any concerns at all and she will be here to advise you. The one thing to remember, Lily, is that, if you are HIV positive, the sooner you begin treatment the better you will feel.'

Eimear squeezed Lily's hand and smiled reassuringly at the young girl.

'We're not here to judge, Lily,' she said. 'We're here to help.'

After all the turmoil and confusion, Lily felt reassured and protected by the health professionals.

'And it's just a finger prick.'

'That's it,' confirmed Dr Shaw.

Lily hesitated trying very hard not to cry. That's all she had done for the last five days. Eimear reached forward and held on to Lily's other hand, careful not to dislodge a line that was providing rehydration.

'OK. I'd like to go ahead with that please, Doctor.'

'Well done, Lily, that's the right decision. I'll leave you with Eimear and come back to see you a little later on today.'

As Dr Shaw left the room, Eimear immediately prepared to take a blood sample from Lily. Within a very few moments it was done.

'That's it. We should have the results before too long and we'll talk about next steps after that.'

Eimear began to make copious notes. The brief silence was interrupted by a tap at the door. From the outline through the glass, Lily knew immediately who the latest visitor was.

'Come in.'

Backlit by the morning sunshine as he walked through the open door, Lily recognised the chiselled face and perfectly honed body. His expression left her in no doubt that he had come for some answers.

'Eimear, can I introduce you to my fiancé, Giles.'

From the young man's demeanour, Eimear realized her patient and the visitor had a lot to talk about.

'Press the buzzer if you need anything.'

As the nurse closed the door behind her, Giles remained at the other side of the room.

'Why didn't you tell me?'

'I was going to tell you, I really was.'

'When?'

'I thought if you found out, you would leave me.'

'Damned right.'

Lily had wanted to confide in Giles every single day since

362

she had become desperately worried she might be HIV positive. She had been plucking up courage to tell him everything while they were in Barbados. It wasn't supposed to happen like this.

'I only found out there may be a risk around my birthday, and in the most horrible of ways. I tried to tell you so many times, but I was ashamed and embarrassed and I couldn't find the right form of words. Please believe me, Giles, I would never do anything to hurt you intentionally, you know that. I love you and I want to spend the rest of my life with you. You have to believe me. This isn't my fault.'

Giles stared at Lily. Tears streaming down his face.

'Will I die?'

'HIV/AIDS is a condition that people live with rather than die from these days, Giles. It's not like the Nineties. With early treatment and medication you can live a full and active life.' Lily recounted the words she had heard just a few minutes earlier from Dr Shaw. 'We could even have a baby if we wanted to. But, Giles, I don't even know yet if I am HIV positive. I'm sure my father was, but I don't know if I am. I've just agreed to have a blood test and I should know later today. I might not be, Giles. Really, I might not be, and then everything will be all right again, won't it?'

Lily's pleading seemed to make little impression on Giles.

'Why didn't you tell me, Lily?'

'I didn't know for sure, and I didn't want you to treat me any differently; I didn't want you to feel sorry for me. I was going to tell you, really I was. Giles, darling, please let me explain. I only discovered I might be infected in April. I needed to know if my mother knew, and then I was going to tell you everything, Giles, I swear.'

'What difference did it make if your mother knew? Lily, you knew there was a risk and you didn't tell me. Why not? I'll tell you why not: because you are and always have been a self-absorbed, self-centred bitch who cares about no one except herself.'

Lily was rocked by the verbal attack.

'That's not true. When I found out that my father might have given me HIV, I thought I was the only person in the world ever to have received such terrible news. I wanted to protect you from it. I'd never heard of a young heterosexual white woman being infected with HIV. I couldn't take it in. I might have an incurable disease that could kill me and all I wanted to do was protect you from it.'

'By having unprotected sex with me?'

'You said you were allergic to condoms. I didn't know what to do. I wasn't thinking straight, Giles.'

'How did you get it?'

'I may not have it.'

'If you have, how did you get it?'

'A blood transfusion from my father. He had it. My mother knew, but she didn't tell me. He died and she still didn't tell me. I found out on my birthday when I was sent a note about what my father had done to me.'

'Shit, other people also knew and still you didn't tell me. Who was the note from?'

'I don't know. I will probably never know. It was from someone who obviously hated my father. Please, please, Giles, none of that is important. What is important is that you are here and that we can be together. I'm sorry for what I did. I'm sorry for not telling you. I'm sorry about how you discovered the truth. Now you know though and you can be tested too. There is a very real chance we will both be absolutely fine and we can begin again. Please, darling, tell me you forgive me.'

Giles remained standing by the door. His vision blurred as he blinked away tears.

'Well, Lily, I'm sorry but I'm afraid this is not a

relationship I wish to continue with any further. I no longer want you in my life.'

Lily began to beg.

'But, Giles, you can't dump me, just like that. My life has been hell for the last few months. Let me tell you what happened. Please don't judge me until I tell you what happened.'

Giles had heard enough. His father was waiting for him at the other side of the door and the plane was on standby to whisk the whole family away from this sorry chapter in their lives.

'I'm sorry, Lily, but it's over. My family would never forgive me if I continued on in a relationship that would bring such shame on them. You can keep the ring. Goodbye, Lily.'

'But please, Giles . . .'

Lily's words went unheard. Her fiancé walked out of the door without a backward glance.

As Giles Musgrave-Rose drove away from St Thomas's hospital supported by his father, Sid Parker was arriving outside. He'd spoken to MW and offered to take over from Michael Montague for a couple of hours so the reporter could 'brush up on his Essential Law for Journalists and avoid us being sued'.

During the cab journey across town Sid had called Steve Stone. After again congratulating the reporter on his world-class scoop, he quickly moved on to the main reason for the call. Sid wanted an exclusive interview with Lily Dunlop while she was still at the hospital. He knew she'd been arrested but not yet charged by the police. That could only be a matter of days if not hours, and he wanted to be able to interview her as soon as possible.

'If anyone can fix it, Steve, it's you, my man. Let me know soonest.'

Now, taking up his position in front of the camera, Sid communicated with the news gallery via his earpiece.

'Hi, Christine, don't you have a home to go to, sweetie? Dinner on me as soon as this is all over. I'll meet you anytime you want . . .'

'. . . at our Italian restaurant.' Christine was immediately embarrassed at finishing the Billy Joel lyric. 'A few words for level, please, Sid,' she added much more formally.

'One, two, three. Talking about this level, I hope you can hear me. I am standing outside St Thomas's Hospital in central London. How's that for level?'

Christine was back in her stride. 'Great, Sid. Thanks for coming out again. I know you had a few days' break planned. It's really good of you.'

'Always desperate to talk to you, sweetheart.'

Christine ignored his flirting.

'Coming to you now, Sid. Suzanna is throwing to you. Here we go.'

Sid smiled his TV smile. Although he knew that his co-presenter would be giving absolutely nothing away in her facial expression, he detected from her tone that she was livid. Sid listened to the long convoluted 'look how clever I am' question from his colleague as she hogged the airtime for every last nanosecond.

'Yes, good morning, Suzanna. Excellent question. I think what you're trying to ask me is . . .'

The subtle put-down would have been missed by most viewers but raised a titter in the gallery. Suzanna needed to be careful; she'd met her match with Sid. He was neither intimidated nor overwhelmed by her. He felt she was a Prima Donna who needed reining in, while Suzanna considered Sid a jumped-up fluffy presenter who knew nothing about real news. The clash of the Titans made for explosive TV and great ratings.

*　　*　　*

As Sid confidently updated viewers on the condition checks of those being treated at the hospital, including young Umair, the boy's father was leaving St Thomas's by a side entrance. Arriving back at the Mandarin Oriental, Ansar was informally greeted by the British Ambassador.

'Hello, sir, I believe you are just returning from the hospital. How is the family? I trust Umair is making a speedy recovery?'

Ansar was in sombre spirits and in no mood to discuss his son's health with an underling.

'Umair and the rest of the family are as well as can be expected, Simon. No thanks to the efforts of your countrymen.'

The Ambassador feigned a suitable expression of contrition to the Prince's chastisement.

'Your Royal Highness, the Prime Minister has once again asked me to reassure you that everything that could be done was done to rescue your family in as timely a manner as possible. Please be safe in the knowledge . . .'

'Yes, yes. Anyway, they are safe now. Umair is recovering well from his fits and we are hoping we can return home within the next few days. Thank you for coming. Goodbye.'

Prince Ansar continued walking towards the elevator that would take him to his suite.

'I wonder if I might be impertinent enough to walk with you, Your Royal Highness.'

'No.'

Ansar didn't even offer the courtesy of a break in stride. The Ambassador persisted.

'I have just one other small matter to discuss with you, sir.'

'Again, no,' repeated Ansar as he reached the elevator and Dmitri pressed the call button.

'I am terribly sorry, Prince Ansar, but I really must insist.'

Ansar stopped abruptly, infuriated by the impertinence of

this subordinate. Dmitri immediately moved towards his master's side and reached inside his handmade suit jacket to rest a hand on his gun. Prince Ansar glared menacingly at Simon Roberts. Despite the presence of this unpredictable hired muscle, the British official stood his ground.

'If I may speak to you in private for just a moment, Your Royal Highness?'

Again the Prince said nothing and Dmitri took a step closer. A little more intimidated, the Ambassador nevertheless refused to give ground.

'Sir, I really must insist on speaking to you. Since you give me no other option, then I'm afraid we must have the conversation here.'

Simon Roberts paused to clear his throat before continuing.

'With respect, sir, the British Government is aware that one of our citizens is being held, potentially against her will, in your hotel suite. I have reassured our security services that it is a simple misunderstanding. Rather that you have been offering Lady Catherine Dunlop comfort and support in her hour of need. Two parents together, worried about their children. Furthermore, I assured MI5 that your concern was primarily to spare Lady Catherine the inconvenience of being so far away in North Oxfordshire. Instead, you very kindly offered her the comfort of a bedroom suite here at the Mandarin Oriental, at your expense. I have this morning reassured the Prime Minister that, now the siege is over, you are in agreement this would indeed be the optimum time for her to be reunited with her daughter.'

Ansar was about to speak, but the Ambassador raised his hand.

'I understand just how challenging a time it has been for you over the last five days, sir, not least with your continuing concern about Umair's health and that he should receive the attention he deserves. As of ten minutes ago, I can inform to you that we have taken the liberty of relieving your security team of the task of guarding your son. That duty has now been undertaken by an elite squad of UK military personnel.'

Ansar tried to interrupt, but Simon pressed on.

'We hope that this move on our part will further aid the reuniting of Lady Catherine with her daughter. Once again, on behalf of the British Government, may I thank you for your generosity and hospitality towards Lady Catherine in her hour of need.'

As the Ambassador finished speaking, Dmitri became aware of several burly men with suits equally as well cut as his own moving inconspicuously towards them.

38

Lunchtime

New Scotland Yard

'I have great news, boss.'

Steve Stone was on the phone to MW as he stood outside the Met Police Headquarters, watching the triangular sign as it turned another of the 14,000 revolutions it made every day. He had news on Lily Dunlop, but unable to speak to Sid, who was live on air, he'd immediately called Miles Winstanley instead.

'Go on then, superstar.'

'Sid asked if I could fix an interview with Lily Dunlop . . .'

'Did he now?'

MW was impressed by his anchor's skulduggery. Suzanna's much-hyped interview with Prince Ansar had come to nothing and Sid was obviously taking matters into his own hands. Sharp.

'Anyway, the police haven't even arrested her yet.'

'Course they have, we saw her in handcuffs outside the vault.'

'Nah, not even cautioned her, let alone charged her. They're waiting for some medical checks or something. They might by tonight, though, so if we want to interview her we'll need to move fast.'

MW was surprised. Relations between Europe News and Scotland Yard were at an all-time low – particularly between him and the Commissioner. He had expected frosty communication between the two organisations would persist for some time, with not the remotest chance of any collaboration. Steve's contacts from his newspaper days had again saved the day.

'Excellent. Why are they being so accommodating?'

'The fuck-up when the vault opened. They want to show how softly, softly they had to be. Hoping that'll explain how Roxy Costello managed to make her star appearance. No better way to make the point than a posh bird in her sick bed. The kid would be even better, but that's not likely to happen any time soon, and the guard is at death's door.'

MW acknowledged the scene with Roxy outside the vault had not played well for the police and an interview with a vulnerable young woman swathed in her hospital gown would offer the public a glimpse of the challenges the Met had faced. Real people with real issues; a gentle approach to the vault opening had been their only option. Steve was right: pictures of the children would have been even better, but given what he knew about Prince Ansar he would never have allowed that.

'Sounds perfect. Let's get on it.'

'There's a catch.'

'There always is.'

'Now all we need to do is persuade Lily Dunlop it's a good idea.'

Steve sounded doubtful. Convincing the police was one thing, persuading a young woman who might or might not have AIDS but was definitely about to go to jail for some time that she should speak on TV first was quite another.

'Don't you worry, I'm sure Sid will have that covered, Steve. Anyway, great job. You are proving invaluable to this organisation. Can you pop in and see me, say next Tuesday? I thought you were top drawer outside the vault; want to talk to you about more on-air time and maybe a bit of camera training.'

'Wow, thanks.'

Steve dropped his phone into his pocket and was almost back at his car before he realised MW had told him he could be on TV, but only once he'd improved his technique!

MW checked the output. Sid was just winding up his latest update from the hospital and threw back to an ever-smiling Suzanna. For all the world they seemed the perfect TV husband and wife, thought MW wryly. He dialled Sid's mobile.

'Sid, thanks for coming in, buddy. There really was no need, but you're doing a great job . . . as always.'

'Thanks, boss.'

Sid paused and waited for the other boot to fall. He knew MW wasn't calling to chew the cud.

'I believe you've asked Steve to organise an interview with Lily Dunlop.'

Aha. Steve Stone needed to learn a few golden rules. Rule one, tell the boss what he needs to know when he needs to know it.

'Yeah, I was going to tell you about that, boss.'

'I'm sure you were, buddy, I'm sure you were. Anyway, he's managed it. Now all we need is for the girl to say yes. Big ask, but if anyone can do it, mate, you can.'

For the last three days Miles had been trying unsuccessfully to contact Catherine Dunlop at her home. He had been told the lady of the house hadn't been there for some days. Not since her appearance on Europe News in fact. Miles had presumed Catherine had decided to remain out of the public eye. He was sure the siege would not be playing well with her family members. With no Mrs Dunlop to ask, Lily was the only other option. She was an adult, she could make her own decisions.

'OK, boss. Well, I have another live with the simply charming Suzanna in five minutes and then I'll wander up and work my magic.'

'I'm sure you will. Let me know.'

Sid ended the call and re-established the line with the news gallery.

'Ready when you are, Sid.'

'Always ready for you, Christine my love.'

By the time Sid had finished updating Europe via his camera position outside the hospital, Steve Stone had driven from Scotland Yard and was by his side.

'Hey, Steve Stone superstar. Believe you've fixed it with the coppers we can do an interview. Great job, mate, but just for future ref, I would rather you'd spoken to me directly rather than via MW.'

Steve had not intended any slight and was immediately embarrassed that Sid might have perceived otherwise.

'You were on air, mate. Sorry, I thought I was doing the right thing.'

Sid decided not to press the point. Steve had worked his contacts. That was all that mattered.

'Understood.'

Steve was immediately relieved.

'Anyway, I've driven over from the Yard because I thought you might need a bit of help with the police guard on the room. I'll leave the nurses to you, though.'

Both men laughed and Sid took off his earpiece before

walking with his hand on Steve's shoulder towards a side entrance of the hospital.

Arriving at the ward where Lily was being treated, Steve greeted one of the armed officers by name and wandered over to speak to him while Sid sauntered down to the nursing station. All of those behind the desk immediately recognised the TV host and melted as he offered his most winning smile.

'Hello, ladies. Goodness, I have to say I'm feeling a little weak at the knee, a nurse's uniform never fails to do it for me. Perhaps I could ask one of you to check my pulse.'

His outrageous flirtation was met by a gaggle of giggles from his instantly acquiescent audience.

'No? Oh well, I wonder if I might be able to have a very quick word with Sister.'

One of the nurses stepped forward.

'That's me, Mr Parker.'

'Goodness even more attractive than I could have hoped, and with authority too. Be still, my beating heart.'

Sid gently touched Sister's arm.

'I wonder if I might have a quiet word, Sister?'

In no time, Sid was inside Lily's hospital room. She was still facing the wall, exactly as she had been after Giles left. Sid had managed to convince everyone else apart from the ward sister to wait outside. The nurse touched Lily's pale hand and the young girl stirred. As she turned her head, Sid saw her face for the first time. She looked poorly, frightened and vulnerable. He could see she had been crying. Poor little thing, she needs a me to look after her, thought Sid. The sister's cough jolted him back to reality.

'This is Sid Parker, Miss Dunlop. I believe your mother spoke to him on TV. Lady Catherine has given him permission to come and speak to you.'

That had been a little white lie told by Sid to the Sister

to guarantee access to the room. Sid was sure if he could find Catherine then she would have said yes, so it was only the tiniest of little white lies.

'Hi, Lily, how are you feeling?'

'What do you want?'

Sid looked towards the Sister, appealing to her for the few moments in private with Lily that he'd requested. A tour of the studios and lunch with him afterwards had been all it took. As the door shut behind her, Sid moved a little nearer to the bed.

'I came to see how you are.'

'Fine, bye.'

Lily turned her face away and closed her eyes. Sid wasn't used to this sort of reaction from a woman, even one in her sick bed, but pressed on. He moved a step closer towards the bed.

'You're quite obviously not fine, Lily. I've come to see if there is anything I can do to help you. Has your mother been to visit you yet, or your fiancé?'

'I haven't heard from Mummy. Giles just left, but not before he dumped me. Please, go away, I want to be on my own.'

Sid eased a little closer still.

'Oh no, I am truly, truly sorry. This is all such a shock for him as well, I'm sure. Give it time and see what happens. What about your mother, have you heard from her?'

'You should know. You said you had spoken to her.'

Caught out at his own game, Sid allowed the moment to pass before pulling up a chair and sitting right next to her bed.

'Lily, I know you are not the ogre they're making you out to be. I want others to know that too.'

Lily didn't reply.

'I want my viewers to see the toll this experience has taken on you.'

'No.'

Too fast thought Sid, slow down. He put his hand on top of hers and waited. Eventually he spoke again.

'I know that you are HIV positive, Lily.'

Lily turned her head to face him.

'I'm not. Anyway, I might not be. I don't know yet.'

Sid was shocked. Not only had Michael Montague imparted confidential medical information live on TV, it might turn out to be completely wrong. That would be one for the lawyers.

'I'm sorry, Lily, if I'm mistaken. All I want is to have the opportunity to interview you and then we can show everyone that you are not the heartless beast the newspapers are portraying you as. I want my viewers to see you as the vulnerable young woman who acted the way she did for a reason.'

Lily looked up from under her overgrown fringe. Her long blonde hair, newly washed by the nurse, lay tousled on the pillow. Sid smiled down at her.

'Seriously, sweetie, I'm your man. This is your opportunity to tell our viewers why you acted the way you did. What do you say?'

Lily didn't have time to answer before there was another tap at the door. It was an unmistakable rat-a-tat that Lily recognised. She immediately turned her face back towards the wall as the door opened.

'Catherine, Lady Catherine, goodness.'

Sid was shocked at the arrival of Lily's mother and stood to offer his hand in greeting. Ignoring the news anchor, Catherine rushed to her daughter's bedside.

'My darling, my darling. I'm here. I won't let anything else happen to you. I am so, so sorry.'

'I'm afraid you'll have to leave now, Mr Parker.' It was Sister. 'Lily can only have one visitor at a time, and of course her mother must take priority.'

Shit and he'd almost had her in his pocket.

'Of course, I completely understand, Sister.'

Reluctantly walking backwards towards the door, Sid paused.

'Remember, Lily, I'm your man.'

39

Teatime

Pacing the corridor outside Lily's hospital room, Sid rang his Head of News for advice. It had been almost two hours since Lady Catherine had arrived and the door to Lily's room had remained firmly shut ever since.

'Her mother's here. I've been turfed out. Worse, Steve's been speaking to the coppers and they say she's going to be arrested and charged within the hour.'

MW was similarly pacing his office floor. Europe News had scored at almost every opportunity on this story, but it looked as though an interview with Lily Dunlop was going to be an exclusive too far.

'Yeah, I know. We've heard from the Yard that it'll be kidnap and false imprisonment. They want to do it within the next twenty minutes. The child, Umair, is improving and it looks like the guard is finally out of danger; a kidnap and false imprisonment charge will round things off nicely.'

'How long will she go down for?'

'Remember Karen Matthews?'

'Not off the top of my head.'

'Held her daughter Shannon prisoner for twenty-four days in Yorkshire.'

'Oh yeah, police found the kid in a flat, under the divan.'

'That's the one. The mother was sentenced to eight years.'

'That's a lot of porridge and watching daytime TV,' joked Sid, playing for time as the realisation dawned. 'So basically, boss, just to be clear, I have twenty minutes to secure this interview before she slips through our fingers for eight years.'

'Yup.'

'No pressure then.'

Sid wasn't worried about the deadline, he worked on a tight schedule every hour of every day, but Lily Dunlop jailed for eight years . . . Technically, she was of course guilty, but it hadn't all been her fault. If he could secure the interview, then others might feel the same way.

'So what's the scoop then, Sid, do we have this interview or not?'

'Not technically.'

'That's like being a bit pregnant,' replied MW. 'You either have or you haven't. Which is it?'

'Leave it with me, boss. I'm on it.'

Steve was still working hard, buying time by making friends with the boys in blue. Sid was watching him in awe when he noticed his crew arriving along the corridor. They'd been dispatched by MW and, though travelling light, they were nevertheless carrying camera, lights, microphones and essential equipment to broadcast live. This might be tricky. The nursing Sister and one of the senior police officers were first to mount the barricades.

'I'm terribly sorry, Mr Parker, but it really is not possible to have so many members of your team here. In fact, I think it would probably be best for you to leave. You have already spent some time with Miss Dunlop and, as you know, her mother is with her now.'

Sid adopted his Colgate smile and, slipping an over-familiar arm around Sister's waist, he turned his attention to the senior officer, reassuring him that none other than the Met Commissioner himself had promised he could have another five minutes with Miss Dunlop, if he would like to check.

Sid's divide-and-rule tactic succeeded in confusing the opposition. The Sister and the police officer hesitated just long enough to give Steve Stone the opportunity to move in from the right flank and continue the assault. Sid tapped on Lily's door.

'Come in.'

Lily lay on her bed. Her mother stood some distance away from her. He could see from the body language between the two women it was going to take his most wily skills to get them to even look at each other, let alone agree to be interviewed together. What had they been doing for the last two hours? Certainly not communicating. Sid decided on forceful honesty.

'OK, ladies, listen to me. We really don't have much time, the police will be entering this room within the next fifteen minutes and, Lily, you will be arrested. They will take you to Pentonville prison to be held until a court hearing is set.

'This is going to be the only time for several months, perhaps even years, that you can explain why you behaved in the way that you did.'

Catherine tried to interrupt, but Sid pressed on.

'I have a film crew outside the door and our Head of News has negotiated with the police to secure us a five-minute interview with you. Of course, the final decision is up to you but the clock is ticking. If it is something that you, Lady Catherine, feel would explain to the British public why Lily behaved in the way that she did, if it's something that you, Lily, feel might help others who suffer from a similar condition, potential condition, to come to terms with their illness, then it is the right thing to do. And if it will give you both the opportunity to reassure viewers, and indeed each other, that a mother's love can conquer all, then now is the time.'

Sid paused. He'd given it his best Churchillian delivery, now it was out of his hands.

Catherine grimaced, every inch of her was screaming that a TV interview was a ludicrous option that would compound her embarrassment, but a niggling thought at the back of her mind wanted others to know that Lily wasn't an evil child. She'd been driven by desperation to behave in the way that she had, and a little embarrassment was a small price to pay to put the record straight. Lily had been crucified in the morning's papers, and Catherine certainly didn't recognise the pariah portrayed on every front page. One even had her sketched as a devil with the scalps of a child and a security guard hanging from her trident.

Lily had taken in little of Sid's speech after his suggestion she could spend years in jail.

'Seriously, ladies, if you are uncomfortable with anything I ask, simply don't answer it and we'll move on.'

Sid looked from mother to daughter. He had wanted the interview in order to stiff Suzanna to show he was top news hound, but now, in the claustrophobia of Lily's hospital room, he felt that he wanted to help, to use this opportunity to change the public perception of her. She had certainly behaved rashly, but she wasn't an ogre.

Catherine was the first to speak.

'If Lily is content, then I do not see an issue.'

Sid didn't wait for Lily's response. He was already walking smartly back to the door.

MW had put the gallery on standby to broadcast the interview live. As soon as the director saw the Outside Source from Sid's camera switch from colour bars to Lily's hospital room, that was the cue to take the pictures live. The director,

Christine and MW all saw the pictures switch at the same time. Sid immediately began the interview.

'OK, Lily, you're live on Europe News. Viewers will have heard your voice, but this is the first time they will have seen you. It's been a tough few days. How are you feeling?'

'I'm feeling much better now, thank you.'

'Can you explain how you found yourself inside the vault?'

'Not really.'

Sid realised this was going to be harder than first anticipated. A monosyllabic interviewee when he was up against the clock was not ideal. He pressed on.

'As I mentioned to you before we started the interview, Lily, only discuss what you are comfortable with. I'm sure our viewers are keen not to judge you, but they do want to know what happened. Do you feel able to talk about it?'

The thought of years in jail was still front and centre in Lily's mind. Slowly, through the haze of fear she realised this was her only chance for a very long time to put right the misconceptions of why she'd done what she'd done. Lily swallowed hard and began to talk about her reasons for visiting the vault, why she had behaved the way she did. As she continued, Sid gestured to Catherine to move a little closer towards the bed.

'So it was something in the security box that you wanted. But why did you take a gun?'

'It was an ornamental gun, I'm not even sure if it works. I was never going to use it, I just needed what was in the box and I didn't think the guard would give it to me without my mother's permission. She was hiding something from me inside the box and I needed to see it. I didn't mean for all this to happen. I just wanted to know the truth.'

Lily dropped her chin and wiped her eyes.

'Don't cry, darling, please don't cry.'

Catherine moved to sit on the edge of her daughter's bed.

'I didn't hide it from you. I put it there to protect you.'

Sid asked the question every viewer wanted to know the answer to.

'What was in the vault?'

'A family secret,' interrupted Catherine.

'Well, it's not a secret any more, Mummy.'

Catherine was about to speak when Lily pulled a legal-looking document from underneath her pillow and thrust it towards Sid. Now was the time she needed to talk about what had happened to make her behave in the way she had.

'This is why I went to the vault, Sid. This is why. It's my father's death certificate. It states that he died of colon cancer, but also that he suffered from HIV/AIDS. My mother hid this document from me in the family vault, even though she knew I could also be infected after a blood transfusion from my father when I was eighteen. I discovered the truth on my twenty-first birthday.'

Lily was now speaking with such emotion Sid didn't need to prompt her.

'I don't know if I am infected, but because my mother had hidden the evidence, any potential treatment has been delayed by months, if not years. Not only that, if I am HIV positive I could also have infected those I care most about. That is all my mother's fault.'

Catherine was shocked by the production of the death certificate, a document that had instilled so much fear in her for so long. But it was just a piece of paper and unimportant now. She reached out and tried to stroke her daughter's hand, but Lily pulled her arms away.

'I've been tested for HIV this morning. I will know by this evening if I have a potential death sentence from my father that was condoned by my mother.'

Only after Lily had finished speaking did Sid turn to Catherine.

'Well, Catherine, I'm sure you must have had your reasons for behaving in the way that you did.'

Catherine ignored the question and spoke instead directly to her daughter.

'I'm so, so sorry, darling. I thought I was doing the right thing. I was deeply shocked when your father died and at first I couldn't take in what the doctors were saying. When I did finally accept how he had died, I felt such intense shame, and I wanted to protect you from that. HIV/AIDS still holds such a stigma in our society, I didn't want you to be tainted by it. Your daddy was your hero; I didn't know how you would feel when you learned that his blood might have contaminated yours. I didn't know how to tell you, I didn't know how to explain. I know now that what I did was wrong, but in my own ill-informed way I wanted to protect you. I read everything I could, and I realised that AIDS is not the killer it used to be.'

'But only if you receive timely treatment, Mummy.'

Lily began to soften. So many things that should have been said so long ago were now out in the open. Both women were relieved to finally be discussing what they should have talked about months, years ago. Catherine was desperate to make amends.

'I know, my darling, I know, and I desperately wanted to tell you. I tried so many times but I couldn't find the words. Time moved on, you seemed so well, not sick in any way, and before I knew it we were making plans for your twenty-first. I planned to tell you after the party, truly I did, but before I could the note arrived telling you everything.'

'The note . . .' Sid was keen to learn more.

'Mummy, I need to know who sent it. Do you know who could have hated Daddy so much they'd have done such a dreadful thing?'

'I'm afraid I have absolutely no idea, darling.'

'It was someone very evil, Mummy. Who could have done such a terrible, terrible thing?'

'Yes, it was an evil, evil person, darling.'

Catherine nodded and paused to blow her nose. In that moment realising exactly who had ripped her family apart.

There was only one other person who knew of her husband's illness, knew how he had contracted it and knew about the contents of the death certificate. Only one other person in the whole world who was aware of the long lonely nights, weeks and months she had spent alone, desperate for her husband's love and support. Just one person who would know how much Lily loved her father, one person who felt that that love was at times misplaced and that Lily was ignorant of what her father could really be like. One man who could deliver a card to Miss Lily without it being traced back to him.

His motive? Catherine could only guess. Perhaps to alert Lily to her potential life-threatening illness while also making it clear it was all her father's fault. His plan was for Lily to finally understand what a terribly selfish man her father had been, while at the same time underlining to the young girl how her mother had had no other choice but to act in the way that she did. That person was a man whose love for Lady Catherine had clouded his judgement and made him act irrationally with a devastating cost to everyone involved. That man was Brian the butler.

'Yes, darling, only someone very evil could have done such a thing.'

Catherine was about to continue when the door opened and several police officers entered. The most senior addressed Sid.

'If I could ask you to stop filming now please, Mr Parker.'

Sid didn't have time to act before the officer turned to Lily and continued:

'Lily Agnes Catherine Dunlop, you have the right to remain silent . . .'

Catherine leapt to her feet, knocking over her hospital chair, and wrapped both her arms protectively around her child.

'No, no, no, it wasn't her fault. Please, take me instead.'

Catherine sobbed uncontrollably, all attempts at composure lost.

As a policeman continued to read Lily her rights, Sid and his crew, still broadcasting live, were guided towards the door by other officers. The shocked anchor collided with a doctor. as they crossed in the doorway. His name badge announced him as Dr Shaw. Sid could just make out the start of the doctor's comments before the door was closed firmly behind him.

'Officers, if I could ask you to leave the room for one moment, please. I have the results of Miss Dunlop's HIV test.'

To be continued . . .

First Ladies

What happens when the power of love challenges the love of power?

Suave Prime Minister Julian Jenson has just been re-elected. The nation's darling, he has an elegance and natural charm in public. But in private the cracks are starting to show.

At his side is his wife, Valerie. Trim, tall, well educated but deeply unhappy – with her son and daughter away at school, alcohol is becoming a trusted friend.

Sally Simpson is at the peak of her game. Powerful editor of the bestselling magazine *Celeb*, she can't wait to take her rightful place by Julian's side.

Sexy TV reporter Isla McGovern has caught Julian's eye, and she will do anything (or anyone) to get to the top.

When the three women meet, so begins a perfect storm, and only one can emerge as the First Lady.

**'Juiciest read of the year.
I loved it'**
Tasmina Perry